The Tides of Men

Niall P MacAllister

Aberdeen Bay
An Imprint of Champion Writers

Aberdeen Bay
Published by Aberdeen Bay, an imprint of Champion Writers.
www.aberdeenbay.com

PUBLISHER'S NOTE

This is a book of fiction. Names, characters, places, and incidents are either the product of author's imagination or are used fictitiously. Any resemblance to actual persons, living or dead, business establishments, government agencies, events, or locales is entirely coincidental.

International Standard Book Number
ISBN-13: 978-1-60830-005-1
ISBN-10: 1-60830-005-6

Printed in the United States of America.

Dedicated to my wife, Theresa

Table of Contents

The Tides of Men

CHAPTER ONE

Kilcoo, and other
"Streets Where They Don't Belong"

Mairead stood by the window, pulling aside the frayed curtains, peering through the dingy glass. She stared from the second floor of the high-rise tenement; the ill famed Divis Flats of the Lower Falls - the slums of west Belfast. Her eyes wide with sadness, fear and something else, she sucked her thumb as she watched the funeral procession slowly passing below.

A little boy about her age, they said, only days ago in a shoot out in the Mournes near Kilcoo. It happened in the mountains, not far above the town. His granddad had also been killed.

Some said the boy's granddad was a terrorist - a Republican, same as her own mam and dad. She'd heard the story; that the boy and his granddad, the Seanache, were very brave - that people from other countries had come for his granddad's funeral, that for the boy now, they'd come from across the world. She wondered why. She remembered she'd lost her dad to the "troubles".

Alone in the house now, her mother working the late shift, she peered out toward the crowd surging toward the City Centre. She saw the growing multitude, bigger by far than for the little boy's granddad; she remembered seeing his granddad's funeral on the telly only a few weeks ago.

Mairéad Donaghy missed her own dad's funeral. She was thinking of the boy. Though she'd never known either of them, the boy or his granddad, she fisted the tears from her eyes as she ran from the bedroom to the living room, following the gathering procession. She opened the window. Singing voices rose to her in a wave from the streets below.

The television announcer was reviewing the events of

the past few weeks.

"From the Victoria Hospital where young Sean died… at first hundreds of mourners, now thousands go by."

Mairéad turned back to the open window. Though she was afraid, having grown up in a world of killing and violence, this was different. Suddenly she found herself running down the stairwell, the door slamming behind her. Somehow it seemed like her dad's funeral now, and she wouldn't miss it twice. Into the street she ran. She didn't want the little boy to be gone without her.

Mairéad reached the growing line. She didn't know the words to the song they were singing, but she'd heard the songs before. She joined in, humming the tunes she knew. A smiling mother reached out to her.

"My name's Mairéad Donaghy, an' I live back there in the flats." The lady nodded, clasped Mairéad's hand, introducing her own children. "We're from the east side, Mairéad - ye'll be all right with us, love." The children smiled at her as they walked alongside their mother. Though Mairéad knew the sorrow and the celebration of the wake they shared, she was happy to be with them – her fears quieter now.

"Where are we going?" she asked her new friends skipping along beside her.

"We're going to Sean McCarton's funeral," the little boy said. "We're going to Kilcoo. They've got the buses waiting by the Ormeau Park." He added happily, "An' the whole world's come to see him off!"

Winding their way down the main road, members of the cortege raised their heads to see a familiar escort appear – an armoured car, its camouflaged, armed, battle-dressed crew framed by the open back of the vehicle. Ranging high above them were army helicopters. Not long after, the menacing presence disappeared. The TV announcer told the story. Security forces had tried to intervene in an event which was attracting world attention. "The moment of historic transition," the announcer called it.

Beyond the "long river of human sorrow, of the final sacrifice", the announcer described what could be a new and different note emerging, "a unique epiphany of joy. The reality of the boy's death now serves as a reminder of other alternatives. The recognition that a moment in time could bring this quarrelling world literally, to its knees."

Immediately behind the hearse paced members of little Sean's own family, his mother, Sheila, his aunt, Theresa. Beside Theresa stood Jack Edwards. Joining them were the wider family, who only weeks before had accompanied the boy's grandfather to his grave. Dan McSorley, freedom fighter - or terrorist - depending on the perspective. Bob Thompson, journalist, new political voice. Paddy Finucane, with Terri Sai and Liu Xiabo from China. Ben Harrari, of the Israeli government, advocate for reunification of the divided Semitic voice. Beside him, slowly pacing, the tall figure of the embattled Irish Taoiseach, John Maloney, and a distinguished confluence of other foreign dignitaries.

Some boarded the waiting buses for Kilcoo. As the afternoon sun darkened the woods of Tollymore Park, the funeral cortege wound its way across the Mournes. On the far side of the glen, sunlight flashed on the Salmons' Leap, the waterfall tumbling in rainbows more than a hundred feet down the side of the mountain.

Further up the glen, nestled among the tall pines, was Clanawillun, above the fairy ring where the Seanache's family lived for over four hundred years. As the bus headed further west, Mairéad turned to look back at the glacier-carved ragged peaks. Distant now, the falls winked in the sunlight. The stone mountains sloped to the sea, their silica glittering sides silent witness among the heather and gorse of centuries.

The sun now hovered low over the mountains, through the wind spun clouds, leaving the distant beaches, the woods and glens of the Mournes in deepening shadows. Slowly they entered the village, its stone cottages crowding the cemetery and the old stone church, with its one storey schoolhouse. They could hear the wailing song of the piper, standing alone at the gravesite.

The great crowd gathered, joining other mourners already assembled in the cemetery. The church bells, like the piper's notes, slowly toned the farewell, carolling, booming, sighing. Some notes in wailing grief, others, it seemed, in angry defiance. The priest stood, white hair blowing in the breeze, commencing the prayers. Still holding the lady's hand, Mairead recited the words she knew by heart. She thought this must have been the way it was for her dad.

A fine rain commenced to fall. Mairéad now heard the memorable words of Fr. Alexander reaching out across the hillside. "The human race was conceived with only the Earth and the creatures of the Earth as each other's only resource. Never having learned to share the resources, to trust one another, they separated, even from their fellow creatures - rather favouring the creed of possessions and exclusion. The havoc wrought was immeasurable, in destruction of their world."

Then as if reaching his own conclusion, a strangely appropriate allusion, "The subsequent generation of grief, of mistrust - the perpetrator becomes alienated from himself, as well as from his fellow man."

Fr. Alexander quoted Gandhi's fifth principle of Sardovaya, an existence in equality and happiness for all who can renounce violence. "And in the words of Confucius, 'the humane man, desiring to establish himself, seeks to establish others, desiring to succeed, he helps others to succeed; to judge others by what one knows of oneself is the method of achieving one's own humanity.'"

The prayers concluded; the coffin was lowered into the ground. Sheila, the dead boy's mother, silently wept. Dan McSorley held her hand and spoke quietly, "You're not alone, Sheila - Sean's not alone. He's with his granddad, and with Frank now."

Mairéad stood with her new friends and their mother, before returning home to the segregated streets of Belfast.

The mourners, friends, family, visitors from across the world, all nationalities, all religions or none, rejoined their own worlds; the stark valleys of Afghanistan, the jungles, the rice fields of Southeast Asia, the deserts, the shifting sands of the Middle East, the rain swept green valleys of Ireland.

Dan McSorley silently stood, retracing the path that

had brought them full circle. His thoughts were now far west of Kilcoo. He could hear the voice of the boy's father, Frank, the quiet hopes, whispered promises they had shared as he stood beside him on a hillside among the Anam Cordilleras; the rugged mountains of Nicaragua.

Above the mourners, helicopters withdrew. From one, later landing in Dublin, its troubled passengers met in a brief but tense exchange with John Maloney, the Taoiseach. Each then returned to their homes, to east and to west – with top security, no publicity. One, a former President from the United States, to Washington. Maloney, standing by the windows, looked out to Stephen's Green, where he'd seen the Seanache approach for their last meeting, then turned away to prepare for the challenge of the days ahead.

Three hundred miles northwest of London, above the weather-beaten granite face of Slieve Donard the eagle flew, on a path unchanged since the volcanic surge, the glacial drift of ages past. More than a hundred feet above the rushing waters of the Trassey River, the fierce old eagle of Luke's Mountain surveyed his domain. Peering curiously, hungrily, gliding on the rising currents of warm air, he rose above the frantic schemes of men, their transient passage. His scream, mournful and wild, echoed across the Mournes, over Slievenabrock, as far south as Ben Crum and northward, over the silvery, windswept beaches of Dundrum Bay. Three thousand miles further west, from the Anam Cordilleras, a distant kin, Thraseatus Harpyja, stared down upon the torrid jungles of the Caribbean.

CHAPTER TWO

Chelle's Children
Moments of choice – young bodies unaware
Old eyes turned to stare – remembering
Yesterdays feverish guitar – forgotten
moments of desire.

Gliding above the turbulent world a thousand feet below, poised on the warm air rising from the distant Costa de Mosquitos, the Harpy eagle peered like Cortes to the far blue horizons of the Pacific and elusive Cathay. Known to the Aztecs as the winged wolf, Thrasaetus Harpyja gazed hungrily for its prey, the sloth, the monkey, the macaw and birds of paradise lurking in the jungles and mountains beneath. Home to the hunter and the hunted, the rugged peaks of the Anam Cordilleras ran their snow or scrub covered spine through the jungles and lakes of Nicaragua.

As the mourners at Sean's funeral resumed their lives – some to their separate paths, Dan McSorley remembered those last weeks with Frank, the dead boy's father, in the embattled provinces of Nicaragua. He recalled Frank's mounting frustration.

"Danny, what the fuck is the use of all this? Worse than fuckin' Belfast. Bloody Americans. Since Vietnam, they've lost their way. One war after another. 'New world order' they call it."

Then, more quietly, "Danny, I think it's time we went home."

Bearded, broad shouldered, Frank turned uneasily, wiping the sweat and rain from his face, his other hand gripping the stock of a shoulder held rocket launcher. He lapsed into an exasperated silence. Dan, a shorter, stockier man, absently singing to himself, made no reply. He'd heard this song before.

Their world was changing again. With a winding down of the Cold War hysteria, the American image was suffering. Budget deficits, a continuing recession, and a growing public disaffection for the costly warrior image – the global Star Wars political agenda. And the residual presence of the Vietnam syndrome all combined to reduce support for the faltering campaign in South America and elsewhere.

Dan and Frank stood in the steady rainfall, in a clearing in the foothills of the Cordillera de Guanacaste.

Frank and Dan, "freedom fighters", "wild geese" on the run from distant battles against the British in Northern Ireland, were members of El Grande, a strike force of the Contras. A motley group of draftees, volunteers and misled young visionaries; Che Guevaras they were not.

They'd gathered in the early tropical dusk - restless, expectant, waiting in the tall grass, their faces blackened for night action. They were preparing to move into the central highlands and attack the Russian/Cuban supply base before dawn.

To one side the Indian scouts squatted or stood; their smooth faces an impassive reflection of an ageless forbearance. Bemused, they watched the frenetic activity of the swearing, sweating, weekend warriors - the gringos from the great white colossus to the north. Yet all insignificant pawns in the Great Game - a peripheral ripple in the priorities of the New World Order.

Washington, Whitehall, all a million miles away as Dan and Frank waited on the remote riverbank in Nicaragua, their future uncertain, their options few, their lives in jeopardy.

"It's this or Afghanistan, Frank, and more of the same." Perhaps Frank was right, thought Dan. Perhaps we should return home. At least there we know who we are and who the real enemy is.

Frank, shaking his head, said nothing. He's already back home, thought Dan. Perhaps remembering the way it started.

*

For Dan, the innocent boyhood days at St. Enda's parish school, St. Columb's College in Derry, a "First" in History and English literature at Queen's University in Belfast. Looking to a promising future in his first year of teaching, he'd seen the Paratroopers, heirs to a brutal tradition, gunning people down in the streets of Derry.

Then the Civil Rights marches, the beatings – the lessons of history forgotten, inevitably repeated. Convictions Dan could no longer deny - the injustice, the brutality. He knew he must make a stand, try to defend his country, his people. He knew where he belonged.

For Frank it had been different. He was a child from the raw, embattled "street school" of Belfast, a target of discrimination, beatings, intimidation - no home, no work, no viable future. In his very struggle to survive he'd found his role, his identity reborn.

He and Dan had met in later years. Frank by then was a hardened "Freedom Fighter" with one goal, to remove the British military presence and all its brutality, its polarizing influence.

On the run following a firefight with a Para patrol near Armagh, Frank and Dan were followed by Execution Squads, the counter revolutionary warfare wing of the SAS. They took refuge in the Mournes near Frank's family with his wife Sheila, his young son, Seanoge, and Sheila's grandfather, the one they called "The Seanache", a legendary figure in the Irish struggle for independence.

After several weeks as fugitives, the net closing in - Frank and Dan made their way to Canada and crossed into the United States. While staying with friends in New York they learned of discreet recruitment efforts for a covert "mercenary unit" to work with American Special Forces in the southern hemisphere. It was a ready egress to avoid an increasingly vigilant FBI on the hunt for illegal immigrants. As Dan saw it, a more authentic representation of the prevailing political ethos in a changing world.

Since World War II Britain and the US were the ultimate

power brokers. The New Imperialists, combining unrelenting efforts to subordinate the political process of the peoples of the third world to the New World Order.

It had been almost three years now since those first, rugged months - three years too long.

*

Frank grumbled to himself, listening to the barking cough from across the river - a hunting jaguar. Glancing upward, Dan watched the half moon rising among the straggling clouds. Around them other members of the strike force were busy checking their equipment, calling to one another in hoarse whispers. Their irritable muttering contrasted with the sonorous dirges of the Miskito Indian scouts crouching motionless in the tall grass, chanting their timeless incantations of life and death.

Frank laughed, "Like you Danny, singin' their war songs, callin' on their gods for divine intercession."

Dan nodded. "Maybe they'll bring us luck. They've endured persecution throughout their history an' they've survived."

The Miskitos lived in their own world. From another age, thought Dan, wondering then, how do they see us? Do they remember, as we remember, the evils perpetrated throughout their history? The story of recurring conquests from Spain, from the Americas, preachers of "civilizations" successively imposed with fire and sword, generation to generation?

In the darkness, the vibrant chant of the Miskito Indians with its low monotone seemed more sinister, melding with the distant chatter of the river water, the pervasive cricketing of the cigarra, the distant barking of the howler monkeys, the squawk of the long-tailed macaw.

The section leaders moved among the men, closely inspecting the blackened faces, reminding them to secure their equipment. Looking over at Frank, Dan saw the sudden change, the totally focused professional, troubles momentarily forgotten - saw him run his hand over the barrel, carefully checking the shoulder rocket launcher he favoured, the belts of ammunition, the string of rockets, once fired, with Frank's renowned skill, so firm and final on their target.

The chanting of the Miskitos suddenly ceased. Glancing around, Dan saw darker shadows slowly coming toward them through the tall grass; the commandant of "El Grande", Cesar Lacayo, and behind him, the stocky bulk of their own captain, El Negro.

Cesar Lacayo, an older patrician figure, moved toward them, nodding to the respectful Miskitos. A former Somacista - whom the Sandanistas had displaced - his goal was clear to Dan and Frank. With the assistance of the Contras - nothing less than the restoration of an American approved, right wing dictatorship - and his own previous, privileged position.

The commandant moved slowly, greeting each one with a vague smile and absent handshake. Dan heard Lecayo's brief exchange with El Negro, following close behind.

El Negro stopped before them. Glancing at his watch, he looked hard at their blackened, camouflaged faces. "You guys - I'm countin' on you tonight. This isn't goin' to be easy." He leaned forward, his expression serious. "Let's make it a good one." Clapping each of them on the shoulder, he added, "See ya' in Chelle's." Chelle's bar in San Jose was a popular off duty hangout for many of the Contra mercenaries.

El Negro gave the section leaders their final instructions, a careful rehearsal of the mission.

"Listen up, Muchachos. Wrap your equipment. A loose piece of equipment or a white face can really fuck us up. He added slyly, "An' that's the way it's always been." Some smiled at the casual humour, all knowing the steely confidence of the man.

El Negro reminded them, "We've seen this stuff before. South of La Flor we'll pick up Conejo's group – then drop our stuff above San Carlos." He looked around. "A lot of you guys owe me one - an' don't let's fuck up! Okay. What are we waitin' for?"

A skilled, experienced professional, respected by his men – his name given according to Contra custom, concise, graphic, depictive; "El Negro" described the man, not his real essence. Indeed, a Black American, he was a veteran of other wars - fighting with American Special Forces in Vietnam. His real name was Buddy Johnson, from New York City. With the Contras now, the total professional - knowing their lives and his own depended on it.

Though El Negro kept largely to himself, Dan and Frank had spent several evenings with him in Chelle's in San José. Apparently, he had served four or more tours in Vietnam, his last two years with some type of Special Forces unit.

Moving in single file, they followed El Negro in a slow jog over the rising slopes. To distract from his growing discomfort, Dan sang to himself, the sound muted by the cadence of the creatures of the night world. The unrelenting rainfall, from deluge to incessant, misty drizzle, reminded him of how it had been back in Ireland. His legs moving automatically, arms relaxed, lightly gripping the shoulder strap of the AK-47, the hostile world around him was soon forgotten.

He could see the rain dance from the mountains in early spring, the clouds, chased by the wind in sudden gusts from the purple heathered peaks of Slievenaman, see the sun dance in the silent green valleys below. Across the Mournes, proud weathered monuments, the shadow plays between the grim, granite shoulders reaching to the sky.

He remembered, as a child, running through the ivy and the blackthorn in the half hidden refuge of the glens. Or out by Eagle Rock, the sunlit quarries, like shining teeth, scarring the slope. As he'd often heard it, like young girls' laughter, the waterfalls, the rustle and whisper from the rocky runoffs. So well he remembered now, all noisily gorged in fish and in spate - all flowing to the long, silent reaches of Dundrum Bay. Oh, to be home again, he whispered.

"Danny boy! What's up? Ye've stopped your song. Are ye still with us?"

Startled, Dan's mind returned from the dream to the sweat and rain running down his back, to the pain in his cramped legs and numb arms. Resenting Frank's intrusion, he heard Frank's continued panting and swearing, struggling along behind him. The wind had picked up, bending the trees, driving the rain into their faces.

Dan heard another sound; distant repeated harsh screams. Frank shouted, between pants and curses, "Do ye' not hear the eagle, Danny? The Incas called it the winged wolf. Do ye' hear it Danny? There it is again."

Dan heard Frank's quick laugh. "One bad, fuckin' bird, they say. They say this bird's an omen. I only hope it's a good one."

Dan strode on silently. Frank rambled on, "Danny –it's time we got goin'. I miss me' wife and son. And better now I know where we both belong, God damn it!"

Frank was homesick for the home and family he might never see again. All his life on the run, only knowing the brutality, still clinging bravely to the dream - God knows how or why. At that point, Dan too, felt cheated, denied. More than anything then, he wanted to bring Frank home.

*

The rain finally relented just before dawn. Dan bumped into the man ahead of him; the column had stopped. He heard the muffled birdcalls of the Miskito Indians signalling the approach of Conejo's group. Out of the darkness straggled the long column of the northern guerrilla force. The commandant of the northern group greeted El Negro. After speaking with El Negro, Conejo's group headed west down the hillside, into the darkness beneath the trees.

Following the others they moved out quickly.Dan was singing again, half aloud, half to himself as they descended toward the protective cover of the trees.

The long file of heavily armed men moved snakelike down toward the distant lakeshore, the scrub pine giving way to scàttered stands of oak. In the darkness, moving more cautiously, they could smell the strong, heavy perfume; the Balsom apple, the orchid sprigs. In the strangely luminous early morning light, they saw the dull yellow glow of the Cortesa tree, the pink fire of the Cabana. Silent, they listened to the morning chatter of the clockbirds, the birds of paradise.

CHAPTER THREE

Other Men's Wars

Suddenly they could smell the unmistakable odour of high-octane fuel. Below them they could see the outlines of the airfield. Cautiously keeping to the tree line they descended, faster now, listening to the reassuring whistle of the point men guiding their path.

A South African mercenary, Mike Wright, originally from Kenya, called back to his mate, Cobber Caine, an Australian. The response was almost lost in the rising thunder as a four-engine transport took off, clearing the brightly lit runway and passing almost directly overhead.

El Negro and the section leaders moved along the column. "Conejo's group should be ready to make its move," he glanced at his watch, "any time now. The detonation of the charges on the fuel tanks is our signal to start firing." He reminded Cobber of the agreed frequencies, the coordinates to send the ready signal within the next few minutes.

The column moved quickly through the underbrush, where the trees thinned out and the perimeters of the base lay directly before them. Fifty yards ahead, they could see the barbed wire fences; less than a mile beyond the fences, the western boundaries of the base. Peering through his binoculars, in the blue glare of the distant arc lights, Dan saw the huge cantilevered wings of the Antonevs, the swept winged Ilyushin - their cavernous cargo hatches open, as trucks, armoured personnel carriers, and a variety of heavy equipment and supplies were being off loaded.

Frank commented, "Danny, there has to be some sort of reserve unit backing this lot up - this is their main supply base. The whole fuckin' Russian air force, guarded by a handful of fuckin' compisteras? I don't like this." Beside them Cobber was muttering into the hand held speaker, his other hand turning the dials, trying to locate El Condor. From the darkness came the soft whistle, the ready signal, the responding acknowledgment from each section leader. There was a moment of quiet - the wind stirring the leaves, a lull in the pattern of take off and landings - hoarse whispers, the subdued rattle of equipment.

Almost simultaneously from Cobber's transmitter, a stream of static - then an urgent voice, volume too high - suddenly reduced. "El Grande, El Grande - this is Condor." The words were hurried, anxious. "El Grande – acknowledge." As Cobber answered, Dan heard an explosive "Holy Christ!" from Mike. "Shit, man!" Suddenly the western sky lit up with a white flash, quickly followed by a rumbling thunder of explosions. Instinctively each man ducked as they saw one another instantly, clearly visible in the reflected glow from the flames of the now burning depot and hangars. They listened to a rattle of exploding ammunition, then to a rising volume of small arms fire, distant shouts - the flare and thud of grenades and rockets.

Dan heard Cobber call out, "A trap! A trap! Conejo's caught it!' Then, the chilling words, "It's the Krauts. The Pommares brigade. They were waiting for them."

Staring through his binoculars Dan saw the chaos - distant running figures, the pinpoint of explosions to the loading area, the watch towers and barracks; heard the distant sound of sirens.

Then he saw them, same time as Mike did. "Fuck!" from both of them. By the main hangars, still intact, were two Russian helicopter gun-ships preparing to take off. Dan could hear Cobber's urgent voice, then static suddenly from the transmitter - unmistakable, the sound of gunfire, followed by a more urgent cry, "The bastards are closing in!"

Ahead of them, truckloads of troops were racing across the airfield toward their positions. Turning, Dan saw El Negro running through the trees to his right, calling out something to Frank on the way. Peering toward the burning buildings, Dan saw no sign now of the Russian helicopters. Perhaps they'd gone up with the hangers. His attention was quickly diverted to the line of approaching trucks. Firing in sustained bursts, the firefight continued sporadically on the northeast corner of the field. Perhaps El Condor was withdrawing.

A number of armoured personnel carriers were heading toward them. Dan was convinced the Germans had been waiting for El Condor's group. At best, Conejo's continuing fight might enable El Negro's group to escape - probably their only chance now. It was a hard decision - a bitter choice, but the only option for El Negro. They'd achieved their objective.

Cobber was still bent over his transmitter, El Negro beside him now. Dan heard "Hold on," or maybe, "Hold out," - then static, or maybe gunfire - a shout - then static. The firefight at the far side of the airfield had subsided, except for random bursts of automatic fire - single shots, an occasional cheer, a distant, single scream.

El Negro crouched silently beside Cobber. There was no word from El Condor now, only static. Cobber kept trying all frequencies with no luck. Suddenly, El Negro called out hoarsely, angrily, "Time to go guys!"

Growing numbers of Sandanistas were running beyond the perimeter toward them, yelling triumphantly, firing as they came. Dan, Frank, Mike and the others tried to slow them down with AK's and M-60 machine gun fire.

El Negro's group was beginning to take casualties. El Negro was helping Mike back to the trees. Suddenly, Dan heard Cobber yell. Cobber was gesturing wildly upwards, his face fearful, contorted. "Time to go! Time to go!" In the same instant, Dan saw Cobber begin firing above and behind him.

Dan heard the clatter of the rotors, the high whine of the twin gas turbines. Glancing up, he saw the sun winking from the offset plexiglass, like predatory eyes. Unseen and unheard in the distracting smoke, the gunfire and explosions of the battle - the two Russian MI-24 helicopter gun-ships had cunningly made their approach from the east, flying directly out of the morning sun.

Some of the Contras scrambled to safety - some fell, hit by the increasing fire coming from the Sandanistas, now sensing victory.

The gunship above them now seemed to pause, hovering, selecting its target. Suddenly Dan saw Frank running up the hillside, turning, beckoning them to follow. Frank was loading the rocket launcher as he ran.

In a second Dan came alive, sighting the hovering gunship - the cabin windows, the side-gunner in the hatchway. He kept firing till the magazine was empty, then threw the weapon aside, screaming in helpless rage and fear. "Down Frank! Down Frank! Jesus! Fuck it! Down, man!"

In another instant the gunship erupted in a thunder of rocket and machine gun fire, churning up the hillside. Dan was hurled to the ground, an explosion almost in his face. For a moment he couldn't see. He thought, the bastards have hit me! He heard a scream - his own - then silence. His vision cleared. Frank stood on the hillside above him. The helicopter had disappeared. The morning air smelled of fuel and cordite. Frank was jumping, arms raised, yelling, exultant - a triumphant dance amid the smoke and debris - watched by the stupefied Sandanistas from the hillside below.

"Danny, we got him! I hit him with the bloody rocket! It's a fuckin' miracle!" Frank was shaking the empty tube above his head, the sky still discharging smoking fragments of the Russian gunship.

As Dan rose slowly to his feet, he heard the machine guns open up from the Sandanistas below. He felt the blow, the sudden burning pain in his shoulder. Stumbling to his knees again, Dan checked his shoulder. Lucky, a flesh wound. Cautiously, he peered around. Occasional small arms fire, single explosions from the far side of the base, told of the final moments of Force Conejo. Time was running out. He turned, expecting a rush from the Sandanistas again moving toward them.

Suddenly, again the unmistakable sound sweeping in around them. In terror, Dan remembered - Jesus, the second helicopter! The world around them lit up in blue white glare. The hillside, the shrubbery and stunted trees flattened in the sudden downdraft. Frantically, Dan scrambled for his weapon lying on the hillside above him. He saw Frank in his strange dance of triumph, still shaking his empty weapon at the sky - exposed, defenceless. Dan watched, mesmerized - an inexorable process, destiny unfolding.

Frank, on a slight rise away from the tree line, finally saw the second helicopter. He looked over at Dan, waving him down. Then, slowly, as from an old projector, frame by silent frame, the irrevocable. Frank, mouth agape in a silent cry. Dan transfixed. The air sucked from their lungs - both struggled to stand. The trees flattened in the backwash from the powerful turbines, the spinning rotors.

Then Dan's unheard scream, "They see you, Frank! Fuck it, they see you!" Dan grabbed his weapon, started running toward Frank, loading as he ran. He saw Frank half kneeling, focused now - the resolute professional, calmly sighting and firing - facing the faceless, the elusive image - on the wrong side of the New World Order.

With a pop, Frank's missile curved upward. As Dan pulled the trigger on his own weapon, he heard and saw the stream of tracer pour from the hovering gunship. The ground around Frank smoked upward. Above Dan, a blinding flash - thick smoke and the sound of faltering rotors, stuttering turbines. Again he heard Frank's cry - a single shout - as the great ship fell off the sky, striking the ground with a thunderous explosion by the perimeter fence.

Dan ran up the hillside to where Frank lay, eyes open, unseeing. Frank had died as he had pulled the trigger, knowing only his final victory.

"Why couldn't you have waited?" shouted Dan in anguished, futile protest, as he knelt beside Frank, holding his head, heedless of the shouts of the others crouched around him.

Fortunately Dan's injury was slight. In guilt and anguish, he insisted on carrying Frank's body all the way.

*

Frank was buried in the churchyard of a small missionary church in San Rafael del Guatoso. Dan asked the priest to put a cross with Frank's name, the date and a brief inscription, "Died for Freedom"; and to be sure to place his name

22

in the church records.

"He has a wife and son, Father. Someday, they'll come looking for his grave."

The old priest nodded and shook Dan's hand. "It's a long way to come, to die," he said.

Earlier that day, at the post office, Dan had collected a white envelope addressed to Frank. Postmarked Paris, France, he saw it had been "expressed" to Frank almost a week before. He read the letter. It was from Frank's wife, Sheila. Dan made up his mind. He collected his savings and Frank's few belongings.

*

At Chelle's bar Dan, Buddy Johnson, Mike, on crutches, Cobber and others met as promised. Chelle's, where Dan and Frank had spent many an evening in talk of home, in revelry, song and laughter. They drank to Conejo, to El Condor, who'd given their lives, and to Frank - who'd saved theirs.

They drank then to Dan's return home. Dan was drunk; he knew he was. Chelle's children, bent in final resolution - appassionata, abandono or veloce! His weary head dropped onto his folded hands and he found he was clutching a small, dully glinting object. It was Buddy Johnson's memento, a small brass key he'd worn round his neck.

"In memory of Frank and the good times we shared." Dan gripped the key as his head drooped towards the bar.

*

Early the next morning, the jet cleared the runway. As the DC-10 banked lazily westward, Dan peered toward the distant rim of the Pacific. He dreamed of the mountains, the shallow valleys. The story he must tell, back home where he belonged, as Frank had said - among his own.

CHAPTER FOUR

China – the Journey
In the beginning of the journey lies the end.

Among those at Sean's graveside in Kilcoo stood Terri
Sai from China, with Paddy Finucane, an Englishman, by her
side. Tightly holding Paddy's hand, Terri's eyes were closed as
she listened to Fr. Alexander's words, quoting Gandhi's fifth
principle, of Sardovaya. "The path is clear – our goal now, an
existence in equality and happiness for all who can renounce
violence." Recalling the words of the Indian holy men over two
thousand years on, "None of us own the earth – only as much as
will suffice to bury you."

At this sight of "weiji", the Chinese expression for both
crisis and opportunity, Terri remembered her friend Aija, their
flight from Beijing and their fateful decision, the road to refuge,
to life and to death for some - a road to freedom for others.

In the valley east of the Tanen Range of Northern Laos,
by the headwaters of the Mekong River, flourishes the glowing
red blossoms of Papaver Somniferum. The sale of the harvest,
the milky sap of the unripe seed pods, feeds the families, the
struggling millions of small farmers in the mountains and valleys
from the Andes of South America to the Taurus Mountains
of Turkey. In turn, the opium refined from the sap, feeds the
fantasies of the children of dreams from across the world, of
affluence or of poverty.

Further to the north, beyond the watershed of the Jhu
Jiand, the Pearl River, for Terri Sai the nightmare had just begun.
With her friend Aija Tsi, who from birth could neither speak
nor hear, both witnessed the killing of their fellow students at
Tiananmen Square in the city of Beijing.

Terri and Aija, then in their twenties, attended the

University of Beijing; Aija majoring in history and philosophy, Terri in languages and economics. They had grown up together. As a child Aija watched as Terri, rapidly touching fingers to lips and finger to eagerly outstretched finger, enabled them to communicate with one another. Never discouraged by their earlier frustrated attempts, sometimes in tears, often in laughter, they grew to share each other's most sensitive feelings. Friends and family called them Shunag, the twins. They were inseparable.

Aija and Terri shared a tiny apartment south of the university, off Tiananmen Square, where they often walked together hand in hand, watching the graceful performance of the ritualistic Taiji movements by the older people in the early morning sunshine. They also noticed the more bizarre movement of the younger boys and girls, black stereo box in hand, volume turned high, the modern intrusion of Western disco dancing and tangos.

More recently they had come to listen to the words of the student dissident groups, the so-called Democracy Activists, with their growing dissatisfaction toward the repression of the traditionalist Communist Government they lived under. It had seemed as if the expression of Democratic ideas was to be an honest forum, to be heard by all the people, their concerns to be addressed by the government.

Patiently Terri discussed this with Aija, who touched her fingers quickly with excitement, nodding her head vigorously. In Aija's mute and silent world she had a bright, imaginative mind, a gifted intellect. Terri was constantly amazed at Aija's ability to grasp the ideas of her teachers. Aija's teachers also wondered at her hunger for enrichment, the range of her voracious reading, her capacity to retain knowledge. They marvelled at the mature scope of the papers she wrote. The thoughts she so eloquently expressed were eagerly sought by fellow students all over China. Those who came to know her were impressed with her energy, mature concern and love of people.

In her papers, Aija judiciously advocated less the need for radical change, than the will to accept progress, furthermore a return to the sanctity of the individual; a restoration of belief in people and their country, in that order. "We are," she wrote, "the modest heirs of our history, its sparse attainments, its myriad misconceptions, and not the origins." She would shyly explain, through Terri, how, "In our history lie the seeds of our destiny." None of them knew what Democracy, what freedom really was. They wondered if they were synonymous.

Terri and Aija joined a young dissident group with their friend, Liu Xiabo. The government had declared Marshall law. Terri and her friends held their ground, feeling that the world would encourage their government to relent. Exhausted, they watched the troops move into the city around them, realising then what this elusive fantasy of free expression might cost.

That night they heard tanks moving through the side streets. Before daybreak, they were startled to hear a burst of what sounded like heavy machine gun fire, followed by shouts and screams, and further bursts of small arms fire. They saw people running, fire and smoke rising around them.

Soldiers were firing indiscriminately at the students who fled through the streets. Terri saw a small group of students standing before the approaching tanks, seeming to be offering the tank crew scraps of paper they held in their hands, waving their arms, crying out to them. The soldier in the turret of the leading tank shouted to his crew below, pointing to the students. In helplessness and horror then, Terri and her friends watched the tank roll up and over the screaming students. Sick and faint, Terri fell to her knees. She realized this China was no longer home; she must leave the homeland she loved.

The rest of the night and the long day that followed, Liu Xiabo stayed with Aija and Terri as they fled south. Liu spoke of heading for Hong Kong and the New Territories. Occasionally they would stop to listen to the broadcasts on Liu's small radio. The government was exhorting all people to turn in the protesters, naming some of the dissidents, calling them "the revolutionaries". During one of the broadcasts, Liu heard Aija's name announced. Her pamphlets on free expression and other topics were the cause of their troubles. Aija was a traitor, they said, a recidivist, who had helped to sow the original seeds of the protest, now a revolution.

"Aija is in grave danger," Liu told Terri. "She must leave the country as soon as possible. The police will be after all of us. They call us the ringleaders."

Terri translated Liu's message to Aija. They concluded that their first plan, to head for their homes in Xian, would be a mistake. The police might well be waiting for them. Seeing Terri's fear, Aija, fingers racing, reassured her, "Do not be afraid, Terri. Freedom is a stronger force than oppression, and we will prevail!"

Intently gesturing then, Aija added, "We must be strong. We must not keep Liu from his chance of escape. We must see him on his way to the New Territories, to Hong Kong, as soon as possible. He can make it alone. We would only hamper his chances."

Impressed by Aija's courage and insistence, Terri reluctantly agreed with her. Terri and Liu both found strength in Aija's resolution. Turning to Terri, Aija concluded, "The dangers are increasing in the central provinces. We will have a better chance if we continue south."

Several days later, in the mountains above the Yangtse River, Liu reluctantly bade farewell to his friends. It was a frightening moment when Terri and Aija watched the tiny figure dwindle eastward, heading for Kwang Tung Province, the Pearl River and the New Territories. Waving to them from a distance, Liu Xiabo finally disappeared into the morning mists still lying in the steep valleys far below.

At that moment, Terri thought of the Buddhist goddess, A-ma, patron saint of the perilous journey. Kneeling, she drew her name in the dust by the side of the road. Aija watched her, smiling and nodding excitedly. They both knew the ancient story of A-ma's long ago life journey. Silently, they asked her to help them take care of each other now, that someday they might return to a free China and to their families.

In Beijing, they had heard of a Chinese lady in northern Laos, Anna Yao, a known temporary refuge for many dissidents. The choice to head south through Yunan Province would be risky, as they would be moving through more densely populated areas. Joining Terri, Aija knelt by her side as they considered

27

the alternatives. They agreed they should avoid Tibet. They had learned that the government was instituting a crackdown in that area. They decided to continue toward the distant Kunlun Mountains. Though a frightening prospect, this might be the safer option. They hugged each other, then gazing westward toward the distant horizon, started out on their long journey. Even as they took their first steps - two solitary figures in the vast, silent landscape - Terri wondered how they could prevail against such overwhelming odds.

Aija and Terri headed southwest through Szechwan Province. The heat and rains of the monsoon season alternately turned the roads to brown mud or soft red dust, clogging their eyes and mouths. In the difficult days that followed, their meagre food sources quickly ran out.

They followed the broad, mud-brown waters of the mighty Yangtse, knowing that they would soon be in the rice fields of southern China. There, hidden among the seasonal, itinerant labourers, the large cooperative farms, they hoped they would find lodging and food.

In their first days among the green fields lush with the rice harvest, they joined a company of young and old on their way to help with the picking of the crop. An incurious, friendly group, they seemed to sense Aija and Terri's predicament, offering them food and shelter. In turn, the grateful girls assisted them with the harvest in the rice fields.

During the long hot days, bending and lifting, or when pausing for water or their scanty evening meals, they would share casual chatter and occasional laughter. Terri learned that many in this group were teachers, civil servants, or even physicians. In an effort to impose their authority, it was the custom of some of the local governments to insist on a token time of shared labour in the fields during harvest time; or assisting in the heavy work, securing the river dykes during the monsoon season.

The older "volunteers" of the group especially, were resentful of these demeaning and demanding obligations. The recruitment of all levels of society was consistent with the teaching of Mao Tse Tung, from the Little Red Book. The initial enthusiasm of the masses for Mao and his teachings, Terri knew, had diminished following the purges of the Red Guard in the sixties.

One night, speaking through Terri, Aija told the group sitting by the fire, "My friends, old customs, old ideas, old cultures and especially old habits don't die as easily as the old people whom the Red Guard so relentlessly persecute. Mao," she said bitterly, "once contemptuously described the Chinese people as 'poor and blank'."

The older people and some of the younger ones, the teachers, nodded to one another, captivated as Terri transmitted Aija's message, keeping her eyes, her fingers, receptive to Aija's every silent word. Perhaps Mao's presumption had been short sighted, thought Terri as Aija confirmed, "With such statements, the old one showed us his own limitations, his own innate contempt for the individual person, whose unique contribution lies in his very individuality in a free society.

"Chairman Mao also said that indeed the people were a blank canvas, upon which the artist may draw beautiful pictures. This," Aija went on, "is where, historically, such benevolent despots fail, where Chairman Mao misunderstood the Chinese character."

Aija had written extensively, analysing the history of the early Chinese emperors and their dynasties. Always, she selected the more positive figures, their contributions and their misconceptions, and often where available, the well known response of the people.

Aija explained how, inevitably, the sanctity of the individual would ultimately transcend transient ideologies. She stressed the exciting cultural achievements of Chinese history, far surpassing those of the Occidental world - finally attracting their envy, their malice, and sometimes the worst of their exploitation.

In developing her own philosophy, Aija had become a brilliant proponent of an original Confucian blend of secular humanism. Yet even further, a timely and unique restoration of the role of the individual and the family, in Chinese society. Its appeal lay only partly in the thirst for alternatives to the rigid Chinese version of the bleak totalitarianism of Lenin and of Mao. People sensed that the ideas Aija expressed offered a characteristically Oriental resolution, a restoration for the long submerged identity of the Chinese people, their true culture.

Through Terri, Aija spoke often of these things. During the long, hot summer evenings the group listened. They seemed to look forward to these exchanges. They watched the smiling, animated figure of Aija as she conveyed her silent message, unable herself to hear, only to see the eager reception of her thoughts.

One evening, several of the young people told Terri they had indeed heard of Aija, even before the recent events in Beijing. They had learned of her new message, they said - of hope, of renewal for the Chinese people. Word of the massacre in Tiananmen Square had already spread across China to the outside world. Her ideas, they felt, were important to young people everywhere. They assured Terri they would protect them from those who pursued them.

Some days later they warned Terri secret police were in the area. Concerned that someone might have informed the regional authorities of their presence, Aija and Terri decided to continue on their journey. Bidding their friends farewell, they headed westward, toward the slopes of the Tahsueh Range. Even further ahead lay the rugged outline of the Ning Ching Mountains.

In those distant mountains, beyond the headwaters of the Yangtse, the melting snows from the high peaks joined the waters of the turbulent monsoon rains to conceive the mighty Mekong. In its broad meandering path, this Mother of Rivers, the rice and opium fields of northern Laos and Cambodia still offered a tempting avenue of escape. To float on the mighty bosom of the Mekong, or follow the jungle trails to Anna Yao in Muong Sing, or even further east, to the delta country of the South China Sea, and to freedom. They considered all these options.

Both were reluctant to leave China, yet afraid to stay. Like A-ma, the legendary goddess, it seemed they must now pursue their odyssey. Solemnly, they vowed that if this were so, someday they would return.

They travelled through the province of Singkiang in the company of a band of Kazakhs, friendly, nomadic stock herders of Mongolian origin. Terri found the unfamiliar dialect of Mongolian and Haka difficult to understand. Aija had less difficulty. Patiently gesturing or, for the children, drawing in the sand, she persisted in communication in her own special way to adults and children alike. She seemed to teach a common language. When her efforts were momentarily frustrated, she freely joined in the laughter.

Curiously, the Kazakhs seemed to understand the words Aija transmitted to them. With Terri's help, Aija would tell them stories as they gathered by the evening fires. Again and again Aija seemed to prove that there were times when the spoken word added little to the graphic sincerity, the ultimate spiritual communion, conveyed from Aija's articulate fingers, charismatic eyes, from her total animation.

As they travelled through the Tan Sueh Shan country they learned more of the continuing campaign of terror by Chinese government forces - of their brutal suppression of the Tibetan people, their culture, their religious traditions, and the power of the Dalai Lama. Terri clearly recalled how Aija had suggested, to Terri's surprise and dismay, that their best chance, their only chance, must now be a path further westward, to Afghanistan. Kneeling in the sand at their feet, her eyes sparkling, intently gesturing, Aija sketched a rough but certain map of the journey before them. Her decision and enthusiasm were infectious, her purpose clear, as her fingers quickly signalled, "We shall find refuge among another brave, oppressed people."

Clutching Terri's hand in hers, Aija went on, "Who knows, perhaps we can share their cause - help them achieve their peace and freedom."

Hesitant at first, Terri was finally persuaded, smiling in wonder at her friend's courage and enthusiasm. Truly, she thought, we are following the spirit of A-ma. All the more, Terri commenced to see Aija as the source and inspiration of her own courage, and of the love and companionship they shared.

Many weeks into their journey, they travelled through the eastern foothills of the Kara Korum Mountains, into an ever changing landscape, brilliant with the perennial wild red rose, the startling evergreen of the richly growing edelweiss. The serene, snow shrouded peaks reached to the clouds. Above the peaks, soaring, the great eagles, their distant cry a lonely echo across the deep, dark gorges. And always, the bitter, intense cold.

As the days passed, the Kazakhs came to regard Aija with a strange and gentle reverence. Camped for the night, warmed by the meal of rice and goat meat, Terri and Aija sat before the blazing fire of Yak dung. The tall Kazakh leader, his weather beaten face wrinkled in smiles, came slowly forward. Gently taking Aija's hand in his, he stood looking down at her. Aija intently watched his bearded lips as he spoke, carefully enunciating each word.

He spoke slowly, with some difficulty, in Mandarin Chinese, so that Terri and Aija would understand. "Aija, Fa Shih, your words are wise and will endure."

All at once they heard the wild scream of the Lammergier, the great eagles of the Hindu Kush, echoing into the snow covered peaks thousands of feet above them. Sensing the sudden distraction, Aija followed their gaze, staring upward. She could clearly see the great birds of prey circling, gliding, far above.

It reminded Terri of the helicopters hovering over the streets during the Tiananmen Square massacre. Below them, the panicked fugitives, running for their lives.

As the screams of the eagles subsided, the leader of the Kazakhs turned to Aija, his face suddenly grave, saddened. "Little one, the great birds, they are a sign to us. They have spoken, and you have been chosen. God go with you."

Aija reached forward, touching his lips with her fingers, smiling, nodding, eyes on his. It seemed to Terri a special moment of strange, silent communion. Without Terri's intervention, Aija had understood this man's words. Terri finally came to accept that many times Aija perceived more than others seemed to see or hear.

CHAPTER FIVE

'Afghanistan – the goat between two lions'
Abdur Rahman Khan 1900

Reluctantly leaving the Kazakhs some days later,
Aija and Terri headed westward into the Wakhan Corridor of
Afghanistan. Their new travelling companions, a group of hardy
Kirghiz tribesmen, the family of Abdul Wahed, accompanied
them through the pass at Wakhjir Dawan, just south of the
barren border of the Soviet Republic of Tadzhikistan.

Normally a fierce and reclusive people, Abdul Wahed
and his family accepted Terri and Aija without question. Again
the women and children seemed to recognize something special
about Aija. They listened with rapt attention to her eager efforts
to communicate.

Speaking little Chinese, they communicated with
difficulty in a mixture of Chinese, their own Altaic language,
and even some English. Terri had taken two years of English
in Beijing. Though less than fluent, this proved useful in her
exchanges with the many different races.

They managed to tell Terri and Aija that they too
were fugitives. Many of their own families were members
of the mujahidin, fighting a holy war, a jihad for Islam and
Afghanistan, against the invading Russian army and their allies,
the People's Democratic Party.

In the next few days, travelling through heavy snow
at over ten thousand feet, they reached the village of Abdul's
relatives. One evening Abdul's brother, Ibrahim, told Terri and
Aija,

"My family and I are from Afghanistan, but first and
foremost we share the faith of Islam. As in China for you, in
Afghanistan, Communism is an insult to our religious beliefs.
Whoever uses these false doctrines to divide us as a people will

surely fail.

"You, sisters, have already fought the same war
in another land. To us you are heroes. You can join in our
great struggle, our jihad against the invaders. You too can be
mujahid."

Looking at Aija, Abdul added, "Silent one, to whom
men listen, to join us is to know only victory. Should you die as
a mujahid, you will be a shahid, a martyr, and," he concluded
triumphantly, "you will go straight to heaven."

Terri explained Ibrahim's invitation to Aija who had
been eagerly following his words. Smiling, Aija commenced
to tell them why she and Terri had come here in their flight
from the same devils of oppression. Aija's animated response,
carefully transmitted by Terri and simultaneously translated
by Abdul, was intently followed by each member of Abdul
Wahed's family.

Aija spoke to them of the embattled history of this
region. She pointed to the high snow-capped peaks of the Pamir
Mountains, to the distant Karl Marx peak, twenty-two thousand
feet above Russian Tadzhikistan. Gesturing, laughing, touching
their hearts, Aija told them, "The young Macedonian, Alexander,
once stood here, surrounded by his enemies, seen and unseen.
Brave, ruthless, and so soon to die. Is it not a strange thing
that where we stand, another young adventurer, Marco Polo,
brought another breed of conqueror on his journey into Central
China almost seven hundred years ago?"

Aija turned to them. "As with my ancestors, is it
not a wonderful thing that those who have passed this way,
missionaries or conquerors, some with no message other than
death and destruction, some with their own heresies, the
Communists, the successors of Lenin and Marx - that they will
all pass, just as those before them? A blink in the passage of
time."

Aija smiled to the children as Terri and Abdul translated
her words. "Afghanistan has withstood the storms of time and
man's follies, and will outlast all the foolish notions, the greed of
these passing conquerors." The men nodded their heads, pleased
at the truths Aija had spoken. Terri wondered at the energy

contained in that tiny, animated body.

Abdul spoke with warmth. "What the silent, little friend tells us warms our hearts. Even the loss of her tongue does not prevent her from speaking. She inspires us, like our Pushtan heroine, Malalai. In the battle of Maiwand, less than two hundred years ago, she led us to victory over the British efforts to conquer Afghanistan."

When they returned to the fire, Ibrahim spoke. "As the fire has warmed our hands and feet, and the food has nourished our bodies, your thoughts, little teacher, have also strengthened our resolve to die as shahids in the great jihad, to drive the evil ones from our holy land."

Aija and Terri decided they would travel southward with Ibrahim's group as soon as the weather broke. The day before leaving a fine snow had fallen. A radiant, ageless image - silent, motionless, ethereal.

Before sunrise, Ibrahim and a small group of mujahidin led the sure-footed pack horses across the frozen slopes. Aija and Terri followed, riding on sturdy Bactrian camels. It was difficult parting from Abdul Wahed's herdsman warriors, the women and children, their hosts since their arrival in Afghanistan. Abdul stood watching their departure, diminishing into the distance, finally dwarfed between the bleak escarpments.

All about them then, a vast silence. The wind blew strongly from the snow capped peaks as they made their way along the mountain paths of the Wakhan Corridor, heads bent, cloaks wrapped tightly around their bodies in the freezing temperature. They spent long, weary days taking turns riding the plodding camels across the mountains, always hungry, exhausted and freezing.

Near Kamdesh, they turned south. A formidable force of mujahidin, armed with shoulder rocket launchers, mortars and heavy machine guns, joined them at Qazi Deh. Terri heard their commander, Jalad Khan, telling Ibrahim, "There is a column of Russian APC's, probably helicopter gun-ships, MI 8's and 24's in the area. We have been warned they are moving north from

Birkot. They should be in our area shortly."

Later that day as they plodded further south, the column abruptly came to a halt. Terri shuddered as she heard the barely audible whine above the whistle of the cold wind among the snow-covered slopes. Quickly the men herded the animals close beside the rocky cliff, while Terri and Aija huddled beneath an overhanging ledge. Ibrahim stood beside them. A light snow fell, drifting softly above the valley. The restless animals stirred by the roadside. The faint whine grew to a close, unmistakable clatter.

"Gun-ships!" Jalad Khan shouted. Terri and Aija held one another, staring skywards. Suddenly, a fortuitous gift from Allah! Dense curtains of snow came sweeping across the valley. The mujahidin crouched, weapons ready as they peered into the blinding softness that poured from the low lying clouds.

Terri and Aija peered down the narrow track along which they had been travelling. Mud-walled huts far below were almost invisible in the gusting flurries.

Suddenly Ibrahim yelled, pointing across the snow swept valley. He aimed his rocket launcher. With deafening clatter, three Russian aircraft screamed around the base of the mountain, flying low and fast to avoid ground to air missiles. Their target, the village, merging snowbound into a featureless landscape.

The helicopters, dark green camouflaged, red starred, turbines whining, hovered above the huddled collection of mud huts, like eagles peering toward their prey. Terri and Aija were horrified to see the houses disappear in clouds of smoke and snow. Explosions followed. The aircraft were momentarily lost to view, muffled in the smoke and increasing snowfall. Beside Terri, two of the men were struggling to keep the animals herded beneath the overhanging cliff. Others lay along the path, their weapons trained on the smoke below. The mujahidin were firing on the Russian aircraft.

Jalad called to Ibrahim, his voice barely audible in the thunder of explosions, the deafening whine of the engines. "The snow has stopped the armoured personnel carriers. They must have turned back!" It was another unsought blessing from Allah.

One helicopter suddenly disappeared in a massive explosion of flame, sending shock waves up the valley, disintegrating before their astonished eyes. Mujahidin from both sides of the valley rose, some with screams of "Allah Akbar!" The remaining two helicopters emerged from the smoke. They watched, speechless, as one helicopter veered wildly off its course, sweeping into the path of the second aircraft. Terri and Aija watched in horror as the two collided with a tremendous clatter. There was silence as the great birds faltered and fell toward the valley floor.

Ibrahim and the mujahidin on the hillside rose, screaming their triumph, noisily proclaimed their gratitude to a generous Allah. Waving their weapons above their heads, they raced for the burning village. Terri and Aija followed, stumbling down the hillside. They came to the smoking, burning remains of the little village.

Some of the survivors were crying, wringing their hands in shock, mourning their losses. Nearby lay the smouldering debris of the helicopters. Miraculously, two of the Russian crew had survived. Dragged from the wreckage, they lay, bloodied, half sitting, terrified. Villagers stood around them, some angrily calling for their execution. Terri saw some of the villagers praying, asking Allah's forgiveness for the prisoners, saying the Russians were hostages of the great evil, too young, unaware of the true God, his great mercy.

Ibrahim and Jalad spoke quietly to the village elders and the Mullah, gesturing toward the prisoners. The mujahidin, their weapons pointed at the Russians, waited for the moment of decision.

One of the Russians, bleeding badly from his forehead, tried to plead for his life. Terri was startled then to see Aija approach the Russians. They watched her, one in sullen trepidation. Aija knelt before them. Reaching forward, smiling, she gently touched their heads. The Russians stared at her. Aija rose, turning to the villagers and the mujahidin. With Terri and Jalad's assistance, she appealed for mercy for the prisoners.

One of the Russian boys watched in amazement. Convinced she was defending them, his shoulders shook as he sobbed like a child. Aija knelt and held his hand. He gazed into her eyes, incredulous, grateful.

In the old Afghan tradition of Nanawati, refuge given even to one's enemies, the villagers and mujahidin voted to allow Aija's plea for asylum for the two surviving Russians. Terri helped Aija care for the young prisoners. One, whose name they learned was Garik Vasilovich, was from the Kazakh Republic. The other, Ilya, was from the Republic of Tadzhikistan.

Ibrahim and Jalad Khan, along with the surviving villagers, all agreed they must leave as soon as possible. The Russians would surely be back. With the Khassadars providing escort, the long column of Bactrian camels lumbered up the snowbound trail. The precious cargo, the regional crop of raw opium, was destined to be sold in the trading bazaars of Peshawar. The long procession moved steadily in the growing dusk. Snow fell heavily; the wind rose. Ibrahim planned to cross the border into Pakistan just north of the Khyber Pass. By travelling mostly at night, they hoped to avoid the high flying Russian MIGs and MI 24's Ibrahim knew were now searching for them.

In the following days, during the brief rest periods, Aija and the Russian boy, Garik, drew close. They spent much of their time gesturing intently, one to the other, sometimes laughing, sometimes touching; one in spirit, just as Terri and Aija had once been. They always seemed to be striving to say so much more than even words could tell.

As his head wound healed, the other Russian boy, Ilya, spoke to no one. He remained sullen, guarded. Ibrahim warned Jalad to watch him, thinking the boy might try to escape. Finally, Garik told them sadly that Ilya was, like too many of the Russians in Afghanistan, addicted to heroin.

As Aija spent more of her time with Garik, Terri reluctantly began to recognise her growing jealousy, that Aija and Garik shared more than a friendship. She realised that Aija had grown from a girl with unusual wisdom, insight and sensitivities, to a woman who loved this lost young man with whom she would never be able to exchange a word, whose words of love she would never be able to hear - yet for whom, it seemed, silent smiles and gestures were all either of them needed.

The love of these two young people seemed to penetrate the lives of all the weary travellers, even the dour, unhappy Tajik, still keeping largely to himself. Aija continued in her efforts to communicate with all of them, especially after the evening prayer at the end of the long, weary days. And always beside her now, the attentive eyes of Garik Vasilovich.

As they approached the border south of Kamdesh, the snow no longer hid their passage. The presence of Russian and Afghan government patrols, the distant clatter of armoured personnel carriers, the whine of the scouting MI 24's, the supersonic scream of high flying MIG 21's, all became more apparent as the weary cavalcade approached Asman and the area known as the North West Frontier.

They were travelling just below the cloud line. Thinking the MIG's and MI 24's had not detected them, they decided to continue toward their goal across the Kunar River. The wind rose unexpectedly to more than gale strength, forcing them quickly to look for a campsite among the trees beside the footpath.

Suddenly warning shouts came from the Khassadars, a thousand feet above the misty cloud line. The wind drove the snowdrifts in sheets as they stood listening to the distant cries. The herdsmen struggled to control the hungry animals, trying to hear, to see through the mist of snow, cloud and fog.

The clouds began to disappear above them, as if a curtain had been drawn aside. Mujahidin were running toward them, waving them off the footpath, into the pitiful shelter of the surrounding trees. Glancing behind her, Terri saw Aija on horseback, her sheepskin cloak drawn around the children she held in each arm. The horse was being led by Garik.

Terri heard the terrifying cry born on the wind from high above them. "Russians!" then louder, from the mujahidin on the path ahead of them, "Above us! Down! Down!"

The scream of engines burst into the valley, the thundering clatter of rotors filled the air. Two dark green shapes with the clear, red starred fuselage circled the side of the mountain, stampeding the animals. The two Russian helicopters were close enough for Terri to see a crewmember crouched over a heavy machine gun.

Incredulous, she watched smoke and flame pour from the machine guns as the aircraft hovered above. A stream of bullets reached toward the animals, the women and children. She heard explosions behind her, the static rattle of gunfire, the cries of the dying. The mujahidin were firing back from the mountainside and the path ahead of her, the fire from the Kalashnikovs striking the armour plating of the killing monster above.

Terri turned, slipping, sliding in the deep snow, searching for Aija. She saw the Tajik, Ilya, running up the side of the mountain. Tripping and stumbling upward, he was screaming and waving to the hovering helicopter. The racket of engines, gunfire and exploding rockets drowned the Russian boy's yells.

Oblivious to the stream of gunfire now moving toward her, Terri saw Ibrahim go down. She saw the Khassadars firing and falling. She saw Ilya frantically reaching toward the aircraft above. Gunfire churned the snow around him. She saw him stagger and fall. Then there was no more movement.

Turning, Terri now saw Garik crouched by Aija at the side of the path. Seeing Ilya fall, Garik's face was contorted with anguish. He rose quickly from Aija's huddled form and ran toward Ilya. Passing Terri, he bent down and picked up an AK-47 from the hand of a Khassadar lying dead in the snow. Looking back at Terri, Garik yelled, pointing toward Aija. Aija was standing motionless, watching Garik. Terri turned back toward Garik. He was firing at the nearest helicopter, less than a hundred feet above him.

Instinctively, Terri turned back toward Aija. She screamed as she saw her friend, her sister, the little magic child running, arms outstretched, across the open ground toward where Garik knelt, firing.

The helicopter circled above Garik, faltered, rotors smoking, then lurched toward the mountainside. The remaining MI-24 turned in its path above the valley. In the same instant,

Terri saw Garik rise and turn toward Aija, saw his expression of anguish. Aija's mouth was open in a silent cry, her eyes wide, arms before her, as if to ward off the gunfire now directed toward her.

Frozen in time, Terri watched, helpless, horrified, as the guns poured a stream of fire toward Garik and Aija. They reached for one another, their love speaking silently above the senseless roar, the gunfire echoing and re-echoing across the peaks of the Hindu Kush.

In the valley of death there was a moment's silence - then a wild, heartrending cry as Terri ran across the hillside calling Aija's name. She threw herself over their lifeless forms.

*

Some weeks after the attack, while recovering from his wounds, Ibrahim spoke to Terri. "We know the loss you have had, a loss we all share. Garik, the Russian boy, is now joined in eternity to the little magic one, the silent one you knew as Aija. Both of them, together, shahids, holy martyrs in the war against the infidel."

Among the people of Afghanistan, the Kirghiz of the Kara Korum and the Wakhan Corridor, the mujahidin and Khassadars of the Hindu Kush, it was said, that when they hear the shrill scream of the Lammergier, they remember and murmur to one another, "Aija, Fa Shih, she will always be with us."

CHAPTER SIX

'The playgrounds of a few silent men.'

Stupefied with shock and grief, Terri remembered little of the following weeks. Jalad Khan and Ibrahim had hastened to bring her and the other survivors through the high mountain passes of Afghanistan to the markets of Pakistan before the Russians reappeared. In the vast refugee camp they joined the displaced thousands of the Afghan war.

Here, near the sprawling city of Rawalpindi, Terri finally awoke from the nightmares. She was young and strong; she knew she must overcome her anguish. If she allowed herself to dwell on Aija's death, the inner strength that sustained her would fail.

It was spring. Bright, fresh fields of orchids bloomed with new life and colour, promising a season of rebirth, rich with opportunity, a new world of busy optimism. Terri felt a compelling curiosity to learn more of Anna Yao, the lady Aija had spoken of. Perhaps Anna Yao, long active in assisting the dissidents from China, could help her. Muong Sing, the refuge she and Aija had rejected in their flight from Beijing, seemed a safer option now. She determined to try to reach Muong Sing as soon as she felt strong enough to travel. Later perhaps, she could travel to Hong Kong and join Liu Xiabo in working to restore a real "people's government", a new China. This the inevitable outcome Aija had so surely believed in. Terri felt renewed strength and conviction to pursue her destiny, her *samsara*. Perhaps, as she and Aija had said, like the Goddess A-ma, to return home from their wanderings.

It was during the Muslim fast of Ramadan that Terri first learned of a new cult of veneration, a mystical obsession spreading across the North West Frontier. The symbol of their devotion - Aija, the Chinese Kwajah, they called her. They had learned of Aija's words of love and liberation, of conciliation, inspiring tolerance and compassion for generations to come. Brave shihad, they said. Terri heard the *Sadhus*, the Hindu holy men, speak of her as a martyr, with reverence for her courageous *shahadat*, her unique profession of faith and love, her final moment of sacrifice.

They came in a growing pilgrimage from many areas of the North West Frontier. It was an extraordinary tribute. Though Aija and her love lay now, frozen in time in the snows of Nuristan, all who came, who touched the stones beneath which they lay buried, it was said, would also share in the spirit of love and forgiveness Aija had spoken of.

The North West Frontier, with its vast bazaars, was a vibrant marketplace of the ancient Mogul Empire, where merchant adventurers from East and West still meet to barter and to trade. Prince and peasant once thronged the markets in the legal exchange of carpets, spices or slaves - more recently, in the illegal trade in drugs, weapons and lives.

As summer approached, everywhere were signs of an increasing trade and traffic in heroin from nearby Islamabad and Peshawar. The opium from Afghanistan, Pakistan and Tajikhistan was shipped to Hong Kong, later sold in the streets of New York, London, Amsterdam and Paris.

As they had journeyed from Kamdesh, Ibrahim had explained how their crop would be sold in Pakistan to support their families, and ironically, in a historic, moral paradox - to purchase weapons needed in their jihad against the imperialists, the Russians, and the puppet government in Kabul.

Terri now accompanied Jalad, his sister Zarghuna, and Ibrahim to the nearby city of Peshawar. The ancient city, once the last frontier of the pre-Christian empire of Alexander the Macedonian, now capital of the Punjab, was also now home to the millions of refugees from the war in Afghanistan and their own factional duelling.

The rugs, whose beauty was extolled by the bearded Turkomen proudly carrying their merchandise across their shoulders as they strolled past the stalls, were not all that was

bartered in the streets of the famous Quissa Khawani Bazaar.
Peshawar was unquestioning host to the purveyors of those
other tools of conquest, the weapons of drugs and dreams.

In the swelter of the afternoon sun, it was a vivid,
sensual paradox, a miasma – the flies, the stench of the
unwashed, the dung of the wandering, sacred cattle littering
the streets. A dense sea of humanity screamed in a dozen
dialects, on foot, bicycle, pedicab or in taxis driven with reckless
abandon. Olympian, remote, among these citizens of Babel, sat
the naked holy men, the Brahman, silent, motionless, a focus of
serene tranquillity. To Terri the discordant uproar, the sense of
violence, disease, and death was overwhelming.

Settling in the stall they had leased, Jalad and Ibrahim
were soon bartering with a group of buyers. Terri, standing
beside Jalad's sister, was mesmerised by the gesturing, the
posturing, the violent denunciation of seller or buyer. Jalad, arms
waving in the air, appealed the niggardly price the group of
buyers was offering. Their spokesman, Zarghuna told her, was a
Hindu from Karachi, a difficult bargainer, a "low caste thief."

As Terri watched the drama, an imposing foreign car
nudged a path through the screaming traders. Its luminous
white hood, silver grille and dark tinted windows balefully
evoked an instant and obsequious respect. It approached unseen
by the frenetically gesturing Ibrahim and the Hindu trader.

The Hindu trader glanced sideways. Seeing the car,
his mouth fell open. He peered fearfully toward the interior.
Ibrahim and Jalad turned to follow his gaze. Terri saw the group
draw back, respectful, watchful. She felt Zarghuna grasp her
arm. The Hindu was bowing deferentially, grinning foolishly,
as they all gazed toward the passengers in the rear seat of the
limousine.

The darkened window of the rear passenger
compartment slowly descended. Two men seated inside leaned
forward, briefly conversed with the Hindu buyer from Karachi.
One flashed gold teeth. The other had striking blond hair, and
spoke with a deep resonant voice, staring briefly, fixedly, toward
Terri and Zarghuna. The window closed then, and the great
white limousine slid rapidly into the evening traffic. Terri stared

after it, its progress marked by eddies and surges in the river of people and animals in the "street of the storytellers".

The Hindu stood mesmerised, half bowed in salutation, staring into the traffic. Quickly then, the exchange resumed between buyer and seller. An agreement was reached, the Hindu now more subdued. Jalad joyously concluded what seemed a generous deal.

Zarghuna turned to Terri. "The men who intervened are rare visitors," she said. "Men of great wealth and power, men of legend. My brother told me some time ago that they are the biggest arms dealers to the mujahidin - even greater, they say, than the Adam Khel Afridis from Kohat who once supplied arms to all the Pathans of the North West Frontier."

Fearfully gazing to either side, Zarghuna lowered her voice, almost whispering, "Known as the *Braderakan*, the Brothers, these men are also the largest buyers of the opium crop, from Kazakhistan to Burma. The man with the gold teeth is known here as the shadow of the blond one, the Imam Zaman. The shadow, he is seen more often around this area, since the war with the Russians. Everyone is afraid of them." Zarghuna concluded, "The word of the Imam is the final word." Terri saw the fear in Zarghuna's eyes.

It was during the early summer that Terri had first heard of the one known by many names. In Urdu, the man was known as El Sadar, the leader. In Arabic, he was El Kaed, or El Algazi, the leader or the conqueror. To the Kurdish people, he was El Ze'im, the anointed one. Significantly, perhaps, in Persian, the man was called the Imam Zaman, the nameless one. In the North West Frontier, with its myriad ethnic groups, many different dialects were heard. Most of the prevalent languages were random mixtures or regional modifications of Arabic, Farsi, and Persian. Terri quickly learned that few had ever seen this man. Even fewer knew him. Yet stranger still, so many knew "of him".

Later that evening, Jalad explained to Terri, "The Imam Zaman does not like to be seen - a reclusive and dangerous man, a deserter, some say, from the Russian army in Afghanistan. There are stories of those never seen again, who have questioned or cheated his buyers. These men are also known in

Afghanistan as far north as the Wakhan Corridor." Jalad went on thoughtfully, "Perhaps they deal in drugs and weapons in Russia. Who knows, perhaps even in China."

Ibrahim confirmed Jalad's words. "On a recent visit to Islamabad, in the Margalla Mountains just seventy miles east of Peshawar, I heard that El Ze'im is now arming our Muslim brothers in Kazakhistan and Tajikistan, as well as others in Iran. The Caucasian Republics are joining them, it is said, in a holy war against the Infidel. A war such as the world has never seen."

Gazing into the firelight, Ibrahim spoke of other arms sellers who had come to the North West Frontier enlisting them to join in one "Colonial crusade" or another - efforts by the Russians, the British, to control the destiny of the area. Ibrahim described others who had come to help them in their more recent battles against the Russians. Among them, Americans, some who had never returned home after their defeat in the Vietnam War. Ibrahim spoke of the British and Americans joining them in their endless war against the Russians. He'd seen one Englishman in the Hindu Kush. "Yet none I heard of," said Ibrahim, "have such power, have instilled such fear, as this man you saw today."

Indeed, Terri would never forget the men in the "Street of the Storytellers". Especially the one who had singled her out from the dense, surrounding crowd, staring directly toward her. She recalled the distinct, terrifying impression, the sense of fear and foreboding that remained with her long after the limousine had disappeared into the traffic of the Quissa Khawani bazaar.

The days succeeded one another in a contrary universe. Terri Sai saw the disease, the despair, the traditional debris of the colonial heritage - sensed the increasing ambience of evil and menace as the ancient world around her shuddered to the new age music, the tremors of the renewed acts of dominion, the pawnbrokers and salesmen of the New World Order.

The U.S. extended their influence into areas of political intrigue, economic dependence. And from Iran, Iraq, Afghanistan to Pakistan, the new voice of Islam emerged. Drugs and oil, for "weapons of mass destruction." The response from the imperial predators to the renewed Islamic unrest was prompt and conclusive. The skies darkened in the smoke of burning oil fields.

Terri Sai wrestled with her decisions, knew the grief, fears, doubts and uncertainties of the sad void in her life. For Terri, struggling to follow her *Kan Khat,* her destiny, the shofar has sounded, as the valley of the Euphrates and beyond trembled to the aftershocks of other wars. It was time to commence the long journey homeward. A time to meet the lady Anna Yao.

Ibrahim had become like a father to Terri. He cared for her as one of his own, and more importantly, shared her veneration for the memory of Aija. Ibrahim and his family reluctantly listened to her decision to journey to Muong Sing. Ibrahim told her he knew of a group of insurgents who were trading opium for weapons in the northern regions of the Burmese Thai border near Mai Sai. There would be an escort of Khassadars accompanying them, to protect the shipment. They would see that she reached Muong Sing safely. Afraid to travel alone, Terri agreed.

Terri and her new companions commenced the long journey eastward. Through the long hot summer days Terri and the Khassadars slowly crossed the massive burning plains, passing south of Darjeeling. In the northern distance, they pointed out the spectacular peaks of Everest, and further north, the majesty of Kanchenjunga, each striding unrestrained to the blue vaults of the Tibetan skies.

In another month Terri and her companions reached their destination. Terri's first view of the Mekong, gorged with mud and rain, and the ancient kingdom of Lang Xan, the land of a million elephants, was an impressive sight. Limestone peaks rose precipitously above the mist-shrouded banks of the broad river. Everywhere a bright carpet of flowers, of yellow daisies as tall as a man, red and white poppies, frangipani and orchids, the colourful harvest of the monsoon season.

Two days journey from the borders of northern Laos, they were met by a Meo tribesman. The short, powerfully built man introduced himself as An Luc. Learning of their approach, the lady Anna had sent him to guide them safely to Muong Sing. The lady Anna awaited their arrival.

Though An Luc spoke Chinese slowly and with some difficulty, Terri readily appreciated the warm and sincere welcome, instinctively trusted him. The Khassadars bade her farewell and continued on their journey northward.

Following the narrow trails beneath the leafy canopy of the tall hardwood trees, Terri and An Luc reached Muong Sing on the evening of the second day. On the outskirts of the town, a primitive collection of native huts, shuttered remnants of the French Colonial presence, stood the crumbling edifice of a French Foreign Legion fortress, like a forgotten scenario for an old Humphrey Bogart movie.

On a hilltop less than a mile from Muong Sing, hidden among the surrounding trees, they came to Anna's house. A sprawling colonial structure peered across green lawns to the valley, the rice fields and the broad banks of the Mekong below. Standing on the balcony, Anna Yao smiled and waved.

Terri sensed that Aija was sharing this special moment with her. She struggled to hold back her tears. If only she and Aija had turned south sooner, following the Mekong to Muong Sing; perhaps Aija would be with them now.

Anna greeted Terri warmly, immediately aware of the incredible courage, the strength of spirit it had taken to bring this vulnerable girl from the vast plains of China. Hugging her, she could not hide her admiration, yet also her dismay on seeing the tiny, weather-beaten figure of this young woman, with her few possessions, the long path she had travelled. As Anna silently comforted her, Terri felt like the wandering A-ma, on her way home at last.

To celebrate Terri's arrival, Anna had organized a *baci*. Terri would long remember that evening, the soft music of the *khenes,* the gentler ringing of the gongs. Then the clear, faultless sounds of a young boy's voice singing the Meo songs of welcome. In the soft glow of coloured lanterns were tables laden with food. Everywhere came the quiet murmuring of voices, warm laughter.

Gathered beneath the glow of the lanterns, in the still witness of a full moon, Terri told the story of her journey. Anna and her guests listened in silent wonder as Terri spoke of

Aija, and their flight from Beijing. Anna and her guests shared Terri's anguish as she said, "So quickly has Aija passed through our lives. Yet so enduring was her impact." To the tearful sympathy, the questions, Terri expressed her own convictions, her commitment now to perpetuate Aija's message of love and tolerance - her belief in the inexorable rebirth of the free spirit of people everywhere. With Anna's help she would carry this message to their friends in Hong Kong and to the people of China.

"Never more timely," said Anna, with warm conviction. "For Aija and Garik, a special destiny, but a sad misfortune. Terri, had you chosen the shorter path to Muong Sing, neither of you might have made it. Chinese security across the border has increased. Aija's words, your mission, would then have been denied. It is our turn now, Terri, our Kan Khat, to help you see that Aija's word reaches everywhere. You are the messenger - you were chosen. Aija's words are not buried in the valley in Nuristan. They are with us still. And when the monsoons have passed, we will see to it that you will safely reach your friends in Hong Kong."

Over the next several weeks, Terri would struggle along the muddy roadways with Anna to visit the busy markets in Muong Sing, or in her morning rounds of the plantation, chatting with the farmers. Like Anna and Terri, many were fugitives from other wars and different countries.

Sometimes seated on the balcony, sometimes walking about the rain swept gardens, or sheltering among the wind bent trees, Terri and Anna shared their stories. Though born in China, Anna was of the *Hmong*, meaning "Freemen", their ethnic origins further south, in Indochina. Centuries before, hunted and oppressed by the Chinese, derisively calling them *Miao*, barbarians, many of the Hmong people fled to the mountains of northern Laos. There, they had resisted successive attempts to enslave them, defying in turn the Chinese, the Vietnamese and the French who gave them the further name, *"Montagnard"* - mountain men.

"Sitting here, Terri, many nights, I have listened to the nearer voice of China, the voice of the Mekong as it tumbles

49

through the cataracts, coursing its way from the province of Yunnan to the South China Sea. It gathers to its bosom the soils of China, of Burma, of Laos, of Cambodia. This river, Terri, is the soul of many generations of our peoples."

Anna gazed toward the distant river. "In so many ways our voice is a confluence of races, our history as turbulent as the rivers, whose energies have provided the life blood for all our peoples."

In the still, humid evenings, the last, reluctant rays of the sun etching the Long Lun Mountains, Terri listened to Anna's story. From the jungle below they heard the muted cries of the night birds, the chattering of monkeys. About them always, the perfume of orchids, and above them, in the sudden tropical darkness, the risen moon riding a cloudless sky.

"We, Terri, are the ultimate lesson in a recurring theme of the history of Southeast Asia, of China, and, it seems, of the rest of the world. Efforts to enslave one minority, ethnic group or another. Or to extirpate the alien voice or vote, as the English delicately call it. It's all the same. Yet all inevitably fail in the face of the increasing resistance of the victims, their succeeding generations providing the human limitations for both." Slowly Anna added, "And so it will be in China, Terri. We will prevail."

Anna had joined the Chinese Communist Party Youth Corps as a young girl. With further dreams for the great socialist victory, she had been recruited during the Vietnam War to work with Chinese government intelligence in North Vietnam.

In the last months of the war, working for the North Vietnamese on assignment in South Vietnam, Anna had unexpectedly made the decision that would change her life. Seeing the cynical use of the drug trade as a weapon against the Americans, their human vulnerability, she felt compelled to reject her role. A sudden victim then, threatened with blackmail, with death, Anna had been rescued by an ex-patriot Englishman, a member of American Special Forces. Anna had unexpectedly faced another moment of fateful decision.

"In many ways, Terri, we were both fugitives. Patrick was an unlikely mercenary - a fugitive, he once told me, from the British social structure. He was the one who gave new meaning to my life. We seemed to find ourselves, as we found each other."

Anna was smiling, her face appearing and disappearing in the play of light and shadow from the lanterns swinging in the warm breeze from the river.

"I was a fugitive then. In the last weeks, we spent much of our time together. When possible he brought me with him on his missions. They were dangerous times. Caught in an ambush in Cambodia, in the last days of the war, we escaped to northern Laos. When the war ended we decided to stay. In a sense, like too many, we are still fugitives from wars everywhere. Neither of us has ever wanted to leave this region. This has become our home," said Anna quietly.

Those first few weeks were a time of peace, and for Terri, sorely needed rest; yet listening to Anna's occasional allusion to the fugitive role, Terri also saw the transient fear in Anna's eyes, heard the change in her voice, sensed the shadows that fell too quickly across the sunlit garden they shared.

In the following weeks, through Anna, Terri began to see a vivid replay of the historic socio-drama of the Vietnam War. With growing fascination she saw the personal, the political intrigue, the lies and corruption. From the extraordinary epic, other tales emerged. One, Terri listened to with a growing sense of dread and fear - Anna's strange saga of the keys, its continuing menace.

It was in the last months of the Vietnam conflict. As many as fifty-eight percent of American troops were on hard drugs - casualties of another war. The demoralised Americans faced impending defeat, in retreat everywhere. The worst debacle, deception, betrayal, in their two hundred year history since winning their freedom from the Mother Country. Withdrawing from Cambodia, from Laos, they left the Hmong people, the Montagnard, to their fate. At best, it was a criminal, political miscalculation.

Anna, then living in Saigon, worked with the Americans, yet as part of a North Vietnamese undercover group had first become aware of the Vietnamese drug sales to American soldiers. Crude but effective, the drug programme was a fortuitous, readily available further weapon. Through local dealers an endless supply of heroin was assured.

As Anna described it, the corruption of the colonial forces had enabled her to deny her scruples. She had seen what the Americans and the French before them had done to her people. She felt indeed that nothing could be too bad in avenging the generations of Colonial oppression, perhaps ensuring the future freedom of her people. This way Anna tried to keep her sanity, to quell the revulsion she felt, seeing the addiction of the innocent as well as of the guilty.

Anna had a dangerous role. Watchful of the local racketeers who could steal the drugs, monopolise or overprice the market or sell abroad, yet not directly involved – hers was a precarious position. Cautious never to reveal her real role, Anna walked a fine line between the merely corrupt and the real enemy, the drug salesmen.

In the drug market in Saigon, among the minor traders, Anna quickly saw the many nationalities involved - Australians, French planters, Americans, Chinese and, significantly, South Vietnamese government officials. Their only fear was that as soon as the war ended, their bonanza would vanish.

"The key figure in the drug conspiracy among the South Vietnamese was General Tung Giang. One," Anna said bitterly, "who suspected my dual role. He survived the victory of the North Vietnamese and transferred a thriving drug operation to Burma. More recently, I'm told, he has moved to this region. He is known here as General Khun Sa, and leads a guerrilla army, fighting for supremacy in the Golden Triangle."

Anna then described an American army colonel, Michael Deevers, who directed the most successful of all drug dealing organisations during the final years in Vietnam. In charge of ordinance and supplies, his activities were well known to the North Vietnamese. Playing all sides, Deevers had the assistance of many in the American and South Vietnamese government administrations.

"We had to keep a close eye on him. He ran a very successful black market, selling weapons for drugs to the northern warlords in Laos and Cambodia. He tried to run an independent operation, selling more through Hong Kong than in the streets of Saigon. Deevers was clever, devious, ruthless. He trusted no one.

"As the war drew to a close, increasing panic, chaos and confusion prevailed. The American colonel became more suspicious, fearing his own betrayal and subsequent exposure. Somehow learning I was Chinese, not from Indochina, he seemed to suspect I might be an agent, perhaps for the Triad or some other Chinese criminal organization. He questioned me, asking if I had ever been to Hong Kong. He mentioned that he had heard from his friends in the South Vietnamese and American administration that an investigation was underway.

"On heroin himself at that point, one night, drunk or drugged, Deevers warned me that he kept a record of all those he dealt with. He spoke of a vault in Hong Kong, of keys that were never out of his sight. He boasted that he held reputations and lives in his hand, that he had enough wealth to buy anyone on either side."

Listening to Deevers' threats, Anna was afraid her time was running out. She considered escaping to North Vietnam, their armies now rapidly approaching the city. But her growing disillusionment, uncertain political identity left her with nowhere to run.

"In Vietnam, I had seen the greedy void of rampant capitalism, 'counterfeit Democracy', the 'Machiavellian illusion'. Deceived, I also began to see the communist perversions of Socialism. Where was I to turn? Was it all a sham? I had to make a choice as I watched the best of men, misled, lured to die in the wars of the arrogant elite - the worst of men!"

As a guest of colonel Deevers and General Tung Giang at a reception at the American Embassy, Anna was introduced to an American major with an incongruous English accent. On permanent assignment to Special Forces, Major Edward "Paddy" Finucane had been in Vietnam for almost three years. That particular evening, indifferent to the suspicious efforts of Anna's escort to deter him, an attentive Paddy Finucane, with his chatter and easy laughter led Anna into another world.

Anna confessed, "I am neither Buddhist nor Christian,

Terri, more a Confucian, perhaps in the manner Aija has described. Yet, I do believe in Kan Khat, a preordained destiny. And so I saw the meeting at that time, with the man who would give me another choice, another chance."

Smiling, Anna recalled his sure persistence, his quick wit and charm, his amusing disrespect and contempt for the rear echelon, the military and political society Anna also despised. An unlikely mercenary; born in Ireland, of English heritage. "A fugitive, he told me, from the British social structure. But the one who gave new meaning to my life."

Eyes glowing, her expression radiant, Anna told Terri, "We left the party, and with this man whom I'd never met until that night, I left my doubts and fears behind and never looked back! Some days later we returned, different people, to the world we'd live in for the rest of our lives."

Anna's life had changed in other ways, too. Shortly after her return, Colonel Deevers called. Angrily, Deevers accused her of betrayal. He was plainly unsure whether Anna worked for the Americans, for those investigating Deevers' own territory, the drugs for weapons market or, for the "drug suppliers", the North Vietnamese. Terrified, Anna listened as he threatened to expose her - accusing her again of working for "others". Bluffing recklessly, Anna wondered if Deevers was also bluffing? How much had he found out? It was only a matter of time, Anna thought. Or, was he more afraid she might now expose him?

When Deevers called again the same night, Anna's questions were partly answered. She was stunned to hear his question. Did she know Major Finucane was working with a Special Forces unit investigating the black market in Saigon? Slyly, Deevers suggested that Finucane probably knew Anna's role, and was using her to reach him. He reminded Anna again of the keys he kept, and their significance. Finally Deevers insisted Anna meet him, alone, at an address in Phnom Penh, Cambodia, April 15. He warned her that if she didn't show up, or told anyone, he would expose both her and Finucane. He said he had enough information to have them both arrested.

Anna sensed Deevers still didn't know her real role in Saigon and was afraid of her testimony if he was discovered. He was, furthermore, wary of her possible access to major figures in the drug world in Indochina and her knowledge of his own activities. Afraid of the protection she might have. Perhaps he was trying to make a deal with her. Though Anna took Deevers' personal threats seriously, she wasn't concerned about his accusations against Paddy. She trusted Paddy - knew he wasn't using her as Deevers implied. Her main concern in fact, was that Paddy might feel she had used him, that she had ruined his career - even risked his life. Reluctantly, Anna realised she must tell Paddy. She never thought of escape. She knew she couldn't leave Paddy now.

Listening to Anna's story, Paddy's immediate concern was for her safety. His instant response was of unquestioning reassurance to her anguished, unqualified confession of her role, Deevers' threats, and of the harm she might have done to his career. He confirmed Anna's love and trust in him and his own love for her. Paddy's understanding of her political scepticism was the final reawakening of all the dreams Anna had lost, or never had. She told Paddy the whole story - her ideals, her disillusionment, her rejection of the excesses of both sides - even of the negative political ideology Paddy now fought for, its conspiracy of lies and greed, that brought so many young Americans and young Frenchmen before them, to die in an alien world.

As Deevers said, Paddy was indeed part of a special unit, investigating the black market in military supplies in Saigon. Until Anna spoke, Paddy had some suspicion but little real knowledge of the extent of his involvement. Paddy described some earlier problems his unit had run into with Deevers and some of the South Vietnamese military brass during their investigations into the black market of military supplies. Paddy had not been aware of the North Vietnamese drug strategy, nor of Anna's role.

Paddy suggested she keep the appointment in Phnom Penh. Perhaps together they could outsmart Deevers in spite of the unfavourable odds. Anna agreed - they had little choice. If they could locate the keys Deevers spoke of and the vault he had described, they might be able to document and expose the extent of his role in the largest black market operation in Southeast Asia.

Without this documentation, Anna and Paddy knew they would likely be the only victims. Anna's testimony, revealed as the word of a former North Vietnamese agent, would not be helpful. Neither would her association with Paddy, already in trouble with the Americans and the South Vietnamese who worked with Deevers. Paddy and Anna, both their word against that of the American colonel with significant influence and resources, might well result in Paddy's court martial. And even worse, in Anna's execution.

CHAPTER SEVEN

Anna's Story

Terri and Anna sat on the balcony, gazing out toward the nearby Mekong. They watched the slim pirogues being poled across the swollen river by the Meo women, their long skirts blowing about their ankles, delicate and beautiful, as in some Korean brush painting. The distant limestone karsks, verdant green, seemed to float above the fog-shrouded rice fields. The mornings were cool, fresh, exhilarating, and the days warm and rain swept, as Anna's story unfolded.

Paddy had instantly reacted to Deevers' timing and location for their meeting. He explained to Anna why April 15th and Phnom Penh, besieged by the Khmer Rouge, continued to trouble him. The location and date were identical to the rendezvous of a Special Forces mission to which he had been assigned some time previously. Perhaps Deevers had other business in Phnom Penh that day. As the day drew near, fear began to stalk Anna's days and haunt her sleepless nights.

Terri watched Anna twist her hands together, gazing toward the river as she continued her story. Advancing North Vietnamese units approached Saigon. Renegade groups roamed the city. In a last minute scheme, members of the South Vietnamese government decided, with the assistance of the American high command, to move the South Vietnamese government gold reserves to a safer location abroad. Paddy's Special Forces group - Spec Seven, was chosen for the unenviable assignment.

To cover all eventualities such as hijack or ambush attempts, Army Command evolved a diversionary plan. Two helicopter flights, designated Eagle Force 1 and 2, each consisting of a Chinook 46 transport and seeming to carry similar loads -

were to leave Tan Son Nhut Airbase.

Eagle One, leaving first under Paddy's command, would carry the gold, and without escort, would rendezvous with a South Vietnamese naval flotilla in the South China Sea, delivering the gold on the first leg of its journey to Singapore. The diversionary flight, Eagle Two, under command of another Spec Seven team member and deliberately rumoured to be carrying the gold, accompanied by two Cobra Gun-ships, would later fly directly to Phnom Penh.

As a further diversion, it was rumoured that the second flight's destination was Bangkok. After completing its delivery, the first flight would join the second in Phnom Penh. Once Paddy's flight landed, he was to radio signal the naval flotilla, which would then convey the gold cargo to the larger transport for the journey to Singapore. It looked too complex to Paddy's dubious eye. Through him, Anna was assigned to the mission as an interpreter.

Though Tan Son Nhut was under increasing North Vietnamese artillery fire, on the morning of the fourteenth the mission left as planned. Eagle One, with Anna and Paddy, delivered the gold and reached Phnom Penh on the evening of the fifteenth. They were surprised to find the airport and Eagle Two under heavy rocket and mortar fire. The Special Forces team and accompanying Montagnards were soon holding a busy perimeter. They had lost one of their aircraft. Evacuation would be a problem.

Perhaps the attack, misled by the diversionary rumours, was an attempt to hijack the gold - or coincidental to a larger Khmer Rouge onslaught. Wondering if Deevers was involved, Paddy and Anna decided to keep their rendezvous.

There were tears in Anna's eyes as she continued. "It was a wild drive from the embattled airport," she recalled. "Our rendezvous was an old French colonial house in the suburbs. In the driveway, we found an abandoned jeep. The keys were in the ignition, the motor still running. Inside, the house was silent.

"We searched the ransacked rooms together and at last found Deevers in a back room." Anna's voice shook as she continued. "He was dead, Terri, crucified, his body still warm.

He had been stripped, and horribly tortured. I was so frightened, wondering if his killers were still nearby. How had they known of the rendezvous? The questions, ever to follow were - who were they, and had they come just for Deevers - or for Paddy and myself as well?"

Anna was pale, trembling, as she remembered the horror, her expression fearful, eyes wide, fingers nervously reaching to the little ornament at her neck.

"Yes, Terri, we found the keys! There were seven of them. As he'd boasted, he'd kept them with him, in the only item of clothing still on his body. Paddy found them hidden in his shoes."

Paddy and Anna made their way back to the airport, where the situation was quickly becoming untenable. Amid constant rocket and mortar fire, the screams of the wounded, the heat and smoke, the Khmer Rough launched repeated suicidal attacks.

Time was running out to accomplish the remainder of the mission. Despite repeated attempts, Paddy failed to transmit the coordinates of the freighter lying off Phu Quoc Island for its final shipment to Singapore. Unless the naval units made their critical rendezvous the gold transport would not be achieved. As Paddy had feared, the costly over-elaborate decoy scheme had failed.

With Spec Seven Task Force still under heavy fire, Paddy and the C/O of Eagle Two agreed it was time to pull out. They had two helicopters, one of the CH-46 transports and a smaller Cobra gun-ship still airworthy. Only one of the assigned pilots had survived. First priority was the evacuation of the wounded. There was insufficient room for the wounded, the body bags, and the remaining survivors of both groups. Anna was offered space - she chose to stay with Paddy.

At this point, Anna remembered, the C/O of the second group offered to fly out the Cobra gun-ship to try to contact the naval flotilla. A crazy scheme, yet if successful would achieve the purpose of the mission. Paddy had later told Anna the C/O had been a "tin jockey", flying for Air American, the CIA in

Cambodia, before joining Special Forces. Anna couldn't recall his name. "A big man - even under fire he was always laughing. He seemed to thrive on the challenge."

Seeing it as their last chance to salvage the mission, Paddy readily agreed, giving the man the last course and location of the naval units and the classified coordinates of the freighter.

On a sudden hunch, Paddy then distributed Deevers' keys to five other members of Spec Seven before departure, giving one to Anna and keeping one himself. That way, if only one of them made it back, the case against the black market operation Spec Seven had been investigating would likely be solved. Deevers' organisation would be exposed. And important for Anna's safety and peace of mind, Deevers' killers would be revealed. As Paddy gave the keys to each one he urged them to deliver them to the Special Forces Commander awaiting their return in Saigon.

In those last moments the Chinook took off, overloaded with the wounded and some of the Montagnards, flying low toward the perimeter. As they gained altitude, it took a hit and exploded in flames over the city. The almost single shout - "Jesus!" - expressed the agony of the watchers.

Having just seen the Chinook go down, the volunteer C/O of Eagle Two didn't hesitate. Anna smiled, shaking her head, remembering. "A wild, crazy man, Terri." Smiling and waving to those left behind, he took off in the Cobra gun ship. Almost at ground level, wildly spinning and dodging, the smaller craft raced toward the river. They watched its course, breathless, silent - as though their chances flew with it. Anna remembered hearing Paddy's cry - the Cobra had disappeared in a sudden pall of smoke - maybe a ground to air missile?

That night the remaining survivors made their way out. Anna and Paddy headed north, following the course of the Mekong, to the Luang Prabang mountain range of northern Laos.

Later, they heard that the naval flotilla had disappeared without a trace. Perhaps the shipment had been sunk as they waited on standby for coordinates to the rendezvous. Or possibly they'd been hijacked by their crew or, more likely, by one of the numerous groups of buccaneers then roving the coast of the South China Sea. During those last days, as some twelve divisions of the North Vietnamese army closed in on Saigon, the Americans evacuated the city. Soon the war to roll back communism in Southeast Asia was over. In the ensuing chaos, all contact was lost with the American Special Forces Command.

As Anna and Paddy adapted to their new life, pioneering in a new world, the extent of the debacle in Phnom Penh gradually emerged. Paddy later learned that all reference to the failed mission was censored, its very existence denied. Further inquiries led nowhere. All other members of the Spec Seven force had been listed Missing in Action, many lives callously sacrificed. Anna and Paddy's survival was known only to themselves. "Then again," Anna said, "possibly Deevers' murderers knew."

Paddy agonised over the bitter implications of his responsible role as the C/O and now, possibly, its only survivor. In discussions with Anna he recalled the controversy surrounding Spec Seven's investigation of the apparent South Vietnamese and American complicity in the black market dealings in Saigon and the eager speed of Spec Seven's subsequent assignment to the gold transfer mission. Then there were the startling developments in Phnom Penh - the ambush, and Deevers' simultaneous presence. Paddy was convinced that Deevers' murder was not a coincidence.

As the days passed Anna and Paddy had focused on a more rewarding mission, becoming involved in the day-to-day life of the region. Anna, happy to be working with her own people, showed Paddy another world; a healing experience. Paddy enjoyed working with Anna and with the Montagnards, whose loyalties he felt had been betrayed when the Americans withdrew. Anna became increasingly involved with the growing number of Chinese political fugitives from across the Chinese border less than five miles away.

Unlike the plundering colonials of the past, Anna and Paddy were content to share equally in the resources of the land and its people, eagerly contributing their energies and skills, the spirit of their love for one another. They immediately confronted a major problem, a dramatic regional proliferation of the drug industry in all phases. Anna spoke of the new drug culture with some sense of remorse. The ultimate irony was the effect her activities in Saigon might have played in the victimisation of her own people, so many years before.

Anna described the drug refining factories in the mountains and jungles of the region, the dangerous regional warlords, debris of the social and political turmoil of the past three decades. She spoke of the enormous profits, some to the corrupt regional governments. The major share of the profits however, went to the distant shoguns; "Deevers' successors", Anna called them. They lived in remote elegance, the best clubs of London, New York, Paris and now, in Moscow.

"And they, Terri, are still in control, as much as they were in Saigon during the war."

Paddy and Anna worked with various regional development programs, some fostered by the governments of Thailand, Burma and an uneasy coalition administration in Laos.

"We transferred our efforts, working with the International Drug Control Office, bringing in substitute crops for the opium harvest. Later, working with the International Drug Enforcement Agency, we were able to increase the commitment to a bean crop that gave the local farmer twice what he was getting for the opium. We brought in weaving, pottery, the cultivation of the silkworm, encouraged other local home industries. For a time our efforts were successful." Sadly shaking her head, Anna continued, "As soon as the demand arose for the new drug substitutes, for cocaine, the market changed again. Drug prices rose rapidly. We could no longer compete with the drug and arms dealers. We had to contend with a whole new influx of international criminals of great ruthlessness, assisted by the very government agencies appointed to control the situation."

Terri saw Anna's expression change. She smiled, quickly chasing the shadows away, as she spoke again of her husband Paddy. "My lord Fucan," she called him, then in London on business. He had been gone for some months, and Anna missed him greatly.

Paddy's father had worked for British Intelligence for some years. Paddy had been persuaded to join the Service, recruited by a former colleague of his father's, then stationed in Bangkok. During the Russian invasion of Afghanistan Paddy and An Luc, his Meo body guard, travelled to Pakistan to work with American and British intelligence against the "Evil Empire" during the seventies. Paddy's further assignment in conjunction with Anna was to assist in a "China watch" capacity.

Though Paddy's visit home to settle family matters was long overdue, the main purpose was official government business. Terri saw Anna's worried expression as she confided, "He is presenting testimony to the International Drug Enforcement Agency conference in Paris, on the increasing drug and arms sales in Southeast Asia." Anna paused. "This is the first time Paddy has left alone, without An Luc. We have led very busy lives, Terri, but we have not forgotten the dangers we share. Paddy's testimony threatens the interests of some very ruthless, powerful people in the region. And again, the Chinese borders are less than six miles from here. The Chinese are well aware of the assistance we have been giving the dissidents. Possibly they are also aware of my former role with Chinese security in North Vietnam. It's not an easy situation."

Anna stood, distractedly staring into the darkness across the forests and the rice fields, to the fog shrouded banks of the Mekong.

Terri recalled her own experience with the drug and arms merchants in the Quissa Khawani bazaar. She remembered the Braderakan, the sense of fear and foreboding she could not shake. The Imam Zaman, the "Nameless One", his booming voice, the hard, staring eyes singling her out.

Her voice almost a whisper, for a moment Anna almost seemed to be speaking to herself.

"There are those who never seem to give up, who seem to follow us. Since Paddy left, the phone lines have repeatedly been cut." She turned to look at Terri, her face in the shadows.

"I love him very much. I'm not so afraid for myself, but for both of us." Again Terri saw Anna reach nervously to her neck, fingering the short gold chain, the small brass ornament that hung there.

"More often," said Anna, "Paddy's thoughts returned to the investigations in Saigon, the disaster in Phnom Penh. He reluctantly concluded that our fears were well founded."

Paddy had felt sure one of Deevers' associates had recognised a window of opportunity to seize control of Deevers' operations and assets. Deevers probably had no intention of returning to Saigon. His presence in Phnom Penh, coincident with the arrival and ambush of the gold transfer flight, suggested a possible bungled hijack attempt. Perhaps his killer had even shared in these plans. Remembering the scene of Deevers' death, Paddy and Anna had agreed, his killer had been a very desperate man. It was never far from Paddy's mind, what had finally happened to the gold consignment, the gold bullion worth many millions.

It was during the last hot, humid weeks before the monsoons, a time of nervous expectancy. One evening, Terri was seated on the veranda, Anna standing by the railing, gazing into the darkness. The only sounds were the persistent chorus of the cicadas, the steady whirring of the slowly turning ceiling fans. They shared the uneasy silence, waiting for the relief, the first drops of rain.

On the warm night air, above the night sounds, came a distant gurgling. The voice of the Mekong seemed different, swollen perhaps, with the carnal debris of human or animal conflict. In the darkness beyond the river, the infinite green sea of the jungle rolled to the mountains in the west. The invisible floral carpet of the valley floor below, a once fluorescent celebration of Terri's arrival, was indefinably sinister now.

Terri shuddered, sensing the whispering night presence, resonant, gibbering, carnivorous. Anna seemed agitated. In the lantern glow Terri saw tears glistening on her cheeks. As if in answer to her unspoken question, Anna knelt by Terri's chair. Impulsively she reached to the chain around her neck, unhooking the clasp. She handed Terri the chain and its stubby ornament, a small brass key. Terri took them in her hand, reaching across to comfort Anna. Anna's voice was soft, almost pleading.

"In these past few weeks, Terri, I have felt that those who follow me draw closer." Before Terri could reply she continued, "They must never get this key, Terri! Will you please keep it for me? It's been a talisman, at times, a heavy burden. Should anything happen to me, please see that this key gets to my Lord Fucan. Our friends in Bangkok will help you reach him." Anna's voice was urgent. "An Luc, who brought you here, he is Khon Kong - has mystical powers of survival. He will get you there safely."

Anna clasped her hands over Terri's. "Terri, promise me!"

North of Muong Sing there was a time of stillness. Even the animals moved stealthily, pausing, listening. Almost inaudible, the distant cries of the boat women poling their shallow pirogues across the broad river. A curious spectacle, their small craft almost invisible, they appeared to stand poised or in slow graceful motion, clearly reflected in the still, silver surface of the water.

In their remote world, Anna seemed happier now. They commenced to explore Aija's writings. Deliberately written in Pia Hua, a common Chinese vernacular, Terri and Anna translated as they transcribed the contents of the little journal and some papers written by Aija that Terri had kept, comprising an imaginative and original political and social philosophy. As Anna commented, it was no less than an alternative way of life, of confronting an endless history of conflict, worldwide.

Aija advocated new priorities for the third millennium, the long sought rebirth of a practical, universal social doctrine. A "family" of tolerance, compassion and of sharing, goal directed challenges to society. Essentially, "from each according to his ability - to each according to his needs."

Terri sensed Aija's presence, standing beside them,

following her own, silent words.

From our first primal inception as a social, intelligent species, wrote Aija, *seeking to realise our purpose, our potential, we have had to recognise our limitations. Even in the face of our solitariness - our only real challenge - the imperative to recognise our biological consanguinity and to pursue the inevitable community and brotherhood of man as its own goal.*

As in Capitalism, the urge to foster, promote and indulge the survival driven instincts and its excesses, polarises the people. Aija stressed the urgency of readjusting the mindless drive to "excel". *Excellence, for the wrong goals, is a destructive, nihilistic diversion of energies.*

Aija wrote of the Western misconstructions of the original Indo-Aryian religious concepts, of the words of their prophets from Buddha to Samsara to Zarathrusta. *True religion, she wrote, preaches the tolerance of diversity! Sadly ignored are the original religious traditions of the early Indo-Aryian beliefs, their enduring resource for man. We must learn to share before we destroy ourselves and our moral and physical environment.*

Pacing on the balcony above the gardens, they watched as the monsoons arrived. The incessant grey, whispering curtains of rain stretched across the rice fields to the Mekong, invisible, in full spate.

One evening, oblivious to the rumblings of the storm echoing to the south, they sat on the veranda. Anna stared toward the Mekong, occasionally visible among the trees. She listened in tears, as Terri read from the journal. *"My friend, my voice, my ears, my first touch of life - I only wish for you to also know such love as I have come to know. The love and care that you have shared with me, little sister, has been my inspiration. For me, never to speak, never to hear - the limits to my physical abilities only inspired me to 'see' more, to try to reach others, as you have reached me. To share the dreams, to help sow the seeds, the harvest that will bring us from serfs to freemen everywhere."*

Terri remembered Aija's words spoken long before the events in Beijing; that freedom was as elusive, ephemeral, as difficult to ensnare, to sustain, as the butterflies of summer!

In those final weeks the monsoons began to recede,

leaving the verdant forest floor and the valleys an exuberant testimony of lush growth; the eucalyptus, the fruit trees, the tall hardwoods, the rice fields were all a rich harvest of bright colours. Full blossomed, the frangipani and the orchid steamed in the early morning sunlight. And rising above the mist were the sudden, evening rainbows - their brilliant spectrum reaching across the gardens of Paddy and Anna's home far above the turgid, rain gorged Mekong. The ethereal colours, some said were an omen, a phantom that would bring ill fortune.

An Luc was in Muong Sing, trying to get the phone service restored. Apparently it had gone down again during the heavy rains. Ever protective of the lady Anna in the absence of "Lord Fucan", he made further inquiries. The news was disturbing. The repeated interruption of the phone service was not, perhaps, a random act of mischief. Not wishing to worry Anna, An Luc called on the Chao Keung, chief of the province, to confirm the rumours.

The old chief, a close friend of Anna and Paddy, insisted on telling Anna himself what he had heard. His greetings to Anna and Terri were solemn.

"General Khun Sa and his army, the Mong Tai," he explained to Anna, "have moved across the Mekong into Houa Kong Province in the past weeks. They are dangerous neighbours, fugitives in this battle for supremacy." His expression was grim. "More powerful groups are coming into northern Burma, the Golden Triangle, and now into northern Laos. I am afraid we have become the battleground once again."

Just as Anna and Paddy had feared, thought Terri, as they listened to the Chao Keung describing the rapidly worsening situation. The control of the production, sale and transport of a new heroin, ultra pure they claimed, smokeable, injectable, now competing with cocaine for the world market.

"Since his arrival in northern Burma," the troubled old man told them, "General Khun Sa has charged exorbitant taxes to protect those who grow, process, or sell the drugs. He has made millions for his services. But he has been replaced in a territorial dispute by a greater lord.

"Chinese criminal organisations," the old chief went on,

"have also moved into the area, followed by Chinese 'Security', supposedly in pursuit of the criminals to stop the drug traffic. More likely, working with them." Terri listened with growing dismay.

The Chao Keung continued. "The newcomer who has taken control in the drug business throughout this region is a Caucasian, *'farang dang mo'*, a sharp nose foreigner."

For Terri, it again reawakened frightening memories of Peshawar, and the meeting with the Braderakan.

After the Chao Keung had left, Anna spoke to Terri and An Luc of the renegade South Vietnamese General Tung Giang, now called Khun Sa. "His local rivals remembered him as a traitor who sold out his country, who led them in corruption." Anna added, pensively shaking her head, "As he draws nearer now, will he remember me as I remember him?" Then turning to Terri, "I wonder if Tung Giang knew of Deevers' plans? And, who is this feared 'farang dang mo' the Chao Keung speaks of?"

An Luc, clearly worried, asked Anna if she wished to leave the area. "For a short time, until we know what is going to happen here - a visit to the Tuan's friends in Bangkok, perhaps?"

Anna shook her head, smiling to reassure An Luc. "This is my home. I won't leave our people. This will always be a refuge for those like Terri, escaping from China. I must be here for them, especially now when great changes are coming. Perhaps," looking again at Terri, her eyes bright, "until Aija's dream has come about."

Unable to sleep, listening to the drumming of the rain on the galvanized roof of the veranda, Terri walked out onto the balcony to find Anna sitting beneath the soft glow of the lantern light.

Troubled by the Chao Keung's warnings, they talked into the early hours of the morning. Anna spoke of her friends in Bangkok, Bill and Mary Whitcombe, Mary working with the International Red Cross, Bill, with British intelligence. They talked about Terri's plans for her journey to Hong Kong. Anna spoke as though Terri's departure was imminent. Later, when the rain eased, Anna seemed more reassured. They returned to sleep the remaining hours till dawn.

Some days later, the phone lines still down, Terri agreed to accompany An Luc to Muong Sing. They started out for the city late in the afternoon. The skies were clear and the jungle steamed, drying in the warm, humid air. The drive took longer than usual; the trail in some parts still axle deep in thick red mud. Finally reaching the city, An Luc delivered crates of corn, beans and raw silk for weaving to the markets, while Terri bargained with the vendors for food and other household supplies.

Muong Sing, the City of Lions - less than six miles from the Chinese border - a frenetic, uneasy scene of conflicting cultures. The enduring peasant grimly struggled to survive among the "new colonials". From all parts of the world they came, a frenetic coalescence of dealers, pimps and sharks. Salesmen of the predatory Western ethos. The incessant turmoil was now closely observed by their giant neighbour to the north - the ever more mistrustful "People's Republic".

Waiting for An Luc on the steps of the old French administration building, Terri listened to the boisterous confluence of a dozen different dialects in raucous exchange. It was a city living in the past, trying to confront a changing world, reaching greedily for the future - a city bargaining, gossiping or plotting, existing remote from reality - in the shadow of the ancient Foreign Legion fortress, a tourist curiosity now on the city's tattered suburbs.

As soon as An Luc had completed his business with the civil administration Terri was anxious to return home. She felt every eye was upon them, every face suspect. As they left, the skies darkened and the rains commenced again. Uneasily, Terri wondered if they could make it back before nightfall. An Luc anxiously peered ahead as he drove, almost blindly at times, through the rain and windswept streets, a bedlam of horns and bells.

Driving past the old Foreign Legion fortress, the rain fell heavier, in wind driven sheets - almost impossible to see ahead. Inevitably, the car skidded sideways in the mud, the engine stalled. With water rising to the floorboards, An Luc shouted to

Terri, they must make it to higher ground. He helped her from the truck, through the knee deep, rushing water to the roadside. They started the long journey homeward on foot, the road now a river of mud and fallen trees. At times, An Luc had to carry Terri across an almost impassable trail. They trudged on in the gathering darkness. The wildly swaying trees above them eerily alight in the recurring flashes of lightning - an instant, psychedelic scene. An Luc leading Terri by the hand, they strained upward into the now torrential rain and gusting wind.

Struggling through the mud, they reached the pathway to the house. In a sudden flash of lightning through the trees they saw the house was in darkness - the lanterns unlit. In a brief hiatus in the storm, above the barking of the gibbons, they both heard it - a long, piercing scream. Then voices, loud shouts, followed by a short burst of automatic fire.

Quickly instructing Terri to wait for him, An Luc fought his way through the tangle of tree limbs, bamboo, mud and vines. In dread and terror, for an instant Terri stood motionless beside the roadway. Already completely exhausted, she began to struggle up the pathway.

Terrified, she stopped again. Echoing above the storm she heard a resonant, booming voice. Brushing the hair from her face in the streaming rain, trying to see, she heard hammering, screams. In horror she blindly stumbled toward the house. Nearer now, she heard the sound of an engine starting. She had barely time to fling herself among the trees when a jeep came careering down the pathway. Engine revving, the vehicle skidded down the hillside. In a lightning flash, Terri saw two large figures in the front seat. One shouted to the driver, holding his hat on his head, looking back at the house. The driver turned as they passed close beside her. Through mud and spray from the passing jeep, in a second flash of lightning, Terri was stunned to see a quick flash of gold teeth - the man in Peshawar!

An Luc was calling her from the house. She struggled on, looking upward. In another fluorescent flash of lightning she saw him standing on the balcony. In panic, hearing the anguished tone of his voice, denying the dreaded intuition - she kept repeating "Oh no! Oh no!" as she ran through the trees, to Anna and Paddy's home - Anna's paradise, among the chattering gibbons, the frangipani and the orchid - "No Shangri-la" she'd said.

CHAPTER EIGHT

The Cobra and the Crocodile

An Luc kept his promise to the lady Anna, escorting
Terri to the Whitcombes in Bangkok. They spent the next few
weeks there recovering. Mary Whitcombe, devastated at the
news, had immediately taken care of Terri, called Paddy in
London and contacted her husband, Bill, then in Hong Kong.

When Mary sadly relayed the news of Anna's death to
Paddy, she told him that An Luc, in accordance with Anna's
wishes, would be meeting him in London. Mary also arranged
for Bill to meet Terri Sai at the airport in Hong Kong, to help her
contact her friends.

Still shocked and grieving from the circumstances of
Anna's death, Terri sat, eyes closed, gripping the arms of her
seat. Her belt securely fastened, she was one of two hundred and
fifty passengers on Air India flight 640, bound for Hong Kong.
The plane shook and trembled as it thundered down the runway,
then climbed steeply above Bangkok. Far below, a variety of
river craft, mighty teak barges and slender hangyao thronged the
busy waterways.

Peering intently, Terri thought she could almost see
the darker green outlines of the Luang Prabang Mountains,
the jungles, the rice fields through which she and An Luc had
found their way only weeks before. Sadly she gazed along the
distinctive silvery coils of the river, to its distant tributary, the
Nan River, down which they had fled from the final nightmare
of Muong Sing and far northern Laos.

Terri closed her eyes. How strange it seemed that she
and An Luc had found refuge with friends in Thailand, in loose
translation meaning Freedom, the name chosen by its gentle

people centuries before. Now far below, the palaces, pagodas, slums and brothels of Bangkok, the City of Angels, merged into the tropical dusk.

Startled, Terri opened her eyes. She declined the smiling query from the attractive Indian stewardess offering her the dinner options. Turning, she saw the concerned expression of the young man seated beside her. Terri scarcely noticed the undisguised admiration in his eyes. She reached up and switched out the reading light, murmuring something about being tired. She closed her eyes again and drifted into a fitful sleep. When next she opened her eyes, momentarily disoriented, she brushed the tears from her face, trying to comprehend the quiet voices, the sudden confines of the aircraft, as they bore her eastward in their flight, rocking gently on the head winds.

The passenger seated next to her spoke, his expression concerned. "I am Peter Ramaiah." He added awkwardly, "You seem frightened. Are you afraid of flying?"

Terri shook her head. He seems so young, she thought, so sincere. She smiled, yet cautious, distrustful. Reluctantly she introduced herself, conceding, "This is my first experience of flying."

Peter Ramaiah told Terri that his business commitments obliged him to travel widely, from Bangkok to Singapore to Hong Kong. He chatted on while Terri looked suitably impressed. Suddenly he fell silent, turning away without explanation. She had the impression he wanted to say more, that he was struggling with some conflicting emotions.

Terri could barely contain her own anxieties. Distracted, she turned to look out toward the night sky. Reaching for the little pouch tied about her waist, she distinctly felt the folds of the small journal. Since their hurried departure from Beijing, Terri had kept the journal as a record of their travels, trials and hardships. Aija would often read Terri's comments, and soon began to add her own. At times the thoughts Aija wrote, or the account of the day written by Terri gave them moments of laughter, of serious or sad reflection, or of intense discussion.

As Terri's fingers fondly caressed the firm bulk of the little diary, they reached further to the key Anna Yao had given her before she too, like Aija, had left her, so violently, in the mountains of northern Laos. Terri fingered the stubby little token suspended from a chain between her breasts. She slept fitfully, starting in her dreams like a child.

In the cabin of Air India, the overhead lights were now switched off. Beneath the dim glow of occasional reading lights, most of the passengers were sleeping, oblivious to Terri's restless stirrings. In her dreams, her nightmares - Terri relentlessly retraced her odyssey, unfolding like the legendary goddess A-ma. Unnoticed, a tall, dark man, Arabic or Middle Eastern, paused in the aisle. He stood, staring at Terri's sleeping form, then moved quickly into the first class passenger area.

Abruptly then, Terri awoke, her mind still in the snows of Afghanistan, her heart still aching with memories of Aija. Terri had the impression she was being watched. She shuddered. Was it a dream? She thought she had seen someone standing over her in the darkness. Clearly she saw the eyes - intense, cold, murderous. Terri struggled to gain control of her fears.

She glanced around. Other passengers were sleeping in the darkened cabin. Somewhere further forward a child cried, muted by the constant rumble of the engines. Startled to see the seat beside her vacant, Terri again felt the cold edge of fear. She wondered if her friend Liu Xiabo had made it safely to Hong Kong after leaving them in Kwang Tung Province. If only he could be there to meet her when she landed. She listened to the smooth rumble of the flight, felt the gentle sway of the big jet as it soared far above the distant China Sea. She thought of An Luc, on his journey to London now.

As soon as she closed her eyes again she saw Aija's face, her smile. She wanted to keep her eyes closed, to live again with Aija. The silent image, so real - the silent laughter that was Aija. If only to touch her lips, her fingers, once again to hold her as they watched the stars.

Would that it had never happened, that she had never come into my life, then her leaving me would not have left such a sad, empty void. Terri quickly rejected the thought. To have known Aija, to have loved her, to have learned from her wisdom, she thought, to have shared her strength, her compassion and tolerance, has given me more than I could have expected from life.

In the darkened cabin, passengers stirred as the fuselage creaked, swayed and groaned. Terri gripped the armrests. She saw Peter Ramaiah moving down the aisle in the darkness. Though she trusted no one now, his return strangely reassured her.

Peter groped his way into his seat and fastened his seat belt. He seemed agitated, nervous.

On the flight deck of Air India 640 the radio operator was exchanging briefly with the weather station at Haik'ou, just off the Liu Chow peninsula of mainland China. A chattering voice intruded on his wavelength. Through the accompanying static, the radio operator heard the repeated identification query. It was coming from the Chinese air force fighter base patrolling off the coast from Chan Chiang.

"We receive you, Chan Chiang." We are Air India 640 with two hundred fifty passengers out of Bangkok and bound for Kai Tek International Airport in the New Territories."

"Flight 640 this is Chinese Government Security. We receive your message. Please inform your captain, you have a passenger on board who is wanted by the Chinese Peoples Government on charges of drug transport."

The radio operator was startled. As he continued to listen, he signalled to the co-pilot, pointing urgently to the headphones. The voice repeated the message, asking for acknowledgment.

"We have notified security at Kai Tek, who will be taking the passenger into custody on your arrival." The security agent then paused, "Be vigilant and cautious. Don't attempt to approach or detain the passenger - we have good reason to believe this person is dangerous."

An intense exchange now took place on the flight deck - calls to the flight tower and security at Kai Tek, who confirmed receiving communication from Chinese Security. The head stewardess was called into the conference. They had no description of the anonymous passenger.

The passengers were unaware of the increasing consternation on the flight deck, the growing anxiety that the unknown person might even be a terrorist or hijacker - might suddenly reveal some crazy, self destructive plan, some monstrous violence.

Captain Rabin Singh had been Air India's most senior pilot for almost thirty-three years. Now qualified for retirement, with a generous pension, he looked forward to spending more time with his growing family.

As flight 640 bore steadily on its course, Captain Singh prayed earnestly for their safe arrival over the New Territories. Captain Singh was concerned at the thought of a confrontation while airborne, the potential loss of life should the narcotics offender decide to hijack the aircraft.

"Hello Kai Tek. This is Air India, flight 640. We are approximately forty minutes out from Lantau Island at thirty thousand feet. We have heavy cumulus below us. Head winds are strong from the north at about forty knots. We await your clearance."

Following acknowledgment from Kai Tek, Singh added, "Has Hong Kong security any further information regarding passenger sought by Chinese government?" Perplexed, he continued before awaiting the reply. "We don't want confrontation on the flight."

The tension on the flight deck increased as the international airport answered. "Chinese government has no other information. They have insisted on being present on landing to apprehend the person. Flight 640," the control tower went on after a short pause, "Hong Kong governor and council have concurred with Chinese demand to identify and arrest the passenger."

Abruptly the speaker broke in again, giving directions for a wide detour. With a growing sense of foreboding Singh acknowledged the instructions. His acknowledgment was followed by an added message, which he listened to with dismay.

"Flight 640 Air India. You will be directed to land at

the Security Terminal building. If you learn or suspect their identity, do not attempt to apprehend the passenger. The person is dangerous."

Terri, eyes closed, was unaware of the frightened crew in conference on the flight deck. The nervous scrutiny of the senior stewardess was well apparent as she paced the aisle. The seat beside her, vacant for much of the flight, was again quietly, almost hurriedly filled.

"Maintain present air speed, stay on your present heading for another fifteen minutes. We will be putting you onto runway fourteen - repeat, runway one four - to security and customs."

The voice from Kai Tek added in a conspiratorial tone, "The Chinese seem to think the person is a woman. The narcotics division in Hong Kong is equally insistent the suspect is a man. Since they also informed us he is a non national, it seems there is some confusion." The perplexed sounding, English accented voice added, "It's really hard to know which one to believe."

In spite of the unhelpful lack of information on their mysterious quarry seated just yards behind him in the aircraft, Captain Singh tried to smile encouragement to his frightened young co-pilot, a novice, trying to maintain his composure. Singh wondered what he would do if they lost control of the situation. One thing he had always secretly dreaded - a shoot-out on the plane. If that happened Singh knew their chances were small. He turned his attention to his instruments.

Terri awoke, startled, haunted by the unthinkable horror of Muong Sing. She stared wildly around, wiping the tears from her eyes. Again she had seen the faces of those she had known and loved. All gone. She felt a great sadness. She reached again to the stubby little key that hung from her neck, aware of its grim significance - then to the small, bulky shape of the journal at her waist. Remembering Aija's words, Anna's commitment, she realised, no! Not all gone. With a sense of humility and pride Terri now felt a stern but comforting sense of purpose. She was the one to carry the message that Anna had helped her translate, transform - Aija's message of hope.

Terri turned from her thoughts. The Indian boy glanced curiously at her. Again aware of the admiration in his eyes, Terri also thought she saw an expression of fear, a haunting expression - the eyes of a boy. For a moment she couldn't recall his name.

"Milady," he began, his words deferential, earnest. Terri found herself smiling. She remembered his name then. She corrected him. "Terri, Terri Sai." He glanced from her face, quickly turned to stare up the aisles, to the passengers in the surrounding seats. He began to speak. At the same moment the pilot's voice came over the sound system. Terri found herself trying to listen to both. She half heard Ramaiah's anxious tones as she also listened to the standard instructions to have passports and landing cards ready.

Suddenly all other sounds were excluded as Terri clearly heard the chilling words, "following you!" She turned to see Ramaiah's worried expression. His voice almost pleading, he repeated, "Miss Sai." He leaned toward her, again nervously glancing around. Almost whispering, breathing hard, he added fearfully, "Miss Sai, we have both been followed since we left Bangkok."

Terri's heart beat wildly. Momentarily glancing around, she remembered thinking she had awakened from her dreams at one point, to find someone briefly standing over her. Collecting her thoughts, she could only stare at Ramaiah.

"Who is following me? How do you know all this?" Terri asked with rising suspicion and dread. "Mr. Ramaiah, who are you?"

The stewardess briefly interrupted, requesting them to fasten their seat belts. Terri kept her eyes on Ramaiah as he stuttered some sort of confused explanation. Again she couldn't help noticing how young he looked, how flustered and clearly distressed. Perhaps, she thought, this is just the fantasy of a boy.

"Miss Sai," he hurriedly stumbled over the words, "As you run from the cobra, you may turn - to see the crocodile awaits you!"

Terri was growing more impatient at his incoherence,

78

his seeming inability to answer her. Ramaiah sensed her growing irritation. As the captain's announcement ended, he told Terri he had been assigned to follow her ever since she and An Luc had arrived in Bangkok.

"They also follow your friend, An Luc, wherever he goes. They want to know what happened to a large amount of gold - stolen, they say, from the South Vietnamese government in 1975. They also want to know what happened to a certain American who disappeared while on a secret mission to Phnom Penh." Ramaiah concluded anxiously, "They think you may know the answers." Worriedly shaking his head, he added, "If they knew I spoke to you, Miss Sai, they would kill me!" Ramaiah gazed at Terri, the fear replaced by a helpless look of anguish.

Terri listened, confused. She remembered Anna's story of the gold - the American who disappeared while on the mission to Phnom Penh. Which American? thought Terri. As far as Paddy and Anna recalled, there were no other survivors.

"Who are 'they'?" Terri asked with rising anger. "I know less than you it seems, Mr. Ramaiah. And why do they think that I would know any of this?"

Ramaiah commenced to tell how they had been watching Anna and the Englishman, referring to Paddy - for many months, in Muong Sing. They knew of Anna's death. They did not kill Anna, but were apparently convinced that Terri and An Luc might know the answers they were looking for.

Scornfully glaring at Ramaiah, Terri asked, "And now that I have seen the cobra, who is the crocodile?"

Ramaiah nodded his head, twisting in some discomfort. His fearful expression unchanged, he said reluctantly, "The ones who killed the lady Anna. We believe they also follow you," he answered earnestly. "I have been watching the other passengers since we left Bangkok. There is another man who has been watching you. He boarded at Bangkok."

Terri felt a cold wave of fear. The figure standing over her - she had not been dreaming.

"Who are you working for, Peter?" Terri asked, her voice shaking, disbelieving, yet grateful for Ramaiah's curious confession.

"I work for General Khun Sa," said Ramaiah. "A very rich and powerful man. A great general with the Americans, against the Communists in the war in Vietnam, before I was born." His expression more fearful, he continued. "The crocodile, Miss Sai, is more dangerous. His master, of an unknown name, is now lord of Southeast Asia. Even my master is fearful of him."

Wheels locked, engines flaring, the shuddering DC-10 reached for the runway. Ramaiah realized his time was short. "I will help you, Miss Sai. I will help you escape." Looking into Terri's eyes, almost pleading, "You must trust me. I will not let them harm you!" Terri sensed his attraction to her, his unhappiness with his assignment. Somehow she felt that maybe she could trust him.

The plane came to a stop. Passengers were rising, sorting out their belongings. Terri glanced out of the window. She was startled to see several armed, uniformed figures on either side, some distance from the plane. Was this routine security? Peter Ramaiah didn't seem to notice. He was reaching to the overhead luggage rack for his briefcase. Uneasily Terri gathered her jacket and hand case. She glanced again out the window - the figures hadn't moved.

Terri heard the thud and rumble of the gangways being connected to the exit doors. She glanced around nervously as the passengers started to move slowly forward; no one resembling the man she thought she'd seen.

Peter glanced back. He seemed to want to reassure her, yet Terri saw his nervous gaze flickering among the other passengers. Occasionally he glanced out of the windows as they moved forward. He too, had now noticed the additional security.

On the flight deck, veteran Captain Singh, now safely landed, rose, wearily reaching for his briefcase. He thought of his wife and children. Glancing around the cabin, Singh breathed a deep sigh of grateful relief.

Terri and Peter emerged from the tunnel of the mobile gangway. As Terri looked across the embarkation area, she immediately knew something was wrong. A large group of customs and police, some in plain clothes, some armed, fanned out across the hallway moving toward them. They seemed to be looking at Peter, some toward Terri.

The other passengers moved on, seemingly unaware. Slightly ahead of her Peter Ramaiah stopped, looked back. Terri saw the unspoken warning. She felt the other passengers pushing, shoving, behind her. Ramaiah pointed ahead. Terri heard shouting. She couldn't hear what Peter was saying, his expression wild. Suddenly she realised that some of the police were Chinese government security. In a panic, she wondered, had they landed in Chinese territory? Maybe the police were coming for her. Terri felt herself being pushed more forcibly. She stumbled, losing her balance. There was more shouting. Peter was in the middle of a group of struggling men, wrestling with a big man holding a gun. In the chaos people began running, falling, screaming. Terri heard Peter's desperate cry, "Run Terri, Run!" She turned – heard shots. Looking back, she saw the big man staring at her as he struggled with Peter.

She fled down the corridor, hearing above the shouts and screams a quick burst of automatic fire. She turned again, this time she saw Peter fall. The man, gun in hand, was free, pushing through the crowd, his eyes fixed on her.

Peter had been right. She now faced the crocodile. Terri ran in terror. She flew down an empty tunnel, running for her life. She thought she heard the man's footsteps thudding down the corridor behind her. Almost out of breath, Terri suddenly saw a side door. Without looking back she opened the door, almost fell down two flights of steps, then paused, panting, listening. Opening another door before her, Terri found herself in a basement tunnel crowded with incurious, bustling commuters. They scarcely seemed to notice her as she quickly joined the urgent rush.

Breathing heavily, she hurried along, trying not to attract attention. Looking at the other passengers, Terri noted with relief they had indeed landed in Hong Kong. She felt a surge of hope. Realising she had evaded customs, she knew it would be difficult to escape. She couldn't believe it - Chinese security, there to arrest her, a political fugitive, with the help of Hong Kong police? Maybe, Terri thought, to arrest Peter as a member of Khun Sa's organisation.

She looked back. Thinking she saw the man's bobbing figure farther back, weaving among the throng, Terri hurried on.

Seeing a door marked "Ladies", she ran in, almost knocking down two elderly women. Breathing heavily, she stood, trying to calm herself.

Terri rinsed her face at the sink. Raising her eyes, she gazed at her reflection. The mirror blurred; for a brief second she thought she saw Aija's face, as she remembered, always smiling. Wiping the water from her eyes, she glanced around. She was alone. She turned back to the mirror, now reflecting her own dark, fearful eyes. She closed them, and for a moment listened to the sound she'd never heard - Aija's voice, whispering in her ear. "Don't be afraid. You are among friends, China's friends, here in Hong Kong."

Terri opened her eyes. In the mirror, where she had seen Aija's face, was now the smiling face of a tiny, elderly Chinese lady. Terri wondered, is this another ghost? She turned to see the lady standing with mop and broom in hand. The lady placed the mop and broom on the cleaning mobile beside her.

"Child, what is it? What frightens you so?" The kindly figure was real, her eyes filled with motherly concern. Reaching for Terri's hands, she murmured, "Don't be afraid, child. You too are from China, yes? My name is Lien Tsieng. My husband and I both came as refugees from China many years ago."

Instinctively Terri reached for the lady's outstretched hands. Remembering her own mother, her family in Beijing, suddenly, impulsively, Terri hugged her. Then embarrassed, she broke away.

Speaking in Chinese, the little lady confided, "I was a teacher. We were driven out after being imprisoned during the excesses of the Red Guard in the sixties." In a moment of love and trust, Terri poured out her story to this gentle soul. The little lady listened with understanding and sympathy. Gripping Terri by the arm, looking into her eyes, her own eyes smiling mischievously, she told Terri not to worry. She would ensure her safe escape from the airport; would bring Terri to her own home in nearby Mong Kok. Terri would have no difficulty contacting her friends in Hong Kong. They hugged one another once more before setting out from the ladies' room in the basement of the terminal at Kai Tek.

Police and security, armed and in great numbers, filled the already crowded corridors of the departure and arrival terminals. Passengers, their families and friends were stopped and interrogated at random. The Chinese were furious. They had been denied their quarry; job botched.

The uproar progressed and intensified down the main concourse through the new passenger terminal. As a little old cleaning lady wheeled her cart, unnoticed, down the hallways, she was smiling, triumphant. Now and then she seemed to be talking to someone; to herself perhaps, thought a security guard, as he turned his attention elsewhere, looking for an international narco-terrorist - a notorious Chinese political dissident - or the armed fugitives they had somehow lost. Momentarily, the security guard thought of the Indian boy who had died. So young, he thought to himself.

CHAPTER NINE

From the Isle of Dogs to the Bishops' Palace

Following Terri's departure for Hong Kong, An Luc
began his own journey westward to London. For An Luc, the
journey was the first in the Buddhist seven stages of mourning, a
via dolorosa of endless recrimination, a constant analysis of what
went wrong, ever sensitive of his failure to protect the lady Anna
and the household he was given charge of.

Shortly after takeoff, An Luc's thoughts were distracted
by the persistent efforts of an elderly, grey-blue haired lady to
engage him in conversation. Seeming slightly eccentric, she was
not discouraged by An Luc's polite disinterest, continuing her
monologue on forty years of missionary life in Southeast Asia.

Now over England, the loquacious missionary, Mrs.
Smathers, finally caught An Luc's attention. He became
fascinated with the unique characteristics of this tiny island
- paradoxically the focus of such wealth and power. Mrs.
Smathers described the enduring character and rustic splendour
of her birthplace. An Luc gazed in wonder, striving to see the
proprietary lines, the curving country roads. Between the even
hedgerows, rolling meadows, stately homes; the fields and
villages. Almost speaking to herself at times, Mrs. Smathers
described the quilted summer patchwork, the hawthorn, the
lilac, the blackberry and the honeysuckle; motionless cows
among the orderly pastures. Rambling across hill and dale were
the barely visible footpaths of rural England.

More distinct now as they descended in their final
approach, among the clustered dwellings, Mrs. Smathers
pointed out the village greens, vicarages and churchyards of
her homeland. Above the trees, reaching toward them were the
church steeples, fingering through the cloud breaks and rare

sudden patches of sunlight.

So this, thought An Luc, Meo tribesman from northern Laos, born to the incessant, turgid sweat, accustomed to a predatory, primal existence, to the flooding, seasonal monsoons - this is England!

An Luc thanked Mrs. Smathers for introducing him to his destination. Upon landing, as they slowly moved toward the exit, he was surprised to find her questions becoming more persistent, more personal. Where was he going, what were his plans? Who was going to meet him? An Luc sensed a warning. He shrugged his shoulders, indicating that his English was limited. Moving through customs, they became separated, Mrs. Smathers joining those with English passports.

Paddy Finucane met An Luc in the terminal lobby. It was a restrained yet emotional encounter; both men strangely comforted on seeing one another. Few words passed between them in those first few minutes. Paddy understood An Luc's distress, saw his undeserved remorse.

As they made their way through the crowded concourse, An Luc was mildly surprised to see the doughty figure of Mrs. Smathers again. She stood to one side of the corridor, peering myopically down the long hallway, seeming to be looking for someone. An Luc raised his hand in recognition. She saw him, smiled, then turned, merging into the surge of passengers from the nearby arrivals gate.

An Luc followed Paddy to the waiting taxis. The little lady with the grey-blue hair moved briskly toward the row of public phones. Carefully placing her glasses on her nose, she slowly dialled a number, then curiously began to whistle several bars of an old German lullaby. She listened for a moment, then broke into a voluble exchange in French. Smiling smugly, she replaced the receiver. Home after forty fruitful years in the sunny service of the Lord - or possibly, registering her satisfaction on the successful completion of a different mission, for a different master.

London-on-Thames lies just fifty miles from the river's broad estuary. Sprawling north and south of the river's sinuous course, its boroughs spread more than one hundred and twenty-five miles. Once a primitive village outpost of the far flung Roman dominions, through the second millennial Norman conquest, to its own "Imperial" epoch - history in transition. Approaching its third millennial celebration, the city confronts a historic metamorphosis. From the Isle of Dogs to the "Bishop's Palace", the city now thrives as the cosmopolitan capital of the Laissez Faire society. Yet withal, London retains its native, quaint, cheery ambience.

In St. James' Park in central London, on a lovely, summer afternoon, it was a time to linger; gentle breezes stirred the waters of the lake, the summer leaves of the sycamore and the beech. Muffled and remote were the distant sounds of traffic from the Mall, the tinkling of the bells of Southwark, the chimes from nearby Westminster. As the rim of daylight fled westward, a misty dusk stole over London, deepening the shadows beneath the oak and the elm. From the lake and marshes the mallard rose in easy flight.

An Luc, seasoned Montagnard war veteran from the distant Houa Kong Province in northern Laos, and Edward Patrick "Paddy" Finucane, Earl from the feudal fiefdom of an alien culture, stood on the bridge above the lake, unaware of the diminishing activity in the park. Each, acutely aware of his own and the other's distress, shared the unbearable bereavement, its horrific detail.

Quietly An Luc told his story, shaking his head as if in denial of his sorrow, his horror or his own shame, reliving the last weeks of rising tension and rumours of the increasing presence of strangers in the area - fugitives from the struggle for power in the regional drug wars. Since that night, awake or asleep, An Luc repeatedly recalled the unforgettable nightmare; sadly, too late to save the lady Anna.

An Luc described the two men, one with long hair streaming from under his hat. In the flicker of lightning, the faces, flashing gold teeth. He stared about, his voice anguished, describing his distress as he found the housekeeper and her children, all murdered. And the lovely Anna, crucified!

It took Paddy a moment to register his shock,

wondering, was it he they had come for that night, perhaps, to prevent him giving testimony in the DEA hearings in Paris? Memories returned of the night in Phnom Penh; Deevers had also been crucified, his body nailed to the wall. Bitterly, Paddy realised that Anna might have been right all along. As she had suspected, they had likely followed them from Phnom Penh, for reasons Paddy couldn't understand. Why had it taken them so long - why now?

He reached to touch the stubby, brass key hanging on the short chain at his neck. Incredible, he thought. One of seven, yet now perhaps the only access to Deevers' unimaginable wealth. Worried for Anna, he had often wished that, by throwing away the key they could remove the threat, deter those who followed the trail. If only it could have been that simple. Paddy struggled with his memory and the conflicting emotions as An Luc spoke. Almost every word confirmed Paddy's suspicions since he'd first found the phone connections to Muong Sing blocked; his letters returned during those last weeks.

An Luc continued reluctantly, his voice hoarse with grief, as he forced himself to describe Anna, transfixed to the panelling, blood everywhere. Gently releasing her, he had laid her dying body on the floor, Terri Sai kneeling, crying, by her side.

With some difficulty An Luc recalled Anna's last agonised, determined efforts; whispered words to a sobbing, distraught Terri, sometimes in Chinese, sometimes in Laotian or Vietnamese. An Luc spoke little Chinese, despite Anna's efforts to teach him. He could only repeat what he thought he had heard, Anna's reference to "friend, friends", calling in Vietnamese, "ban, ban dong hanh". Finally, Anna's reference to keys, pleading with An Luc to flee before they returned, to get Terri to Bangkok as quickly as he could; then safely to her friends in Hong Kong; that they would surely follow them. Her final words were to, "warn lord Fucan", and of her love for him.

"There were other words I did not understand. In Chinese, some reference to 'the crazy man'." An Luc appeared puzzled as he continued. "To the 'man who never died', I think she said."

An Luc wept silently, describing how they had buried Anna in the garden beside the house. They had quickly set out that same night for Bangkok.

Agonised, Paddy tried to focus on the implications of that awful night, of Anna's words and warnings, her crucifixion, its terrible significance. He should never have left her. Yet, as An Luc reminded him, Paddy was likely the real target. An Luc, a khon kong, a Buddhist, would stay with Paddy now, according to his beliefs, his kan khat, until he was satisfied Paddy had found the truth, satya - and his samsara, his destiny.

St. James' Park now lay in misty darkness, reflecting the sombre mood as the two men walked away beneath the trees, across the bridge and beside the still waters of the lake. Reluctantly accepting the grim reality, they resolved to confront the inevitable threat that cast its long shadow from Southeast Asia to London.

Early the following day Paddy and An Luc paused at a busy intersection by Charing Cross. Accustomed to a more tropical climate, An Luc raised the collar of his jacket. Though the sun had risen, the fresh, English morning air had a penetrating chill. They continued their short walk from the hotel to Paddy's morning appointment with Sir Geoffrey Gordon at Horse Guards.

"You mustn't blame yourself, An Luc. I too believe in destiny. Anna warned me they would return someday. I had become complacent, distracted. She was right and, from what you have told me, Anna recognised something about them - something that will lead us to them, perhaps before they find us. Why they killed her the way they did - a warning, maybe. I don't know at this point. But," continued Paddy, "as Anna told you, if they came for the keys, they never got them. As you said, Anna's key is with Terri Sai now."

Paddy looked at An Luc. "We should hear soon if Terri is safe with her friends. You did all that Anna asked of you, more than anyone could have expected, in the true tradition of your people."

They passed beneath the clock tower, through the cobble paved archway of Horse Guards. To either side of the archway mounted troopers stared ahead, motionless, like toy soldiers. An Luc curiously eyed the red uniforms, glinting swords, burnished cuirasses and plumed helmets.

They walked up a flight of steps and through a short passage monitored for security. Paddy described the itinerary for the day, their later flight to Paris for the International Drug Enforcement Agency meeting the following morning. A uniformed policeman requested identification. He saluted Paddy, then directed them into a carpeted, low ceilinged reception area. Its lead-paned bay windows gazed out across the largely deserted parade ground.

A dark suited receptionist again requested identification. The burly figure scrutinized Paddy's ID. "Sir Geoffrey Gordon is expecting you, sir." Paddy followed the man into Gordon's office. An Luc took a seat by the windows.

Sir Geoffrey greeted Paddy warmly, motioning for him to be seated. Geoffrey Gordon had been like a father to Paddy over the years. Paddy thought, how old, how worried the man looks.

Sir Geoffrey gathered some papers from his desk. He distractedly thumbed through them as he reviewed with Paddy the material Paddy planned to present at the DEA meetings in Paris. Most importantly, the security arrangements, both for the DEA meeting, and more critical, Madam's arrival in Paris. Sir Geoffrey worriedly commented how any one of a number of terrorist organisations might see the occasion as "open season". Representatives from all the major powers drew world attention. An opportunity for the powerful political persuasion of terrorism to deflect attention to their own compelling cause, not to speak of the worldwide television and media publicity they could obtain.

From his own experience, Paddy spoke of other organizations - a criminal hegemony that fearlessly promoted its trilogy of oil, drugs and arms - that might seize the opportunity, by some act of violence, to dissuade any concerted international intervention. He described a world of vast territories no longer under the control of their regional or national governments, held to ransom by these Taipans; racketeers of a new mafiocracy; their quasi respectable, international image, and the difficulty in recognizing the extent of the corruption.

Gordon's expression was grave, clearly impressed at the scope and implications of Paddy's description. Then, realising more personal priorities, he expressed his sympathy and concern for Paddy's recent loss. Sir Geoffrey was no stranger to tragedy and death in his own family.

"Have you had any word about who might have been responsible, Paddy? These new criminals you speak of, do you suspect their role in Anna's death?" Then as if embarrassed, he apologised for intruding into such recent pain.

Paddy reassured Gordon, then told him of An Luc's arrival in London, describing the circumstance of Anna's death. Paddy mentioned the possible role of some new regional drug lord as Anna's killer.

Gordon murmured his concern. He rose, slowly paced before the windows, hands behind his back. Hesitant, but with growing enthusiasm, he began. "Paddy, things, God knows, have tragically changed for you in the past few weeks. A stroke of cruel fate. Perhaps this is not the time - yet the opportunity might not come again." He paused, leaned forward, his fingers braced against the desk. "I had always hoped we might work on a closer basis, this is a well-earned opportunity for your future with the service; to return home."

Curious, Paddy listened as Gordon pursued his purpose.

"I believe your work in Southeast Asia over the past few years - in Afghanistan, and more recently with us here in London and Paris has been first rate, and God knows, we need someone responsible like you. Someone experienced in these sensitive areas. Someone who can help us administer British intelligence operations abroad - especially, Paddy, in these very difficult times in southern Asia."

Paddy remained silent. Gordon, arms folded, stood before him. "Bill Whitcombe is due for retirement shortly. He's on the New Year's honours list. We were looking for someone to act as his interim deputy. You would be ideal for the assignment." Gordon slowly continued, "I have taken the liberty of submitting your name, placing you on the short list for that post."

Carefully choosing his words, aware of Paddy's scepticism of "the Establishment", its "favoured" traditions, he quickly added, "I spoke with Whitcombe the other day. He's most enthusiastic and in agreement with your well deserved promotion to DDG, Combined Intelligence Far East - pending his retirement. This, Paddy, with a view to your ultimately assuming the position of Director General of CIFE in Bangkok."

Gordon concluded, "Consistent with the routine vetting process, Madam is to review this, following the Paris meetings. Your appointment should be no problem." As though Paddy might reject the offer out of hand, "Paddy, your father would have been proud."

From the parade ground below Paddy heard the distant shouts of command - the changing of the guard. Both men faced the open window, the curtains billowing slightly. Each wondered what Paddy's father might really have said.

It was not an easy subject. Paddy thought of the bitter irony of this sudden opportunity, the long road he had travelled - Gordon's role in the whole unlikely scheme of events. Gordon, Paddy's father's close friend, was appointed Paddy's guardian following the unexpected deaths, first of his mother in a hunting accident - later, of his father, while with the service, under mysterious circumstances, never fully explained.

After public school, Paddy, still unsettled, had a brief career with the Irish Guards. His "promise" never fully realised, he had been cashiered for striking a senior officer while on station in Northern Ireland. Only through Sir Geoffrey's intercession had he been spared a full court-martial. Venting his anger and disillusionment - still haunted by the mystery of his father's death, Paddy left England for the United States. There he joined American Special Forces heading for Vietnam.

After Vietnam, while Paddy was living in Northern Laos - another close friend of his father, Bill Whitcombe, discovered his location. Perhaps with a view to relocating Paddy, Whitcombe recruited his assistance during the Russian-Afghanistan affair. If nothing else, Bill Whitcombe realised

Paddy's need to resolve his father's will and estate - a matter too long postponed. Paddy remembered his initial reluctance to leave Muong Sing. Despite her own fears, Anna had finally persuaded him to go.

Paddy knew he owed it to his father - to Anna now, and lastly, to himself, to look for a new future. He would give Gordon's generous offer serious consideration.

From Horse Guards below, Gordon heard the muted commands curiously blending with the cries and laughter of children, visitors and tourists. He was remembering his visit to Harrow long ago, to tell Paddy - a sullen, distant, sixteen year old - that his father was missing, presumed dead in a plane accident. He never mentioned to Paddy, then in grief, that he was now lord Finucane, the hereditary Earl of Clanrickard. Nor did Gordon mention that Paddy's father, at odds with some in the service at a time of growing internal mistrust, had been sent abroad to a CAZAB conference in Australia. He had been "lost" on the return trip, off the coast of Malaysia, somewhere in the South China Seas. This incident coincided with the anger and mistrust following the assisted departure of the scheming Philby, to Moscow - an escape that wrought havoc in an era of betrayal and recrimination on both sides of the Atlantic.

Gordon pondered the paranoid contradictions of *the times*. He was reminded of his own father's troubles some years before, another victim in the endless "mole hunt". It seemed no one escaped, except those of the Oxbridge fraternity.

Gordon glanced at Paddy, wondering if he would accept his offer. Perhaps the posting in Southeast Asia, away from England, might help him to forget old grievances. Yet the close proximity to the site of his father's death might also remind Paddy of unanswered questions.

"Thank you Geoffrey, for all you've done. I appreciate your efforts. I'm inclined to accept your offer," Paddy said quietly, "but I don't want to mislead you. I have other priorities. I need time to reorganise my life. But first, I must concentrate on the DEA conference, and assisting MI5 in organizing security for Madam's meeting in Paris."

Gordon readily agreed. "Take your time, Paddy. Let

me know as soon as you've decided. This conference might be an occasion for you to check with the SDECE, French security, and American Special Intelligence. It's a very real opportunity for investigating the links you spoke of among terrorist groups from Southeast Asia to the devolving Russian Republic. As you have said, an opportunity for criminal groups from any of those regions to disrupt a concerted counteraction, including those of our old nemesis, the IRA, eager to use any occasion to take a stand."

Gordon warmly shook Paddy's hand. He asked quietly, "Are you sure you're up to this agenda in Paris? We could find someone else to present your material for you."

Seeing Gordon's troubled expression, Paddy replied, "Perhaps it's better for me to be busy at this time. Don't worry. With An Luc, I am well protected."

There was more to be said, but it was too early yet. Paddy knew Gordon's father had also been in the service. Like Paddy's father, his career had ended tragically. Gordon never married, had dedicated his whole life, Paddy suspected, to a fruitless crusade to expiate his own father's mistakes, trying to vindicate a forgotten history, for a disinterested generation. Gordon had recently been given his "reward" for dutiful service, being appointed Director General, MI5 – had been knighted in the New Year's list. Despite these tokens of appreciation, Paddy felt that Gordon would never be wholly at peace.

For Paddy it would be different. He would learn the facts of his father's story, and if he found the explanation unsatisfactory, he would confront those responsible. He felt sorry for Gordon, inheriting his father's guilt, whatever it might have been, Gordon just another victim.

They walked into the reception area. Paddy introduced An Luc to Sir Geoffrey. "I had the privilege of serving with his father, a brave comrade, during the Vietnam War."

Gordon shook An Luc's hand. "I now know Lord Finucane is in safe hands." An Luc smiled proudly.

Sir Geoffrey walked them to the stairs. "I'll see you both in Paris." As Paddy and An Luc descended the broad steps, the clock tower at Horse Guards struck the hour, a thin, tinkering sound. Across the parade ground, the Lifeguards - toy figures in a stiffly moving pageant - attracted the attention of a group of Asian tourists. Cameras aimed, shutters busily clicked.

CHAPTER TEN

Paris – City of Life

Paris - for some, city of light - for others, city of gloom.
The morning smell of freshly brewed coffee, fresh baked
bread. The flowers in the Champs de Mars dance lightly in the
gentle breezes to the music of summer. In the Gardens of the
Tuileries, the rich green foliage, the rustling lime trees bewitch
the transient visitor, just as they once enchanted the original
designer, Gabriel. His master, Louis XV, so admired this once
rural retreat, with its arboured pathways, from capital to
countryside - now the majestic Avenue des Champs Elysees.
Little did the dissolute and ineffectual monarch guess that the
garden he so much admired would one day serve as the site of
the guillotine, and those arboured pathways would become the
final route down which the drunken, screaming Paris mob, the
Canailles, would drag the tumbrils, carrying so many of his regal
relatives to their execution.

The square, first named after Louis XV, where a small
plaque remembers the execution of the brave queen and mother,
Marie Antoinette - would be renamed the Place de la Concorde.
Today it is busy with tourists, resonates to incessant clamour;
polluted with the fumes of buses, cars and taxis.

Paddy and An Luc were met at Roissy-Charles de Gaulle
Airport by Michael Weatherby of MI5, a friend of Paddy's, with
whom he had been working for the past month on security
measures for the DEA conference and Madam's subsequent visit.

The drive along the broad, multi-lane expressway
took some forty minutes. An Luc stared, fascinated, as the
new expressway swept past, a marvel of French engineering.
Michael described a growing unrest in the city - labour strikes,

95

unemployment, a devalued currency, increased cost of food and petrol, recent student riots, terrorist bombings in the subways. "Not good for the coming meetings, Paddy. And it's a bit dicey for British residents, over some territorial disputes on North Sea fishing rights." Michael was smiling, "A great welcome, eh?"

He glanced back to An Luc, who sat, mesmerised at the growing city skyline. "Paris," Michael told him, "has one of the largest Southeast Asian populations in Europe, mostly from Indochina, Cambodia, Vietnam and Laos - and from the Philippines." He laughed, "This crazy driving probably reminds you, An Luc, of your home, Vientienne."

An Luc smiled. "Not quite as fast, but people the same the world over, it seems."

Michael, like Paddy, had attended public school at Harrow some years before. Again, like Paddy, he had joined the Guards. During Madam's Falklands campaign, Michael transferred to the Parachute Regiment, later, to Special Air Services. The following year he was invited to join British Intelligence. He had been with MI5, Section D, counter intelligence ever since. He lived with his wife Beth just north of the city.

It was after five when they reached the Saint Simon Hotel. Paddy and An Luc showered and changed, then joined Michael at a nearby restaurant for dinner. Ever wary of the invisible, hostile world around them, An Luc stared about, watching for the intruder, the sudden confrontation.

Paddy and Michael discussed Paddy's earlier conversation with Gordon. Michael congratulated Paddy on Gordon's offer. He understood Paddy's scepticism. Michael saw it as another voice for Gordon and MI5, with the "hereditary institutions".

During the conversation, Paddy sensed a change in Michael since their earlier weeks together - an element of distraction. Not wanting to pry, Paddy knew there'd be time later.

Around them, in the soft glow of the table lamps, amidst the discreet tinkering of cutlery, glass and china, Parisiennes sat at tables, savouring their own scene, evoking a busy, intriguing ambiance.

Outside the bistro, beneath the street lights and the trees, the colourful evening parade of beautiful women walked with their dogs and their wealthy, older escorts; the strolling accordeoniste, the ragged clochard - the homeless and the transient - all in discordant harmony through the side streets and parks near the Champs Elysées.

As they sat drinking coffee after dinner, Michael sensed that Paddy needed to be alone. He'd been with Paddy when he received the call from Mary Whitcombe about Anna's death. An Luc's arrival had certainly reopened the pain. Still early, a lovely, summer evening - Michael offered to take An Luc on a brief tour of the city. An Luc readily accepted. Paddy excused himself to make preparations for the meeting the next day.

In the cool darkness of his hotel room, Paddy sat staring out across the flickering lights of the city. Above the trees of the Champs Elysées, between the elegant domes and the pinnacles of the Grand Palais, he could see the glittering lights of the Eiffel tower climbing toward the night sky. The window curtains stirred in the cool, evening breeze. From some nearby discotheque came the rhythmic drums, the Moorish twang and quaver of guitar strings. Paddy heard the soft vibrancy of a woman's voice singing a wistful, Moroccan love song. The plaintive lament, echoing the ache in his heart, was soon lost in the roar of the passing traffic.

Paddy had written to Anna when he first arrived, telling her that when he brought her to Paris he would have the Eiffel Tower lit up to celebrate her arrival. He listened now, and from the streets below heard the light chatter of the passing parade. Then, startling - came the booming clamour from the bells of Notre Dame, and successively, from Montmartre, the musical peal from the church of Sacré Coeur.

Paddy rose and paced the floor. He thought of Sir Geoffrey's offer. Perhaps the position in Bangkok would give him the intelligence access and facilities to find Anna's killers.

Paddy tried to stem the flow of memories. He walked to the window, the lights before him now unseen, the sounds unheard. He reached to his neck to touch the key that hung there. He remembered those first happy months with Anna, before Phnom Penh. He shuddered, picturing Anna, like Deevers, nailed to the wall, tortured, desecrated. He couldn't face the horror.

Crucifixion - so bizarre; even in his long years in Vietnam, with all the savagery, deliberate mutilations, Paddy had never seen an instance of such brutality until Phnom Penh. Not typical of the region, nor the times, crucifixion was an ancient, ritualistic punishment, perhaps of intimidation. Introduced into the east by the Greeks in their conquest of Persia, it was used by the Romans to put down rebellions, against the Greeks, the Carthaginians indiscriminately against the Jews, the slaves and the Christians. But why now, in Southeast Asia? And by whom?

The manner of Anna's killing, like Deevers', excluded a mindless act by some random guerrilla group. More likely a deliberate warning - a reminder perhaps. The manner of Anna's death confirmed her own predictions that their nemesis would return some day.

Paddy recalled An Luc's agonised struggle to interpret Anna's words, to convey some message. Perhaps Anna had remembered faces they'd known, names forgotten; her reference to the keys they'd come for and never found. An Luc's confusing reference to "the crazy one" that "never died". Anna's puzzling repetition of "friend, friends", in Vietnamese, then in Chinese. Paddy felt sure Anna had said more in Chinese than An Luc would have understood.

Paddy was impressed with both Terri Sai and An Luc's dedication to Anna. Before all phone communication had failed, Anna had spoken to Paddy of the Chinese girl, Terri Sai, with such admiration and candour. Anna described their time together, translating the story of the heroic Aija. Perhaps Terri Sai would know more. He knew he must go to Hong Kong as soon as possible to find this Terri Sai.

The city of Paris, long asleep for some, was for others still in restless search of distraction. Music still played, dancers still moved, wine still flowed. And for a few, whispering

silences, passionate words that hurried on. For Paddy, now gone
- the song that was forever.

Seated by the window, his mind in relentless pursuit,
Paddy thought of those who had moved into the area of Houa
Kong Province before he had left. And many other groups later,
as An Luc had said, some who might have perceived Anna and
Paddy as a threat. Khun Sa perhaps. Or even the Chinese, Anna's
old nemesis - seeing her as a traitor, or a dangerous enemy - her
home a refuge for political fugitives. A less likely threat, perhaps,
to the regional drug lords who'd been there throughout the
years, satisfied with their own domain. Paddy remembered An
Luc's rendition of the warnings of the Chao Keung; a Caucasian,
a Russian deserter perhaps, "the farang dang mo". Paddy
wondered which, if any, had been Anna's killer. Again Paddy's
hand went to the chain at his neck, ironically the only lead he
had.

He glanced at his watch. Midnight in Paris, near midday
in Bangkok. It took the operator longer to put the call through
than it did for Mary Whitcombe to answer. Relieved to hear his
voice, Mary told Paddy she had called Gordon's office in London
earlier, looking for him. Terri Sai was missing.

In response to Paddy's question, Mary confirmed, "Yes,
Terri was on the flight. I was with her when she boarded the
plane in Bangkok.

"Bill had been at the airport to meet Terri. There was a
shooting; an Indian boy was killed; drug related, they told Bill.
As far as Bill had learned, no one else was hurt. There is more
to this, Paddy," Mary explained. "Chinese authorities had been
there to apprehend one of the passengers."

Mary's voice changed. "There is one other passenger
missing, involved in the shooting. They saw him running from
the scene with a gun. Chinese authorities are blaming Hong
Kong for bungling the job.

"Perhaps Terri was being followed. Bill feels sure Terri
somehow found her way out of the airport. He is still looking for
her. We are just hopeful that she is safe. Hong Kong authorities
are also looking for her and the other passenger. They have
checked the hospitals - no reports of any unexplained gun shot

injuries."

Mary promised to call Paddy as soon as she had any news. She mentioned that the incident at the airport had been curiously suppressed, apparently at the request of the Chinese government. Promising to stay in touch, Paddy ended the call. He wondered if the shooting at the airport had merely been a coincidence, or were Anna's killers already on Terri's trail?

He drifted into restless sleep, listening to Anna's voice from the darkness, as in Muong Sing, long ago - "Don't let him find us, Paddy!"

Wide awake now and shaken, Paddy stared up into the darkness. He felt sadness, yet also a cold rage. As soon as he could, he and An Luc must travel to Hong Kong to learn more about those last moments for Anna. Finally, exhausted, he slept.

During a hurried early breakfast Paddy briefly told the worrisome news from Mary Whitcombe. Not wishing to alarm An Luc, Paddy reminded him no one else had been reported injured. They would likely hear from Terri, or from Mary shortly. An Luc listened, shaking his head. "It is what I had feared."

An Luc and Paddy now stood at the entrance of the hotel, waiting for Michael Weatherby to bring the car. During last night's dinner he had offered to drive them to the DEA meetings, due to start at eight o'clock this morning. An Luc drew Paddy's attention to an odd older couple, a man and a woman, standing together on the far side of the street. They appeared to be waiting - the man reading a newspaper, the pages flipping in the breeze. Occasionally he raised his eyes, stared at them over the top of the paper. The woman looked away as Paddy gazed toward them.

"They have been watching us since last night," said An Luc, "ever since our arrival. It seems to be more than curiosity, Tuan."

They drove off, Michael cautiously steering into the busy morning traffic. Glancing back, Paddy saw the odd pair still standing beneath the trees. Both watched the departure with undisguised interest. Soon all he could see was the flapping newspaper, the formless faces, the eyes peering after them; then lost among the gathering throngs. Coincidence? Imagination? Paddy couldn't be sure.

Shortly after their arrival into the auditorium at the Navy Ministry, An Luc and Michael seated themselves among a sizeable audience. Paddy was introduced as "Regional Consultant" to the Office of International Drug Control, Southeast Asian section. His was a special presentation.

In the darkened forum, Paddy delivered the familiar material, illustrated in a rhythmic succession of slides. Briefly his mind was distracted, thinking of the elderly couple who had watched their departure from the hotel - suddenly remembering An Luc's comment about an inquisitive elderly lady beside him on the flight from Bangkok to London.

Paddy focused then, his words now following the slides, illustrations of the escalating yearly production of the coca leaf - up almost a hundred thousand tons in ten years. Opium was up over five thousand tons, doubled in the 90's - and an estimated population of addicts exceeded three million between the Americas, Southeast Asia and Europe, growing daily. Paddy spoke of the rapid increase in refineries throughout Southeast Asia, described the "new routes" and their increasing traffic, from the historic Silk Road through China to Hong Kong, through Malaysia to Singapore, Iran and southern Turkey. Or again, from Soviet South Central Asia, the Middle East, Syria and South America, to Europe and the United States.

In the darkness, the flickering light of the projector, An Luc noticed the forum was packed, the doors open, latecomers crowding into the aisles.

"Recent figures have shown that more than half the heroin sold in the United States and Britain at this time is produced by the flourishing new drug empires of Southeast Asia. Déjà vu. Once west to east, now east to west - a tragic irony, the mirror image of the Opium Wars in reverse. In this region alone, from Afghanistan to northern Laos, the area under cultivation by the big drug refineries has increased from a million to two million acres in the past decade. This," Paddy added, "does not take into consideration the vast new harvest

101

from Central Asia - from Tadjikistan to the Caucasus - a new and thriving source of drug production."

Paddy then described the infrastructure - how the crops grown in the villages, processed in the laboratories, the "Special Farm" refineries were now the harvest of a sophisticated, high tech international corporate network. A select number of the wealthier and more powerful drug Czars, empowered through their own dependant bureaucracy of dealers, distributors and street hustlers were now responsible for a sophisticated distribution network, its world market expansion and protected by their own well-funded political connections.

"All part of the rapidly expanding new world embracing drug empire and its 'new emperors'. Only this," said Paddy, "is now larger than any preceding empire, larger by far than that of Britain and Rome combined, and is still growing."

Paddy occasionally walked to the screen to point to some relevant figure, quietly telling the story of the "new currency", as he called it - the "new corporate hierarchy" and the incredible profits in this new global enterprise. Amounting to trillions of pounds yearly from Southeast Asia alone, with over six hundred billion dollars laundered annually, worldwide, through illegal banking enterprises. "This, more than the total assets of the seven richest oil companies put together, more than any of the major nations spend in their annual, total military budgets."

Paddy, distractions forgotten, began to sense his own outrage, his own growing frustration with the unrestrained banditry and murder and the continuing criminal immunity from prosecution the cold statistics did little to illustrate. He concluded, describing the poor results of their efforts to plant substitute crops, to develop cottage, local farm industries.

"None of them were ever able to realise more than a dollar a bushel. The local farmers in northern Laos tried, but it was just no competition. This, while opium resin was selling for one hundred dollars a pound - ten times as much as the traditional alternative crops. Alternative crop substitution has largely been abandoned. The hunger for drugs in the salons or streets of the western world, for food in the jungles or slums of the third world, drives the market – both sadly accompanied by a rapid escalation in the incidence of violence, incurable diseases, of HIV and of AIDS. We live in a world where greed reigns."

The lights came on. Collecting his papers, Paddy was surprised to hear the volume of applause that followed. Looking up, he quickly saw the size of his audience - some now moving down the aisles toward the podium. For several minutes he responded to the questions of the group gathered about him. Some from multi-national drug enforcement bodies - American, European, Asian - questioning statistics, sources. And especially from the press representatives - would he name the "new emperors", "drug czars", "illegal banking enterprises" referred to. Paddy substantiated figures he'd presented, deferring some answers until further investigation.

The room began to fill again for the next presentation, the new speakers taking their places on the podium. Paddy excused himself, joining Michael and An Luc, who congratulated him on the success of his efforts.

Passing another auditorium with its doors open, they paused, making way for the emerging audience. Paddy heard the moderator thanking the audience and members of the panel. Something about the voice, the face, stirred his memory. Asking Michael and An Luc to wait for him, Paddy walked toward the stage. The room was busy with audience members talking among themselves, passing up and down the aisles. Halfway down the aisle Paddy stopped.

The moderator was gathering his notes. Looking up from the podium, the man's eyes were drawn to Paddy, staring curiously up at him. Drawn as if by a magnet, they approached, eyes fixed on one another. Paddy searched his memory for the man's name. He saw the slight, balding, stooped figure, the glasses, the opaque stare, uncertain smile. He sensed the man's growing discomfort. As he extended a hesitant handshake, Paddy remembered.

"Victor Perry, isn't it?" said Paddy.

The older man murmured, "many years ago," looking furtively around, reluctant to meet Paddy's eyes. Paddy remembered a younger, shadowy figure in an immaculate uniform, one of the more than ninety percent of U.S. forces in Vietnam who never saw combat, except in the Judge Advocate's office or courtroom - their engagements, in the social circles of the wealthy Vietnamese government or the American administration bureaucracy.

To Paddy's question, Perry nervously explained that he now worked in some capacity with the American section of the United Nations Aid for National Development, the committee on environmental protection. A suitably obscure, bureaucratic designation, thought Paddy, as he remembered more clearly now the man from more than twenty years ago - an army lawyer, with the Provost Marshal's office - later with Roger Moorefield, Chief of Army Intelligence, stationed in Saigon.

Clearing his throat, Perry commented he had been surprised to see Paddy's name on the programme. "Working with the British team now, eh?" He smiled ingratiatingly. "I caught some of your presentation, dodged in as you were speaking - was most impressed. I hadn't known you were here till I was assigned to moderate this program, on short notice."

Paddy sensed he was lying. In response to Perry's successive queries about his designation, he made some noncommittal response. Perry blurted, "You may remember Roger Moorefield? He's now in Defence Intelligence, Liaison Officer, European sector, I believe. Stationed at the American Embassy in London." Perry, in a stream of nervous chatter, impulsively added that he himself would be leaving for the United States shortly. He was returning to London tonight.

Perry was running out of trivial talk, growing increasingly nervous. There was no further mention of memories related to Vietnam as the conversation faltered to an awkward silence. Finally, reaching to shake Paddy's hand, Perry stammered, "I'll be seeing Roger tomorrow, in London. I'll tell him we met. We're almost neighbours now. Perhaps we'll meet again."

Paddy nodded, shook Perry's hand reluctantly. Perry, obviously anxious to be off, moved aside as a group of television people passed up the aisle, preparing for the next meeting. The panel of speakers passed between them, followed by some of the audience. As they separated, Perry's words came through to Paddy. "Sorry to hear about Anna - lovely lady." The rest of his words were lost as a sound crew came by carrying wires and other equipment. Surprised, Paddy peered across. The next session was about to begin, the moderator calling for order. There was no sign of Perry. He wondered, how had Perry known of Anna's death?

Michael and An Luc were now beside him. "I think they're ready to begin in here." Michael and An Luc started moving up the aisle. Paddy turned, following Michael toward the door. Remembering Perry's role a little more clearly now, his aggressive investigative effort to indict Spec Force Seven, accusing them of murder in the "termination" of a South Vietnamese officer involved in Colonel Deevers' black market operation. A friend of Tung Giang, as Paddy recalled, caught stealing truckloads of American supplies, was shot while "resisting arrest". Perry, then an arrogant prosecutor, also a friend of General Tung Giang, was unable to obtain a conviction - Spec Force Seven were the final victims; assignment to the Phnom Penh mission their reward - and punishment.

Paddy remembered Perry's presence, with Tung Giang or Deevers, at many of the social functions given by the American Administration in Saigon. He wondered how close Perry had been to Deevers. Curiously, as Paddy had listened to Perry's evasive lies, his nervous chatter, he had felt Anna's angry presence, warning him.

Still not used to the finality - echoes of receding footsteps - Anna seemed to be everywhere, beside him now. Words of condolence, even from a friend, were painful. From this man Perry, with all the pain and anger he brought back, the words were a harsh reminder - curious, even bizarre.

Paddy saw Michael regarding him worriedly. "Someone I knew in Vietnam," muttered Paddy. "Never thought I'd see him again." Then again to himself, how did he know about Anna? He followed Michael and An Luc, now checking their programs for the next session.

CHAPTER ELEVEN

Our Own Worst Enemy – The Enemy Within

Beneath the linden trees, protected from the heat of the late afternoon sun, a line of tourists moved slowly forward. They boarded the buses parked in rows along the Avenue Montagne. Few noticed the tall bearded man as he passed the lines of visitors emerging from the Palais de la Decouverte. Fewer still noticed a man and woman, an older couple, standing together by the intersection of Roosevelt and Montagne.

As the bearded man emerged from beneath the trees of the Palais, the elderly man lowered the newspaper he appeared to be reading. His slightly younger companion discreetly waved toward a blue Citroen parked near the intersection.

The bearded man, briefcase in one hand, walking stick in the other, passed between the buses. Glancing up the Avenue des Champs Elysées, he stepped into the street. He passed in front of the blue Citroen now waiting for the light to change. The man appeared to stumble, almost falling into the street. The Citroen moved forward; two men jumped out. They hustled the man into the car, briefcase and stick falling to the street. The car started moving, then abruptly stopped. A man ran back, picked up the briefcase and quickly re-entered the car, which now moved rapidly through the changing lights.

The event went unnoticed by the grim faced guards behind the barriers surrounding the residence of the French President in the Palais de L'Elysées.

An alert gendarme, however, witnessed the scuffle and retrieval of the briefcase. He walked quickly across the intersection, picked up the walking stick and made his way back to his station before Le Grand Palais. Somewhat out of breath, he stared after the car, now long lost in the surge of late afternoon traffic. He examined the walking stick. The handle, a curiously rounded, gold plated knob, had a small wrist chain attached. He looked closer. He hurried then to a nearby police phone kiosk.

Elsewhere, from just outside the city, a different call was placed. "Monsieur," the operator responded brusquely, "You did say seventh arondissement? Now monsieur, the number again? Thank you. No monsieur, you must add a 16-1 when calling from outside the city. You must add a 4 to the Paris code before dialling such a number."

The caller spoke in agitated tones, "I am calling from a pay phone. I could walk to the city in shorter time than it has taken to put this call through!"

It was warm inside the phone booth. Time and patience were running out. The operator's voice gave the rewarding news, "Monsieur, your number is ringing now. We hope you have a more pleasant weekend."

"Hello. I have had great difficulty in getting through. I am outside the city. I don't feel safe. I trust no one now. No, I am not sick!" After listening to the firm voice, the instructions implicit, "No, the meeting was attended by both of them. I did not realise he would be giving evidence. There were a lot of relevant figures - I believe he must be aware of our plans. I heard he'll be appointed to Bangkok. He still has many connections here. It's my belief he's going to go for the source. No, nothing specific. I had to leave, I was assigned to another panel." A pause, then, resentfully, "I tried to avoid him. I was surprised he recognised me." He listened to the intense interrogatory voice.

"He watches me, the other one. As far as I know they are both stationed in Paris now. No, I didn't think anyone had survived, until you told me about the lady." As the exchange continued, the caller became angry and defensive. Another pause, a moment's perplexed thought, then an uncertain response, "No, I scarcely knew her."

An intense denial came from the increasingly distressed caller, one hand wiping the sweat from his forehead. "No, Madame!" Then, loudly, "With Weatherby, yes - D Section, MI5. Yes, a short, muscular man, some type of bodyguard perhaps."

Then, tartly, "Weatherby, Jewish? How would I know that? I've no idea."

The caller pushed open the door of the booth as he continued, agitated. "You must speak for me, Madame, I leave for London tomorrow." There followed a pause during which the distressed caller listened with obvious exasperation.

"Madame," his voice had taken on a pleading, wheedling note now, "I am getting too old for this." In response to what must have been a series of terse remonstrations, the caller, his voice almost sobbing, suddenly shouted into the receiver.

"I never betrayed my country! Never intentionally harmed my countrymen!" Almost out of control, he continued on a high note, so that a passerby hurrying to the nearby Metro turned to look, then hurried on.

Perhaps only the man himself heard his own final words. "I've had enough!" Then recklessly, desperately, "Don't let them forget - I have more on them than they have on me!" Suddenly frightened - "Hello! Hello! Operator - oh no! I've been disconnected!" Distraught, he listened to the recording politely requesting another twelve centimes.

He fumbled with the phone, reached to his pockets, dropped his glasses while calling into the receiver helplessly, "I'm out of change!" Hopelessly, to himself then, "Out of time now, too." Slowly he replaced the receiver and left the booth. He had almost two hours yet to pack and catch the plane to London. Looking around for the distinctive yellow sign of the Metro, he fumbled in his pockets for his rail pass. Then, the slight, balding, stooped figure, unaware of the light rain that fell, briefcase in hand, walked quickly toward the Metro station at Courbevoie.

After leaving the talks at the Navy Ministry, Michael and Paddy attended a meeting at the British Embassy to finalise security arrangements for the Lady Prime Minister, due to arrive early the next day. Sir Geoffrey Gordon and a group from MI5 would be arriving tomorrow morning. The Chief of Protocol and the Under Secretary discussed in some detail the plans for the special meeting with Madam, and the reception to follow. As far as Paddy could determine, the meeting was a top secret, no agenda, "counter-terrorism" strategy session.

Following the briefing at the embassy, Michael suggested that they stop for a drink at his favourite Paris pub before dinner. After a quick change at the hotel, Paddy met An Luc and Michael at the reception desk.

As they drove off from the hotel, Michael handed Paddy a copy of the evening paper, directing his attention to an article inside the front page. Paddy read - *Distinguished Scientist, Professor Henri Senjaye, Missing - Believed Kidnapped.*

"Interesting, Paddy - that man is quite controversial, has been a recurring focus of attention. He's an expert on chemical and biological weapons, and an ardent Islamic nationalist to boot. He is disliked by the Turks, by the moderate Islamic vote, a very subdued voice now. There's more to this than meets the eye. The questions - to which 'zone of contention' was he kidnapped - and by whom?" His expression worried, Michael continued.

"For me, it all seems more relevant now. Professor Senjaye is perhaps part of the puzzle. The situation is highly combustible everywhere. The conflict in the Middle East, southern Russia and Southeast Asia are all worsening situations. And the Balkans, never a side show in the European imperial arena. Hidden games and schemes played in each area, trying to exert control. And now China, the ultimate confrontation."

Further across the inside page, Paddy's attention focused on another late news summary, *Amnesty International Cites British in Questionable SAS killings in Gibraltar.* It was a brief notation, describing how the European courts had found the British killing of two young Irish men and a young Irish woman, some weeks before, all shot in the back without warning, as "counter terrorism, unjustifiable." The decision would have embarrassing consequences, leaving the question undecided - who now, the "terrorist"?

Seated apart from the other patrons in the inner sanctum, the snug of "Ma Place", Michael and Paddy, sipping Scotch, An Luc, black coffee - discussed the issues Paddy had raised at the DEA meeting. Dim lit, intimate, with a well-worn, comfortable brass and leather ambiance, Ma Place was a popular lunch and dinner bar on the west bank. The tables and bar were not yet crowded.

"Paddy, the American you spoke with after your talk, have you known him long?" Michael's expression was curious as he waited for Paddy's answer.

"I knew Victor Perry," said Paddy, "during the Vietnam War. I haven't seen him for over twenty years. He works for the United Nations, he tells me, in some capacity with Aid for National Development. It was a surprise to see him," Paddy added. "Brought back some bad memories."

Briefly Paddy described Perry's former association with the American military administration in Saigon. Paddy told Michael of his investigation into the rapidly worsening black market in weapons and equipment.

"Perry was among some American and South Vietnamese government officials suspected of racketeering and corruption in the very lucrative, black market scheme - some only exposed during the last weeks of the war."

Michael listened intently. Then almost reluctantly, he said, "It seems we have similar stories to tell. Paddy, An Luc, I trust you both as my friends. I have not spoken of this to anyone else."

Nervously looking about the room Michael continued, "As you described in your talk, on the international political scene, corruption prevails - so too now, in England. In the past few months, I've discovered a growing conspiracy. Recently it's become a lot more aggressive."

Michael continued with a sense of urgency. "Since you told me about Gordon's offer, the intent, perhaps, to return you to the fold. Yet I am sceptical. From what I have learned, your return is viewed with reservation by some. Your placement with CIFE, Far East station, would be a plus for some in the new party, Britain First. Some older members view you, Paddy, as a maverick - a Lawrence, or Wingate perhaps. Others might see you differently, questioning your 'affinities'. Those remembering your father's story might wonder if you will be inclined to dig up secrets. They would be happy to see you remain 'exiled' as it were, in Bangkok. They don't forget, or easily forgive. I am even concerned that their aim might be to silence you - one way or the other."

Seeing Paddy's look of growing concern, Michael added, "After you received the news about Anna, I was reluctant to further burden you. Yet, after listening to your talk today, and now your story about this man Perry and his possible role in the drug and arms trade - I believe we all share a common danger." Michael paused, sipped his drink.

"As I see it," Michael said, "this new party, Britain First, appealed to a spirit of renewal, a reassertion of traditional, national pride. Originally, it was the subject of derisive comment, media satire. The party is now serious business. An old game with a new face. In the art of political deception, Britain First is strong on both sides of the House - in the government and in the cabinet. They have achieved a 'fait accomplit', quickly assuming an international role. Nor is that quite what it appears. Though the public voice of Britain First, from all sides of the House, is now 'the voice' in National Policy at home and abroad, the real intent is still deliberately obscured."

Michael stared around the room. "Circles within circles, Paddy. The inner circle - the core of this overtly innocent, nostalgic public voice is, in its final expression - the carefully crafted ideology of PASS and its members. PASS - acronym, pseudonym for those espousing the real goals of Britain First - Protestant, Anglo-Saxon Supremacy - a coy label for a ruthless band of latter day buccaneers and right wing fanatics."

Michael described the "new" colonial strategy of those in PASS. "A global economic device for returning all the former colonies to the fold."

Paddy wondered how he could ever have expected Britain's colonial mind set to have changed in a mere twenty years. He could see the "great games" as still the national pastime for the "favoured few".

"Economic empowerment," said Michael, "the strategy. No visible divisions needed here. Only the untraceable currency you spoke of this morning Paddy - oil, drugs, the arms trade -

and a few good men."

Michael paused, again scanning the room. "As in other times, those legendary buccaneers from Drake, to Clive, to Kitchener - the Philbys of times past - father and son, and all their successors. Now it's our turn. And presto! You have realised the objectives of those in PASS. A new world order, the colonisation of the third millennium!" Michael leaned forward, his voice almost a whisper, "I have recently learned, Paddy, that PASS is a major investor in what they call the China Scheme - one of the most aggressive, rapidly growing international financial enterprises - a global investment empire with interests in Southeast Asia, Hong Kong and China. Here your friend, Victor Perry, has some role. I have been watching him for months, reporting to some people in SIS and D Branch. Strangely, they seemed to discount his importance. Yet he really gets around, Paddy. I keep running into him at embassy functions. He is ever chatting up some select members of the government." Michael leaned forward. "Especially in the last few weeks, Perry has been a pervasive presence. He's supposedly working for the United Nations, for American interests. He's playing a curious and dangerous double role."

Paddy watched Michael again peering about the now busier tables. He realised Michael's discovery, its disclosure, came at a price. Paddy remembered other times, other victims of such discoveries. The bizarre trail of betrayal, suicides and murder in the history of the British and American intelligence services before, during and after World War II. Perhaps, like Paddy's father so many years ago, Michael's curiosity had not gone unnoticed. Might he not also be seen now as a threat to those involved in the conspiracy?

Some later arrivals were lining up for tables. An Luc scanned the faces, ever more watchful of the chattering, laughing, passing throng. For An Luc, the City of Light - host to lovers, the gourmet, the gourmand, the painter and the poet - could now also be host to the unknown assassin.

Driving west toward the suburbs of Neuilly sur Seine, Michael explained how he had been stationed in Northern

Ireland for a short period before the Falklands sortie. As if weighing the priorities, reaching a conclusion, Michael continued. "Paddy, the other item in the news - the shooting in Gibraltar - is not what it appeared. I knew the SAS personnel involved in the hit. The three Irish Republicans, one a female student at Queen's University, thought they were negotiating an arms deal with the Libyans. Unfortunately for them, they discovered too late they'd blundered into a much bigger game. A Brit/US, British-American intelligence drug/arms deal with the Syrians, arms going to southern Russia. Hearing the Irish Republicans, en route to Libya, had learned of the deal, Brit/US were afraid they would expose the British-American drug connection. This misconception led to SIME - Security, Middle East silencing them with the assistance of an SAS hit squad. Two of these received special promotions - the other, an OBE." Michael shook his head, still incredulous. "The Syrian plan was directed by the same MI6 'hot jocks' that organized the BCCI scam. And now Paddy, I believe they're in again - same company." Michael considered his last revelation.

"God, this is a festering sore, Paddy."

Paddy had grown up with, learned first hand the traditional, hardened indifference to human life, the cold arrogance of these self appointed custodians, the established "lords of the realm". He knew their fervid dislike of the crusading zealot who might uncover the cynical plans of these supercilious, as Michael expressed it, "sons of the better breed". Self-styled toffs, feral dilettantes, generation to generation, their antics designed to sustain their own ascendancy, immune from prosecution.

It was the environment that Paddy had fled from. The recurrence of the circumstances of which his own father had been a victim. Was Michael, Paddy wondered, perhaps now replaying his father's role?

Michael's tone was bitter. "We'll hear it all tomorrow – Madam's 'final solution'. I believe MI6 and many in PASS have organized the presentation. From what I hear, with Hong Kong in the process of liberation, she has agreed to make the Irish problem, her last colonial toehold, a shining example of stubborn

113

British resolution."

Michael swore as he narrowly missed an errant French driver. The driver made an obscene gesture, followed by mouthing soundless invective and disappeared at perilous speed into the oncoming traffic. Unperturbed, Michael responded to Paddy's question of the penetration of PASS into government circles.

"Even to Cabinet levels, Paddy. The number two man, Wolsey, I've heard, is a secret supporter. The involvement among MI6 is more extensive. DeVeere, the Director General, and his deputy, Blount. It's less in MI5. And, I'm told, members of both the upper and lower house, Lords and Commons. Britain First has also a more general appeal, in a patriotic sense perhaps, to national pride - a restoration as it were. PASS, a more subtle ideology, has evolved gradually and is seen from two perspectives. One's a potential right wing, Fascist regime of violence. The other, those with global aspirations, anticipating a restoration of wealth and power. A law unto themselves."

To Paddy's further question, Michael confirmed indeed those in PASS might well be aware of his views. Michael had not been too discreet. Too many had heard his adverse comments and occasional criticisms.

They drove in silence now down the historic avenues, passing the monuments, stern or eloquent reminders of earlier empires and their self-destruction; from the dreams of liberty, equality, fraternity unrestrained, to the nightmares of "the terror", "the Commune".

Michael's wife, Beth, met them at the door of the apartment off a quiet, tree lined side street in Neuilly-sur-Seine. Greeting Paddy and An Luc warmly, Beth briefly but sincerely expressed her regrets to Paddy on his recent loss.

Michael and Beth had been married almost a year, and in the next few months would be expecting their first child. Beth was a lovely girl, bright and cheerful. Reaching for Michael's hand, she told Paddy and An Luc the story of their meeting. Beth was a student at the Sorbonne, finishing her Masters in Hebrew law and history and Michael was taking courses in French while stationed in Paris.

"We were drawn to one another," Beth smiled, "for different reasons. Michael's flawed French, my imperfect English - his English reserve, my Jewish chutzpah!"

Curiously, Beth's mother and father had also met and married in Paris. Beth's father had come from Israel to study law at the Sorbonne. Her mother had been a visitor from England. Beth's parents now lived in Israel, visiting Paris frequently. When Beth spoke of them Paddy saw the distant, worried expression. In spite of her laughing manner Paddy could see Beth was distracted and nervous.

They enjoyed an elegant candlelit dinner, Beth amiably chatting of her studies, her life in Israel, and their life in Paris. After dinner, Michael brought them coffee and brandy. While responding to Paddy's questions about her parents, Beth suddenly fell silent. Gazing from one to the other, her voice slightly trembling, she apologised.

"I feel increasingly afraid. Michael shares many of my concerns. He tries not to worry me. And this," said Beth, her voice choked, "makes it more difficult for him."

Michael reached for Beth's hand, trying to console her. Beth shook her head. "No Michael, there has to be a better answer. Tonight we are among real friends. In Michael's job this doesn't happen often. There are so few you can trust. I feel the situation is rapidly getting worse - not alone for Michael and me, for my parents in Israel - but now for our child. I worry about the world he'll be born into. We're all aware of the growing tension and mistrust, everywhere, it seems."

Paddy saw a sense of helplessness in Beth's expression. With tears in her eyes, she continued.

"My father writes to me almost every week. He called me this morning. He is afraid of the recurring cycle. Israel, ever the ready target - the sacrificial lamb - to be betrayed again. Just as before, one sell-out after another. All to placate, to reward bigotry, prejudice and greed!" Beth's voice was growing angry.

Michael tried to calm her, murmuring something about rumours, media exaggeration, sensationalism, but Beth shook her head.

"No Michael, this is different. Today, at the university,

115

everyone was talking about the kidnapping of Professor Henri
Senjaye. I read and listened to press reports. They said he was
recently criticised for his experiments in virulent viral cloning.
His projects caused great concern about the potential for
chemical and biological weapons of pandemic proportions." Beth
fell silent, anxiously looking from one to the other.

Paddy gazed through the windows beyond the tree-
lined streets. So much was at stake with so little known.
Following the years in Vietnam, he remembered thinking
he'd seen it all, heard it all - until one night on the North West
Frontier. Hearing Beth's distress, he told the story now. Near
the end of the Russian-Afghanistan war, one surprise succeeded
another in a harsh enlightenment, as he had been silent witness
that night to the "Great Game" - Michael's "circles within
circles".

Paddy had heard the "other voice," that of Islam, an
unfamiliar view, describing the deliberate division of the people
of the Middle East. Paddy, remembering it now, told the story of
the colonial mirage of deception and lies - obscuring history to
exploit the people and their resources. As Paddy had first heard
it, a re-moulding of history, offering a different future for those
in the land of Sumeria and Canaan - of Jew and Arab and their
resources. Both, children of Abraham, both victims of the covert
strategies of the Gertrude Bells, the more militant "Rambos" of
Imperialism and their greed.

As they listened in the candlelight; other voices, other
shadows from the past seemed to slowly fill the room. As he had
learned that night in the mountain kishlak near Ryandzh, Paddy
was convinced Beth's forebodings would all soon change. Israel
was not the final target of the new Islamic restoration – the "new
Imperialism" was. This was the threat all were now facing, the
new version of the old nemesis - "our own worst enemy - the
enemy within."

Paddy recalled the scene late in December of '88, in
Afghanistan, near the Pakistan border. Paddy and An Luc had
been accompanied by a mujahidin unit and their guide, Ahmed
Shah. They were on a dangerous mission, trying to arrange a
new weapons source for the mujahidin.

Though the primary payer was "Deep Pockets," the American representative would not be present. Paddy, working part time for CIFE, was receiving instructions from Whitcombe. On this occasion "London" had decided, for discreet reasons, to retain the strategic, political initiative.

Paddy, An Luc and Ahmed met their local contact who brought them to their new supplier, a handsome, self-assured Chinese man who spoke flawless English. Within the hour they had concluded a favourable deal, a seemingly inexhaustible supply of high quality weapons from all sources.

Traders, dissidents and deserters, sometime "freedom fighters," "terrorists", briefly "friends" emerged as the story unfolded. Among them Usnakov.

Usnakov had described himself as a deserter who decided to leave the dying to his comrades, bitterly claiming the Americans lured them into Afghanistan to "see us drown in our own blood! Greed the driving force – 'nifak', to divide, their strategy." He told them how meeting an Iranian Mullah, the missionary of God, had changed his life, had given him purpose in helping Muslims of all nations realise the Islamic mission, "to seek peace with our Semitic brothers."

Like many Paddy had seen in Vietnam and after, Usnakov was surviving, but at a price, his hopes precariously balanced on fragile, transient political destinies. On learning that Paddy was British and had served in Vietnam, Usnakov became more friendly. "You too, like the mujahidin, brave warriors, now fight for the 'Great Satan'. As with our brothers in Israel, all of us guns for hire - victims of Imperialism, Russian or American."

For a brief moment Usnakov was not alone - his troubles, their common experiences, now shared as friends, fellow warriors - in other men's wars.

CHAPTER TWELVE

Nifak and the "Divided Family"

Warmed by the fire, the wine, Paddy recalled the words
of Rashid Safarov, a freelance journalist, covering the war in
Afghanistan. Safarov had once been a writer for Tass. Safarov,
Jewish, had defected from the Soviet Union after the Vietnam
War. Afghanistan, once the focus for British and Russian
aspirations, was now the strategic launching pad of conquest.
War was inevitable, Safarov had said.

Paddy recalled Safarov's comments on developments in
the Middle East, the recurring Asian conflicts viewed by many
as the beginnings of the ultimate pan-Islamic jihad against the
West. Beth and Michael listened intently as Safarov's words,
through Paddy, continued. "Evil times. Too many knew too little
- too many, too much."

In the Middle East, Safarov had to confront his dual
heritage, his transient political philosophy as a Russian and
his enduring heritage as a Jew. The "holy land" for some, was
the site of spiritual rewards. For others, it became the killing
grounds for murderous hordes crusading in the name of
Christianity.

"Beneath the sand, oil - the world's most profitable
resource. Middle Asia reaped a harvest of hatred and violence;
impoverished and vandalised by predators, profits were
channelled westward.

"The Brit/US alliance pandered to the greed and
pride of the wealthy Arab families, awarding the sheiks their
'emirates' in exchange for a guaranteed flow of oil. The emirates,
each a puppet emperor enthroned."

Safarov spoke of his return to the land of Canaan,
his own growing awareness of his heritage, and of a shared

suffering. "Israel, perpetual adversary in a hostile environment, was forced to act the pawn; Arab and Jew, easy prey, their real enemy invisible. Like many I spoke with in Russia, later in America, we awoke from the dream to find it had left us.

"Now is the greatest challenge to all the peoples of middle Asia - the time and wisdom to confront and overcome the deliberately sown mistrust and jealousy. For Arab and Jew to take charge of their own common destiny and share their bounty.

"There are many types of enslavement," Safarov claimed, "best achieved through the Apartheid of the colonial inheritance. Like the Russian distortion of communism, the New Imperialism will subject people worldwide to exploitation, leading to subsistence in poverty. Unless we make a stand."

It was after midnight. From the room, it seemed, the shadows withdrew. Beth and Michael felt reassured in hearing that other victims of colonialism, of nifak, shared their concerns.

Driving Paddy and An Luc back to the city, they thanked Paddy for giving them a different perspective, more aware now of the shared tragedy, shared threats. Israel was no longer the sole victim, but one among many.

In his hotel room, Paddy lay on his bed. He turned on the TV. The newscaster commented, "Still no trace of Professor Senjaye, nor any clues to the identity of his kidnappers." Paddy turned off the screen. The room curiously reflected the lamplight from the streets below. The wind rose, stirring the curtains in billowing folds.

Paddy wondered if Safarov had returned to the new emerging Russia. The era of communist oppression had self-destructed, Capitalism now rampant. Perhaps Safarov had returned to embattled Israel, to help find a way to resolution.

Paddy recalled Safarov's reference to a different source of arms from the Middle East, from Kurdistan. A nameless one, first on the scene in any area of pending strife, even rumoured to be in Kabul before the fighting had commenced. Paddy wondered if the "nameless one" Safarov had spoken about was still in business, arming other conflicts.

There was much work to be done. He began to see an immediate path at hand, to help Michael reveal the true purpose of Britain's new movement, PASS, perhaps shedding new light on old mysteries, and to see what corruption the "China Scheme" might be a party to. First, he must unravel the mystery of Anna's death. He drifted off to sleep, dreaming of Anna, sensing once again the smiling warmth of her presence.

Some hours later, alert in the lively Parisian ambiance of a fresh summer day, Paddy called Michael. They would meet at the Foreign Ministry within the hour.

Paddy and An Luc walked along the busy streets. By the Pont des Invalides, the crippled veterans huddled, unseen and unsung heroes of other campaigns. The incurious pedestrian work force hurried by. Everywhere, baroque monuments, silent witness to the city's two thousand year odyssey.

For Paddy, the great chateaux once built to instil envy, fear and subservience sustained an eloquent paradox. They stood, gilded citadels of pride, lining the majestic avenues in elegant apotheosis, empty mausoleums to the greed and theft of another age, to the inevitable mortality of beggars and kings.

For An Luc, from another world, Paris was an imposing city, a macabre paradox. Paris once, and still, the capital of excess and indulgence; a city too often the bloody site of revolutions to change its destiny.

On the steps of the French Foreign Ministry, Sir Geoffrey Gordon stood with his staff and several stone-faced security figures. Greeting Paddy, An Luc and Michael, he took Paddy aside, warmly complimenting him on his presentation the previous day. Gordon informed him that copies of his talk had already been circulated to London. Paddy was pleased but sceptical.

"Madam and others have read your report, Paddy. Madam told me she was impressed. Seemed to find your reference to an international criminal conspiracy timely and interesting. Perhaps," added Gordon cautiously, "it suits the strategies she is promoting. Madam looks forward to speaking with you later today."

Gordon mentioned Madam's reaction to the decision of the European Court of Justice in the Gibraltar affair. "She is most upset and humiliated. She speaks of interference in British affairs from every side, from the Americans especially."

Gordon and Paddy moved across the marble foyer. They stood apart from the others, Gordon looking hard at Paddy, his expression querulous. Paddy realised Gordon was earnestly pressing for his acceptance of the appointment to CIFE. Gordon cautiously glanced about, his voice low.

"She is keen to learn more concerning the Senjaye kidnapping. She feels this has other implications. Thinks you might be of some help here. Madam plans to discuss these affairs at the conference this evening."

Paddy and Sir Geoffrey Gordon entered the hall. Paddy stared around the large, elegant room. Even in the dim light he could see the gilded empire ceilings, the ornate drapes at the floor to ceiling windows. This meeting, another forum on regional drug enforcement issues, presented by the French section of the International DEA team, was already in progress. Paddy and the other members of the delegation were led down the aisle to their seats.

Before taking his seat, An Luc and Michael close behind, Gordon said, "Look forward to seeing you all at the reception later." He slid past Paddy.

Paddy stared distractedly around the darkened auditorium. He found himself recalling the disturbing encounter with Victor Perry the day before.

An Luc suddenly touched Paddy's sleeve, pointing toward the podium. Paddy's attention refocused. Nodding, An Luc handed Paddy a set of earphones.

Paddy listened. Surprised, he heard - "since the American departure from Vietnam, the Russian forces from Afghanistan, and now Tadjikistan, a scene of increasing regional conflicts has emerged." The slides being shown, the maps, the graphics; much of it was familiar. The data summarised statistics much like his own, showing regions of increasing narcotic production in Southeast Asia - arrows pointing to increasing markets in southern China. Paddy listened with quickening interest, realising the information expanded his own data.

"Too many," said the speaker, "are successfully involved in all phases of the drug business. They are of all nationalities - Iranians, British, Australians, Russians, as well as Americans - and now, from China."

They were now listening to the question and answer period. Seated to one side of the auditorium, Paddy strained to either side, trying to see the speaker's face. It was not uncommon, he knew, for people involved in the vast and complex assortment of international agencies abroad to be working only miles from one another, yet neither aware of the other's presence.

Paddy slowly made his way toward the stage, closely followed by An Luc and Michael. Members of the audience surrounded the speaker. He was in his late forties, of slight stature, with thinning hair. Paddy glanced at the nametag placed on the speaker's dais. He slowly read the name. He looked again, raising his eyes to meet those of the speaker.

Walking with a noticeable limp, the man came toward Paddy, both hands extended, eyes alight, his expression one of recognition. "Paddy, is that really you? Mon Dieu, I can't believe this!"

For a moment Paddy couldn't reply. "Jean, Jesus - it is you, Jean!"

Seeing each other for the first time in more than twenty years, each thinking that the other had risen from the dead, both men warmly clasped hands, smiling broadly. "How can this be?" "I must be dreaming!" "This couldn't be true!"

They stood with an incredulous shaking of heads. For both, a rush of memories. As he looked now at Jean Claude Davost, Paddy remembered the tough veteran, the last hours they'd spent together as members of Spec Seven at Phnom Penh.

Still savouring the moment, Paddy hastened to introduce Jean to Michael and An Luc. Laughing, Jean again reached over impulsively and shook Paddy's hand. With the other hand, unselfconsciously, he reached to wipe his eyes.

"We have much to talk about, Paddy," said Jean happily.

Jean collected his notes and, using a cane, slowly descended from the stage. He laughingly explained to Paddy, "a result of the difficult journey home from Phnom Penh."

One question followed another. Outside, Sir Geoffrey and other members of the British delegation met them. Once again, introductions all around. Sir Geoffrey joined the others in wishing them a happy reunion celebration.

"Your presentation was so similar to Paddy's. A remarkable coincidence from many points of view." Adding that he looked forward to seeing Davost at the embassy reception that evening, Gordon turned to go, reminding Paddy and Michael, "Don't forget our meeting - six thirty."

As they descended the steps of the Foreign Ministry, Jean smiled to Paddy, "What a fantastic coincidence that we met now. You and I were working in the same area. We never knew how near we were. I'm surprised at your choice to stay in Asia - this intrigues me."

Paddy laughed, "And now our decision to return. Yes, we do share more than a secret past. We really have much catching up to do."

Jean insisted Paddy and An Luc be his guests during the rest of their stay in Paris. "Everyone must come to my house now, to meet my wife and tell our stories."

Paddy and An Luc accepted the invitation. Michael thanked Jean, excusing himself, saying that he had some preparations to make for the evening meeting, but that he looked forward to seeing them all later at the reception.

"See you about six, Paddy," he said. He turned to go, hurrying after Sir Geoffrey Gordon and the other members of the British delegation.

Jean suggested driving Paddy and An Luc to their hotel so that they could collect their belongings. Jean and his wife, Nguyen, lived at Saint Germain en Laye, just outside Paris. "We should have plenty of time to run out to the house," said Jean, "meet my wife, and be in good time for the reception."

Paddy and An Luc waited as Jean went to bring the car around. "An Luc, your father knew Jean well. He was born in Vientiane, his father died at Dien Bien Phu. He never wanted to leave Laos - it was his home too. Jean is one of those I never thought I'd see again. First Perry, now Jean Davost - the bad and the good - like old photos of the past." Paddy smiled. "What a contrast."

An Luc saw "Lord Fucan" come alive again, seeming more assured. The sadness and grim purpose of the past few days was lifted. It was as though the lady Anna, intent on protecting her Lord Fucan, guided their footsteps, leading them to friends once thought lost forever.

"Monsieur Davost's arrival is a timely miracle," An Luc commented, "I feel strongly, in the many ways of samsara, the lady Anna is with us still."

"I agree," said Paddy. "Davost's arrival is a miracle! Lady Anna is with us and we need her, in many ways."

Jean's beautiful wife, Nguyen, was French Vietnamese, born in Vientiane. With her long, shiny black hair and eyes almost as dark, Nguyen reminded Paddy of Anna, the gentle, attentive manner, the similar beauty and heritage, the intelligence, quick laugh and sincerity.

Paddy, Jean and An Luc joined Nguyen in the flowered peace of a summer garden. In the late afternoon sunlight they sat chatting, sipping wine and eating sandwiches Nguyen had prepared. Nguyen was not unfamiliar with the experiences Paddy and Jean had shared in Vietnam. She fully appreciated the significance of their meeting.

Nguyen showed An Luc the gardens, closely followed by Jean's two borzois - graceful dogs, languid companions, as they strolled down the walks between the fruit trees. She and An Luc shared memories of Laos, recalling the land they had both once known as their home. In explaining his own presence in Paris, An Luc told Nguyen of Paddy's recent loss, Anna's death.

Jean and Paddy sat in quiet conversation. Jean was surprised on Paddy's mention of Victor Perry's reappearance.

Describing his own escape, Jean commented, "Hearing Saigon was already surrounded, we trekked westward, a very difficult journey. We ended up reaching Bangkok some weeks after. After arriving home, I made many enquiries about who had survived, always met with "no comment". But I've kept my memories of my friends."

Paddy told Jean after Phnom Penh he and Anna had spent their lives together until her recent death. Jean was shocked on learning the circumstances.

"So well I remember Anna, a lovely lady of great courage." Jean reached across, gripping Paddy's hand. He affirmed that he would be available any time to assist Paddy in whatever way he could, to help find those responsible for Anna's death.

An Luc and Nguyen returned from the garden. Briefly touching Paddy's shoulder, Nguyen expressed her heartfelt sympathy on learning of Anna's death. Paddy quietly thanked her. Nguyen refilled their glasses, then excused herself to change for the reception.

An Luc and Jean exchanged memories of their childhood world. Vientiane served as the government centre of French Indochina; some of the old French families still unable or unwilling to leave. "Permanent colonials," Jean laughed.

Into their reminiscences came the sound of Nguyen's voice from the landing, gently reminding them that Paddy had a meeting to attend before the reception. She came down the stairs, her smile radiant, her dark hair falling around her shoulders, a colourful ao dai, like a gossamer cloak flowing about her. Nguyen deserved Jean's proud compliments.

Again Paddy was reminded of Anna. Strangely at peace now and among friends, he was beginning to accept her death. As if in another dimension, warming, reassuring, he felt her continuing presence.

Happily chatting, the little group moved into the courtyard. Paddy loudly expressed his hope that perhaps Nguyen might prefer to drive as Jean had missed his calling as a Grand Prix driver. Nguyen laughingly assured Paddy and An Luc that Jean had an unsullied record.

"Not a land speed record, I hope," said Paddy, as he fastened his seatbelt. They commenced another precarious race through the suburbs of the city.

Jean drew up before the embassy. The pavement

outside had been roped off. Special Security, British MI5, and French DST stood by the steps, all visibly armed. A uniformed member of the embassy staff, accompanied by several plain clothed security immediately approached the car. British security checked their identification.

In the foyer, identification was again closely and impersonally scrutinised by French and British security.

Moving into the crowded hallway, Paddy recognised other members of the embassy staff. Michael and Beth Weatherby came across the foyer to meet them. Beth warmly greeted Nguyen and Jean as they were introduced. While Nguyen and Beth talked, Beth gazed nervously around. Paddy sensed her distraction.

Michael reminded Paddy it was time for their meeting. Looking back as he followed Michael up the stairs, Paddy saw Beth staring worriedly after them.

CHAPTER THIRTEEN

Another 'Final Solution'

At the door to the conference room, Michael and Paddy's identification was again carefully examined by security. Paddy noticed a tall, heavyset man in regulation dark suit watching them. Momentarily the man stared hard at Michael, then eye to eye with Paddy, cold, insolent, appraising.

Inclining his head he beckoned them, "This way, Lord Finucane, Captain Weatherby," leading them to seats at the rear of the room. Paddy noticed a hard twang in the accent, Australian, or East End, maybe.

During the introductions, Michael whispered to Paddy, "Some are members of SIS, MI6. Others from Watchers include a special group of MI5 from the Northern Ireland Office. E4A they call them." He bent close. "The chap who showed us to our seats is Graham, a strong supporter of Britain First and a core member of PASS. He made a name for himself with SAS in the Falklands."

The first speaker, Michael Deicey, Director of SIME, Security Intelligence Middle East, answered some impromptu question on the kidnapping of Professor Senjaye. He had no new leads.

"There are at least two main areas of concern: the New Russian voice and the Islamic revolt. And God knows there may be another voice emerging, perhaps fuelled by a desire for Kurdish autonomy."

He concluded, "Mossad tell us there are new threats. Their goal is an extension of Israel's safe perimeter, engaged to see that the voice of Kurdish nationalism is not misused to threaten Israeli security. The region is under constant satellite scrutiny. It is not a reassuring picture."

After some discussion, attention focused on Margaret Aylward, a stern looking, not unattractive woman, possibly in her thirties. Michael whispered to Paddy, "She's the newly appointed Director of the Joint Intelligence Committee. Her specialty is leaks and moles. Except for a bitter personal animosity with Madam, the reigning government 'monarch'."

"We are at a stage of peculiar crises," Aylward began, "before an empowered European community, in a world of gathering violence. There's dissension on the home front. Abroad, we learn of increasing problems with the incoming Chinese administration in Hong Kong, an increase in international criminal activity, continued regional conflicts. And the recent threat of a major conflagration affecting all our interests, especially those in the Middle and Far East."

There was a sudden flurry of activity near the door. Preceded by a retinue of security, a covey of scurrying aides and officious secretaries flustering about, Madam Prime Minister entered the room. Sir Geoffrey Gordon and his deputy, Morris Stanfield accompanied her. The unvarying teflon image, the supercilious, glazed expression, the hard eyes gazed about as she conversed with Gordon, the overbite incisors in a fixed feline smile.

Aylward quickly collected her notes and returned to her seat, scarcely acknowledging Madam's arrival.

Madam and her entourage made their way toward the front. Madam nodded to the occasional acquaintance, functionaries in favour. Among these, Paddy saw Colin DeVeere, DG of MI6, and his deputy, Blount, eagerly moving forward to share the conspiratorial touch or whisper.

Geoffrey Gordon stepped to the podium. Briefly he introduced the small, middle-aged lady, so carefully coiffed and coutured. The focus of international attention, national controversy and bitter, regional venom, she needed no introduction.

Madam moved eagerly to the podium. Authoritative, imperious, enunciating each word clearly, Madam came straight to the point.

"I want to make this perfectly clear, I am not going

to tolerate the resurrection of the Irish Question in any shape or form – certainly not as a matter to be discussed by any so called international civil rights body. In questions pertaining to the North of Ireland, Great Britain has sole dominion in their resolution."

Madam commended the action of the Special SAS unit in stopping the terrorists in Gibraltar, then launched into a self-righteous tirade. Some of her listeners shifted uneasily, embarrassed by the too obvious loss of emotional restraint.

"With our American cousins, we intend to pursue terrorism wherever we find it - in whatever guise it assumes."

DeVeere and Blount nodded vigorously, calling "Hear! Hear!" Margaret Aylward stared grimly straight ahead.

Paddy had heard it all before by others in bygone years. Claiming a threat to national security was sufficient reason to infringe human rights. As Paddy knew, the designation of terrorist depended on perspective. To demonise was for some a useful strategy. This was easy to apply in Afghanistan against the Russians. The Russians were the "axis of evil", the "terrorists". The latter designation, in the Middle East and in Northern Ireland, was now more selectively prescribed. Former freedom fighters were now terrorists.

Paddy was impressed. As Michael had predicted, Madam had just belligerently proclaimed the propriety of "sole dominion", domestic sovereignty of England's curious claims to a piece of the island of Ireland, public opinion irrelevant.

Madam continued, never loath to preach on the "great moral precepts," of freedom and terrorism, while she simultaneously planned her own covert, selective elimination. Paddy saw Michael shaking his head.

In recent weeks, Paddy had read Madam's statements in support of the ethnic minorities in the Balkans, and against the ruthlessness of a policy of ethnic cleansing. He wondered how this Oxbridge prodigy seemed to have such myopic vision when it came to Ireland. Its liberation a traumatic labour, though finally coming to deliverance, surely on a similar "great moral basis" as America, the first colony to successfully reject the same oppressor. Paddy listened, more alert now to Madam's tirade.

"We have good reason to suspect that the IRA, common terrorists, have been trading over the past few months with a dangerous, fundamentalist Islamic movement and other totalitarian regimes. They have been in contact with enemies from Libya, Syria and now across the Arabian Peninsula to Iran, home of sectarian bigotry and their proscriptive fatwas, their jihads - all constraints to the voice of the freedom we cherish.

"The vital interests of both Britain and our American friends are now at stake in this region," Madam stressed, "and no one region is strategically separate from the larger picture. From Belfast to the Balkans, the Irish vote in American politics - all acutely affect our own voice and vote at home."

Glancing at Sir Geoffrey Gordon seated to one side of the podium, Paddy saw a distinctly uncomfortable expression, eyes fixed somewhere beyond the high curtained windows as Madam set forth the principles of survival in an incorrigible society.

Scarcely believing, Paddy was now listening to the specifics of Madam's plan to put a stop to "IRA terrorist" activities. Paddy saw Madam glancing curiously about the room as she described the measures to be taken in conjunction with "our friends" in the United States. Measures including obtaining information, condoning torture, detention without trial at the pleasure of the Secretary of State. "All those bent on driving the British from Northern Ireland or elsewhere by intimidation will find they've met their match."

Momentarily unguarded, no one's mother, no one's child - the predatory instinct, carnivorous, poised to strike. Looking about the room with a thin smile, "We have decided to call this final solution 'Plan Ajax'. To be kept top secret, of course," Madame warned.

DeVeere and Blount nodded an approving "Hear, hear!" Across the room, Geoffrey Gordon sat motionless. Paddy was conscious of Michael, tense beside him. It was becoming more difficult even for Paddy to sit in silent assent amid the posturing, the entrapments of power and its callous indifference.

Paddy remembered the family values he'd grown up with, principles preached and accepted during his Public School years. His own grandfather, Paddy had learned, was a member of the British team negotiating the troubled emergence of the Irish Republic. Paddy's father had seemed reluctant to discuss the subject. More curious perhaps, since the family fortunes had been so closely associated with events in Irish history. Their "stolen" estates or titles, "grants" in the plantations that were won or lost again, incidental to England's uncivil wars in the struggle for a legitimate royal progression. Once again it seemed his embattled family heritage and its uncertain course had returned to haunt him.

With a nudge from Michael, Paddy realised Madam was addressing him from the podium, something about grateful recognition of his valuable services abroad. "As we heard your message yesterday – the story of your gallant efforts to forestall the inroads of the Asian drug traders, to whom your family recently fell victim. Our sympathy on your recent loss, Lord Finucane. Your personal knowledge and experience in this region is of importance during the transfer of power, particularly during the increasing difficulties in our exchanges with the Chinese government."

Madam was at first solicitous, then warmly smiled. "We hope that Lord Finucane has returned to his rightful home, to take his place among us soon, as Deputy Director, CIFE."

Paddy was aware of the congratulatory nods and smiles of some, among them Geoffrey Gordon, who may well have asked Madam to make the unusual commentary. A premature recruitment nudge, or signal of her support perhaps. Some stared back, faces expressionless, among these DeVeere and Blount.

Madam paused, then in serious tones announced, "Before closing I must mention that the Chinese government, in the past few days, has conveyed its grave concern over the increasing intrusion of drug merchants and other criminal enterprises into southern China in recent months." Looking over at Paddy again, Madam continued, "A problem, Lord Finucane, which you spoke of at some length in your presentation. Of great concern to us are allegations by the Chinese government, of the involvement of British subjects - among them members of the former Hong Kong administration in some perhaps related, criminal transgressions." Glaring about the room, Madam promised, "This we will investigate!"

A tense silence prevailed. Most eyes remained on the speaker. Some, Paddy noticed, looked busily elsewhere. He heard Michael's exasperated muttering.

The precise tones concluded, "There is speculation that these irregularities may affect Hong Kong's special position in the ongoing administrative transfer to the Chinese government – Britain's continuing investment in the Hong Kong economy. Your presentation, Lord Finucane, has been most timely and has encouraged us to request a postponement of the transfer of power, pending the results of a United Nations fact finding commission." A half smile, of satisfaction perhaps? Madam, confident the Chinese might discover a continuing British "economic presence" essential to sustain Hong Kong's stability.

Madam glanced around the room, looking for some response to her gratuitous query, "Any questions?" There were none. Gordon, looking troubled, moved toward the podium. He murmured a few words, barely heard. Some had risen from their chairs, looking about as if preparing to leave.

Michael suddenly rose, barely withholding his anger. "With due respect Madam, speaking for myself, perhaps for others, I hear a catalogue of deception."

There were startled exclamations. All, including Madam, stood back, scarcely believing the unexpected interruption by a little known, temporarily appointed MI5 Station Chief.

"Again history repeats itself, again a betrayal of the trust of people everywhere." Michael looked about the room.

He spoke quietly, expressing his profound frustration, each word resounding in the ominous silence. His stunned audience seemed too surprised to react. Paddy winced in anticipation of what would follow.

"When will we confront our mistakes? The Irish nationalists, IRA, or whatever we call them - have been a voice that we have refused to negotiate with. Our policy only reinforces our historic colonial image, gaining us well-deserved international condemnation. We have advised others to sit at the table - to talk. But the much proclaimed Brit/US doctrine of dialogue and decommission, only for the quarrelling Irish. For Brit/US, our only response is war. Just as we abhor terrorism - tactics that intimidate the civilian population - doesn't this apply equally to us?"

Michael glanced about as he spoke. "Terrorism is the weapon of despair - of last resort. When used by a major power it's inexcusable!"

There was an embarrassed or angry silence, a shuffling of feet, some perhaps even admiring Michael's reckless audacity. Michael paused to look across at Madam, who stared back coldly.

"In Madam's own words, 'The lesson of this century, that countries artificially put together will fall apart.' Nationalist identities in Ireland or elsewhere cannot be denied or suppressed."

Michael continued, almost without pause. The passion of his quick delivery postponed the inevitable interruption. "There are two standards of hypocrisy - one when you fool yourself, the second when you fool each other. One for those who believe the civil charade we present, and one for those who know we're lying. There are those of us with a different dream, those who don't feel the need for a 'Greater' Britain. Britain for us, never greater than when it returns to being England."

The die cast, Michael rushed on, sensing a recovery from the initial surprise and the growing hostility. "Let's stop trying to deceive ourselves and others as we have done for too long. Our manner is the badge of our deception. Christianity, commerce and civilisation be damned."

This was met with cries of protest, more restless stirring.

Michael looked directly at Madam, confronting her hostile stare. "How do we think we can get away with this program of discrimination, deception, and now of selective assassination? Supposed leaders of a free world society."

Paddy saw Graham standing by the door, glaring. He knew Michael's stand was likely to be his professional requiem.

"More alarming now is the possible international criminal activity you referred to, into the Hong Kong administration."

Curiously there was a momentary nervous silence. "It is my conclusion that the Chinese government would do well to reflect who really owns Hong Kong, or indeed the Chinese economy. The Opium Wars of the third millennium, only this time we're not the ones pushing the drugs. This new China Scheme could be part of an extensive global scam, involving the transfer of ownership of economic resources of the region to an unknown other party. This time, we're among the victims - some of us seduced by our own greed - some by the greed of others."

Michael's allegations had touched some raw nerves. Interruptions became more frequent, louder, yet attention still focused, shocked - expressions genuinely worried. More curious, thought Paddy, was Madam's pause before leaving the room, anxious perhaps, to hear him out. As if on signal then, Madam and her staff moved toward the doorway.

Paddy saw Gordon move to the podium as DeVeere, Blount and some others from MI6 hastily followed Madam's exit. Members of the audience stood about, angry or dismayed, appalled at Michael's condemnations.

Paddy reached to draw Michael's attention, to persuade him the show was over. He found himself forcibly countering several hard-eyed security types, among them Graham. There was no mistaking their intent.

Graham turned to Michael. "You're more fuckin' trouble than you're worth - you'd better bloody watch it!"

At that moment Gordon came up. Graham glared at Michael a moment longer, then turned and left the room.

Visibly distressed, Gordon addressed Michael. "Michael, I don't understand. Really quite a blunder. Madam was very upset by your comments." Michael straightened his jacket and tie. Gordon looked from Michael to Paddy. "We must discuss this further - definitely raises problems." Shaking his head, Gordon moved toward the door. "Call me later, both of you."

Their departure from the reception was earlier than planned. Jean and Nguyen, knowing things had not gone well at the meeting, insisted a troubled Michael and Beth join Paddy and An Luc at their home for "a drink and a chat". Beth reluctantly agreed.

Madam, standing beside the ambassador in the hallway, bid the departing guests goodnight. Her chilly acknowledgment did not go unnoticed as Michael and Paddy left the reception. Geoffrey Gordon was nowhere to be seen. Graham stood with security at the top of the steps, staring after Michael as he went to collect the car. A few minutes later Paddy looked again. Graham was no longer there. On the drive to St. Germaine en Laye, Paddy found himself occasionally glancing out of the rear window at the following traffic.

Beth and Nguyen sat quietly chatting in the drawing room. The four men sat around the dinner table in the pleasant aura of cigars, brandy and coffee. Though Michael was distressed by the hostile reaction to his message, Paddy could sense his feeling of relief, the burden lifted. Knowing they could trust Jean's discretion, first Michael, then Paddy described their growing concerns.

Michael explained to Jean his impression of the China Scheme. "Government, in name only, will have become the hired broker of some international conglomerate – a silent conquest in an invisible transaction in the new global imperialism."

Michael rose from his chair, stood before the fireplace. "In the Oxbridge tradition, the Philbys, Dulles, Casey - almost every year another one, immune from accountability or even identity. For the Americans - the CIA spy turned CEO, the CEO turned spy - through the revolving doors of the largest weapons conglomerates - the supra national corporate mogul now determining foreign policy - and the rules." Paddy realised Michael was feeling an increasing sense of isolation, with the added threat of retaliation.

"Michael, you had the courage to express what some of us also feel. Seeing the reaction, you really got to some of them."

Arm in arm, Beth and Nguyen walked into the room. The four men rose to greet the ladies. Smiling, Beth apologised for the interruption.

"What a great evening I've had. How glad I am to find

135

I'm not the only one to forget the time among friends. Made me forget my troubles - but we'd better be off. We both have an early morning. I've a lecture at the Sorbonne - Michael to the embassy, right, Michael?"

Michael nodded, smiling grimly. "If I've still got a job."

Beth and Michael thanked Jean and Nguyen for their hospitality. Nguyen hugged Beth, telling her that they looked forward to the new baby's arrival and the good times they would have together.

The group stood in the courtyard as Michael helped Beth into the car. She rolled down the window as the car pulled away - again thanked them all, telling Nguyen she'd be in touch. Michael called back as the car passed through the gateway, "See you at the embassy, Paddy." Then they were gone, passing out toward the highway and Courbevoie.

Paddy and An Luc, Jean and Nguyen stood staring into the darkness from the steps of the old house as the lights of the car disappeared from view. It was a cool night, the evening rain had stopped. Between the clouds a full moon rode the night sky above a dark, featureless landscape. Paddy recalled such nights in Vietnam, the "hunt and kill" expeditions of Special Forces - a "hunter's moon", they'd called it.

The men sat before the fireplace in the great family room. Nguyen brought them coffee, then sleepily excused herself. Kissing Jean, Nguyen left them to the firelight.

Jean asked, "How badly did things go for Michael? He seemed to think he'd really blown it."

"It was a bad scene," Paddy answered. "He didn't hold back. Took on the whole reigning British political hierarchy - and the Anglo-American alliance." Paddy was silent for a moment.

"His last remarks relating to the China Scheme, suggesting that some in the government might be involved in the drugs and arms sales in Southeast Asia, broke up the meeting. The mood turned violent. I don't know what we can do at this point, other than help him with his investigation. I'm beginning to see a link with the groups you and I spoke of, and An Luc saw, in Southeast Asia." An Luc silently nodded.

They sat before the great fireplace, faces occasionally

lit by the flickering light of the burning fire. Jean and Paddy inevitably returned to the memories shared in Vietnam, sometimes in laughter, more often in troubled recall.

They remembered the shooting of the South Vietnamese officer caught removing truckloads of military supplies from the main depot in Saigon - murder, the administration called it. The ensuing "hearings" were the frantic efforts of both South Vietnamese and American civil and military administration to put a stop to their investigative activities. Victor Perry's role in the "trials" diminished, in fear of what might be revealed.

Jean recalled the enormous profits Colonel Deevers and the South Vietnamese General, Tung Giang, were realising in those last months of the war. Paddy told Jean the story of the keys, their significance for all who had known or worked with Deevers. The threat, Deevers' warning of instant exposure to anyone he feared. The challenge, Deevers' enormous wealth, to which the keys might provide access. Paddy told of Deevers' threats to Anna – then finding him crucified, in Phnom Penh, the site of the gold transfer.

"Anna felt sure those who murdered Deevers would not stop looking for the keys - maybe suspected we had found them. Listening to An Luc's account of her death, Anna was sadly proven right." Paddy gazed into the glowing fire, his expression a mixture of anguish and conviction. "After all these years."

Jean suddenly rose from his chair, excusing himself. He returned after some minutes, carrying a small box. Reaching inside he withdrew a tiny key.

"I well remember when Anna gave this to me. You keep it, Paddy." Paddy gratefully accepted Jean's gift.

An Luc exclaimed, "The path of destiny, Lord Fucan - step by step."

Paddy told Jean of his constant efforts to understand the significance of Anna's last words. "Who could it have been, I ask myself, trying to recall Deevers' other associates - Tung Giang, the one who tried to have us court martialled?" Paddy repeated An Luc's information - Tung Giang's re-emergence now as Khun Sa, the powerful regional drug lord in the area of the Golden Triangle.

Briefly then, Paddy described his surprise to see Victor Perry at the DEA meetings. Jean, remembering the Perry they'd known in the attempted court martial in Saigon, was equally sceptical of any legitimate role he might have in drug enforcement - more likely involved in some way in the corruption.

The three men sat gazing into the flames, their flickering reflections sending tall shadows around the walls of the room. They spoke in low tones, recalling another night long ago, the words weaving a strange spell. Deja vu - the crackling logs before them, gunfire now; they crouched in unceasing bursts of automatic fire; the flames, thudding explosions of rocket, mortars and grenades - beside them screams of the wounded, joined by the taunts and threats of the Khmer Rouge. Paddy and Jean wondered in quiet, awed voices - how had they survived?

"I can remember, Paddy, the increasing incoming fire, B-40 RPG's. Mon Dieu, the screams - I can hear them now. You and Anna crawled up - she gave us those keys, told us to get them back to Saigon. The Chinook took off, loaded with the wounded. They went down - exploded over the city. The Cobra took off then. The pilot - C/O of E2, Kerkorian. He loved a challenge. Remember the Afro-American? A great soldier. Johnson, Buddy Johnson."

Jean paused, looked at An Luc. "And among the Montagnards I remember your father, An Luc, among the bravest."

Paddy too was remembering the faces Jean recalled. "Even with special equipment we still couldn't raise the naval flotilla. That was when Kerkorian volunteered. Sounded crazy to me, but we'd no alternative." He paused. "Yes, he'd try anything!"

The faces all came back to him - loyal Buddy Johnson; Ben, the Jewish boy; his friend, the Irishman, Jack Edwards; the macho super jock, Kerkorian - defiant of regulations or discipline, with his wild tales of the "Companions", legendary warriors from history. He'd called the Spec Seven group "a band of brothers".

Again Paddy saw the Cobra streaking nose down

across the airfield, as the Khmer turned every weapon on them. The explosion just beyond the perimeter seemed to engulf the aircraft. When the smoke cleared there was no sign of the Cobra. Paddy remembered his certainty that Kerkorian had met his fate - the last hope of achieving the goals of the mission dying with him.

In the momentary silence, Jean quietly asked, "Paddy, whatever became of the gold shipment?" the question Paddy had asked himself and so many others, in the months after the evacuation.

It seemed as though Paddy hadn't heard Jean's question. He was remembering the sudden ending of one life after another - their voices, their faces, disembodied before him. Turning to Jean, Paddy slowly shook his head. "I never learned what really happened to the naval flotilla waiting for the message that never came. Wherever I enquired, no one knew - perhaps hijacked by its crew. The shipment never arrived. Some suggested the gold was stolen by pirates, or lost at sea on the way to Singapore. The flotilla was never seen again."

In the room the shadows deepened. Paddy and Jean, in their own time warp, shared a world long gone; yet the echoes and reverberations still touched their lives.

They were startled to hear Nguyen calling. They met her in the hall as she hurried down the stairway. Breathless, she spoke. "It's Beth - quickly Paddy, she's on the phone. Something about Michael!"

Paddy followed her to the hall phone. As he picked up the receiver he tried to stifle a sudden cold dread. Beside him, An Luc, Jean and Nguyen anxiously waited. As soon as he spoke her name, Paddy heard the tremulous words.

"Paddy, I'm frightened. It's Michael. He left to meet someone - he's not back yet - he hasn't called. Something's wrong! God, it's nearly four a.m.!" Beth made a choking sound. Paddy tried to calm her.

"Paddy, soon after we got home, after one - a call woke us. I answered - the English voice seemed familiar, asked for Michael. I was barely awake. Michael was on the phone quite a while - seemed surprised, worried."

She continued, her voice trembling, stifling an occasional sob. "When he got off the phone I asked him who it was. He just told me not to worry. Paddy, Michael always tells me where he's going, or who it is. When I insisted, he told me it was something to do with his talk at the meeting yesterday - people involved in the China Scheme."

Paddy almost held his breath, glancing worriedly from An Luc to Jean as Beth's voice hurried on. "After Michael left, I looked outside. The car was still there. He must have taken the Metro." As if trying to reassure herself, "Sometimes he leaves the car for me. But this was after 1:30 in the morning. It's all wrong Paddy - maybe I should drive over to Montparnasse now?" Paddy interrupted, strongly advising her not to. "Oh Paddy, I don't know what to do!"

Paddy tried to control his own mounting anxiety as he spoke gently, firmly. "Beth, stay by the phone - don't leave the house." Thinking quickly, he asked, "Where had they planned to meet?"

"To meet in an hour at Place Denfert Rochereau, opposite the Paris Observatory, Michael told me, by the entrance to the Catacombes. It was then after one. They should have met over two hours ago! I asked him to call me. He said he would."

"Hang in there, Beth. An Luc, Jean and I will head over to Montparnesse right away. If Michael calls tell him we're on our way."

Turning to tell the others, Paddy himself was not reassured. He wished Michael had called him first. He could see it now - Michael conscious of the liability he now posed, trying to go it alone.

Jean knew the location - they could reach Place Rochereau in thirty minutes. Nguyen, hurrying up the stairs, called down to Paddy, "I'll drive over to Beth's. Give me the address - in Neuilly, yes?" Jean was placing a call to a friend in French Security. As soon as Jean hung up Paddy tried to call Beth. The number was engaged. Waiting a few moments he tried again - again busy. Jean and An Luc were ready to leave. Paddy turned to go. Maybe Michael was calling Beth, or perhaps Beth was calling the embassy. Pausing at the hall door, Paddy looked up to see Nguyen standing at the top of the stairs. "Nguyen, I've tried to reach Beth - her phone's busy. Please call her, tell her you are driving to her house."

It took Jean less than thirty minutes to reach Montparnasse. Cruising slowly, Paddy, An Luc and Jean peered down the dark side streets. The Place Rochereau was deserted, from the Metro station to the entrance to the Catacombes. They parked on a nearby side street. As they emerged from the car they heard the urgent hee-haw, hee-haw of emergency vehicle sirens somewhere in the city. Jean suggested they split up. They would meet back at the car in an hour.

Checking their watches, they set off at a fast pace. Jean crossed the street, heading back toward the Cimetiere. An Luc and Paddy, at a half trot, scanned the empty streets off Rochereau. Above them, rising unseen, the pale glow of dawn chased down the narrow alleyways, feathered the rooftops, the towers - humble garrets, ornate bastions and basilicas. Slowly the city awoke, Paddy and An Luc among the first hurrying figures, as the homeless, the dishevelled clochards rose from the benches - straggled from the bushes and the parks in the early morning mist.

People passed them, hurrying toward the Metro, each oblivious of the other. Paddy and An Luc moved faster now, peering anxiously about the streets for any sign of Michael. Reaching the fountains, Paddy glanced through the trees toward the parks and hidden recesses of the Luxembourg Gardens. Above the trees in the early morning light - northward, serene, unseen - the distant towers of Notre Dame - and above the city through the early morning mist, the distant dome of Sacré Coeur.

It was well past five. An Luc and Paddy glanced at one another, silently sharing the mounting anxiety. They began to jog along the pathways - passed the fountains, trees, ponds and hedges of De Medici's formal gardens.

Suddenly An Luc grabbed Paddy's arm. They stopped. An Luc pointed ahead. Through the trees, to one side, Paddy saw the flickering lights - police cars or ambulance. Suddenly the harmonious sounds of an awakening city echoed again to the strident dissonance - the hee-haw of a police or ambulance siren, directly ahead of them. Instinctively both men set off running. Paddy found himself quietly calling out Michael's name.

In minutes they drew up to a taped off area beyond the trees, a pathway leading through the park. The area was surrounded by gendarmes and uniformed Special Police. An ambulance was drawn close to the pathway, engines running. Their flickering emergency lights cast an eerie rhythmic glare on the face of an approaching gendarme, hand raised, shaking his head, as Paddy and An Luc stepped over the tape. Scrutinising the identification Paddy quickly produced, he led them to a small group of civilian clad officers in charge.

A grim-faced older man came forward, introduced himself, apologised, and immediately expressed his sympathy. "A terrible tragedy - a callous killing." Paddy, in horror and disbelief, barely heard him. The Inspector and a member of French Security, leading Paddy and An Luc to one side, spoke the words Paddy had dreaded to hear. "Your friend, Jean Davost, called me. We found Captain Weatherby only a short time ago. I'm sorry - Jean told me that Captain Weatherby was a close friend of yours."

They were too late. Michael was gone - his reckless, brave crusade stopped. Asked if he wanted to see the body, after a moment Paddy nodded. Michael had been shot several times in the chest - from close range, the French Security agent told him. Paddy knelt by his friend. The eyes closed, the face pale, expressionless - almost childlike. At peace, Paddy thought as they replaced the cover over Michael's face.

The Inspector offered to drive Paddy and An Luc back to their car. They found Jean waiting for them. The Inspector told Jean the details; the news was a harsh shock - a friend so quickly come and gone. Jean turned to Paddy, expressing his sorrow. Silent, numb, they dreaded the next step - their thoughts now focused on Beth.

The Inspector returned to his car to place a call to Sureté. Suddenly he called Jean over. He covered the receiver with his hand, telling them he now had worse news. Nguyen, not being able to phone Beth, had driven to Neuilly.

Beth had indeed left the house - perhaps to drive to Montparnasse or to Nguyen's. The car, which Michael had so thoughtfully left behind, as far as they could now determine, had been booby-trapped. Beth's death, and that of her unborn baby, was instantaneous.

CHAPTER FOURTEEN

"England! What shall men say of thee, before whose feet the worlds divide?" Oscar Wilde

It was a warm, summer evening off the Rue de Fauberge St. Etienne. In the massive telephone exchange complex for central Paris a call was transferred to a phone booth in a pleasant rustic setting outside the Noah's Ark Pub, near Effingham in Surrey, barely forty minutes train ride from London.

The lone figure standing inside the booth hummed cheerfully to himself, then glanced at his watch as the phone rang. He allowed it to ring twice. Picking up the receiver, he softly whistled several bars of a familiar German lullaby, then listened silently. The instant response was clear and precise.

"Bonjour, Monsieur le conquistador." There was a pause. "C'est le jour. Madam c'est la cible." Again a pause. "Le soleil range s'eleve aujourdui, n'est pas, monsieur?" Without waiting for a reply, the caller added, "Bon chance, mon ami."

The recipient of the phone call softly whistled several more bars before replacing the receiver. Leaving the booth, the dark-skinned, casually dressed "whistler" passed into the dim lit intimacy of the Noah's Ark. Moving through the crowded tables he joined his companions, a man of similar appearance, and a woman, seated at one end of the bar.

Some of the early evening customers turned to view the attractive woman now bent forward in earnest conversation with her companions. Indeed the one who saw it all, and who would later testify, was Henry Lavery, sole proprietor of the Noah's Ark. Lavery prided himself on a constant awareness of the priorities – business and customer satisfaction.

Busily pulling pints of draught, Lavery chatted with the noisy regulars. Turning to work the cash register, he snatched a quick glance to the mirrored wall behind the bar, noting the busy reflections of a larger than usual midweek crowd - ever aware of the reflected profits. With its rustic village location, its proximity to London, the historic inn was a favourite gathering place not alone for locals and visitors from the city, but for tourists as well.

The prevailing public sentiment was less evident in the superficial exchange of a village pub. Yet beneath the talk and laughter was a mood of denial and desperation, many unwilling to confront the depressing prospects at home and abroad. Lavery had listened to their stories, drunk or sober, of increasing unemployment, labour exported to the third world and so on. A government out of touch with the people. Everywhere, the threat of another outbreak, from the Balkans to southern Russia and Iraq. And always from the Middle East, and Northern Ireland.

Henry Lavery was a man of the people, yet of distinguished Irish ancestry. After the IRA bombing of a pub in nearby Guilford, he had taken to denying his Irish heritage. It was everywhere, nowhere safe. There had been increasing 'terrorist' activity in the past weeks. In Paris, the recent kidnapping, and the assassination of the British intelligence agent and his wife. All of it was the IRA's fault, they said. Lavery was sceptical. It was bad for business everywhere.

The group at the end of the bar arrested his gaze. The two men were expensively dressed. Saudi or Syrian, he thought. His gaze lingered on the lady, noting the dark eyes, dark hair, the perfect white teeth, the deep, rich colour of the skin - a real beauty. Lavery noticed the girl staring toward him. She smiled. Lavery grinned self-consciously in return.

Guiltily he glanced over at Miriam, his wife, chatting with those at the bar, joking and pulling pints. Bending once more to the task, he listened to Miriam's busy chatter as she matched him pint for pint. Life was good for Henry and Miriam.

In the mirror, again Lavery watched the three at the end of the bar, still in busy conversation. Suddenly the girl looked up, staring across the room. Lavery's eyes followed hers. A more distinctive group of arrivals approached, drawing wider attention. Fit looking SAS in civvies, shaven heads, from the nearby camp, headed for the snug.

The SAS, mostly officers, kept to themselves. They were

a hardy lot, Lavery knew, jocks and mercs from all countries
- guns for hire. Generally well behaved, they had their rowdy
moments. He appreciated their patronage as steady customers.
Over the years he had come to know some of them personally.

One of them, the Australian, Stephen Tracker, stopped
at the corner of the bar to talk to the dark-skinned girl. Lavery,
watching through the mirror, saw the earnest exchange. The
girl spoke rapidly to Tracker, her companions leaning forward
to listen. Glancing up, catching Lavery's curious stare, the
Australian spoke one or two words to the group, turned and
rejoined his friends.

Strange bloke, thought Lavery. Over on rotation as an
instructor, he had been told. Stephen Tracker was not the type
for casual acquaintance. The Aussie never had much to say. A
big man, his scarred face, his physical presence said it all. The
people he'd just spoken to, Lavery had never seen before. Odd
lot, he thought, vaguely troubled. He remembered the comment
Captain Grey, a long time patron, had made some weeks before,
about the time Tracker had first arrived. "A real pro", Grey had
said. Captain Grey, a Welshman, was a more friendly sort.

Lavery wiped the sweat from his brow, scarcely hearing
the plaintive thump of the jukebox, hurriedly responding to the
loudly repeated call from the heroes of the Falklands, Nicaragua
and northern Ireland - "Eh Lavery, another round 'ere mate!"
Happily he listened to the rising clatter and ring of the till.

It was about five in the evening. The army lot was about
to leave. As they'd passed through the public bar they'd waved
to Lavery and his wife. The Australian had again stopped to
speak to the girl and her friends. No sooner had Tracker left
than the three strangers followed. Lavery remembered waving
goodbye to the lady, and again she had smiled at him. He'd been
staring after her when he'd felt a nudge in the ribs.

"Henry," said Miriam, "I'm going to have to keep my
eye on you. Couldn't take your eyes off her, could you?"

Through the streets of London a surge of cars, taxis,
vans and double decker buses crawled impatiently past the
historied elegance of Whitehall, Horse Guards, the Admiralty.

146

Incongruous amid the grit and grime, window boxes bloomed, flush with yellow primroses, pink peonies and purple pansies.

Engine fumes gathered as London, sweltering in an unexpected heat wave, sought to take itself to the crowded beaches of Herne Bay, of Brighton, or Southend on Sea. In warm-bodied droves they poured, bag, bucket, sandwiches, suntan lotion and sullen mother-in-law, through the boroughs of London to points south, east and west of the broiling metropolis.

Later that day the city was strangely still. Down a quiet, shadowed side street, on the steps outside a Georgian townhouse, the revered portals of ministerial power, police constable Edgar Patrick Hennessey stood. Of considerable bulk, Hennessey, Irish scion of the London Metropolitan Police Force, son of generations of policemen and a loyal resident of Whitechapel, moved his feet restlessly to ease the discomfort.

His shift had been a busy one, watching, saluting, opening doors, assisting various dignitaries or ministers as a succession of official limousines arrived and departed #10 Downing St. As his brain simmered under the police helmet, once again Hennessey sprang to attention as a large blue limousine drew up. The slight, older man leaving the car was Sir Geoffrey Gordon, MI5, Director of Intelligence, accompanied by the Chief of American Intelligence, a tall, grey haired American. Hennessey had seen him some weeks before, visiting Madam in the first few days of his appointment to London. Like many with peculiar English antipathies, Hennessey had some natural resentment of "Yanks". "Rich an' loud", his mother had described them, "think they can buy anyone."

As Hennessey saluted, Sir Geoffrey and the American passed into the reception of Number Ten.

Shortly after Gordon and the American had left, Hennessey felt sleepy. He stood in the shade, head nodding. A limousine drew up; he hadn't seen its arrival. Startled, he noted the Irish flag on the fender. He rushed to the door, embarrassed at the slip, just in time to nod and smile to the emerging Irish Chargé d'Affaires, Higgins, and his secretary. Both greeted Hennessey by name, as was their usual custom since discovering the shared ethnic seed.

147

Constable Hennessey and the security detail had failed to notice on this busy, heat stressed, Thursday afternoon that the arrivals and departures at Number Ten were also being closely watched by an older couple. Slowly pacing arm in arm, they came to stand in touching tribute at the foot of the Cenotaph opposite Richmond Terrace.

The gentleman leaned on a cane; the lady held a bunch of flowers. As the afternoon wore on, they stood, their eyes fixed, not on the memorial, with its faded bunch of poppies at the base, but on the street beside them, carefully noting every arrival to or departure from the nearby shadowed entrance to Downing Street.

Within the hallowed residence of #10, the "First Lords" of Treasury, of prime ministers, from Disraeli to the profligate Lloyd George and his Mrs. Stevenson, to Chamberlain's "peace in our time", home to the pugnacious Churchill - a memorable house indeed. Distinguished occupants, each of whom had guided or misguided the nation and the affairs of its empire through evolution and decline.

The day's schedule for Madam was now winding down. She had been frantically busy, the way she liked it. The early hours were given to preparation for question time in the House. This proved to be an adrenalin provoking challenge, facing her adversaries on both sides of the House. There was a lengthy discussion on the question of the European hegemony and the reduction of Britain to a lackey role in the new European community – quickly outvoted. Rather, Madam advocated Britain forge an ever-closer association with "our cousins" in the United States. "Brit/US", the new alliance.

Ever an aggressive exponent of the "imperial ethos", Madam shrewdly determined to control events, with an unswerving support of their combined aspirations and shared interests in the northern and southern hemispheres.

No sooner had Madam returned to 10 Downing Street than Alan, her secretary, shared with her other matters requiring immediate attention. With little time to spare, she greeted Sir

148

Geoffrey Gordon, bringing the newly appointed American Regional Intelligence Representative, European theatre, Roger Moorefield.

Moorefield, a veteran of the Vietnam War, a thoughtful man of few words, had impressed Madam. During the sombre re-exploration of the sad events in Paris, Geoffrey Gordon confessed there were no further leads in the Weatherby assassination. Roger Moorefield reassured the Prime Minister American intelligence and the National Security Agency were working both in Paris and the Middle East on the Weatherby affair as well as the kidnapping of Professor Senjaye, following up on all signal traffic from target areas in the Middle East, and exchanges between Republican elements in Northern Ireland and other countries. He would keep her informed of their progress.

After Gordon and Moorefield left, Madam momentarily secluded herself, instructing her secretary to hold all calls. The fate of the Weatherbys in Paris had reminded her of friends who had died in the endless Irish wars. She thought of the terrifying explosion at the recent Party meeting and her own narrow escape.

Since her return from Paris, she'd had a call from DeVeere of MI6. As with the Gibraltar affair came mixed signals, no go ahead on Ajax. Despite Weatherby's bizarre outburst, Madam was determined that the IRA would follow their comrades, as in Gibraltar.

One thorn in her side all these years was Sean McCarton, known by his followers as the Seanache. Grimly sure his time had come, she would have her revenge.

The phone rang, interrupting her thoughts. Irritably she picked up the receiver. Alan was reminding her of the visit by the Irish Chargé d'Affaires - he was already waiting. Peremptorily she ordered him sent in.

The Irishman, Dermot Higgins, was a man she had little use for - his ingratiating, fawning manner, his sometime insolence. "Ghetto Irish" she called him. Added to her irritability was an underlying uncertainty. Madam wondered if the Irish government could possibly have been informed of the new

149

security plan. An indiscretion from someone at the Paris meeting perhaps? With Weatherby now dead, who might it have been?

Neither side trusting the other, she listened grimly to Higgins's official protests. She would extend her charade to marathon levels, exposing the impatient IRA to further international opprobrium. She would gain further support for Ajax. Madam well knew the southern Irish government didn't have the moral fibre to stand by their brothers in the north and did not wish to pay the price of an all island re-unification.

After at times, heated exchange, veiled threats and warnings from both sides with neither side listening, Higgins made an abrupt departure.

Alan entered the room. Rarely intrusive, he had the unnerving knack of sometimes approaching unseen. Unaware of his presence, he heard her muttering, "Shiftless, snivelling, spineless lot!" He was concerned. Ever since her Ladyship's return from the funeral of the Weatherbys in Paris and the mounting troubles at home and abroad, Madam was not her usual confident self.

"Can I bring you a cup of tea, a sandwich perhaps - while we gather up the reports of what, may I say, Your Ladyship, has been a most successful and productive day?"

Madam started, momentarily flustered. Composing herself, she grimly replied, "Thank you, Alan. I agree, it has been a productive day. And yes I will - not tea mind you. I need something stronger."

As Alan left the room, Madam rose and stood before the window. It had been a violent week. What had Weatherby got himself into? Such a sorry end to a promising career. A misguided idealist. Some of what he said she couldn't deny, but not in the national interests to peruse or divulge, especially now. And his comments on the China Scheme were a great source of worry to her. His rash accusations were indiscreet and reckless. His insinuations against those in PASS; hotheads perhaps, but a radical conspiracy? Never!

"Preposterous!" Madam muttered, peering above her bifocals. Yet she was not convinced.

Geoffrey Gordon had agreed with her conclusions

that the deaths of the Weatherbys were a brutal terrorist act, though perhaps Weatherby's wife was an unintended victim. Weatherby's shooting was in retaliation, Madam supposed, for the much publicised ruling from the European Courts on the Gibraltar incident. The deaths of the Weatherbys were just the sort of retaliation she would expect.

Madame remembered some lines then from her days at Oxford:

> *Set in this stormy northern sea,*
> *Queen of these restless fields of tide,*
> *England! What shall men say of thee,*
> *before whose feet the worlds divide?*

Irritated, she remembered the author was the Irish dissolute, Oscar Wilde.

Alan had quietly reentered the room, hearing her last remarks. He stood, tray in hand, beside her desk. "Please, Madam, try not to show yourself to the street below."

Startled, Madam turned from the window as he set the tray on her desk. He crossed the room to straighten the curtains she had set aside.

"Thank you, Alan." The prime minister poured herself a stiff shot of malt, adding a splash of water. She nibbled her favourite cress sandwiches as she sat at the desk and commenced to review the newspapers, enjoying the first tranquil moment of a long day.

Not two blocks down the street, yet worlds apart - another pair sat in the late afternoon sunlight. Before them, the Cenotaph, withered flowers at its base.

"In remembrance, love, of my two uncles - and five hundred thousand others who died that spring, April 1916. One in France, at the Somme, the other in the same spring rains, for a different cause, in the Rising in Dublin. All the brothers, husbands, sweethearts in France, too young, too ignorant to understand, fighting for the same imperial executioners killing their own people back in Ireland." The old gentleman whispered a quotation from another age, the mistrusting iron-eyed Tudor Queen, Elizabeth I of England, "To become thrall to a foreign nation is the greatest misery that can happen to a people."

Madam finished her second drink. A gentle, fuzzy euphoria supervened. She rose from the desk, smiling and talking with Alan as they methodically stuffed their briefcases. Madam seemed to have found renewed energy, bustling about, preparing endless notes in anticipation of the weekend's homework.

The lady prime minister had invited Alan to join her and her family for the weekend, to share some work that had to be completed. As she carefully folded her papers into her briefcase, Madam was relieved that she would be home for dinner. They would share a family evening.

Her secretary hurrying along behind her, briefcase in either hand, the Prime Minister emerged from Number 10. Aloof, not a hair out of place, she barely nodded to Constable Hennessey and the bowing security contingent rushing for the door of the limousine. The black limousine disappeared around the corner of Downing Street into Whitehall.

By the Cenotaph, the couple rose, the man making a quick sign of the cross. Then both hurried, hand in hand, across the street to the phone booth on the corner of Richmond Terrace.

The beflagged limousine slid past the Ministry of Defence, past Horse Guards and the Admiralty. So imperative, so enduring, so secure, thought Madam, peering to either side, as though seeing London for the first time - the still figures of the Household Brigade - their imperious flash of scarlet and white, the silver cuirass, gleaming swords beneath the archways of Horse Guards - still for Madam a moving sight.

They drove swiftly to the Charing Cross Pier where the Prime Minister's helicopter waited. The pilot, Wing Commander Brian Alcott, greeted her.

"Good evening, Madam. Conditions look excellent. We will be flying at low altitude. The view should be a splendid one."

"Always a pleasure to be leaving before nightfall,"

replied Madam, then boarded the aircraft. With stunning rapidity the engines screamed into life. The helicopter slowly rose, then, nose down, slid out across the suburbs.

Far below, the elderly couple walked rapidly toward the Hungerford footbridge, pausing for a moment to watch the aircraft slide across the cloudless sky. Now a speck in the early sunset, it disappeared in the orange glow over the still waters of the Thames. They continued then, each in silent thought, across the river toward Waterloo and the first leg of their long journey home.

"Hello Sea King One. We have you on vector 347. You are clear to Landstone. Have a good flight, and good wishes to her ladyship."

Within the soundproof quietness of the cabin, Madam peered across southwest England, reflecting on the achievements of the past few months. She glanced down to where her family awaited her arrival. To the west, the sun was setting, a ball of crimson above the Cotswolds and the Wiltshire Downs. Far below, the rolling meadows of rural England led to the distant invisible spires, the byways and lanes, to fond memories of the halls - "high table" and the cloistered walks of Oxford.

She glanced to one side. Alan, busy as ever, sorted papers, making hurried notes. In his hand she saw the thick document titled "Top Secret". The code name, Ajax, the only copy, always kept in her personal folders. He was nodding reassuringly as he placed the document in the briefcase.

In the pilot's cabin, Alcott shifted controls, coming around now over the rolling hills and moors of Surrey. Effingham and Madam's destination lay below. "Landstone, do you read me? We are on our final approach."

Glancing downward, his attention was suddenly distracted by a bright flash from among the trees almost directly beneath.

Gazing eagerly toward her home and her family, like a child again, home for the holidays, Madam saw it too - the bright flash from among the trees. The missile seemed to rise almost lazily – then, quickly fixing on its target, closed with terrifying accuracy and speed. Madam knew and died in the same instant. Above the busy Noah's Ark, a crack, like distant thunder. And seen by few - a sudden ball of fire, then smoke. Madam's dreams of vengeance, of Empire restored - were now history.

CHAPTER FIFTEEN

The Return

In the northern parts of the world, the osprey climbs high on the thermal currents, its beady eyes surveying the rolling tides. Far below, the fierce grey herring gulls scream, wheeling in arcing flight above the silvery, sweet fish meat in the rumbling draw and foam of the western tides.

In the cities and across the country families watched the morning television news. Some sat transfixed, listening to the ongoing reports of "the ultimate terrorist assassination!"

The announcer grimly described the events, trying to recreate the scene. "Within seconds, in a clear sky, the Sea King helicopter exploded. A flash, a puff of smoke, seen only by one or two. There were no survivors. The experts, at this point, have no tangible evidence, yet conclude unanimously that Madam was the victim of some as yet unidentified terrorist group. No one is claiming responsibility. Possibly a rocket or bomb on the aircraft - though security claims the Sea King had been closely inspected before takeoff."

Pictures of Madam, of her home and her grieving family flickered hour by hour across the television screen. Among those interviewed, the hastily appointed interim leader, Sir Arthur Wolsey, promised a ruthless pursuit of the culprits.

In the following days of international disbelief and outrage, the hunt was on. Terrorism, high on the agenda, was foremost in people's minds. Hundreds of police and security fanned out across the region - suspicious visitors in the area over the past few weeks were narrowed down to several hundred - a seemingly hopeless task. Among them, however, a dogged police inspector had noted an odd report - the appearance of three strangers, described by the owner of a nearby pub - "maybe Arabs, Saudis or Syrians" he'd said, "a couple of days before."

It seemed innocent enough, vague on the surface. A long shot, but progress had been slow. Public and media criticism was gathering. Arab or Irish "terrorists" were ever-popular suspects - especially after the affair in Paris. On further questioning by the inspector, the pub owner, Henry Lavery, noted to be of Irish descent - came up with a curious story about one of the three strangers, the woman. "Quite young she was. A real stunner." With some embarrassment, "Well, Inspector, it was her eyes," he'd said. "When you looked at her, she almost seemed to know what you were thinking." Much later that day Lavery tried again to explain this to the detective from Scotland Yard, and yet again to "Special Intelligence". As time passed Lavery's story was regarded with growing scepticism. The police or intelligence people grew bored; looked at him with some disbelief.

There were other matters - the briefcase Lavery had found outside his pub the night of the "accident", the delay in delivering it to the CID inspector and an angry and frustrated "internal Security" officer - causing intense interdepartmental wrangling and mutual suspicion. Lavery expressed shock and dismay on learning his tardiness might be critical - the briefcase was one of the few intact pieces of distinguishable debris surviving. Further, Lavery's final confession, that he had peeped into the contents of this Top Secret repository of Madam's innermost thoughts on matters of State - placed Lavery in a very suspect position. Lavery's ethnic background had not helped, nor indeed that the business of the Noah's Ark had unhealthily thrived following Madam's tragedy.

Lavery had not mentioned to CID, nor to the various security people questioning him, nor to the hordes of journalists, television gurus and opportunists that descended on the Noah's Ark in the following days - the presence in the pub that evening of the SAS group. Nor that one of them had seemed to know the "lady with beautiful eyes". Why should he - they were all Madame's loyal subjects, weren't they?

*

"Passengers from United States, Trans World Airways, flight 447 from New York, now arriving at Heathrow, London, gate 24." The flat mechanical tones reverberated throughout the busy terminal.

Emerging from the gate, American passenger Jack Edwards headed up the corridor to the main terminal. He had plenty of time. His flight to Belfast left in two hours.

Above the chorus of announcements, a melée of multiracial commuters in multilingual chatter were hurrying back and forth. Jack saw little of this, his mind elsewhere. He took a seat in the main terminal, set his hand luggage nearby and turned to a copy of the London Times he'd picked up at the newsstand. It was a special edition, with several pages on the assassination, but no more informative than the television reports. The Times, in its traditional posture, a stern but civil mentor, promising harsh Cromwellian retribution for those responsible.

The official voice reassured its readers that there would be an immediate response, with the assistance of their American allies; the forces of NATO and the UN were on standby. Jack knew things would never be the same. He recalled one despairing Arab comment, describing the ever-turbulent tragedy of the continuing Arab-Israeli conflict, "Shades of Belfast, forever!"

A professor of political science and law at Johns Hopkins University in Baltimore, Jack Edwards was on his way to a lecture engagement at Queen's University in Belfast. Born in England, of Irish parents, Jack had spent his first years in England before returning to Ireland.

Jack could see the greening fields, the cowslips bright yellow in the sunlight, could hear the harsh call of the corncrake. And across the uneven pastures, the rambling hedgerows, pale red or white, the honeysuckle and the clover - all the vivid memories of childhood. On the mountains now, the purple heather, the foxgloves, stirring in the summer breeze. And among the white sand beaches, the long combers rose and fell on the empty strands.

Some months before, Jack had called his father. It
had taken his father awhile to come to the phone, still slightly
confused following his recent stroke. Jack's mother had passed
away several years ago. Jack found himself repeating, "Dad, it's
me, Jack. I'm coming to take you home again, to take you home
Dad - can you hear me?"

It was as if the very words, home again, had blown away
the cobwebs and the confusion. Jack could almost see his father's
smiling face as he heard the delighted exclamation, "Oh Jack,
that would be wonderful! When are we leaving? When are we
going home?"

I'll be there soon Dad, to take you up North again, just
you and me. We'll drive up from Dublin, up the cliff road by
Kilkeel, past Maggie's' Leap and up through the Mournes, to
Clanawhillun."

He remembered his father as he'd last seen him. His
youthful and exuberant spirit impatiently contained in the
reluctantly aging body, the bent frame but quick step - the strong
handclasp, the certain gaze, the smile, as they warmly grasped
each other hand and arm, then stood apart, embarrassed at the
intensity.

Jack's father had been too frail to make the journey.
Aged ninety-four, he had died in his sleep, just two days after
Jack's call. With some regret Jack wished he could have been
with his father in his last moments. To hold his hand, to reassure
him as he left us, thought Jack, again hearing the strong laughter,
remembering the great athlete, accomplished pianist, Irish folk
dancer, the gentle counsellor, successful celebrant of life who
was his father and his friend.

Of his family of seven siblings moving from Belfast due
to an unfriendly political climate, Jack was the only one to be
born in a little seaside town on the southwest coast of England.
He had enjoyed the lazy, unfocused life, seemingly endless years
when the world had seemed so young. The infinite succession
of still, summer mornings were followed by long, cosy winter
evenings. On windswept beaches, the sand blew in high clouds
across the dunes to the storied marshes. And always the promise,
from the remote, tidal estuary, of another distant world.

Jack remembered his pride as he cycled to pick up the evening press, to read his father's name in print, well known across the southwest of England for his feats in golf, as champion and county captain. Beneath the shy manner of his mother lay the steely enduring religious commitment, the contrary mix of stern, Calvinist moral perspectives and an embattled Ulster Catholic, of gentle but indomitable will. She was a constant, patient presence as Jack and his siblings passed breathless and chattering from childhood to youth.

His family moved in later years back to Ireland. After boarding school, Jack commenced university studies in Dublin. Restless for other options, uncertain where his interests lay, with his father's encouragement and much against his mother's wishes, he decided to emigrate to America.

Yet again, America was at war. Jack decided to join the growing commitment in Vietnam. This decision was largely influenced by his chosen specialty, to seek an answer to the recurring failure of a political solution, the failure of negotiation, of alternatives to a philosophy that only led to more wars. Jack felt he might benefit from a short course in practical politics. He enlisted in '72 with the United States Marine Corps. Before the end of his first year Jack had been promoted to Lieutenant, twice decorated for bravery, and had won a purple heart - fortunately a minor shrapnel wound. During his convalescence he decided to re-enlist for a second tour. He found he enjoyed the danger; felt he needed to learn more, joining the best of America's special forces - the Green Berets.

"Passengers for Belfast, Northern Ireland, British Overseas Airways, flight 227, departing 12:30 p.m., gate 16. Please check in by twelve noon." The polite monotone continued, "Have passports and identity cards available. Thank you."

It was just eleven o'clock. Picking up his hand luggage, Jack rose and moved into the nearby lounge. He settled himself in one corner of the bar, ordering a Scotch and seltzer. He took a slow sip, remembering his good fortune; one of the lucky ones to get away in the last few shiploads from Saigon in April of '75. Jack clearly knew his goals now. The anguish and horror of his

159

experiences in Vietnam had given him added incentive to sort out the political alternatives to the misery of war. And, further, to seek out the origins, political and economic, to the conflicts that seemed to recur with greater frequency, generation to generation.

Jack had taken degrees in political science and law, then in economics. He was a member of a Washington "think tank" on international conflict. His writings on "Alternatives to Violence - The Resolution - Different Perspectives" - had drawn a growing following as he continued with what was now his life's work. He was also a consultant and sometime advisor to the Central Intelligence Agency.

Jack Edwards took another sip of his drink. He glanced around. Across the tables he saw the solitary figure of a nun in traditional white wimple and black veil. Perhaps a message from his mother, Jack thought, smiling. The nun seemed to have been watching him. Even across the lounge, within the veil, Jack saw a very attractive woman. Her eyes returned to the pages of the book she held before her. Was it her breviary or, Jack wondered playfully, some lewd novel? A good thing his mother couldn't read his thoughts.

The nun was now joined by two "brothers of the cloth". One seemed rather young for a priest, maybe in training? Jack noticed that while these people were ostensibly reading their breviaries, they were also carrying on an intense exchange. Intrigued, Jack watched more closely. The two men seemed to be arguing. As the nun intervened, her companions listened respectfully. Suddenly the nun glanced up and saw Jack's curious stare. Embarrassed, Jack looked elsewhere.

The lounge was almost full. He looked around at the ruddy cheeked faces, so typically Irish. Even among the young the climate dealt harshly, with the skin well weathered. White haired older women, like his mother, aged before her time. The quiet, strong features of the men, the "Celtic" nose, prominent cheek bones. Jack saw the unforgettable mannerisms, the spontaneous giggle and laugh, ready smile, the childlike nudge and joke. Or among those not quite so young - the brooding stare of hard times.

He heard the strong north of Ireland accent, "British Overseas Airways for Belfast, flight 227, now boarding. Please have your boarding passes ready." He drained his glass and bent to gather his luggage.

Following his fellow passengers to a more remote area of the airport, Jack noticed the mood had become more subdued, with hushed conversation.

For each in their own way, the sudden and violent death of Madam Prime Minister had its own particular impact. Jack had the impression that the people shared a uniform sense of guilt. This behaviour, Jack knew, was an inculcated subservience learned over the centuries: victims of a deliberate political strategy. Madam, another arrogant voice from history, a lightning rod, the unsubtle spark to light the conflagration. Northern Ireland's tragic history, Jack knew, overshadowed its unrealised economic opportunities, the rich culture of its normally friendly peoples.

Armed special police stood about, some in plain clothes, some in army battle dress, eyeballing the passengers, scrutinised by the cameras overhead. The beefed up presence of security was a stern reminder of the condemnation of the "Paddies". More likely, Jack knew, under the present circumstances it was domestic surveillance units of MI5. The expressions of each were grim, insolent.

Metal detectors scanned Jack's person. A Customs official perfunctorily, brusquely, reefed through the luggage of an Irish passenger ahead of him. Jack's own suitcase, briefcase, recorders and camera were given a slow, careful and deliberate search.

At the door of the plane, Jack was greeted with a cheery, "Good afternoon, sir", in a soft Irish accent. The dull bulk and purpose of British security was now replaced by the smiling contrast of the fresh, if restrained sexuality and pert figures of the flight attendants. Locating his seat, Jack placed his camera and briefcase on the seat beside him and stuffed his shoulder bag into the overhead luggage rack, then settled into the window seat.

Someone had left a copy of yesterday's *Belfast*

161

Telegraph on the seat beside him. Jack noted with amusement the front-page commentary on the continuing "peace talk" strategy. Madam's team had made no effort to "persuade" the intransigent Unionist to meet with the sceptical Nationalist. The inevitable polarisation furthered mistrust, driving the more radical elements of both sides into more desperate measures.

For those for whom the only resolution was the removal of British presence, the faltering talks were perceived as a serious ambivalent threat. Jack regarded with major concern the distinct possibility that Madam's devious strategies had only perpetuated the conflict. She, possibly now its victim.

Jack sensed America was aspiring to England's colonial role, the goals of justice and liberty now a sham. As a senator in Washington recently expressed it, "Politics is broken - people have lost faith in the political process." As Jack saw it now, particularly in England and the United States, people were eager for a new voice, sick of the violence and greed, seeking a return to fundamental values, where justice is a definable virtue - honesty, fairness, caring and sharing, all recognizable goals.

The voice of pilot Colin Campbell growled from the cockpit to the control tower, "This is British Airways flight 227. We're already fifteen minutes overdue - and now another hold-up?" He turned toward his co-pilot, placing his hand over the mouthpiece. "Mr. Stephens, room for three more. Special security clearance."

Co-pilot Stephens stood by the door to the passenger section in quiet, earnest conversation with Sheila, the senior flight attendant. Occasionally one or the other glanced toward Campbell.

Running a finger down her clipboard, Sheila shook her head. She spoke quickly, nervously. "Brian, I don't like this." Looking again toward Campbell, she pushed the door closed behind her and bent forward, speaking to Stephens now in a lower, urgent voice. "Why security clearance at the last minute? Do you think they know, Brian?"

"Not to worry, love. Maybe front runners for this increased security assignment to Northern Ireland." Sheila's expression led Stephens to add, "They do this all the time. Probably a couple of old service Johnnies trying to hitch a ride home for the weekend." Sheila tried to smile, turning to leave. Brian placed a reassuring hand to her shoulder. "Let us know when they're boarded, love."

Brian Stephens knew he had sounded more convinced than he felt. He realised the situation was dangerous. He quickly resumed his seat, replacing his headphones, as he saw Campbell beckoning, pointing to the headset. Campbell looked over and nodded, thumb raised. "Looks like we're ready to go."

Stephens, staring out across the terminal, wondered if Sheila was right. Was the irregular security request a more significant signal? To distract himself, he joined Campbell in checking the controls.

*

"I'm sorry to trouble ye'."

Jack looked up on hearing the deep, husky, strong north of Ireland accent. He looked into the direct gaze, the attractive, open smile of the nun he had noticed in the waiting lounge. "Not at all, my pleasure."

Feeling foolish and strangely embarrassed Jack hurried to move his briefcase and camera from the seat beside him. He introduced himself as she settled herself into the seat.

"Pleased to meet ye'." She was looking into Jack's eyes. "It's Professor Edwards isn't it?" Jack nodded, surprised. "I'm Sister Theresa." Jack felt the firm clasp of the small strong hand that shook his; saw the cool, level glance as he again admired those lovely eyes. He felt his mother nudge him in the ribs - still a nun, remember?

Fastening her seat belt, Sister Theresa went on, "We know who ye are. We've read some of your writings on Northern Ireland and seen some reference to your work on television interviews. Your original ideas on the human conflict interest many of us - but we've yet to meet all the players here in Ireland, Professor Edwards - an' to have a fair game, ye need all the players. Your visit, especially now, will certainly be

163

welcome." Jack thanked her, explaining the invitation to talk at Queen's, the focus of his visit.

"Perhaps we shall be seeing more of ye over here then," smiled Sister Theresa. Jack saw her glance up, saw her smile disappear, her mouth harden. Immediately above them stood a burly figure, extricating himself from his wet raincoat. Wiping the moisture from his face with his handkerchief, he looked down at his ticket, then showed it to Jack. "Believe you're in my seat sir." The tone was not unfriendly - just matter of fact. Jack reached for his ticket. The man was right. He was in the right row but across the aisle. Jack rose, apologising.

Ignoring Jack and Sister Theresa, the big man went on. "Bloody wet out there." He was pushing his raincoat into the overhead luggage rack. Jack glanced at Sister Theresa. She was looking at him, shaking her head. She whispered hurriedly, "No - please, let me take the seat across the aisle." Sensing the alarming urgency, Jack nodded. In an instant Sister Theresa quickly moved into the vacant seat. The latecomer, busily drying himself off, didn't seem to notice.

Jack rose and moved aside to allow the bulky figure to struggle, swearing, into the window seat. He was chilled to glimpse the unmistakable black butt of a 9mm automatic in a shoulder holster beneath the man's jacket. Settling in, the man calmly returned Jack's stare.

Jack resumed his seat, wondering, what is he, some type of crazy hijacker? The man certainly didn't look or sound Irish - the shaven hairline, the cockney or colonial accent - Australian or Eastender? He wondered, should he challenge him, or talk to the stewardess? The thought occurred to Jack, possibly he was airline security. Not entirely reassured, Jack reasoned the man could never have got on the plane through airport metal detectors unless he had some type of security role.

"Name's Charlie Graham." Jack saw the large hand extended.

"Jack Edwards," he responded, shaking the man's hand.

"You an American then, Mr. Edwards?" Jack nodded.

Graham smiled. "I knew it soon as I saw you." Looking at the camera in Jack's lap, Graham asked, "Back to find the old roots then?"

Sheila was moving slowly down the aisle checking seat belts, answering questions. Looking worried, she stopped by Sister Theresa, who appeared to be sleeping, bent down and spoke quickly. Jack saw the instant response, a brief, intense exchange.

Jack was puzzled to see the instant familiarity between the two women. The flight attendant moved on down the aisle. Sister Theresa glanced toward Jack, her expression tense, anxious. She seemed to want to say something, then changed her mind, smiled and looked away.

Graham was muttering something about the weather. "Bloody rain. Never fails. You'd think we were in Ireland already." Jack followed Graham's gaze through the windows to the overcast skies.

The plane thundered down the runway, quickly airborne, then in level flight. Glancing once more across the aisle, Jack saw that Sister Theresa seemed again to be sleeping, eyes closed, hands holding her purse in her lap.

Jack listened to the rumbling profanity beside him as Graham leafed through the pages of the *Belfast Telegraph* he'd found. Sheila and the other flight attendants were moving up the aisle, wheeling the refreshment cart. Jack ordered a scotch and soda with ice. Graham leaned across, ordering a double scotch and water. Peering through the newspaper, he asked, "See you Yanks in for another election. One's the same as the other right?" Graham sniggered at his own joke. Jack said nothing as Graham continued, his voice and humour quickly changing to muttering anger. "What do you think of this bloody business? Didn't have a chance - blew the bloody chopper out of the sky!" He thumped the paper with his finger.

The flight attendant handed them their drinks. Closing the newspaper, Graham took a deep draught. Then in an oddly conspiratorial way he glanced around, leaned across to Jack and growled, "I'd have no problem settling the score with this lot - an eye for an eye, right?" Graham looked out the window, his hand gripping the paper in his lap. "My answer, same as that bloody M.P. - I'd arm the bloody Unionists an' pull out - let the

bastards eat their own. Bloody cannibals. That's what I'd do."
He turned to Jack as if for approval. Jack again said nothing as
Graham, taking another deep draught, continued a rambling
diatribe, followed by a string of muttered expletives, as if Jack
wasn't present.

Graham fell silent after a while. He looked across the
aisle to where, it appeared, Sister Theresa slept. Turning again
to Jack, his expression suddenly changed. He was grinning
now - took another swallow, nearly emptying his glass. "You
a journalist or something?" Jack shook his head. Graham
concluded, "Maybe something more than the 'old roots' for you,
right?" Without waiting for an answer, his mind made up or
indifferent, he changed topics. "Were you ever in one of the big
ones then, since WW II? Not one of them Yankee 'spats' - Cuba,
Granada, Panama, Haiti, Nicaragua, the Gulf or the likes. I mean
the real thing - Korea, Vietnam, the Falklands. We did it to those
bloody Argies, without your help either. An' we hauled your
bloody arse out, mate - more than once, didn't we - the bloody
wogs. In that Gulf bit, knocked 'em back for six, we did."

Jack had little option but to listen, occasionally nodding.
Graham didn't seem to need any encouragement. Jack wondered
what fuelled his resentment of America and his hatred of the
Irish, and anyone else between. He had not forgotten the 9mm
automatic only inches away from him.

Jack's ears perked up as he heard, "An' in Nicaragua,
your contra thing - we picked that one up for you. An' the ones
in Africa. I was there, mate, in Angola - the 'nigger wars'. I saw
it all. Before your Gulf piece we did it to them. For diamonds
an' oil, right? In Dubai, in Abu Dhabi, in Oman, we had those
bloody wogs kissin' our feet - places you've never heard of
mate. I was with the best of them - Landon, Aspin, Green, an'
one of yours - Buckley. They tortured him to death. I've seen it
all, mate. An' we did the fighting for you, in the holy place, they
called it. We took 'em out in Mecca." Graham was staring at Jack,
his silent audience.

Jack doubted anyone else could hear Graham's voice,
low and intense, over the sound of the engines. Just as well - he
sounded more than a little drunk now.

Graham, his gaze focused on Jack, again asked, "Were you ever in any of the big ones, mate?" This time he waited for Jack to answer.

Jack didn't like to think about it, much less talk about it, but there seemed to be no escape. "Yes, I was in Vietnam with Special Forces, and not as a journalist."

Graham looked distinctly uncomfortable. Perhaps he had misjudged this American.

A passing flight attendant refilled their glasses. Both men now sat silent, staring out the window. The charade was over, as each remembered the realities that the trivial, drunken rhetoric had obscured.

The pilot's voice came on, announcing their location some twenty minutes out of Belfast. Jack wondered if his cousins would be there to meet him. He glanced across the aisle and saw Sister Theresa returning his gaze. She smiled, then turned away quickly. He wondered had she heard Graham's angry words.

CHAPTER SIXTEEN

Finally Home Again

From the pilot's cabin Colin Campbell kept his eyes
on the gathering storm clouds ahead. Brian Stephens was idly
scanning the instrument panel. Suddenly both were alerted to an
urgent voice, occasional static.

"Hello, 227. This is RAF, Denbigh North Wales.
Emergency transmission, do you read me? British Airways 227
for Belfast - do you receive me?"

"Denbigh RAF, this is British Airways 227, Heathrow to
Belfast," Stephens responded, "What is your message?"

"You have a security problem on board, just confirmed
by Military Intelligence, London. Two, possibly three, members
of IRA, suspects in the recent Paris murders, also possibly
involved in the Prime Minister's assassination." Stephens knew
the IRA had no role in either killing, yet in British management
of Irish affairs one was guilty till proven innocent.

Colin Campbell was unaware of Stephens' other
connections on this flight. As the impact of the announcement
sank in, from different perspectives, both felt the cold rush of
fear.

"227, it is urgent you transmit this information to the
special security agents on your flight - the late boarders at
Heathrow, ASAP. Belfast has been notified. Keep us informed
and good luck." The voice fell away, leaving the two men, each
with his own particular nightmare, twenty-seven thousand feet
over the Irish Sea.

Campbell turned to Stephens. "Jesus Brian, let's hope
they don't find each other. And we won't tell them, not till
they're off the plane. Then they can start shooting. Jesus, if they
find out sooner, it could be a midair massacre! Get Sheila up

here with the manifest. You'd better call Belfast and check the preparation for our reception."

Stephens had other concerns, Sheila's worst fears now confirmed. He reached to the intercom, then, changing his mind, pressed the flight attendant button. How much did the security group know? He worried for their three friends, now targets. He felt sorry for Campbell. Neither he nor the passengers deserved this. He was especially concerned for Sheila. If they had trouble - if the investigation looked into Sheila's background and learned about her husband Frank and her family's connections with the Republicans, there would be grave repercussions. If they discovered how he had supported her application to British Airways, both of them would be prosecuted for assisting in the escape of known fugitives, or worse.

Brian Stephens contacted Belfast, receiving confirmation and "ready state" preparations. Doubly grateful that Campbell had agreed not to inform the security agents on board, he could only hope they remained unaware, till after the landing. A crazy thought occurred to him. An early exit for his friends might be arranged. In the confusion they might get away with it. He leaned toward Campbell.

"Colin, I'm requesting assignment to the emergency runway. It will keep us out of the public area in case of trouble."

Campbell agreed. The desperate plan began to take shape. Stephens knew Belfast Airport; had landed there hundreds of times in all kinds of weather. The emergency runway was in a more remote part of the airport. Security would be gathering at the main arrivals gate. They were now less than fifteen minutes out. With any luck, a last minute change in docking procedure would disrupt the reception for a short time. Time enough, he hoped.

Stephens turned his head to see Sheila standing by the doorway. Disconnecting his headphones, Stephens left his seat and joined Sheila. He knew she was still mourning the recent loss of her husband, Frank, killed fighting with an American mercenary unit in Nicaragua. Ironically, Dan, one of the "targets" now on the plane, had been with Frank when he was killed.

With a wary eye on Campbell, quickly, quietly, Stephens outlined his plan. Sheila tensely agreed it was a chance worth taking. Studying the manifest, Stephens saw the focus of concern would be Graham, the security agent seated across from Theresa. He wondered if Graham already knew.

"Warn Theresa and the others as soon as you can, Sheila. Tell me quickly if anything starts to go wrong." Knowing how much she had already given and how much she'd lost, Stephens added, "Try not to worry." Nodding grimly, Sheila turned and left.

Resuming his seat, replacing his headphones, Stephens wished there was more he could have said. He nodded to Campbell's silent query. Sheila had indeed been warned.

The phone call Sheila had received in the early hours had increasingly worried her. She'd confided in Brian that morning. The call was an urgent request from contacts in Paris, describing the plight of an IRA group, among them their friends, targeted by a special assignment unit carrying out a recently discovered plan to assassinate selected members of the Republican Front. Sheila was asked to facilitate the group's passage through security at Heathrow. With Stephens' help, she had seen them aboard without incident.

Campbell glanced over, giving Stephens the go-ahead on their descending path toward the coast of Northern Ireland. Stephens switched on to the passengers, announcing their approach to Belfast, hoping to distract as Sheila delivered the warnings to Theresa and her two companions in the rear section. He felt his hands sweating as he now took the controls, glancing over at Colin, who nodded reassuringly, totally focused on the approach. Stephens knew the main risk would be the sudden rearrangement of landing patterns in a busy airport. Fortunately Belfast was less busy than some.

Stephens gradually reduced power on both engines as the heavy, rain-streaked 737 thundered through the grey cumulus above the loughs and rolling fields far below. He wondered how Campbell would react to the coming adjustment in their plans.

Sheila slowly walked down the aisle, trying to control

her rising panic. She steadied herself as the plane wavered in the descent, found herself looking into every face, man, woman and child, guiltily wondering about the risks ahead.

Drawing closer, Sheila saw Theresa watching her. Looking past her to the rear of the plane, Sheila saw Cormac and Dan also watching her. Cormac smiled and waved. As her gaze returned to Theresa she saw the American, Edwards, looking up at her. Beside him, her eyes caught the curiously hard stare from Graham. She quickly looked away.

Now opposite Theresa, Sheila bent to retrieve the purse that had slipped to the floor. Bending forward, she hurriedly whispered, "Brit Security on board – in window seat across the aisle. Preparing to pick you up on landing. We're providing a getaway. Be ready. I'll tell Dan."

Sheila moved on, Dan and Cormac watching her approach. Across from them, the other two British security agents seemed unaware - one looking out the window, one reading. Seeing Cormac's smile, Sheila tried to smile in return. He reminded her of her husband, Frank. Despite Cormac's tough dedication, he was still a boy.

Thinking of Frank, Sheila grew calm, cold inside. She thought of her son, Seanoge, so recently deprived of his father. She knew she would not hesitate to give her own life. At least, unlike Frank, it would be on Irish soil. Quickly she brushed the thought from her mind. With only minutes to go she bent to speak with Dan.

Further up the aisle, Jack was seated beside a more restless Graham, gazing around, straining to stare out the windows to either side. He repeatedly checked his watch, gripped the armrest. Jack had overheard the quick exchange between the flight attendant and Sister Theresa. Remembering the weapon Graham carried, Jack sensed an approaching problem.

Suddenly unfastening his seat belt, Graham rose. Pushing past Jack, he started up the aisle, grabbing the seat backs to steady himself. Jack kept his eye on Graham, more disturbed now, as he saw him continue on into the pilot's cabin.

"Mr. Edwards, we need your help!" Jack turned,

surprised to see Sister Theresa bending across the aisle toward
him. Her expression was strained - her dark eyes wide. "No time
to explain." She added hurriedly, "The man beside you is part
of a Brit undercover hit squad. Two others in the rear." To Jack's
incredulous expression she added, "We're leaving as soon as
they land. If he moves to stop us, don't let him use the gun he
carries."

Sheila hurried past and reached the galley as Graham
emerged from the pilot's cabin. He brushed past her and
commenced an unsteady progress down the aisle, his eyes fixed
on Theresa. Suddenly another pilot's announcement, the voice
urgent; almost strident.

"Flight attendants take your seats - we're on final
approach." To either side, the familiar purple and green, the low
mountains and fields of Ireland reached toward them.

Sheila's eyes fixed on Graham ahead of her. "Take your
seat, please - we are landing now." Graham ignored her, almost
stumbling as the big jet banked and rocked toward the runway.

Jack looked up. Graham stood above them, holding
tightly onto the seatbacks on either side, staring at Theresa. Jack
released his seatbelt. Instinctively he knew this was it.

"Bitch!" The growling expletives followed, the menacing
eyes never leaving Theresa's face. "Put your bloody hands in
front of you - terrorist bitch!" Jack was already moving as he saw
Graham's hand reach toward his open jacket, toward the 9mm
hanging from its holster. A nearby passenger screamed. At the
same moment the plane touched down, bounced and swayed,
momentarily throwing Graham off balance.

Jack followed old reflexes, memories of Special Forces.
With one hand he yanked Graham's arm across his chest, tore
his jacket down and in seconds pinned the man's arms. With
one foot he drove the big man down. As Graham stumbled back,
he fell into Sheila, both falling to the floor. Standing above the
cursing, enraged and drunken Graham, Jack believed the bastard
would likely have shot Theresa.

Jack was surprised to see Theresa had been even faster.
When Graham stumbled, his 9mm had fallen from the holster.
She knelt in the aisle now - both hands holding the automatic,

trained on Graham.

"Move an' ye'r dead, Brit bastard!"

Jack reached to help Sheila to her feet. At the same time there was a shout from the rear of the plane - a shot – screams, followed by moaning. With the gun fixed unwaveringly on Graham now lying, his hands on his head, Theresa shouted loudly, "Cormac, Dan, answer me!"

Jack looked back to see Cormac and Dan, the two "brothers" he'd seen in the departure lounge reading their breviaries, now holding the two agents in the aisle.

"We have 'em. One's down. Watch him, girl, an' let's get ready to move!"

The plane was now shaking and shuddering with the application of reverse thrust. Without turning Theresa called back, "Up front, Cormac. Dan, cover them!" Sheila had turned and was running toward the pilot's cabin. Cormac came up, his gun now trained on Graham, who was still cursing.

"Damn, fuckin' Yank - you're crazy. These are a bunch of fuckin' terrorists!" Jack heard the thud, the yell as Cormac's boot drove into Graham's side.

"It's you who's the bloody murderer you bloody ignorant Tommy, the same bastards that did it to Mairead, to Bobby Sands and the fourteen in Derry!" Jack could see the young boy was shaking with rage.

Theresa reached toward Cormac and shook her head. "Sister" Theresa had lost her veil and coif in the struggle, her dark hair curling now about her shoulders and face. Impatiently she brushed it aside. She looked over at Jack, her expression saying it all. She peered out at the more slowly passing trees and fields, then ran up the aisle following Sheila to the pilot's cabin.

Jack had little time to think. What had he got himself into? In the rear of the plane, some of the frightened, screaming passengers became quieter, surprised to hear a deep tuneful baritone voice. In the terrified silence, Dan was singing some old dirge - maybe a song of home and friends. The rich, resonant notes had a strangely calming effect.

The singing stopped. Dan moved up the aisle with his prisoner stumbling before him. Reaching Graham's prone figure,

Dan ordered the second man to lie beside him. Dan moved past Cormac, now covering both men. He nodded to Jack.

"You're a man - beside this trash on the floor – you're a real man." For a moment Jack saw the contrast, so unlike Graham. Dan's red hair, the blue eyes, the incongruous, deeply tanned skin. Dan moved on up the aisle as the plane was coming to a halt.

Theresa, Sheila and Brian Stephens emerged from the pilot's cabin. Quickly Sheila moved to unlock the exit door. Dan turned to the passengers then, their faces in various expressions of fear and confusion.

"We're leaving you now. Sorry it had to be this way, but you've seen the real 'terrorists'. Not the Republicans, but the Brit garbage on the floor where they belong." Some of the faces looking back seemed understanding, some hostile. Theresa was beckoning, moving toward the door. "Dan, come on!"

Dan called down the aisle, "Time to go Cormac!"

About a mile from where the plane had come to a stop, heavily armed units came running, heading for their vehicles. Cormac, peering out the window, quickly called to Dan and Theresa, "Don't wait for me, I'll follow you!" Dan shouted back, "See you man!" Guns in hand, Dan jumped down first, followed by Theresa. Cormac backed up the aisle, his gun still trained on Graham and his partner. Jack glanced out to see Theresa and Dan running for the fence less than fifty yards away. Looking to the other side, he saw the trucks moving out of the parking lot.

Sheila, now at the rear of the plane, was bending to check the wounded British agent. Cormac shouted again, "Move an' ye'r dead, Tommy!" Jack could see the trucks coming closer now; shooting had started, single shots, short bursts. He heard Theresa and Dan's shouts from the fence, from behind him Sheila's anxious cry as she ran back up the aisle. "Cormac, go, for God's sake!" Jack turned to see Cormac bending to look out the doorway.

Suddenly Jack heard a scream from beside him. Graham was up - he had Sheila in front of him. His partner had also risen, handing Graham a gun he had concealed in a leg holster. Graham yelled, "Drop your gun IRA or you're dead!"

174

Sheila was screaming, "Cormac, shoot the bastard - shoot!"

Graham fired, striking Cormac twice. Jack leapt for Graham and his partner, driving both to the floor. Cursing, Graham scrabbled around the floor for his weapon. Sheila, freed, ran to the exit, crying, "Oh no! Oh no!" Jack quickly joined her. They watched, anguished, helpless.

Cormac was limping slowly. A short distance from the plane, he stopped. He waved to Theresa and Dan waiting for him by the fence, then deliberately turned away. Dan struggled with Theresa as she tried to go to Cormac.

Paras and SAS units were firing, closer now, heading for the fence. Cormac stood, returning fire. Massively outgunned, Jack saw the young man hit again and again. Cormac slumped to the runway. Sheila hid her face in Jack's shoulder; he could feel her shaking with anguish.

Paras and others were running for the fence, Theresa and Dan now disappearing into the woods. The shooting had stopped. Inside the plane, the sound of children and others crying, the quiet sobbing of Sheila as she stood by the exit. The two security men knelt by their wounded partner at the back of the plane.

Jack jumped from the exit, followed by Colin Campbell and Brian Stephens. They stood by the still figure of Cormac. Cormac lay, eyes gazing sightlessly at the grey clouds above. As the slow moving clouds drifted on, a shaft of sunlight threw their shadows across the dun, green fields of Ulster. The blood still flowed; and Jack knew he was finally home again. He turned and walked slowly back to the plane.

CHAPTER SEVENTEEN

A Phone Call

In his cousin's house, later that night, unable to sleep,
Jack listened to the night sounds of the city. In Belfast, guard
dogs, barbed wire and barricades - ever wary of the night
prowler. Voices were raised in a dissonant, drunken chorus as
midnight reveille from a late night pub, or the housing estates on
the Falls.

Jack felt the tremor, at first a distant flutter, rising to
rhythmic clatter, then resounding, penetrating vibrations, as a
pair of low flying helicopters swept over west Belfast. "Spotters"
on the prowl. For Jack, it brought back memories. In Vietnam,
their presence had been reassuring. Again from a distance, he
heard an occasional shout, the shrill sound of a whistle, then a
burst of automatic fire.

Jack stood by the window. A clear moon lit the night
sky. He stared out toward the darker shadows of the Cave Hill.
What a day it had been. Not the homecoming he had anticipated.
Two worlds; one, with warm memories of friends and family he
could never reclaim. The other, with its obsession with death, the
world his father had tried to escape, but had never really left.

After Cormac's death, Jack recalled the uncanny pause,
the gruff self reassuring pantomime of professional toy soldiers
in maroon berets, armed to the teeth, self consciously acting out
their prescribed role - utrinque paratus, anything goes. Cormac's
body had been unceremoniously dragged aside, his brief role,
his fierce passion so quickly played out.

In a room at the terminal that served as a temporary
command post, with the Paras officer, security and a suddenly
very sober Graham among them - accusations and counter
accusations flew. Threats to detain Jack for interfering with a

176

security officer attempting to apprehend. Jack described his shock on observing Graham's drunken disregard for the other passengers on the plane.

An infuriated, red-faced Graham accused Jack of being an accessory to terrorism.

They were interrupted by the stormy arrival of a distinctly tall, dishevelled, overweight individual. Cigar in his teeth, angry and harassed, he complained,

"Can't get anywhere near the airport, with all the bloody road blocks and barricades! It's an infringement of fundamental rights - freedom of the press. Bloody worse than Russia!" He strode over to Jack, introduced himself as Bob Thompson, independent journalist, writing for *The Times*.

Disconcerted, the Para officer ordered Jack not to leave the building; he and Graham then abruptly left the room. Jack and Thompson were left alone, awaiting the American consul.

Thompson's presence at the airport was no coincidence. Interested in the escalating problem in the north of Ireland, Thompson had learned of Jack's visit through a notice in the *Belfast Telegraph*, a brief reference to his source background. The title of Jack's presentation, "Alternatives to Violence", had intrigued him.

Thompson had learned of Jack's heroic role from the flight crew. "That was some quick thinking. A shame about the boy who died."

Jack had seen violent death many times, in Vietnam, and in the urban jungles of America. Rarely had he seen the same willingness as that of the boy, Cormac, to state with his life his deepest beliefs. Jack was genuinely troubled. The common factor in America - the disenfranchised, dispossessed, Afro-American - their only perceived options, drugs and violence. No different for the discrimination and oppression of the Irish and their children, fewer alternatives - to die in the streets, to turn their backs, or to confront overwhelming odds to be heard.

Reaching for common ground, like schoolboys exchanging secrets, Bob Thompson and Jack Edwards explored their past. Both discovered an academic preoccupation in history and political science; more important, an instant trust.

177

Thompson described his experiences as a journalist in Vietnam and elsewhere, his recent involvement in the Irish scene. "For England," said Thompson, "Northern Ireland is our Vietnam, and we don't know how to get out." Thompson then spoke cautiously of his suspicions of a covert operation he'd recently learned of.

After some time the Para officer and Graham returned with the American consul, Tom Feely, accompanied by an English representative from the Northern Ireland Office. Feely promptly reminded them that they could not detain Jack, an American citizen. An increasingly heated exchange took place then, between Feely and Graham.

Graham's growing chagrin was evident as Thompson related more of, "our detained guest's background - a visiting professor, distinguished lecturer at Queen's University. Also," Thompson added, "an authority on alternatives to violence, right, Professor?"

The English representative from the Northern Ireland Office, troubled by Thompson's information, tried now to reduce the significance of the "unfortunate mishap". Bob Thompson heatedly disagreed with the little man, describing the affair as inexcusable, unauthorized mayhem. Thompson was unsparing.

"Too long have decent English people, uninformed, put up with devious schemes." Jack noticed Graham's startled expression as Thompson continued. "In foreign places, the excuse, if any is given, is 'national security', 'strategic significance'. Here, too near home, these excuses are irrelevant."

Evidently, Thompson was on his own crusade. Jack was impressed with his sincerity and courage. He liked the man's sardonic wit and humour, flair and aggression - an outspoken political critic - a dangerous occupation now, in some parts of the world.

Thompson and Graham nearly came to blows before Graham stormed out. Ignoring the Northern Ireland representative's apologies for the "inconvenience", Jack agreed to be available for further questioning.

Tom Feely insisted Bob Thompson and Jack accompany him to Belfast. As the embassy car pulled out from the terminal building in a heavy rain, Jack looked back to see Graham staring grimly after their departure. Thirty minutes later, just outside the city, they were stopped at a roadblock by uniformed soldiers.

"Parachute regiment, 'warrior elite'," Thompson told Jack. "They send them over here to get experience in street fighting. 'Shoot to kill', or 'beasting the Paddys' they call it," Thompson explained.

Thompson and Jack joined Feely, who had stepped out of the car. One gung ho, blackened, pimply-faced recruit aimed his rifle at Jack.

"Fuckin' Yank - heard about you!"

Thompson dangerously grabbed the muzzle of the soldier's rifle. Jack jumped forward. "Easy guys. Let's leave the guns out of this."

Handing his rifle to one of his mates, tearing off his smock and flak jacket, the boy started forward. Jack waited, watching the approaching trooper roll up his sleeves like some sort of boy scout. A young, fit looking officer intervened.

"Back off chaps."

Feely pushed between Jack and the soldier, introducing himself to the officer. The officer addressed Feely,

"Lieutenant Wilson, Special Unit, 2nd Parachute Regiment. We have terrorists on the loose - can't be too careful, can we?" His fruity tones were incongruously out of place with grim camouflaged battle dress, red beret and other war paint.

Feely and the officer briefly spoke, quickly resolving the episode. The troopers sullenly waved them on; they continued on their way. Feely told Jack and Thompson the officer had indeed been aware of the incident at the airport, also knew Jack's identity. Jack instantly recalled Graham watching their departure.

Past vacant lot and rubble, they finally emerged on the Falls Road. Thompson informed them this was a war zone as they hastened past the segregated ghettos of the Divis Flats - to eventually reach the concrete bunkers, barricades, gun ports of the Andersontown Barracks - the security fortress at the point of the Falls and Glen Road. Peering through the rain, Jack counted the houses up the deserted street to where his cousins lived. It was almost midnight when he rang the doorbell.

He was immediately engulfed in the concerned and relieved reception from his cousins, Brigid and Rosaleen, the household where the happy spirit of his father still danced, and the voice of his uncle, long dead in other wars - in traditional Irish song and dance, still sang.

Standing now by the window from which his mother and father had often gazed, Jack realised his arrival home was a stern reminder of the intransigent colonial role - the "north of Ireland", a historic, economic and political pawn. Was this what his mother and father saw? Was this what they knew, what his father called home? They grew up, finally forced to leave the violence and discrimination.

Restless and uneasy, Jack lay on his bed, closed his eyes. The harsh events of the day had rekindled the sleeplessness, the nightmares he'd once known in the months following his return from Vietnam.

The clatter of the helicopters receding, half asleep, Jack relived another colonial war, with his Special Forces unit - running through the streets of Saigon, April of '75. Above the city, helicopters were spinning out toward the Mekong Delta, the last Americans to leave. Once more Jack stood on the deck of an overcrowded fishing boat, peering at the receding docks of Kan Hoi. Among the faces of the thousands lining the dockside, staring silent, haunting - Cormac's face emerged.

Jack awoke with a start. Memories of Vietnam were bitter. From his dreams evoked curious similarities - devious duplicity, as now in Northern Ireland. In Vietnam, "British Indian" troops had rearmed the captured Japanese, to restore the brutal French colonial rule. As General Douglas Mac Arthur commented on learning of the British "strategy", "If there is anything that makes my blood boil, it is to see our allies in Indochina re-conquering the little people we promised to liberate."

Jack slept fitfully the last few hours until dawn. He heard the phone ringing - heard his cousin's footsteps on the stairs. "Jack, are ye awake? You have a phone call."

"Be right down, Brigid." Jack quickly zipped on a pair of trousers. His mind uneasily ranged over the possibilities. Feely or the Northern Ireland administration, or security, with unpleasant news - perhaps even Queen's University, to cancel the engagement.

Jack wasn't prepared for the familiar, easily recognised voice. He was thrilled to hear the unmistakable tones - remembered her as he'd last seen her, calling out to Cormac before Dan dragged her away, under fire.

"It's me, no names - we know who we are. I called to thank you for your help." The low voice continued, a note of sadness in the Scottish burr of the northern dialect, the accent of Jack's mother and father, unchanged over the years.

"He was so brave. He gave his life to save us - gave his life for Ireland, no questions asked. Read it as he saw it. It was hard to leave him."

There was a moment's silence. She continued then, "He was sure he'd see it in his lifetime - Irish men and women, of all faiths - together." With surprising quick change, "Be careful - ye've accidentally touched on a bad situation - an' the one ye'r up against is a real bad actor."

"I'm glad to hear your voice. Don't worry about me," said Jack, "It's you they're after." He commenced to describe the exchange with Graham and the para officer in the terminal building but was quickly interrupted. "Be careful what ye say on these phones. They're all tapped. An' watch where ye go. Your cousins will see ye right. We know them - good people." There was a pause. "Good luck in your talk - we'll be listening."

"Take care of yourself," Jack replied. "I'll be looking for you." He added quietly, "Perhaps I can help with the problem."

"Take care," she answered. "Keep your eyes open."

The phone went dead. Still holding the receiver, Jack heard a secondary "click". He realized he was in a more difficult position than he'd thought. His life was changing. In a sense he felt he was already committed - his expertise, his unique position giving some advantage - a weapon these people, his family, never had.

Brigid was standing by the open kitchen door watching

him. Jack replaced the phone, laughing self-consciously. "Sorry, Brigid, I was distracted." He ran up the stairs, a boy again - his first morning home from boarding school. "Brigid, you know what I'd love for breakfast?" He stood at the top of the stairs, the violence of yesterday, the restless night forgotten. He felt great! Looking down the stairs at Brigid, he thought for a moment he was looking at his mother's face - saw her expression of joy and bewilderment.

"Just like your father, Jack. What is it ye'd like for breakfast - as if I didn't know already?"

"You're right, Brigid, same as it used to be - the potato bread - the baps and farls and all the trimmings!"

The kitchen door closed below. Above his cousins' chatter Jack could hear the sizzling sounds - could smell the salty Irish bacon, the black and white pudding - could taste the strong, sweet tea.

He looked in the bathroom mirror, smiling to himself. For a moment he saw his father's face, smiling too. Probably from the same mirror he had gazed into as a younger man - before he descended the stairs to dance for his family, for his friends, for Peter or Pat - perhaps when he'd come on Christmas visits, to brighten their season - to entertain them with his laughter and stories.

Jack descended the stairs, humming a tune to himself - a tune his father had often sung to him when he was a small boy. He was really home now.

CHAPTER EIGHTEEN

A Terrible Price

South of the Chiltern Hills, above the placid valley of the Thames, a lone sparrow hawk flew in easy circling flight. Its predatory gaze ignored the busy traffic of the Great West Road from London, fiercely focused in stereoscopic vision on its inevitable victims, helpless prey among the grass and reeds far below.

Paddy Finucane's mind was in turmoil. He had been called to Geoffrey Gordon's office in London. On hearing of Madam's death, Paddy's first thought was of the IRA. Had the IRA, whom Madam so maligned - finally caught up with her? As he heard the details from Gordon, doubts began to gather. The execution was too sophisticated, too faultlessly planned. Recalling how the IRA had bungled previous attempts to settle their score, Paddy felt it just didn't have their signature. Even Gordon had expressed doubts. The Irish problem was only one of a broader cast now, from east to west, a world at war with itself. Reminded of Michael's warnings of corruption, of the ongoing investigation of the China scheme, Paddy sensed a wider conspiracy.

From Geoffrey Gordon, he learned of the shooting at the Belfast airport. One IRA and one SIS Special Security agent had been shot. Gordon was worried about the involvement of an American, which could likely become an international incident. Among those figuring in the shooting was Graham, apparently following an IRA group from Paris. Paddy remembered Graham standing by the door of the embassy that night in Paris watching their departure; the night of the Weatherbys' murder. And now the shootings in Northern Ireland. For Paddy, Graham now assumed a more sinister image.

Victor Perry sat in the departure lounge at Heathrow,
nervously sipping his drink. Fidgeting with his ticket, he
tried to avoid the eyes of two of his three companions, Paddy
Finucane and An Luc, holding sporadic conversation with Roger
Moorefield.

Paddy had earlier met with Roger Moorefield, recently
appointed CIA, EU station representative, at the Weatherbys'
funeral in Paris. Geoffrey Gordon had introduced them, unaware
of their experience together in Vietnam. Roger's recollections
were no different from the others, that no one had survived the
Spec Seven mission to Cambodia - all members MIA. Roger was
pleased to hear of Paddy's reunion with Jean Davost.

Aware of the ongoing investigations of the China
Scheme, Roger was interested to hear of Victor Perry's possible
role in the promotion of the enterprise. Paddy had described
Perry's strange behaviour in Paris, his association with Deevers
in Vietnam. Roger remembered Deevers' suspect role, never
confirmed before the hurried evacuation.

Paddy was not surprised to learn that Victor Perry
was returning to Washington, not alone to give his report
on developments at the DEA meeting, but had also been
subpoenaed to testify before a Congressional subcommittee on
national security. This, Roger Moorefield surmised, probably in
relation to the China Scheme, following complaints regarding
irregular British and US trade dealings with China. As Michael
Weatherby had suspected, the scheme's link with criminal
organisations, especially in the growing drug and arms trade
into China, was rapidly emerging.

At Roger's suggestion, Paddy had quickly agreed to
accompany him in seeing Perry off to the States from Heathrow.
Knowing he would soon be facing a grim interrogation, public
indictment, accusation and exposure of using his role with the
DEA to advance the corrupt activities of the China Scheme, Perry
might be willing to talk before departure. If Paddy's, and now
Roger's suspicions were correct, both reasoned it might occur to
Perry to turn government witness, as a plea bargain was perhaps
his only option.

For Paddy, this might also be the remote chance to shed

light on Anna's assassins, or on the identity of the killers of Perry's former partner, Deevers, those who may have assumed control over Deevers' affairs in Southeast Asia. Word perhaps, even to the mystery of the missing gold bullion.

Paddy glanced at the clock on the far wall of the airport lounge. Seated across from him, Perry was nervously chatting with Roger. Paddy was growing impatient.

An Luc's attention was directed elsewhere. His gaze was fixed on two men standing together across the departure lounge, and a woman seated beside them. Dark skinned and expensively dressed, the group had repeatedly stared toward his table since their arrival. An Luc, more than casually observant, practiced the extraordinary extrasensory skill not uncommon among the Shaman, the Buddhist holy men of Northern Laos. He watched the objects of his curiosity, their clothes, their carriage, their gestures. Completely focused, he read their origins, the spoken dialect. It was even possible, it was said, to interpret the words of those so closely observed.

The attractive, dark-eyed woman, wearing a purple and gold sari, glanced toward An Luc. She looked away quickly, aware perhaps that she, too, was now being watched.

Victor Perry, drinking steadily since his arrival, spoke louder now, with repetitive comments about Madam's unexpected demise. Paddy decided he must make a move before Perry became too drunk. As if reading Paddy's mind, Roger Moorefield rose, nodded toward Paddy, and excused himself.

Paddy leaned forward, eyes fixed on Perry, who nervously returned his gaze. "Victor, the day before they were murdered, Michael and Beth Weatherby told us of their concerns about your role in the China Scheme - actively promoting it."

Perry looked startled. Paddy closely watched him. "Victor, this hearing in Washington, regarding the China investment plan - what exactly will you tell them? Any link to the Weatherbys - dangerous witnesses, now no longer with us?"

Victor shook his head, staring warily about. He mumbled, "I can only tell them what I know. All I know, Paddy. All they want to hear."

Paddy was afraid he was too late. Victor seemed too

185

drunk. Paddy continued questioning. "About those involved in the Hong Kong administration and those in the government of the UK?"

Perry's eyes fixed on Paddy with a trapped expression, as Paddy pursued his interrogation. "Not all they want to hear Victor, but the real facts - what you've hidden all these years. More recently, about the new Asian connection. And from Vietnam, Victor - the continuing American connection."

Perry said nothing. He sat before Paddy, mouth open, mesmerised, listening to Paddy's quickening interrogation.

"Victor, we have all the keys."

Victor's eyes grew suddenly wide. He looked about, as if for a way to escape. Paddy continued, relentless. "The keys to the Southeast Asian connection - the links perhaps, to the business in China, in Hong Kong, in Australia and elsewhere." Then suddenly, "Who is the missing link, Victor?" Paddy sat eye to eye with Perry, their faces now only inches apart. "Where are they?"

"Links, keys - what links, what keys?" Perry muttered, trying to appear perplexed. Paddy, quickly unbuttoning his jacket, drew out the tiny icons to the past.

"For these, Victor, too many have died. Blackmail and greed, the reason, one or the other why you became involved - why you are still a victim, in bondage to the long dead Deevers."

Again Perry looked startled. He stared at the keys, confused, shaken. "I never knew what happened to them," then quickly, "to him. For a while I thought Colonel Deevers was still alive, or maybe that he'd been a casualty related to your expedition. Maybe, that he'd gone to Cambodia or somewhere buying stuff. No, I never saw those keys before."

Perry's voice trailed off. His expression became more cautious, more cunning. He muttered something about the confusion of those last days and his own narrow escape.

Seeing the change as soon as Victor saw the keys, Paddy was convinced. Victor may not have seen them before, but he'd certainly heard of their existence - and their significance.

"Anna and I found Deevers, crucified, in Phnom Penh. Whoever did it didn't find the keys. We have them now, Victor.

And whoever killed Deevers, whoever killed Anna, they're after both of us now."

Victor's face transformed to instant shock. Paddy was surprised that this was really news to him.

"They killed Anna," Paddy continued, "but again they never found what they came for. How did you learn of her death? Who, Victor, is responsible? Who took Deevers' place?" Perry was muttering incoherently, his hands trembling, clasping and unclasping his empty glass.

"Victor, I hold the last key for you now. Tell me the story and perhaps I can testify for you. Soon the media will be onto it. Then what story would you have me tell them?"

Victor looked even more flustered. "I never knew of your wife's death till recently. Someone told me, probably at the Embassy. I didn't know what happened to Deevers. Tung Giang told me Deevers was joining your expedition to Cambodia. A secret mission, he called it. I never saw Tung Giang, nor Deevers again." Perry's eyes looked haunted, remembering those last days.

"Lucky, I thought, to have escaped, I never knew it would come to this. When I came to Paris I received phone calls, orders – threats." Looking at Paddy he asked, "Tung Giang still lives?"

Paddy nodded. "A leading drug kingpin in the Golden Triangle."

Victor's face was pale. Paddy was convinced. Victor, working for the State Department at home, still worked for the 'Asian Connection' abroad.

The harsh metallic announcement interrupted Paddy's thoughts. "TRANSAIR flight for New York, now boarding."

Perry quickly fumbled for his briefcase. Paddy rose and leaned toward Perry. "Victor, they crucified Anna; they tortured her. They're going to catch up with you. This may be your only chance - tell me their names."

Victor stared up at Paddy. "I know little about them. They have a base in Paris, yet I never see them." Perry rose unsteadily. With Paddy close beside him, he moved slowly forward, following the other passengers toward the boarding gate.

Paddy leaned closer to Perry. "Victor, the roles have been reversed, don't you see? Deevers', perhaps Tung Giang's plan, was to hijack fifty tons of gold. It never got to its destination. It vanished. Someone got it; likely the one who murdered Deevers. Perhaps, the same one who is now blackmailing you."

Victor stopped, looking back across the room. Roger Moorefield was returning. Looking hard at Paddy, Perry asked incredulously, "Gold - fifty tons?" A growing anger began replacing his surprise.

"You have allowed them to blackmail you, Victor." Paddy now added his bluff. "We have the keys to the only hard evidence, and to your freedom."

Silent a moment, confused, Victor looked at Paddy. "I didn't know what else to do - they hounded me." Seeing Roger was approaching, Victor continued in a rush.

"Paddy, I had no choice. They warned me they would expose me. In these hearings, perhaps I will be the one to see to it that they are now exposed. I have to give my story first, Paddy."

Then, with a sly look, "If I gave my whole story too soon I might lose the opportunity to win a reprieve." Victor's expression was now one of self-importance. "The information I have, as you say, might bring me a role as a government witness - with proper timing."

Moorefield was now only a few yards away. Perry's voice changed to an almost triumphant note. "Soon I will be on the stand, and then it's all over... for them that is."

Moorefield joined them, reached to shake Perry's hand, wishing him a good trip. Perry turned then and disappeared down the ramp.

Across the lounge, An Luc had remained seated, watching the foreign group. Curiously, none of them boarded the flight. As Victor Perry followed the other passengers, An Luc watched the dark-eyed lady make her way to a nearby phone. Speaking slowly in English, she gave a brief message to a cell phone in the Western Hebrides of Scotland, then glancing briefly toward An Luc, followed her male companions from the lounge.

An Luc now shared his information with Roger and Paddy. "The woman is Bhutanese. Her friends come from Pakistan. They did not come to travel, Tuan, they came to see Mr. Perry leave."

"Something else interesting, Paddy," said Roger. "My office had a call from Gordon. The American involved in the shooting in Northern Ireland is one Jack Edwards, professor of political science - sometime consultant with National Security." Seeing Paddy's amazement, he continued. "Wasn't he one of your group with Spec Force Seven?"

Jack Edwards stood among the gravestones of Milltown cemetery. Brigid and Rosaleen had gone to pick up their cousin, Mary, coming off night shift at the Royal Victoria Hospital. They had arranged to drop by for Jack within the hour.

Unable to return for his father's funeral, he had come now to pay his respects. Jack wandered the gravel pathways, pausing to read the names - Campbell, Johnston, Mc Glade - loving mother, loving father - beloved son or daughter. Above the grassy mounds, Celtic or Coptic, lichen covered crosses ran like iron or granite tears across the hillside. Among the broken vases, he saw the fresh turned earth of the recently departed, covered with the fresh bright flowers of the recently bereaved.

About to retrace his steps, suddenly in front of him hung a series of granite obelisks, with black, gold or green ornamentation, Celtic crosses, with names inscribed. Above the names, pairs of crossed Irish flags. Jack read the names and the ages, each followed by dates and the letters IRA. Many were in their teens. Dozens of lives, dying for the elusive dream of nationhood, each as they saw it. Some, like Cormac, in the public arena - others in some back alley, street corner or tenement.

At a crossing in the pathways, Jack read the long list on one weathered memorial, the stark inscription, on hunger strike. A terrible price to pay.

Jack was dismayed to read the name of the young girl, Mairead, murdered in Gibraltar only weeks before, by "security" forces. He found himself reaching to touch the cold stone of a life and spirit lost too soon. He knew some day this is where Theresa might lie, and others, unless someone found a way to resolve the enigma.

Jack looked across the sloping perimeter of the cemetery. In the silence, he felt the impact of a thousand voices, too late to testify. He could almost feel his father's presence.

Brigid and Mary were standing by the gate, waving. "Did you find your mum and dad, Jack?"

"No, but just as well. I'd rather remember them the way they were - dancing and singing, telling their stories - the way we knew them best." He really didn't want to see their names in stone, in these acres of silent mounds and monuments of dead flowers and granite crosses. Jack thought of Theresa as he walked toward the gate. He knew he didn't want to see her name here either.

They drove slowly through the late morning traffic, listening to Mary, fresh from a busy shift in the operating room. Mary was nodding toward the hospital buildings they were now passing. "The Royal Vic., where I've worked for the past twenty years, Jack." Pointing to one side, "Right up there on the third floor, in emergency surgery: that's where I spent the whole of last night."

The sprawling compound was surrounded by high, red brick walls topped with the inevitable rolls of razor wire, the traditional iron spike fences, disfiguring reminders of the morbidity and mortality of a city at war.

Brigid drove a meandering route. "Part memory lane, part pilgrimage," she explained. Turning into one of the dingy side streets, she pointed out the graphic artistic conceptions, the sectarian graffiti and murals of political or religious affiliations adorning the sides of buildings.

The colourful portraits and wistful assumptions were not unfamiliar to Jack. He recalled similar graphic displays on the walls of tenements or high-rises in the slums and ghettos of New York, Baltimore, Washington, or Los Angeles. The street artists all sang variations of the same song, as victims of oppression, discrimination, apartheid, in a world seemingly blind to their suffering, a defiant cry of anguish and hope rising above the squalor.

"That's an insight into our worst problem Jack. A prevailing fear, not of the violence, but of obscurity and irrelevance, a loss of identity." Jack nodded in agreement.

Brigid pointed out the burned out buildings, vacant lots, staring women, children, their canny faces, older, watchful eyes: landmarks of conquest and neglect. At the street corners Jack saw idle groups of men chatting away the endless, hopeless days, or staring vacantly or sullenly at the passing traffic.

Jack saw the unvarying sameness in the serried rows of red brick Victorian hovels of the indentured workers, the "willing cannon fodder" – the street names commemorating the Somme and other sites of Imperial carnage.

"Shankhill to the Falls – it's all the same misery," said Brigid, shaking her head. "This is where the conflict begins," Brigid nodded toward the far side of the street.

A group of shabbily dressed teenagers, in jeans and hooded jackets, were exchanging insults with another group of teenagers, dressed in flak jackets, camouflage Dennison smocks, and wearing the distinctive maroon beret of the parachute regiment Jack had already seen too much of. Boys, trying to look like men, trained their SLRs from rooftop to roadway, playing a provocative game designed to impress and impose, to the irritation of the watching teenagers.

Brigid passed through the city centre, moving into an older part of town. Shouldered between successive grim Victorian edifices, Jack saw a more elegant façade, its spires stoutly reaching above the encroaching cupolas of commerce and trade. Beneath the soot and grime, law or insurance offices gave way to the baroque, ornate entrance to an old church. Its cornices, niches, plaster cherubs and ancient water font were mute testimony to its vital role in the embattled lives of its congregation.

"St. Malachy's, the church where your mum and dad were married, so many happy years ago," said Brigid, pulling into an empty parking spot across the street. "Go ahead, Jack. Mary, Rosaleen and I have things to do - we'll see ye back here shortly." Adding in her inconsequential way, "An' say a prayer for us as well."

Jack stepped up to the heavy oak doors, the world around him quickly receding. He found himself in another time, among a ghostly group of laughing faces, the men dressed in their best suits, the women wearing summery hats and dresses. The great doors opened; the crowd gave way. The bride and groom, in a flurry of confetti, flushed and laughing, passed through the oak doors and ran down the steps.

It was dark and cool inside the church. Jack's eyes adjusted to the dim candlelight. The altar to one side, the pulpit lay among the shadows. Slowly Jack touched the water font.

He remembered his mother telling him the way it had been that morning; the insistent clamour of the bells, the bustle and fleeting glamour for two eager, hopeful lives. Little did they dream, as his mother had said some seventy years later – that almost fifty years of such mornings lay before them. Jack knew that memorable day had made it worth all the sacrifices, the hardship and the modest victories of their working lives, living in the crucible of another pending conflict - and growing old in a world again in another "war to end all wars".

Jack drew some coins from his pocket and inserted them into the offering box. Lighting a candle from one of those already burning, he carefully placed it beneath the statue of the maternal figure of the Virgin. Her eyes seemed to watch him as he stood back in the candlelight, silent witness to his visit, to their celebration that long ago day. Mother and child posed, her enigmatic smile frozen in time.

Ironically, that same spring day of celebration for Jack's parents, those first happy years in Ireland, were also final days of tragedy for many others. In the killing fields of Flanders and the Somme, it had been a year of genocide on an unimaginable scale for generations of young Irish men and others. And in Ireland, in a bloody spring of another more selective execution, of the young and the not so young, of the poets and the dreamers, heroes all, when "A terrible beauty was born".

Jack found himself genuflecting as he had done morning after morning during those long years in boarding school. The old church, enduring and unchanging, begrimed with the soot and pollution of the Industrial Revolution and its social consequences.

Jack turned toward the door, reluctant to re-enter the world of uncompromising violence. Dipping his fingers into the holy water font, he blessed himself, then passed through the archway, closing the heavy doors behind him.

At a police barracks in the seaside town of Newcastle at the foot of the Mourne Mountains, less than an hour's drive south of Belfast, an urgent phone call was received.

"This is Inspector King. What can I do for you?" His voice was polite, reserved. A grey-haired, fit looking older man, King wore the sombre uniform of chief inspector of the Royal Ulster Constabulary.

"Inspector, this is Charles Graham, British Special Security."

King responded with a curt acknowledgment. With no further preliminaries Graham, his voice brusque, impersonal, continued, "They tell me you're our man covering the area of the Mourne Mountains – "

King interrupted. "Not exactly. That's a long reach. You've also got Johnson, Rathfriland and Mc Garrett in Newry. They're also our men."

Graham ignored the comment. "We're over here following an IRA group likely involved in the recent shooting in Paris and possibly also in Madam's assassination." His pause met with no response. "We've reason to believe they are hiding out in the Mourne area."

Inspector King grunted a monosyllabic response. He had little time for this kind of interference in Northern Ireland affairs. The inspector had received a call the previous day from the Northern Ireland office in Belfast, updating him on events since the shooting at the airport.

"Graham's his name - from MI6, in charge of an anti-terrorist strike force. They say he's got special 'emergency powers' since Madam's assassination. And he's moving fast."

King listened now with impatience as the gruff voice blustered on. "I want to set up a meeting tomorrow, to follow up a lead we've had. We'll need your help to stick it to them, right mate?"

King, a solemn, responsible, senior officer in the constabulary, made a non-committal response. The common English address, *mate,* irritated him.

Graham went on, "Among the names high on our list is the one they call the Shanassy."

"That's Seanache," corrected King.

"Whatever. He's right up there, a primary target – er, suspect, that is. He's out there in the Mournes, and we're informed the others are with him."

"What you say may be true," King answered cautiously. "The Seanache is well known. He's given us trouble in the past. The man is older now. As I'm aware, he hasn't broken the law recently. We keep an eye on him." King added sarcastically, "An' we're short of men here, an' in no position to mount some sort of round up."

"Not what we had in mind," said Graham, his voice more arrogant now. "Short or not, Inspector, I would appreciate your beefing up patrols in the Mournes. Keep an eye on the old man until we arrive. And keep your eyes open for any of the others. The one they call Sister Theresa is an accomplice in the shooting of one of my men. Tomorrow we will be sending a Sea King recce over the area. Later, helicopter patrols will arrive from Lisburn, and SAS units from Bangor." Then slowly, distinctly, "I remind you, Inspector, I am authorised to carry out this mission as I see it, and that is my intention." He concluded with a peremptory, "I expect your complete cooperation. We'll be in touch in the morning."

King reluctantly attempted a stiff, conciliatory tone. "We will try to increase our activities here until the arrival of the additional forces you mentioned." He couldn't resist adding, "Though we could probably handle the situation better ourselves, if we had the personnel."

There was a moment's silence at the other end of the line, then abruptly the phone was hung up.

King was still smarting at the patronising tone.

"Stupid arrogance!" he muttered to himself as he poured

himself another cup of tea – added a stiff shot of Jameson's from the top drawer of his desk, then stood at the window, staring out across the distant tide rolling in from Dundrum Bay. A beautiful land. A God given country, with a God forsaken history. It's strange, King thought, how, Monday morning to Saturday night, we can laugh and play together, share our ways in song and story and dance, until Sunday - when whatever religion we belong to separates us - then fear, guilt, anger and shame commences.

Though a confirmed Unionist, King had always considered the label meaningless. You have to be something yourself first, before you look for a union with something else. It had a meaning in times gone by – with the historic threat of "Home Rule" from the south. Political opportunists had played the game, firing and inspiring the unsuspecting loyalist lackeys of the day to retain their sovereignty in Ulster, outfoxing the southern nationalists - driving the two apart with a "God save the King!" Times had changed. King sighed. All we're left with are the drums, the poppy parades, and the mindless "royals" we once died for.

King had always had an unshakable belief in the resolute practicality of the north in their ability to remain a force to contend with. It occurred to him that in any arrangement with the southern part of the country, without the Brits, the northern Scot could more than hold their own. The south, King thought, would follow our economic leadership, our industrial aggression and genius. The south, for all their blather, are as afraid of us as we of them. In any settlement, we would lead the country then. It was something to dream about, but a thought King had never shared with friend or family.

Quickly walking to the doorway, King shouted down the corridor, "Are ye' there, Willie?"

His sergeant emerged from the ready room, buttoning his jacket. "What can I do for you, Chief?" Willie followed King into his office.

"Willie, I'm goin' to need a wee hand. We'll have to raise operations west of Newcastle an' into the Mournes. They're goin' to start a search out this way tomorrow, first thing in the mornin' - helicopters, SAS, the whole works. Would you put a call through for me - to Johnson, Rathfriland, an' Mc Garrick at Newry - an' get me the names of all we can call in for tomorrow. Now off with ye' Willie."

"Right ye' are!" said Willie, running from King's office. As soon as he reached the ready room he shut the door and put the first call through, hastily transferring it to King's office.

Willie listened in to the conversation for a moment, then gently replaced the receiver. Cautiously tiptoeing toward the pay phone on the wall of the corridor, he reached for the receiver and dialled a number, bypassing the regional exchange. It seemed to take ages for anyone to respond. Then, with a sigh of relief, "Is that you, Sean?"

Almost at the same time as Willie and Inspector King were making their separate and very different phone calls, Victor Perry awakened from the nightmares that peopled his drunken sleep. He had no time to express his regrets for the betrayal of the mission to Phnom Penh, no time to think of the keys, no time to wonder who had taken Deevers' place. No time for public hearings, senate committees, public revelations, the heroic role denied. No time to languish or linger - to agonise in guilt. Only time for the final harsh retribution.

Victor had been waiting for his executioner for weeks, almost unable to eat or sleep, ever since the Paris phone call; startled at every unexpected sound or innocent daily confrontation.

He had been dreaming about the lady he'd seen watching him at the airport less than an hour before. His dark-eyed nemesis perhaps - the beauty of her eyes, their steady gaze, beckoning him to his final nuptials. Now, in smooth flight at thirty thousand feet over Kilbrannon Sound, Victor had to wait no longer. He felt the instant terror, yet equally, the instant relief.

Only as he died did Victor receive the clear revelation of who killed Deevers and Anna, who must have assumed Deevers' role. In one wild second, suspended between mortality and the infinity of space, did Victor scream the name. His cry was never heard.

He found himself spinning in another dimension as he rose in silence, chasing his parts among the constellations toward the sun. In a jeering clown dance to the awful sounds of that instant audio-byte before the final disruption, the shrieking and screaming, or was it laughter, derisive hilarity? Victor fell before the moon and among the stars.

Sadly, his dissolution had compelled the involuntary attendance of some two hundred and fifty-seven innocent guests - falling now like tiny stars, glowing incandescent across the universe, mocking the complexity of their creation, atomised amid the transient fumes of high octane gasoline. The slavish computer, the final executioner, rocketed to self-destruction.

High above the rolling estuary of the Firth of Fourth, the beady eyes of a solitary fish hawk, in long swooping flight, pierced to the silvery fish shoals running before the rising tide far below. Accipiter, sleek, cruel beauty in smooth, soaring perfection - her wild scream rose and fell hundreds of breathless feet above the grey seas.

Almost motionless on her broad, stubby wings, she suddenly sensed the distant thunderous explosion - felt its hot shuddering impact through the stratosphere, perceived the momentary blinding glow brighter than the sun.

Undeterred, she focused - her eyes on her victim moving through the foam and surge beneath. From above the purple, misted cliffs of Kintyre, she dived, as around her the elements appeared to dissolve in spinning stars – in smoke, cloud and spray. She struck - her talons driving to the living flesh and blood of her prey - the innocents that moved unaware through the chill seas, off the deserted moors and rocky beaches of Kilbrannon Sound.

CHAPTER NINETEEN

The Real Victims

On arrival at Queen's University, Jack was surrounded by a noisy crowd of students, and even more of the general public was gathered by the entranceway. Some carried Unionist or Republican signs. Some seemed to be shouting words of encouragement. Others waved banners addressing the wider focus, against Capitalism, the World Bank, or the expanding U.S. role everywhere, chanting, "bloody Yanks." Some responded, angrily denouncing, "Union flunkies!"

A television crew was filming outside the hall. Though no reference was made to Jack's embattled arrival at the airport the day before, the noisy reception served to confirm his growing notoriety. Inside, the American Consul, Tom Feely, closely followed by the journalist, Bob Thompson, greeted Jack and his cousins.

The auditorium was filled to capacity. Those turned away at the entrance crowded the open doorway. Jack noticed a strong security presence, constabulary, university personnel and curiously, British paratroopers, weapons in hand, scanning the crowd. Inside, the president of the student council had some difficulty in quieting the raucous cries, calling repeatedly for the audience to take their seats, as Jack was introduced from the stage.

After gratefully acknowledging a professionally flattering introduction, Jack commenced an academic review of the history and possible resolution of existing conflicts worldwide. He imagined he saw his father seated in the front row, saw the intent gaze, the proud grin, nodding with every word. He found himself speaking directly to him, explaining why he'd left Ireland, the path his life had taken.

"Arriving in America in the late sixties, a freshman in college, it was my first major adjustment. Since the assassination of John Kennedy, America had been in a state of turmoil and cynicism. Camelot, a receding memory - its people rudely awakened from an illusion of innocence. From Cuba, America briefly confronted Armageddon, the countdown to nuclear holocaust. The threat of Communism, replaced in the following decades by the faceless, imperial fantasy. Anyone, anywhere, the enemy now. Invisible tenants of the "pinnacle of evil", setting the pace for the next century. From the Gulf of Tonkin to the Iran-Contra affair to the other Gulf wars, all the 'wages of deception', a hidden agenda. As Napoleon once described it, 'a different set of lies' seen from a new perspective.

"The further turbulence of the sixties produced a decade of lynchings, mob violence and the continuing struggle for civil rights. The storm gathered with the murder of Bobby Kennedy, the assassination of Martin Luther King and the bombing of black churches. Despite the eloquent plea of Martin Luther King's 'dream', discrimination was still not overcome. The voting franchise and equal treatment before the law was still a dream; for some, a nightmare. Embattled minorities, still living in an enclave of terror."

In the audience there was uneasy silence. Slowly the question emerged, "Does this sound familiar? The American dream unrealised – and now, for Northern Ireland, no different."

The audience stared ahead, avoiding each other's eyes. The crowd at the door stirred restlessly, murmuring amongst themselves or straining to listen to the evolving analogy. Alert young paratroopers scanned the faces, sensing the change.

"As a survivor of the war in Vietnam, I returned to the United States. I returned to an America in worsening turmoil. The next generation, with scarcely time to breathe - more cannon fodder for the militant corporate lobby - sent to disruptive conflicts from Angola to South America and ready to go in Afghanistan. In the Middle East, another big one brewing - targets set on the oil fields."

Jack told his listeners America was suffering the effects of increasing international isolation, resentment and hatred. It was the beginning of decades of corruption, lies, and increasing mistrust in government. Once the great society, America was now at war with itself.

Some in the crowd grew angry, some shouted support as they saw the parallel, realising how they too were being duped.

"Three costly years in Vietnam were where I realised the concept of my thesis on the "Alternatives to Violence". I found myself fighting for the sick strategy of Apartheid – of Imperialism under whatever name, against a people who fought only for their sovereignty – a free, undivided Vietnam. Democracy, I discovered, was a much-abused term."

Another pause, fewer catcalls, some shouts of support.

"In Vietnam I learned the realities of the world we live in. I discovered the other face of capitalism, of colonialism, who we were fighting and why. Much of it suppressed, censored or sanitised." Even the paratroopers seemed to be listening as Jack told a story few had known: how the British had enlisted the surrendered Japanese army to defeat the recently liberated Vietnamese people, to restore French colonial rule.

"Like the French before us, we too were defeated. In 1975, Vietnam was united, and regained her freedom. And the real victims," Jack told them, "were the Vietnamese people, who had lived through the wreckage of their country, diseased, divided, impoverished. We departed, with bitter memories, some in shame, some in search of other prey."

The crowd outside seemed oblivious to the light rain that commenced to fall. Jack had seemed to capture their gradual understanding of a different point of view, the cautious support of most of his audience.

"From the Americas to Southeast Asia, more than fifty ethnic wars still in progress, and the conflict intensifies. They play on your fears: of sudden death, of being alone in an alien world. Afro-American, Caucasian, Arab or Jew, Serbian or Christian, Hindu or Moslem, Protestant or Catholic. What are the alternatives to this bizarre trilogy of conquest, oppression and exploitation - this parody of justice - one man's saga of the prevailing ethos of greed and abuse? Don't be misled. As members of the human race you share more than divides you. The real threat today is the dislocation of our role in the economic spectrum. Our major concerns, with the new technologies, are the coming 'end of work'."

The audience seemed calmer. The American apparently had a wider focus than some had expected. His range of experience, different perspectives, fascinated them, had won their respect. This is where our paths diverge, Jack thought, as he headed for the more controversial decisions.

"From the civil and human rights violations I have witnessed in America, and as consultant to the State Department in endless conflicts, Northern Ireland is no different. Shorn of the distraction of the historic grudge or religious bigotry, in all instances we share a common factor, the presence of the colonial agent - and now the corporate godfathers - their vested interests little different, imperial power and profits."

Jack saw one or two stirring uneasily. Among those listening, Jack knew, were a fair section of the children of the favoured few, from the wealth of Knocknagoney to the Malone Road. A division of the marginalized, the very rich, the very separate and the very greedy. The implications were clearer. So far, their faces were attentive and expressionless.

Jack described a dangerous situation, the resurgence of fascism in Europe, communism resurgent in Russia. "And in Northern Ireland, an economically subsidised cocoon, you are not immune, but are increasingly vulnerable and dependent on this divided island economy."

Those listening outside could hear a ripple of interruption from the auditorium within. The president of the student council had some difficulty in quieting the raucous cries. Above the speaker's voice, a random call for "Question! Question!" A scuffle broke out in the back rows. Some figures were quickly wrestled toward the door. Jack waited as the interruptions grew quieter.

"Your only option, in Ireland south and north, is to confront the trans-national corporate rapacity as a single economic unit, for the benefit of both your families. Borders, political, religious or ethnic diversions, are irrelevant distractions now. Separatism in the Irish geographic entity is unaffordable."

Objections were voiced from the back of the hall. Jack reminded his audience, "As for the French in Algiers, the Americans in Vietnam, for Britain, now is the time to withdraw from its first and last colony. Britain's continuing presence here and everywhere else ensures a non-solution. Negotiate now for your own economic future, united, for the shared profits that are rightfully yours."

Jack concluded, "For those in power in the Northern Ireland colony, there is nothing to fear but fear itself. No one can take from you what you don't or shortly won't have."

The audience again became disruptive, differing loudly with one another. There was an increasing thunder of stamping feet and clapping hands. With rising fervour singing voices commenced, "We shall overcome."

Forced to stop in the crescendo of interruptions, Jack was startled to recognise the bulky figure of Graham entering the door at the back of the hall. Graham was surrounded by a group in civilian clothes; with them, several in the uniform and the buff beret of the SAS. As violent eruptions escalated, a member of the university security approached Jack, suggesting a postponement, for his own safety.

Suddenly Jack was surprised to hear again the familiar, clear tones, the deep voice, the strong accent. The singing and stamping ceased. The startled audience listened as the words came from a shadowy figure on the darkened balcony, closed for Jack's presentation.

"A cara. His points are well taken." Then, with dry humour, "Our civil rights marches here were greeted with the same enthusiasm as in America. One of the differences - our legislature has a strong reluctance to pass any legislation for an equal franchise, remove discrimination from the ballot, restrain police brutality, or the selective unemployment Professor Edwards speaks of.

"As Prods and Taigs we're all equal victims of this embattled colony. Those of ye here today, you're the lucky ones, the more socially fortunate. Ye can't afford to ignore the less fortunate victims of the wars that separate us, a Whitehall that keep ye an' your Mercedes in comfort. It's not the religious differences – and you're all too blind to see it!"

Theresa's words penetrated above the rising objections.

"In the words of the Republican, Oliver Cromwell, to the British Parliament, 'In the name of God: be gone!'"

The audience erupted with loud jeering and counter cheering. Suddenly, the lights flickered and dimmed. In the semi-darkened auditorium, fights broke out. Paras moved in, trying to separate the combatants. Jack saw some of the paras running toward the balcony. Uniformed figures running for the stairs found them barred. Voices shouted through megaphones, calling for those on the balcony to come down with their hands up. As the doors to the balcony were broken open, Jack saw Graham. At that moment the lights in the auditorium went out completely, leaving them in near total darkness.

Suddenly above the uproar, the unmistakable explosive crack of a single shot. Jack crouched behind the podium. He sensed the shot had been fired toward the stage. Within seconds a stampede, screaming and shouting, headed toward the doors. Several professors sharing the stage with Jack joined their fellow faculty in an unseemly scuttle for the wings.

Jack hurried after them, worried now about his cousins. He felt a tug on his arm. He looked down to see the anxious face of a young woman beside him. A piece of folded paper was thrust into his hand.

"A note from your friend," she shouted in his ear to be heard above the noise. "She'll see ye in the Mournes at midnight. Drive to Kilcoo. The old man at the garage will be waitin' for ye'. He'll tell ye where to go." She turned and was quickly lost in the crowd.

Jack's cousins were anxiously huddled below the stage waiting for him; Bob Thompson and Feely were with them. Hurriedly they joined the struggling bodies making for the exits. Outside, the rain fell as security tried to control the unruly crowd. Briefly, Jack explained his decision to head for Kilcoo. Brigid insisted Jack take her car for the journey, handing him the keys as she described the main route heading south. Tom Feely would see his cousins safely home.

Thompson cautioned Jack, "I've seen their plan, Ajax

they call it. The lady who spoke tonight, Sister Theresa, she's high on the list. The shot that was fired could have been meant for her. There's more to this than we know and I'm betting Graham's involved. Stay away from him, he's a dangerous lot."

Remembering Brigid's hurried instructions, Jack headed for Kilcoo. He was driving now through torrential rain, peering through the sweep of the windshield wipers to the unfamiliar roadway ahead, listening for the sound of police sirens, glancing to the rear-view mirror, waiting for the reflection of flashing lights. Exhausted by the succession of events of a near sleepless twenty-four hours, jet-lagged, dazed, listening to the hypnotic, steady thud-thump of the windshield wipers, Jack tried to stay awake. He turned on the radio, sifting through the static.

Suddenly more alert, he listened to a news report, "... TRANSAIR 747 lost over the coast of Scotland this afternoon, with over two hundred and fifty passengers aboard, including some members of an American DEA team who had been attending the recent International Drug Enforcement Meeting in Paris. Sabotage is suspected." Jack was troubled as the voice added, "On the occasion of this meeting, a member of the British Embassy staff in Paris and his wife were assassinated. The identity of the assassins or the motive in either tragedy remains a mystery."

CHAPTER TWENTY

"The fault, dear Brutus, is not in our stars - but in ourselves that we are underlings." Julius Caesar - ACT I - Scene II

"Yea, though I walk through the valley of the shadow of death - I shall fear no evil - for I am evil - SAS." Spray painted graffiti on a wall near Andersontown, Belfast.

In the front seat of the armoured patrol vehicle Graham sat, flashlight in one hand, squinting at the dimly lit street map. He shouted to the driver.

"Corporal, the second turn-off, fucking watch for it!"

Realising he'd missed his opportunity at Queen's, Graham headed for the air base at Bangor. He planned to get a jump on his quarry, a late night or early dawn ground and air reconnaissance. With 2 Para sections coming in across the Mournes from Rathfriland and the help of Inspector King in Newcastle the net would be closed.

Occasionally Graham growled into the mouthpiece of a radio receiver, exchanging with the O/C at the RAF base at Bangor. He was intent on converting another bungled job to a last minute success. Unfavourable weather conditions, the late hour, an uncooperative regional bureaucracy, inter-service rivalry and his inability to fully reveal his mission all added to a total cock-up!

Corporal Evans, a Welshman from 2 Para - the "Maroon Machines" Special Patrol Group - gripped the wheel, recklessly careering the heavy armoured Saracen through the rain-slick streets. He silently cursed the arrogant MI6 agent beside him.

Largely ignoring Graham's frustrated outbursts, Evans made no response. He knew better. Twice "back squadded" to private for insubordination, he was crawling back up the ladder. Since joining Counter Insurgency - Military Reconnaissance Force, Evans had racked up three notches on his belt. IRA shot, allegedly, "trying to escape". Many more "beasted", with broken limbs or heads, he added to his credits. Provies, Stickies, Taigs, Loyalists, Orange Orders, UVF - all one and the same to Evans. But for the first time he could remember, Evans knew fear, not of the action ahead, but of the straining animal he sensed beside him.

The recklessly driven Saracen was followed some distance further back by a four-tonner, packed with the main group of 22 SAS, Graham's strike force. Cam-creamed, eager young robots, they sat with their automatic rifles. "Hot jocks", ready to shoot to kill designated or other targets of opportunity.

Graham sat silent now, arms folded, staring grimly. Since hearing of the downing of the TransAir flight some hours earlier, he had been convinced something else was going on. Before Weatherby's self-destruct, he'd felt those in PASS were immune. Nearer home, with Madam's assassination, his world was reeling out of control. At first he was sure the IRA was responsible. Now, with the sabotage of the TransAir 747, the kidnapping in Paris and other unexplained events in the past few days, he was less certain.

Relentless rain and low clouds precluded any chance of a helicopter sweep tonight. Perhaps it would be better before dawn as Wing Commander Hawkins, the C/O at Bangor, had suggested. Graham withheld final judgment till they arrived at the RAF station.

Temporarily deprived of his quarry, Graham's thoughts returned to Jack Edwards and the disastrous confrontation on the plane. Probably a fucking set up. In the circumstances, Graham knew he'd been lucky to turn the tables. Pity he didn't shoot Edwards while he had the chance! And the other one, Dan, Graham had learned, was wanted for the deaths of nine members of 2 Para, ambushed near Armagh over a year ago. Special Branch, RUC and MI5 were doing background checks on the flight crew as well as the American, Jack Edwards.

Graham had since learned of Edwards' role as consultant

with the CIA, and worse still, for the most secret of all think tanks, the Institute for Defence Analysis. That's all he needed - a fucking international incident on a top-secret mission!

Graham recalled the arrival of Thompson at Belfast Airport. A coincidence? Thompson's insolence, startling reference to events in Paris, accusations - challenging Graham in front of the American Consul. Graham had barely restrained his response, with a promise of later satisfaction. Tensely he wondered if there was another game - another adversary stalking the arena? MI5, he'd heard, had their eye on Thompson for some time now.

Graham had a special aversion to "Toffs of the Oxbridge sorority". Following service in the Middle East, he had come to share the traditional British antipathy to Semitic peoples. Jews, Wogs, all the same to him. Thompson, like the Weatherbys, was a Jew, Graham now decided

Graham perceived Thompson as a renegade journalist, best known for his controversial articles that called the voting public "Britain's silent majority", Britain First, the "controlling minority". And now Graham had seen it with his own eyes, collaborating with the American; siding with the terrorists. He shook his head in disgust. Edwards and Thompson were traitors, dangerous.

The brief appearance of the IRA woman at Queen's had taken Graham completely by surprise. He had not anticipated her reappearance after her escape at the airport. High on the list, given the right opportunity, he planned to eliminate her. And now perhaps, to arrange a fortuitous accident for Thompson.

At Queen's, again he'd seen both Edwards and Thompson supporting the same platform. Fucking reborn Marxists! Same as Weatherby. Graham trusted none of them. No telling whose side they were on or what game they played.

When the lights went out, the electrifying sound of a single shot matched the almost inaudible "pop" of the silencer on his own 9mm Browning. Immediately Graham realized three possible targets for the other marksman - Thompson, in the auditorium, Edwards, at the podium, and the IRA woman in the balcony. Momentarily, before the blackout, he'd recognised the SAS 2 I/C - the Australian, Major Stephen Tracker, near the balcony. They had exchanged glances.

As the convoy now swept along, Graham's anger and impatience increased. By this time he was sure his targets had probably reached the Mournes. Graham waged his own clandestine war now, a silent warrior on another disclaimed top-secret mission. It was less than a week since he'd received the orders for the implementation of Plan Ajax. His other mission, 'snow drop' – the deliberate delivery of drugs into Ireland south. For Graham and his mentors, a drug addicted society was a further disincentive to a reunified Ireland. Dependency reinforced, the IRA demonised as the guilty party. In the Kafkaesque world of Star Chambers, the subversive agenda would be unaccountable.

Graham's assignment required dangerous commitment, entailing immeasurable risk. A standard Intelligence option, yet in this case absolving MI6 from what would be a criminal transaction, and for which Graham, disowned by MI6, could spend the rest of his life in jail, if not "silenced" in the process.

Graham glanced at the driver. Evans sat hunched forward, maroon beret pulled down to just above his eyes, intent on maintaining speed. I was there once, thought Graham.

His circuitous route to MI6 was not an easy road. Unlike others in MI6, Graham was not born to wealth or privilege, had not attended Public School or University. Growing up in a succession of orphanages, always at odds, he decided to join the regular army, a precocious eighteen year old, fresh out of Grammar School.

Within a year, a rebellious misfit, Graham transferred to Paras. Emerging first in his class - he was recruited to a different world, as an officer candidate to the elite ranks of Britain's best - the SAS. Graham had found his course and pride in a new identity and a new life. The regiment was the parent he'd never known.

In the following years Graham's aggressive drive was recognised, as he became a first choice for the "foreign mission" campaigns. From the mountains of Rhodesia, of Nicaragua, the Gulf to Mogadishu, he took part in strategic expeditions for the prized currencies of power. Graham had spent what felt like the whole of his life with 22 SAS. Here he won acclaim of a different sort - the nickname, "The Terminator". Finally for Graham, warrior was king.

The early disciples of PASS, those within the intelligence circles, had seen a role for Graham, his recruitment to the normally unattainable, exclusive ranks, the impregnable tribalism of the "old boys club", MI6. Graham, restless, ever seeking new dimensions, had watched the aggressive evolution of Britain First and the more furtive PASS. Feeling he could use his position in MI6 to further his own goals, he decided to accept their offer to join Britain First and PASS. He easily identified with the reassertion of power for supremacy and domain. Graham was confident he would attain the leadership role that seemed to beckon.

For Graham, Britain's MI6 and its traditions had a peculiar and well earned reputation. With their partners, the American intelligence services, NSA, their liaison officers formed a special relationship. Existing in their own shadow world, they set their own rules; their loyalties were their own choice and decision. Their creed, in the words of a former member of The Club, there is "no chain of command... it is the spy who is the main guardian of the nation's security." Graham, now among them.

Right now the focus of his anger, the Irish, were a recurring source of problems, every fifty years a focus of rebellion. His commitment was to Ajax, the final solution, a solution no less ruthless than the famines and the genocide of colonists of bygone years.

Graham knew the urgency of his mission; the window of opportunity could quickly close. Occasioned by Madam's death and by the other recent events, the international focus on terrorism might justify a radical anti-terrorist strategy. The public perception of the frightening threat of a global apocalypse would help to demonise the voice of nationalism from Ireland.

Graham felt sure he could speedily achieve his goals, despite the warnings of the gurus of Whitehall, to be discreet in counter terrorist tactics in Ireland. Too near home, too near the fractious and vocal European Courts of Human or Civil Rights.

Evans was slowing down. Graham saw the high razor wire fencing of the RAF base. The rain was easing off. Perhaps he could still talk them into a night operation. The element of surprise would surely be on their side.

In a rare moment of indulgence Graham smiled to himself. He knew which would prevail, *Utrinque Paratus,* ready for anything. Better yet - who dares, wins! Graham chuckled as Evans glanced nervously at him.

CHAPTER TWENTY-ONE

The Old Eagles of Slievenaglogh

"Ye'll know it soon as ye see it - the top of the big mountain, Slievenaman. Keep your eyes skinned. Right there ye'll take the first turn down into the glen. Clanawhillan and the Trassey River lie below." His mouth fixed in a toothless grin, the old man stood, oblivious to the pouring rain. "They'll be waitin' for ye. *Dia's Muire guit.*"

God and his mother be with you, the old man called as Jack drove away down the empty street, lit by the single street lamp, past the few shops and the row of cottages of Kilcoo. He drove cautiously in near pitch darkness, peering beyond the beam of the headlights to the narrow, winding road ahead. Jack had been this way once before many years ago. Much younger then, his father had taken him to visit his grandfather's grave, then to the ancestral family home.

Jack saw to his right the approaching bulk of Slievenaman. Ahead of him he saw a bobbing glimmer, two figures standing by the roadside, one holding a flashlight. He drew up alongside them, relieved to recognise the stocky figure of Dan. Jack emerged from the car.

Dan reached to shake his hand, introducing his younger friend. "Martin here'll take care of the car. We've a wee ways to go, you and I, on foot."

Jack followed Dan's striding figure down a rocky footpath beneath the trees. As on the plane, he heard the tuneful, impromptu song ahead of him; Dan, singing to himself. Noting the familiar stock of an Uzi carbine strapped across Dan's back - a favourite once with Special Forces in Vietnam - Jack realised the increasingly hazardous role he had inadvertently assumed in less than seventy-two hours.

211

Occasionally glancing over his shoulder, Dan spoke. "Your family was from this country they tell me. They'd be proud of you Jack. You did your best for poor Cormac - for all of us."

They stopped at an old stone wall. Dan's voice was gruff. "I had to carry her away. Theresa would have gone back for him. They'd have got all of us. It would have made his death a useless sacrifice. Thanks again for what you did – you're a brave man." He turned quickly, climbing the wall, Jack not far behind.

High above them, electrifying, a scream echoed among the mountains.

"That's the old eagle of Slievenaglough," said Dan. "They say she's lived up in these mountains for generations." He laughed. "They say she's been screaming across these mountains ever since the 'flight of the earls,' since the Irish chieftains left for Spain. She'll stop when her sons return, when the English are driven out."

On rising ground Dan broke into a steady loping trot, moving with easy grace. Jack hurried to catch up, breathing heavily. Not as fit as he used to be, he painfully recalled the same, enduring pace they'd travelled on night missions in Vietnam. Jack wondered where Dan had acquired the practice.

Just as Jack was about to call a halt and take a break, Dan called, "Gets easier, Jack, we're almost there." Finally Dan stopped. Jack stumbled up, panting. Dan grinned. "You did well, man." He raised a hand. "Listen." Jack heard the gurgling and rustling. "That's the Salmon's Leap."

Dan led the way across the short grass. The rushing of the falls grew louder. Easily hopping the fence, Dan turned to Jack, beckoning. From the clearing in the moonlight, Jack could see a high, arched stone bridge. Beneath the sturdy span he could hear the river's busy rush and gurgle. At the bridge Dan stopped.

"This is the Trassey River. This is where I leave you, Jack. Theresa will be coming down that path." He reached out his hand. "Take care, man."

Jack heard the long forgotten departing salute, "Gia Sao", as Dan disappeared up the path. He wondered where Dan might have picked up the Vietnamese expression.

Listening now for Theresa's approach, he recalled her different images; the quiet spoken nun in the terminal at Heathrow; then on the plane, the courageous young woman, confronting British security with such resolute self possession. Later at Queen's, her confident words provided an instant metamorphosis. And, she was a very beautiful woman. He was eager to see her again.

Over Slievenaman, a vault of pale stars in an ageless world bore silent witness to his return. Leaning on the parapet above the river, Jack's thoughts returned to the old man at Kilcoo. "They'll be waitin' for ye". He wondered had he meant not alone Dan, but the spirits of Jack's ancestors. Jack sensed the gathering of past generations among the shadows. He remembered his father's words, "From Tollymore Forest to Luke's Mountain - the garden of memories, and my father's house."

He saw their faces, some he'd heard of, some he'd known. His uncle Charlie, a red bearded bear of a man, a legendary hero of the "Tan" wars, his laughter, his songs hiding the torment of his memories. And strangely now, beside Charlie's face stood the haunting image of Cormac.

Jack had been cast centre stage, his cherished hypothesis, "alternatives to violence", now more tenuous. What had been quiet fireside recollections of bygone years - ancient folklore, bedtime stories, snapshots from a family album - all now suddenly, literally, exploded from myth to brutal reality.

"I see they failed to stop ye, Jack."

Startled, Jack turned.

She was chuckling as she spoke, the sound deep and low. He saw her, a darker shadow beneath the branches of the blackthorn. Without a sound Theresa moved toward him, her hands deep in the pockets of the bulky anorak, her head half covered in the hood, an Uzi over her shoulder. The scarf around her neck, the boots, all seemed too big for the small frame. So vulnerable, yet he remembered, in confrontation, so formidable.

She drew nearer. Jack stared, feeling foolish, his heart racing like a boy. As she came into the moonlight she reached out to him.

"I think I woke you from another world." The cloak fell from her head, her hair darker than the night, blowing in the breeze, her eyes shining, her smile radiant.

"I'd have thought Dan would have warned ye to never stand out in the moonlight. It's not too safe." She smiled mischievously.

He held the small, strong hands in his. "Theresa, you're safe, that's all that matters."

Her laughter, low and rich, at that moment filled his world. Remembering Thompson's warning, "a target high on the list," Jack knew he would do all in his power to protect her.

Catching his troubled expression, Theresa smiled, "Forget the old nightmares for now, Jack. Come on. Up the hill, they're waitin' for us." She looked back, laughing, "Don't worry, just a wee ways up the road."

Over Slievenaman the sky was clearer now. The full moon rode stray rags of storm clouds far above the Mournes. In the half-light, they watched their footsteps along the rocky path. Theresa looked back, "The summers and the winters come and go - and the great rock face bears no mark of our passing. Makes ye think doesn't it?" She stopped, pointing ahead. "We're finally home, Jack."

In a gathering of gnarled old trees stood a low roofed farmhouse. Jack saw the rough stone walls, the dim light from its deep-set windows; above the roof, a drift of smoke from the stunted chimney. An old sheepdog slowly came forward to greet them. Standing in the light from the open door Jack saw two figures: the tall, upright frame of an older man - the other a boy. Both were calling greetings as they crossed the yard.

Theresa introduced Jack. "We're all family here, Jack. Seanoge, the young one, and his grandfather, Sean McCarton. The Seanache," she added proudly, "the wise one".

The older man reached for Jack's hand, modestly protesting, "I often wonder why they call me that - they don't listen to me any easier." He laughed.

The Seanache, of childhood stories and memories - one and the same. Indeed Jack had heard from his uncle and his father the name of this legendary figure in the perpetual Irish struggle. A sturdy older man, windblown white hair, weathered face, troubled smile. Jack had heard how the Seanache's endless efforts to bring the travesty of the British occupation of Northern Ireland before the eyes of the world, had earned him the unrelenting hostility of the Anglophile constituency. Always pitted against him were the unremitting efforts of British propaganda to demonise him as a dangerous terrorist. Jack wondered at the ageless energy of the man, surprised by the vigour and strength of his grip.

The Seanache's eyes narrowed as he leaned close. "I know who ye are Jack. Before ye came we heard of the talk ye were to give. Theresa told me ye did well. But on the plane, Jack, that was somethin' else. In the words of the ancient Jewish Talmud, Jack: 'Whoever saves one life, saves the world'".

Quickly switching to easy laughter, the Seanache invited Jack into the old farmhouse. Intermittently lit by reflections of leaping flame and shadow from the great open fireplace, it was clearly a home, a place of friends and family. Here were the roots of the generational Irish Diaspora, with their memories of hard times, of the penal years, the persecution and famine.

Theresa caught Jack's troubled gaze as she reached to unstrap the Uzi from her shoulder. Turning away she placed it on a shelf beside her. She was smiling again as she asked Jack, "Would ye care to join us in a bowl of hot soup, to warm your bones - a drop of spirits to warm your blood?"

Seated before the welcome warmth of the open hearth, Jack answered, "That would be great. To warm the bones, stir the blood - that would be just fine."

"It's the chill and the damp will slow ye down over here," said the Seanache, adding dark bricks of peat to the glowing hearth. Young Seanoge filled the glasses as Theresa poured the thick, hot soup. Jack watched her. Bustling about, she was the focus of all the warmth and good cheer. Theresa, again a person of many roles - now the homemaker.

"They called again, Theresa," Seanoge was saying. "Granddad answered." Trying to sound casual, the Seanache responded, "It was from Willie again. Nothin' new. They'll be into the mountains at first light, with helicopters." He glanced quickly at Jack, smiling to conceal his concern.

"Same as always," said Theresa, also trying to sound reassuring. "Who knows? There could be a heavy fog across the mountains in the mornin' - enough to keep them grounded for a while."

She handed each of them a glass of whiskey. Sharing their first toast to "health", they each proposed a toast - the Seanache, to "friends and family" - and Jack, warmed by the occasion and the amber spirits, to "Ireland".

Looking down at young Sean, an arm around his shoulders, Theresa smiled protectively, gave him a quick kiss. She laughed. "There's one man well fed, and well past his bedtime! Seanoge, time for sleep."

Climbing the narrow stairway at the end of the big room, Sean asked, "Grandfather, we're Irish - an' Jack's American, isn't he?" The Seanache nodded. "Aye, Seanoge. But Jack is both - the best of him's Irish, the rest's American!"

Young Sean joined in their laughter. Moving slowly up the stairs, looking over at Jack, he called, "Tomorrow we'll take ye to the falls - show ye the Salmon's Leap - right, Theresa?"

"Right, Sean." Theresa added, "Say your prayers and sleep well, love."

Seating herself beside Jack, Theresa spoke, grittily trying to smile. "So brave. Some months ago young Sean's father, Frank, was killed fighting in South America. Dan was with him, lucky to survive." She turned her head, wiping away a tear. The stewardess you met on the plane, Sheila, that's Sean's mother, Frank's widow. Sean's story is only one of many. But the situation, as ye know, is rapidly getting worse."

"Like everything else, Jack, there's more to it than ye see." The Seanache shifted in his chair. "A brave, hard life. What a savage waste. I have been where young Sean is today, many long years ago - my father murdered and my life in disarray." He paused.

Her eyes appealing, Theresa asked, "What is the answer, Jack? It's easier said than done. I believed your words at Queen's. As ye say, the hard-core establishment knows how to set them one against the other." Theresa's voice now sounded angry. "An' Frank an' Cormac must die - an' every other mother's son - at the hands of these mindless janissaries!"

The Seanache's eyes filled with a world of sadness. "We're sorry, Jack, that ye return to such grief – an' no end in sight."

"Don't apologise," Jack answered quickly. "This seems to be why I'm here now. To seek a path to resolution - for Cormac, for Frank; for Dan and for Theresa."

Outside, the rising wind rattled the window frames, creaking the joists and beams of the old farmhouse. The sheepdog rose, padded his way from the hearth to place his muzzle on the old man's knee. The old man reached to rub the old dog's ears.

"You've already done more than anyone could ask with your talks, but that's the way of it - reason to ask ye to do more - too few of us are left." Jack watched the firelight play across the lined, earnest face, the dark, anguished eyes.

"Madam's assassination, though I can tell ye we'd no hand in it - was a lucky accident, but there are other deeply troubling matters. Following the murder of the British agent and his wife in Paris there is word, Jack, of a 'hit list', selected Irish Republicans. Ajax they call it. And with the transition of Hong Kong to Chinese administration, there's further news of a brewing global scandal, based in Hong Kong. The so-called 'China Scheme'. With the sabotage of the American plane over Scotland some hours ago, all these events Jack, I believe, are linked. British Intelligence, it seems, is involved in all spheres."

Jack and Theresa waited as the Seanache sipped his drink. He stirred restlessly in his chair, then rose to throw more peat on the fire.

"Your presence, Jack, is most fortunate. We've helped to wind it up, and the clock, it seems, is about to strike. Time to tell the world the story. Such an opportunity might never come again. Just over twenty-four hours ago I returned from a hasty visit with John Maloney, the Taoiseach, an' members of his government. I've had little time to talk about this - even with Theresa, since my return." He glanced worriedly into the smouldering flames.

"In my lifelong struggle to free my country - to return the voice and vote to all the people of Ireland, I've been a fugitive, Jack, always in the shadow of the hunter an' his paid assassins. And," he added grimly, "in that I'm never alone."

CHAPTER TWENTY-TWO

The Third Nemesis

His deep penetrating voice almost a whisper, the Seanache leaned forward, gripping the arms of the chair. "For over sixty years now, Jack, I've been on the run, in search of weapons, financial and other support to achieve our national goals. An' those from MI5, MI6, my first nemesis, they've followed me, intelligence services and other hired assassins from abroad. More recently, from drug runners in the Middle East." Jack saw Theresa's troubled expression as the Seanache described his experiences with British agents, SAS to SIS, he'd confronted through the years.

"I've led 'em on a long chase, Jack," the Seanache laughed, "always one step ahead." He looked from Jack to Theresa. "Suddenly the shadows grow taller, new ones I don't even recognise."

He paused, his voice almost pleading, "I need more time. I'm not getting any younger." Seeing the fear in Theresa's eyes, "Age, my second nemesis, love. A fact of life. It's taken a lifetime to find the truth. And, God help me, Jack, I've lived to tell it!"

The Seanache looked at Jack, his head slowly nodding. "As ye spoke of it at Queen's, Jack, it's a heritage of hatred to deceive our young; to have them kill one another. In the past century, callous sacrifice of their own military lads, sent to their deaths in the swamps of the West Indies or the mud holes of Verdun, the Somme.

"I've told the southern government the time will never be more favourable. The Brits no longer have exclusive control of the media. They can't mislead the public now. In a world of quickly changin' values, people are no longer hesitant to challenge what has stood for proper government. With instant media cover, televised or computerised British deception and murder can be exposed."

Restlessly the old man paced, his eyes peering into the shadows. He thanked Theresa as she refilled his glass. Seated again, he leaned back in his chair.

"The southern government over the years has largely been indifferent to our plight, at times a sceptical or reluctant partner to the 'northern colony'." He looked from Jack to Theresa, hands on his knees, his gaze intense. "I told the Taoiseach, Maloney, of the threat of Ajax; my own name and Theresa's among the targets." Jack wondered where the Seanache, and Bob Thompson, had learned of the British Intelligence plot.

Unable to repress his excitement, his voice a harsh, conspiratorial whisper, the Seanache stared from one to the other. "Finally, I told Maloney and members of his cabinet the truth I'd uncovered. Evidence of British deception in the infamous Treaty negotiations of 1921, a deception that involved a love affair between Lady Edwina Granart and Michael Collins.

"'The Chief', they called him. Collins recruited his own close disciples - the Apostles, hard men he could trust. My father, a young man then, was one of those twelve. The Chief and my father, among others, were selectively murdered in the civil war that followed the Treaty negotiations. Recently I found out how and why they died. The same games, Jack, that are being played across the world today."

Shadows leapt about the walls, the turf flared and smouldered – voices, living half forgotten memories.

"This Jack, was a segregated society, east to west. The multi-headed Medusa - in which Collins, the socially naïve, brawling, fearless Irish country boy - was surely out of his depth. In December of 1921 Collins found himself, with his colleagues in London, negotiating the freedom of the whole island of Ireland. The Irish team, inexperienced and already divided among themselves, now fumbled, faltered and anguished."

Once more restless, the Seanache rose and paced - hands in his pockets, shoulders bowed. "With Lloyd George's threat of all out war, Collins and his fellow emissaries were outfoxed.

Collins, convinced there was little alternative, also persuaded by the beautiful Lady Granart and her friend, a young Irish peer, finally yielded. Cunningly deceived, Collins and Griffiths, troubled and confused - each signed copies of the 'treaty' – each, later found different from the final version. Both misled, the Lady Granart told me."

Resuming his seat, the old man sadly described the final tragedy. "Within six months of the signing of the treaty, Collins, Griffiths and my father were dead. Collins and my father were assassinated, their silence too important to leave to chance. Their murder, I learned, arranged by British intelligence."

"What happened to the others?" Theresa asked in a low voice.

The Seanache answered in a tone of quiet wonder. "The beautiful widow Granart remained a recluse, lived with her secret to a great age. Too late she realised her love for Collins. In growing self recrimination, intent on some day exacting vengeance and resolution, she kept a journal of the intrigue, the assassinations. It was the only true account, other than those in secret British archives.

"She sent for me some months ago. By her own confession I learned of her callous enticement of the infatuated young Collins, misleading his overburdened conscience, betraying his trust. Sadly she described how she had anguished when she learned of his assassination, and that of my father, his friend."

"When I returned to read Lady Granart's diaries, I was too late. She had died suddenly, her papers left in trust to the estate of her long dead friend, the Irish peer. I assumed the further evidence might forever be denied me. I thought I'd reached the end of my journey. And now with the help of others such as yourself, Jack, I have enough support perhaps, to have Lady Granart's papers released, the deception revealed."

A shadow seemed to cross the old man's face. His tone troubled, he now spoke of others who continue to follow him, his 'third nemesis' - those from Europe and the Middle East, possibly from missions in which he had been involved for too many years.

"They have some evil men there, dealing in drugs and lives." The Seanache's face broke into an uneasy smile. "The Brits, my first nemesis. My years, my second. The third, that is another story." He gazed into the fire.

Theresa rose from the table, took the bowls to the sink, then poured two glasses of whiskey and set them beside the two men.

"The Irish peer, what became of him?" she asked. "The surviving heirs - those who hold her papers?"

The old man slowly nodded, remembering, "He was elevated to the rank of Earl, to reward him, or to ensure his silence. Later, a conscience in remorse perhaps, he rejected the society that had nurtured his role among the Irish ascendancy. He was forgotten, spent his remaining years drinking. He died, his story untold."

He leaned forward, his expression troubled. "I learned the heir to his title had run into some trouble in England, had joined American forces and was declared missing in action in the Vietnam War. He was the last Earl of Clanrickard. There were no surviving heirs."

The words left Jack stunned.

CHAPTER TWENTY-THREE

'Who Dares Wins'
Motto of the SAS

More than forty miles to the north, in the pre-dawn darkness, the RAF station at Bangor awakened to the disciplined hustle of a new day.

Graham's efforts the night before to persuade Wing Commander Hawkins to undertake a late night "recce" into the Mournes had been unsuccessful. Hawkins had been adamant. He had no interest in risking the lives of his pilots. He did promise however, to undertake the operation at first light, weather permitting.

Graham had tossed restlessly all night. Again facing the woman on the plane, he'd hesitated. The fatal pause. Her eyes cold, smiling; he'd felt the life draining impact of the rounds, tearing bone and tissue, spilling his lifeblood across the floor.

Suddenly he found himself wide-awake, sweating. He wondered why he hadn't shot the IRA woman while he had the chance. Shoot to kill, as he'd learned as a Para recruit. Perhaps he'd been unsure of his ground. With a return of fire, the whole plane would fall, a flaming Roman candle into the Irish Sea. Perhaps he was getting too old for the job.

He rose early, long before the first stealthy glow of sunrise from the distant Scottish coast. Hurriedly, he shaved and dressed, resuming his secretly comforting other image: uniformed anonymity, Dennison smock, buff beret with winged dagger badge - Graham, cool hunter-killer of the SAS. In the cold, damp mist he headed for the flight operations centre.

Psyched to go, Graham was impatient to get the job done. His thoughts briefly returned to the encounter he'd had with Stephen Tracker, second in command, a last minute replacement. The officer originally assigned had gone missing

223

the morning the SAS unit took off from Aldershot. Graham had been given the information only hours before the 2 I/C joined the unit.

The Australian, Tracker, was unusual in that his experience exceeded Graham's. He had seen service in the last years of the Vietnam War, and had been since assigned to other missions, classified details, especially in areas of Southeast Asia. The resumé described expertise in regional dialects, and in the use of rocket projectile technology.

Stephen Tracker seemed familiar with the situation in Northern Ireland, and more than familiar with the names of those on the "list". Remembering Tracker's questions about Sean McCarton and "Sister" Theresa, Graham had commenced to fabricate his report, shrewdly connecting both "Sister" Theresa and Dan McSorley to Madam's assassination, saying they had been spotted arriving at Heathrow that same night. Tracker had made no comment as Graham concocted his elaborate fantasy.

As he proceeded now toward the Flight Control Centre, Graham refined the script. Both Sister Theresa and Dan were suspects with other accomplices in Paris in the killing of the Weatherbys. Graham had just such a likely accomplice in mind - an IRA leader now living in Paris. Things might well work out. He'd done it before and the gamble had paid off.

He allowed himself the momentary indulgence. He saw himself, from the silent ranks of the unseen heroes of SAS, receiving the accolades from a grateful nation. Foremost, the solution of the Northern Irish problem. A smile crossed his lips. The irony, the Borstal boy on the New Year's Honours Lists. As those in PASS might see it, a well-deserved recognition for assisting almost single-handed in the restoration of Madam's posthumous strategy, Ajax.

Listening earlier to a news broadcast, Graham had been surprised to hear, among those who died in the 747 over Kilbrannon Sound, a name he remembered, Victor Perry, a curiously strong proponent of the China Scheme. Graham wondered, was it sabotage, and why so soon after Madam's assassination? Whatever the stories implicating the IRA, it was least likely in this case.

There emerged the distracting possibility of another player. He felt a cold, untrusting premonition. For Graham, no other trust existed outside of Special Forces. No forgiveness, no prisoners – that was his creed. Outside their cloistered, furtive, Spartan ranks existed another world, different values: many faces showing a different deception.

The single story structure of OPS bustled with the restrained urgency of imminent departures. The prefab frame building resounded to the static echo of brief personnel announcements. Graham strode through the swing doors, studying the scene. He searched for his unit.

The now familiar figure of the Australian, Tracker, emerged from a nearby room. Without preliminary greeting, he called to Graham.

"The lads have eaten. They're assembling on the tarmac." Tracker led the way up the corridor, coolly ignoring the salutes of the passing airmen and NCOs. His accent was a broad caricature of Graham's own cockney twang. "The OPS bloke says they'll have us out within the hour."

Graham said nothing. He was irritated with the Australian's cold authority and arrogance. Tracker had shown a complete lack of deference to Graham's seniority as Lt. Colonel. Tracker was obviously not intimidated.

Though he knew he might have to count on Tracker's cooperation and discretion at some point, Graham was bothered by the uneasy feeling that he couldn't control this man. He felt a momentary urge to reach for shared ground, shared loyalty.

"Lost too many SAS over here. Owe it to the corps not to fuck up. An eye for an eye, right Major?" With no response, Graham forged on, adding recklessly, "Needless to say Major, should you make a target sighting, don't hesitate. Shoot to kill." Tracker just nodded.

Several young pilot officers stood idly chatting by the door to Wing Commander Hawkins' office. They fell silent on Tracker and Graham's approach. Several of the pilot officers came to attention, saluting as they saw the discreet ranking insignia of both men. Graham reflexively returned the salutes.

Tracker gave no response.

Graham had little use for the cavalier helicopter jocks with their jokes, flippant references to occupational hazards. In spite of extensive combat experience, Graham had a well-guarded secret - an enduring fear of flying. Only his conditioned, steely resolve and competitive pride enabled him to complete his jumps with Paras over the years, without revealing his phobia. No one had suspected his white knuckled, breathless terror as he rose in flight, or worse, fell under a billowing chute.

"Morning gentlemen." The brusque, cheery greeting came from Hawkins as he opened the door of his office."We'll be ready to move in about thirty minutes." As the pilots joined them, he added, "Weather conditions have improved. Predictions are for a raised ceiling, fair visibility over the Mournes for the next few hours." To Graham's irritation Hawkins seemed to be addressing Tracker.

"Have your group ready over by C building."

"The men will be ready," Tracker replied, "I'll take one group and Lt. Colonel Graham the other." He turned to Graham as if for confirmation. "As you suggested last night, I've arranged with the wing commander for our unit to be flown in two groups to Newcastle. From Newcastle we'll make our sweep into the Mournes, staying in contact with the land unit." Graham had no choice but to nod in agreement.

Graham was irritable. Bloody Australians, an aggressive lot. Tracker must have made his arrangements before Graham had risen. The Australian was taking over the operation without properly consulting him.

Hawkins moved to the door. "We'll be taking the Chinooks to Newcastle and two smaller Sea Kings for your mission into the Mournes." Graham and Tracker nodded, then turned to leave.

They walked with heads bent to a light rain. Increasingly irritated, Graham hoped the Irish drizzle might let up by the time they reached Newcastle. If visibility remained poor they would be reduced to combing the Mournes from trucks and on foot. The chances of sighting their target would be significantly reduced.

Ahead of them the distant limits of the airfield took shape. In the eerie blue fluorescence of the arc lights they saw two transport Chinooks, rain-slick and camouflaged, their huge, weighted rotor blades poised for lift off. The sudden whine and roar of the starting engines fired and inspired the two men like restless predators.

Suddenly, unexpectedly, the *Times* journalist, Bob Thompson, appeared. Thompson insisted on accompanying them, on the strength of his special security press permit. Wing Commander Hawkins felt Thompson's high national profile left little option but to include him on the mission. Graham and Tracker saw it differently.

The exchange between Graham and Thompson quickly deteriorated to a violent argument. Thompson, insisting on his rights as a member of a free press, with top clearance, threatened to contact "friends" in Whitehall and the Northern Ireland Office. Graham hastily relented, offering to have Thompson accompany the motorised units from Rathfriland. Thompson, unfazed, insisted on a place with the aerial patrol.

The Australian, Tracker, adamantly rejected Thompson, calmly explaining that the safety of the men was his concern. Under no circumstances would he permit Thompson on his aircraft. Out of options, Graham reluctantly agreed to have the journalist on his flight.

The SAS troopers boarded, trailing their bergens, SLRs, automatic rifles, ammo pouches across their backs. The SAS were a mixed bag, wayward adolescents, soccer thugs, cast-offs in an underprivileged society. Some of them, like Graham, were ex-Paras or ex-Territorials, members of a fit, "enabled" group of rational killers. Or as they preferred it, the "warrior elite" Stirling had once envisaged from World War II. Glad now to be on target, they shuffled aboard, the camouflage paint glistening on their faces below the buff berets.

Tracker had given them their orders. Each knew the designation of "Provies" as targets, the clear implications. In the dim lit interior of the Chinook they sat silent, wiping the rain from the barrels of their cherished "bunduks". The vaunted image, "ready squadron", prepared for the only options they knew - to sleep, to eat, to fuck, to kill.

Graham and Tracker crouched, holding onto their berets in the sudden down draught as the huge rotor blades picked up, spinning above their heads. They glanced at one another - mouths open, words lost in the thunder of the engines. As they separated, unheard by Graham, Tracker called, *"Gia Sao"*, then to himself, "My last fuckin' job!"

White knuckled, Graham gripped the sides of his seat. In the other Chinook, Tracker laughed to himself. This day would bring him release and reward to keep him in luxury the rest of his life. No time lost since his assignment. All goals so far secured.

The Chinook slowly rose, then, nose down, surged forward. Graham clenched his teeth, eyes closed. The hunters - both worlds apart - were on their way.

CHAPTER TWENTY-FOUR

The Fairy Ring

It was well after midnight when the old man concluded his story. "Enough," he said with a deep sigh, "Enough for now."

Turning to Theresa, he hugged her, smiled. "I know, I never spoke of this before. But, 'tis said, there is a time to every purpose under heaven." He turned to Jack. "The night's half gone. But if ye've a mind to it, Theresa's goin' to take ye' to see Clanawhillun, home of your family for almost four hundred years. Farmers, Jack; in war and peace they persisted with poor crops, no crops and famine."

Once again Theresa guided Jack along the rough path, almost invisible beneath the fern and bracken. Above the rumble of the falls, Jack listened to Theresa's breathless words of admiration for the Seanache. "I had thought he was indestructible, till tonight. He trusts you, Jack."

Hearing the warmth in her voice, Jack felt his own admiration for the courage and purpose of this woman.

Theresa stopped to catch her breath. "Why the surprised expression when the Seanache mentioned the Earl of Clanrickard, Jack? Had ye heard of him before?"

"It is an extraordinary coincidence, Theresa. The Earl of Clanrickard I'd known was my close friend, Paddy Finucane. We served together in Vietnam. A small world indeed! Sadly, as the Seanache learned, Paddy was listed missing in action - never returned from a mission."

Theresa took hold of Jack's hand, guiding him along the wet path. "Here it is, Jack, Clanawhillun. 'The glen of the holly leaves'."

They walked across the cobbled yard. Jack pushed on the

sturdy wooden door beneath the shadowed lintel. Lodged with generations of cobwebs, weeds and dust, the ancient structure slowly yielded.

"The return of the prodigal son - feels like they've been waiting for us."

"Makes you wonder, Jack, what was it like?" Their hushed tones echoed throughout the empty house.

Standing beside her in the musty room, Jack wondered indeed what it would have been like. Theresa smiled, listening to Jack's whispered words, sharing the scene the way it might have been. Beneath the great lintel stone lay the empty hearth, where fires of logs and turf had burned for over three hundred years. Hanging from the great iron hob, steaming pots of soup or stew boiled for the family meal. Before the blazing hearth they gathered, to warm their feet and hands before the sun had risen; the children on their way to school; the men to the fields. The older ones standing or seated by the fireplace, and the younger children playing about the stone floored rooms, or running and laughing up the narrow stairway, watched by his father and mother.

Grandfather and Grandmother too, in smile and talk, in song and in laughter, in sorrow and in joy. Too often, scenes of departure, to America or elsewhere, some never to return - the inevitable bereavements, or again, the occasion of happy celebrations, birthdays, baptisms, the shy weddings and the summer night dances. Theresa could almost hear the clapping of hands, the rhythmic clatter of agile feet.

One arm around her now, Jack looked down at her. "We return to the spirits of generations - to tell them our story, Theresa, to see them, as they now see us."

They imagined the great room in flickering candlelight. From the shadows by the doorway, happy faces crowded in. They could see his father's broad smile as he introduced Jack and Theresa. In the corner by the fireplace, Jack saw his mother's warm smile, her eyes shining with pride and love.

"They'd truly be proud of ye, Jack," said Theresa softly. She saw his intensity, his eyes fixed on hers.

"And they'd think I was a very lucky man, Theresa, to

have met you."

Without hesitation she responded quietly, "Me too." She laughed shyly.

Jack looked down at her in the dim light. Seeing her now, her dark hair falling in loose curls about her shoulders, she seemed so frail in the bulky folds of the anorak. He held her more tightly. She looked up at him, her expression strangely at peace.

"This struggle in Ireland, Jack, it's my life. We owe it to them. We can't abandon their sacrifices. This is a great burden for you to share, makes it very difficult for you in your position. You owe your loyalties to another country now, to other responsibilities."

Jack smiled. "It's my commitment now to you, and to the principles we both share. I've discovered that you can't happily compromise your standards of morality, justice, fairness and truth, no matter what your documented nationality. And that is also my career, Theresa. To make the world a better place, where successive wars have only proven how useless they are in resolving any problem. God knows, if we can't make it work here, we won't make it work anywhere else." Suddenly self-conscious, "Sorry, I got carried away. But don't forget, this is my home too."

Theresa turned to face him. "Since I first introduced myself to you as Sister Theresa, I knew I could care a great deal for you, Jack."

She buried her face in his shoulder, then looked up, her eyes twinkling, gently teasing, "Ye get carried away very well, Jack. I listened to ye before, remember? And just as when I heard it at Queen's, your words made me realise how lucky I am to have you with us."

Grasping her gently by the shoulders, looking into her eyes, Jack spoke quietly, "Theresa, you have really brought me home. Your life has become mine." He held her tightly, his mouth in her hair, whispering her name.

Strangers only three days ago, three thousand miles apart, they kissed, cherishing something neither expected in two such passionately dedicated, committed lives. Priorities hadn't changed, only modified, merged, and now shared. Both recognised the tenuous partnership, realising their fears for each other, and their unlikely future. Faintly they heard the chuckling, gurgling waters of the Salmons' Leap, and nearer, the Trassey River, chattering on its course to the beaches of Newcastle.

Suddenly Jack spoke, his voice eager, excited. "There's something I'd like to show you. Something I remember from family folklore." He led Theresa to the deeply recessed window. Standing close, his arms around her, they peered through the cobwebbed, broken panes, looking out across the still dark valley. The rain was easing. The moonlight drew delicate patterns of light and shadow through the grimy panes, dancing past the branches and across the floor as Jack pointed beyond the house. In the moonlight above the mist, Theresa saw the solitary ring of dark trees rising from a surrounding low wall of stones and shrubbery.

"The Fairy Ring. Just as my father described it," said Jack, "cherished relics of the past that have endured." He laughed. "Another family secret you and I now share. In the Penal times, he told us, gathering from nearby farms beneath those trees and within the stone circle is where they hid, to celebrate Mass with the fugitive priest.

"The Fairy Ring, my father told me, where his own father had sworn the spirits of the little people still lived. To harm the trees would bring bad luck, he said. My father, as a boy, once dared to defy the old superstitions, carving his name on the bark of one of the trees." Jack laughed again. "For my father, the spell was broken, for his father the spell was cast. They were forever at odds with one another from that day forward. Happy days, so quickly gone."

Theresa quietly shared her own memories. An only child, her father died when she was young. Yet she spoke cheerfully of the hardship of their lives, of her mother's undiminished optimism. Her mother had raised her with a love of history, reading to her stories of Ireland's heroes, of her own heritage, her dedication to Ireland's fight for freedom. Her mother had special pride in Theresa's admission to Queen's, won with scholarships; her joy in knowing, before she died, of

Theresa's commitment to the national cause. The "educated commitment", her mother believed, was the real key to resolution. "It was hard to deny the resort to violence," Theresa said. "A futile option, yet one we couldn't change." Theresa turned to stare toward the window.

She described her mother's stoic acceptance; to give your life for such a cause was only second to that of the religious vocation. As she would remind Theresa, to "take the veil or to swear the oath" was the ultimate goal that anyone could aspire to. For her and her generation, there would be no compromise.

Jack's fears for Theresa's safety were growing. He saw the same willing spirit as Cormac's, as Mairead's, pulsing within her. As with the hunger strikers, Theresa would not hesitate to use the ultimate weapon, to see the dream realised, justice achieved. Gratefully Jack accepted that she wanted to assist in its delivery, rather than give her life for it. Convinced a new era was dawning, a new voice emerging, perhaps she and Jack might achieve this together. He gazed toward the fairy ring, as if searching for an answer.

It's unreal, thought Jack. My family's past reaches out to draw me back into the struggle, first with violence, and now with overwhelming love for this woman, on whose small shoulders the mantle has fallen to continue the fight.

"As though all my life was a preparation for this day," he said aloud. Secure in his arms, Theresa smiled.

The wind sighed down the empty chimney. Daylight would in all probability bring in the hunters. Jack knew the significance of the choice he had made. Instinctively, he felt the conditions had already been set, realised full well the scope of their Herculean task.

In the cool first light, the old farmhouse, sunk in the heathered, granite hillside, peered blindly across the glen. Far above the harsh, granite peak of Luke's Mountain, the moon was still visible in the west; to the east, a misty morning sky hung above the Mournes. In a moment of love and warmth the old home had not seen in a hundred years, the silence of Clanawhillun seemed unbroken, in a world of heather, gorse and summer flowers.

CHAPTER TWENTY-FIVE

A Still Primitive World

The clattering racket of the helicopters echoed across the waters of Dundrum Bay as they flew beneath the grey cumulus clouds. Nearing the temporary base at Newcastle, the tense figure of Graham sat hunched, rigidly gripping the sides of his seat. He swore as the aircraft swung in the gusts.

Thirty minutes later, in the Mournes, the sun had risen, sending flickering leaf shadows across the rough walls and ceilings of the ancient, weathered farmhouse. Jack and Theresa watched as a faint mist rose from the river, so that the trees appeared to float suspended above the valley floor. Through the fairy ring a light breeze set the leaves to whispering.

In Jack's arms, Theresa started. "Jack, listen!" She broke away from his embrace. "Helicopters!" Theresa hurried for the door.

Jack could hear it, unmistakable. How quickly Theresa had changed, her face pale and tense, her expression cold, remote. He struggled to drag the old door open.

Pulling his jacket on, Jack followed Theresa across the cobbled yard, running for the path across the hillside.

"My God, Jack we've got to move fast! I hope Dan an' the others are alert."

They listened as they ran, trying to hear above the sound of their stumbling footsteps, panting breath. The clattering chorus rose and fell. Jack knew they were flying a reconnaissance pattern, peering across the glens, slowly, inexorably progressing toward them.

His throat dry, heart pounding, Jack was literally on the run, less than seventy-two hours after his arrival in Ireland. A fugitive – *apatrides* and without the law, victim of the

234

clandestine world of terror and assassination. Everything he had experienced had grimly confirmed the Seanache's testimony. Legs aching and breathing hard, he strained for the shelter of the farmhouse.

Ahead, standing in the doorway, the Seanache frantically waved them on. They ran for the house. The Sea Kings paused momentarily above. Jack saw Sean McCarton's worried frown as he turned to bolt the door. The racketing clatter seemed to shift back toward the falls.

Theresa's voice broke in. "Seanache, the boy, Seanoge, where is he?"

Anxiously they glanced about. They headed for the stairs, calling the boy's name, with no answer. The Seanache stopped halfway up the stairs, then glanced back, his expression horrified. Pointing to the open back door, "He was there before I went to let ye' in." He was shouting now, staring wildly from one to the other. "He's out there. Where could he be?"

The old man looked around. "Theresa - the armalite - where is it? I left it on the table. It's gone!" Then a frightened, "Jesus, no. God willing, he can't be too far!" Ignoring Jack's warnings, Theresa's pleas, the Seanache ran across the yard, then disappeared beneath the trees.

Theresa grabbed her weapon and started for the door. Jack intercepted and gently took the Uzi from her grasp. "Theresa, one of us must stay, the boy might come back." He saw her mixed expression of anger, fear, of love. Reluctantly, she agreed.

"Wait here for us!" With that he was out the door.

Moving quickly, Jack called the boy's name, focusing between the trees and occasionally upwards. A light mist still lay across the path and the glen. The Uzi held high across his chest, Jack reflexively checked the safety. Legs aching, he ran the familiar pattern.

No sooner had he left the cover of the trees when, high on the bare slopes of Slievenaman, Jack saw two figures. Even at that distance, he knew it was young Sean, struggling upward toward the cloud line, the armalite clutched in his small fists. Not far beneath and closing came the Seanache, his white hair a windblown halo.

Filling the glen with the ominous clatter and whine of engines, the helicopters came sweeping over Luke's Mountain. Jack quickly stood, desperately waving his arms and shouting. Undeterred, the aircraft swept toward the moving figures on Slievenaman. Appalled, Jack heard the rapid fire of machine guns, saw the smoke trail, the lethal stream swiftly engulfing the climbing figures. He saw the boy go down.

Hearing a scream of agony from behind him, he turned to see Theresa emerging from the tree line. Jack broke into a run. Crossing the rocky bottom of the valley, wading and stumbling through a small stream, he emerged on the slopes of the mountain. He saw the boy struggling to stand, arms steadying the armalite. Incredibly, he fired at the thundering helicopter above him, then fell forward.

By the fallen figure of the boy the Seanache picked up the weapon. A wild figure, biblical - braced against the slope. Bullets churned the ground around him, striking the old man, throwing him into the air.

Cursing, Jack dropped to his knee on the rocky slope. Bracing the Uzi against his shoulder he fired in long bursts, aiming for the auxiliary tanks beneath the missile pods. Emptying the magazine into the murderous, rocking shape now hovering beneath the summit of Slievenaman, he heard the roar of the second aircraft approaching.

Above the thunder of both aircraft, Jack heard a great shout. Looking across the valley he saw the masked figure of Dan emerge below the cloud line. Rocket launcher to his shoulder, Dan fired; the missile flamed skyward.

Jack heard the deafening explosion, felt the shock waves, saw the rain of debris from the helicopter. The second helicopter seemed to hesitate, then fired one long burst in the direction of Dan. Moving toward Jack, the aircraft fired a short burst, then rose abruptly, disappearing into the clouds.

Jack fell to his knees, dropping his weapon. Feeling the pain in his shoulder, seeing the blood on his arm, he realised he'd been hit. Rising slowly, he saw Theresa and Dan climbing toward him. Stumbling through the gorse toward the still figures of the boy and the Seanache, Jack heard only an awful silence, louder and more ominous than the devastating explosion of the helicopter.

He reached the Seanache, his tattered figure sprawled across the hillside. The debt had been called. Jack was anguished at the terrible waste.

Theresa ran past, calling Seanoge's name. She bent over the still figure of the boy, then turned to Jack. "He's alive! Quick, let's get him to the house."

Jack bent to check the boy. Sean was bleeding from a chest wound, breathing with difficulty. Theresa asked, tears in her eyes, "The Seanache's gone, Jack?" Rising, Jack nodded. Seeing the blood on his shoulder, Theresa asked, "Are you all right?"

"It's not serious. I'm O.K. It's the boy I'm worried about."

Dan approached with a grim expression.

"The Seanache's gone Dan. The boy might make it, if we can get him to hospital. Let's get him to the house. We'll call for air transport, the car may be too slow."

They clambered down the hillside, Dan carrying Seanoge, Theresa and Jack close behind.

Beyond the silent valley, in Saracen, truck and staff car they came - the "lunatic fringe" – Paras, Constabulary, the SAS 'Strike Force'. And across the bleak, heathered slopes of Slievenaglogh, the scream of the old eagles - timeless refrain in a still primitive world - echoed and re-echoed.

Landing at Newcastle, the heavy thud of rotors subsided, the shrill whine of turbines whispered to silence. The cabin door slid open with a crash. Sunlight poured in. A member of the ground crew peered blindly inside. "Awright in 'ere?"

Graham moved quickly to the doorway. Another mission a total disaster. How ironic that Thompson had been assigned to his flight. Graham wished the journalist had ended up with the Australian, ashes in the Mournes. Ever the ultimate professional, Graham was already anticipating the next step, busily devising his story.

Equally in his own world, Bob Thompson shed his shoulder harness and wrestled his bulk from the seat across the aisle, emerging into the warm sunlight. Thompson made his way toward the trailers and Nissen huts, the temporary command post.

Wing Commander Hawkins sat listening to the pilot's rambling account of the recce into the Mournes. The shaken pilot recounted the shouted commands of the intelligence officer ordering him to move in. Troubled and ashamed, he described his efforts to control both himself and his aircraft.

"I heard this struggle back in the cabin. The journalist an' the Lt. Colonel were goin' at it." He had contacted the base at that point, calling Hawkins for direction. In support of the pilot's claim, Hawkins had heard background shouts between Graham and Thompson. Hawkins had immediately ordered the aircraft back to base.

The pilot almost collided with Graham, who strode through the door muttering, impatient to be heard.

"That fucking journalist! I should never have let him on the mission. A bloody anarchist! Lost an aircraft and a lot of good men. Bloody traitor. He should be shot!" Graham, for all his bluff and blather, ensured that the best story was told.

Hawkins listened to Graham's tirade, sickened as the implications began to sink in. There would be a major investigation. Those of sufficient rank would shoulder the blame. He had, by this time, dissociated himself from the intransigent perplexities of the Northern Ireland scene. He had lost interest in the regional conflict. His focus now, only to make sure the "showing of the flag" was carried out efficiently and safely.

Thompson now entered. Face to face with Graham, heated words were again exchanged. Graham moved threateningly toward Thompson. Hawkins stood, both hands on the desk, his voice hard, incisive.

"Graham, you're out of order! What in the hell do you think you're doing? This is my command! It's difficult enough without this hooliganism! I'll be talking to Mr. Thompson now. Please hold yourself available outside my office."

"Excuse me," Bob Thompson calmly looked from Hawkins to Graham, deliberately choosing his words. "The 2 I/C might like to note my comments for the record. Commander, I deeply regret that good men have lost their lives today, but I believe you have been misled. This mission was an illegally authorised plot known as Ajax. It's purpose, to assassinate selected members of the Irish Republican movement. There is no evidence that the people they were pursuing had anything to do with Madam's assassination. This is a wide stretch of the so-called Counter Revolutionary Warfare strategy; contrary to human rights and any basic principle of International Law."

The room was silent. Graham glared at Thompson. "You bloody, bleedin' heart liberal bastard! Your actions today cost us the lives of our men. Illegal, hell! These same people most likely sabotaged that American plane yesterday. Anything goes with these terrorists. There are some of us know how to take care of them, and have the balls to do it! It's traitors like you that fuck us up."

Hawkins raised his hand. "Enough of that. Back off."

Graham stared at Thompson, who calmly ignored him. "Whoever the C/O was on that flight deliberately shot to death at least two people, clearly not attempting to apprehend, or even to identify them. Only one appeared to be armed, and he looked like a boy to me." Graham was beginning to look alarmed.

"This man," Thompson briefly pointed to Graham, "further incriminated the operation, trying to kill a third person. My story will be told to a wider audience; then perhaps, we'll see if MI6 still runs the affairs of the country with its own agenda."

The phone rang. With a brief acknowledgement, an orderly handed the phone to Hawkins.

Watched silently by all in the room, Hawkins gripped the receiver, making an occasional, barely audible, monosyllabic reply. He scribbled some notes on a pad. Promising a quick response, Hawkins replaced the receiver, his expression weary, anxious.

"That was the emergency health service - an ambulance is being sent to a farm in the mountains. There'd been a shooting and a boy, they say, is bleeding badly. They called the Medivac unit from the Royal Vic in Belfast, but they're already on a call. They need our help to evacuate the boy."

Hawkins, visibly shaken, looked over at Graham. "They spoke of an American, also wounded." Thompson looked startled. "There's also been word of an exchange of fire at Rathfriland, holding up the Para and RUC group there."

Hawkins shook his head in response to Thompson's anxious question. "They gave no names." Looking over at Graham, he asked, "Jesus Christ, what have you got us into?"

As Hawkins prepared to leave, Graham said, "Let's warn the field units about a heavily armed terrorist group somewhere in those mountains. You spoke of an exchange of fire at Rathfriland. We can't afford the possibility of another ambush."

Hawkins nodded. Looking at Thompson and Graham, he added firmly, "Both of you will accompany me into the Mournes. And unless ground units are already engaged," addressing Graham, "we must tell them to hold their fire. There will be no more killing today, if I can help it."

CHAPTER TWENTY-SIX

In the Glen of the Holly Leaves

With a stutter and cough the turbines started up. The limp blades lifted into spinning life as the Sea King, like some bird of prey, rose slowly, heading south along the beach, then westward toward the Mournes.

In the crowded interior, Thompson watched the hunched figure of Graham, capped in his SAS beret. His fraternity badge, thought Thompson. This man was a dangerous maverick.

Since Madam's assassination, Thompson had known he was at least one step behind. He and Feely had seen Jack's cousins safely home; only then had he been able to trace the destination of Graham's undercover unit to Newcastle.

Thompson knew he'd been lucky. A different roll of the dice and he'd have been with Tracker, on the wrong aircraft! He remembered Graham shouting encouragement to Tracker. "Go for it! Jesus, you got the buggers!" Thompson's futile shout, "Stop this bloody murder!" had been quickly rebuffed. Deciding enough was enough, Thompson had ripped off his harness; half fell, half dived for Graham, who was firing toward his targets. The struggling figures had been separated by some of the SAS as the pilot brought the aircraft back to base.

As the Sea King now flew once more into the Mournes, Thompson and Graham both stared ahead, swaying to the torque and thrust of the powerful turbines, not a word spoken.

In the Glen of the Holly Leaves, above the Silent Valley, the troops closed in. Inspector King's Special Patrol ground units, the RUC, 2 Paras from Newcastle, and the CRW squad of SAS from Rathfriland, finally reached the Seanache's farm, running quietly for the cover of the stone walls. On the mountainside, the heather still smoked from the debris of the helicopter.

Inside the dark shadows of the old farmhouse, the boy regained consciousness. He looked toward Theresa. In great pain, his eyes wide, he whispered to Theresa, "Where's me granddad? Where's the Seanache?" Seeing Theresa's tear stained face he asked, "Will I be a hero too, like Cormac, an' like me Dad?"

Theresa stifled her tears. Sean coughed, grimacing in pain. He stared into Theresa's eyes. "Am I goin' to die for Ireland too?"

After carrying young Sean to the farmhouse, Dan had returned to the hillside, bringing the body of the Seanache back to the cobblestoned yard. Not too long ago, he'd carried Frank, young Seanoge's father, to his final resting place in Nicaragua. The Seanache lay, partially covered with a blanket, his sightless eyes gazing skyward. Far down the glen, the old eagles of Slievenaglogh spoke their lonely, keening, voice.

The Sea King hovered above the farmhouse, scouting for a suitable landing site. Wing Commander Hawkins had succeeded in making radio contact with Inspector King's ground forces. Inspector King had been unable earlier to contact the aerial reconnaissance units, or anyone else at Newcastle. Their radio transmitters had been malfunctioning for several hours. Between bursts of static, Hawkins managed to learn the identity of the three victims of the morning's shooting.

Thompson saw Graham's triumphant response as the name of the Seanache was mentioned. Graham swore as they both heard the name of Jack Edwards.

Graham braced himself for the confrontation, yet again, with Jack Edwards. Just who was this Jack Edwards? If indeed Edwards worked for American Central Intelligence, what was his mission? Perhaps if the American became another casualty, the leak could be secured. Graham brushed the thought from his mind. Already, especially with Thompson as a witness, the event could soon be an international incident.

The Sea King slowly settled, straddling the broad, flat surface of the barnyard, away from the house and surrounding trees. Suddenly Graham and Hawkins turned, staring through the Perspex, listening to the quick succession of single popping sounds, and the distant rattle of automatic weapon fire. Hawkins swore. "The lunatics! Can't get enough of killing each other!" Graham, misreading the message, grunted, "Bloody IRA." Thompson struggled through the exit, following the SAS unit, Graham and Hawkins.

Graham shouted to his troops, "Spread out and take cover!" Unslinging their weapons, the troopers disappeared, surrounding the barns and farmhouse.

Hawkins shouted, "Hold your fire! That's an order!" Thompson saw two unarmed men standing together by the door of the house. One of them called out, "Hold your bloody fire! We have a wounded boy in the house!" Thompson immediately recognized Jack Edwards. Graham moved across the yard toward the ground troops. Thompson followed Hawkins to the courtyard. Jack came forward to meet them, one arm wrapped in a bloody sling.

"Bob Thompson! Boy, am I ever glad to see you again." Jack nodded to Hawkins, then introduced the man beside him. "This is Dan McSorley, a brave soldier and good friend. Dan, this is Bob Thompson, journalist from *the Times*." Bitterly he added, looking toward Hawkins, "The Seanache's dead. Young Seanoge's badly injured. He needs immediate help."

Hawkins spoke. "The Medivac is on another call. We came to bring you and the boy to the emergency care unit. They're waiting for confirmation."

"What did you bring the bloody army with you for?" It was Dan's angry voice. "And the same bloody murderers that came in this morning!"

Hawkins frowned. "We don't know the whole story, Mr. Mc Larnin. We also lost a lot of good men. There'll be charges - and there'll be a hearing. Right now, I'm concerned to get the boy and Mr. Edwards to the hospital."

Dan turned abruptly and led the way into the house.
Hawkins, Jack Edwards and Thompson followed. In the dimly
lit room, Hawkins blinked, trying to adjust to the darkness. On a
large sofa near the fireplace he saw a young woman bent over a
small, motionless form. The woman looked up, then turned back
as the small figure stirred and moaned.

Bob Thompson recognised her from news clips. Sister
Theresa, as Thompson remembered, was the voice at Queen's.
Wanted for questioning following Madam's assassination,
and more recently, the shooting at Belfast airport. He noticed
the shrouded figure by the stairway. "Sean McCarton - the
Seanache", Jack whispered, standing beside Thompson.
Thompson knew of the legendary figure. He followed as Jack
joined the group gathered by young Seanoge.

Hawkins was regarding the boy as he engaged in earnest
conversation with Dan and Theresa. He rose, then moving
hurriedly across the room, picked up the phone.

At that moment, Graham and Inspector King entered,
accompanied by three bulky figures in full battle gear, weapons
in hand. They stood by the door watching the scene. Jack,
standing by Theresa, ignored the arrival of Graham. All eyes
were riveted on young Sean. They listened to the boy's attempts
to suppress the moans, the muffled, sucking sounds of his
painful, laboured efforts to breathe.

Sean lifted his head, trying to focus. Gritting his teeth,
looking at Jack, he spoke, his words a harsh whisper. "Tell...
them... what the Brits... did to us." He coughed, spitting blood
and saliva. Blood was seeping through the sheets across his
chest. Theresa, tears flowing, begged him to rest. Sean's eyes
brightened. "I'm... a good soldier... right? Like me dad? I tried
to... to stop 'em... didn't I, Jack?"

Jack quickly replied, "Sean, I've seen brave men. You
Sean, are the bravest; a credit to your dad and your Granddad.
And I can promise you Sean, we'll see the world knows." Sean's
pale face struggled to smile.

Wincing in pain, gasping for breath, Sean closed his eyes,
trying to stop the tears. His straining ceased as Dan lowered his

head to the bloody pillows.

Kneeling by the bed, Dan whispered, "You're a brave man Sean, and you'll have your medal. I've something for you." Jack saw Dan reach behind his neck, then slowly remove a chain and tiny glinting ornament from beneath his collar.

Two of the troopers moved toward Dan; one placed a hand on his shoulder. Dan shrugged it off, eyes fixed on Sean. Leaning forward, he placed the dully shining ornament around Sean's neck. Jack heard the words Dan whispered to Sean. "A little trophy, worn by brave men. It was given to me in recognition of your father's bravery." Dan added softly, "He was the best, Sean - and he's proud of you, boy."

In the dim light, the SAS and RUC moved forward, their bulky gear throwing giant shadows across the room. Inspector King, in his sinister, Darth Vader, black uniform, read Dan and Theresa their rights.

"I'm placing ye both under arrest for conspiracy against the state - for possession of arms and other weapons - for armed insurrection - for membership in an illegal organisation - for causing bodily harm and injury - for the destruction of one of her majesty's aircraft..." the words droned on.

Graham interrupted, suddenly moving forward. He stood before Dan, his voice low and menacing. "You're also wanted in connection with the sabotage of Madam's helicopter, resulting in wanton murder." The words were thick with hatred. "And, McSorley," he continued, "we will be questioning you relating to the sabotage of the American aircraft over Scotland. I've only begun to settle your score, you fucking terrorist!"

In a second Dan was on him. Two of the SAS and two RUC pulled them apart. Straining and tugging, they stood eyeing one another. The RUC constables placed handcuffs on Theresa and Dan.

"Won't be long Graham, before they lock you up in a lunatic asylum." Dan's voice was strangely calm. "Or for a murdering Brit like you, a seat in the House of Lords, God help us!"

Theresa's voice, deep and hard, warned, "Ye'll be punished for the murders ye planned against an old man, a woman, an' a boy, an' this time we've got the witnesses. Your time is up Graham, an' your game is up in this country."

Jack spoke quickly. "There's been enough delay. The boy must be moved to the hospital immediately."

Thompson looked at Hawkins. "If you don't carry this boy in soon, you're going to have another death on your conscience. And if that doesn't bother you," he shouted, looking over at Graham and King, "none of this is going to sit well with the British public, who pay your salaries. By the time we're finished, we'll all learn the Northern Ireland strategy - the whole bloody, tragic farce!"

Hawkins, just off the phone, heard Thompson's last words. Standing by the doorway he called, "They're waiting at the Royal Vic - time to go."

Thompson nudged Jack, pointing across the room where two RUC constables were leading Theresa and Dan to the door. He saw Theresa's worried glance back to young Sean, lying motionless now, unconscious. Two SAS troopers prepared to place him on a makeshift stretcher.

Jack moved quickly to Theresa's side. "I'll be with you as soon as I see Sean to the hospital."

"Don't worry about us, Jack," Theresa said bravely. "Have your shoulder seen to and don't leave Sean. Don't leave him!" They looked at each other for a long moment. Jack whispered, "I love you."

He nodded encouragingly to Dan, then walked over to the boy, now being slowly carried from the room.

"Edwards, we'll be looking into your role - again interfering - trespassing, or worse, in areas of National Security. We'll be launching a formal protest with your government." Graham turned and followed Hawkins out to the courtyard.

The helicopter rose above the ancient valley. It was a brief journey to the trauma helipad at the Royal Vic. Time enough for Hawkins to put calls through, informing Sean's mother of her son's transfer, and to call the American consul, Feely, to notify him of Jack Edward's situation.

Considering Graham and the other representatives of brute force masquerading as "the law", Jack knew his involvement was now likely to become an embarrassment to the State department. This would probably finish his consultant role with Central Intelligence – perhaps indeed his career. His only regrets, the loss of life - and that he had waited so long to find his place in the real world. Once a member of the remote audience of academe, pronouncing on the human conflict, Jack felt humbled and horrified by the murder and deception he had witnessed; chastened and inspired by the love he had come to know.

CHAPTER TWENTY-SEVEN

We Are the Children of the World

Within minutes it seemed, the aircraft settled onto the helipad at the Royal Victoria Hospital. Sean was rushed into the emergency triage and stabilisation unit. Figures in scrub clothes performed a hurried assessment; a succession of quiet orders commenced treatment. Jack, less urgent, was ushered into a nearby cubicle across the hallway. Thompson waited with him.

Truculent and sullen, SAS stood nearby. Hospital security kept a host of foreign and domestic reporters and TV cameramen at bay. Peering across the hallway, Thompson saw the stern faces of persons from the Northern Ireland Office or Administration talking with nervous looking hospital officials.

Shortly Jack was attended by a nurse and a staff physician. After giving him a mild sedative, the nurse removed the bloody dressings from his shoulder. The physician made a careful examination of the wound. "An inch to the left could have been a disaster, Mr. Edwards." Numbing Jack's shoulder, the physician deftly made the repair.

Drowsy with the sedation, Jack heard his cousin Mary's voice. "Hang in there, Jack. They tell me you're doing fine. We're working on Sean. I talked to Brigid and Rosaleen. Tom Feely told them he'd keep an eye on you. He's coming shortly. See you later," she called as she hurried back across the hall to help with Sean.

Jack slept for a short while, waking as the nurse began to bandage his shoulder. He heard the surgeon's voice. "You'll be staying with us for an hour or so, Mr. Edwards, till the sedation wears off. We'll check with you before you leave."

Still drowsy, Jack was moved from the examining table to a wheelchair; the curtain was drawn briskly aside. Tom

Feely stood with three men beside him. Jack heard the words, "There's someone I'd like you to meet." He struggled to place the smiling face of the one closest to him. Feely introduced him, "Roger Moorefield, with Central Intelligence, in London now." As Moorefield shook Jack's hand, he said, "I was with military intelligence in Saigon, not too many years ago." Jack slowly recalled the face and figure - older now, but recognisable.

The other two figures moved forward. One was Asian, the other, Jack immediately knew. Paddy Finucane? Couldn't be! The Seanache just two nights ago had confirmed it, MIA in Southeast Asia. Jack closed his eyes. He must be dreaming. As he opened them, it was indeed Paddy Finucane striding forward, hand extended in greeting.

"Jack, never thought I'd see this day, but for me these surprises have been happening regularly now." Paddy, with a wide grin, clasped Jack's good hand.

"Good God," said Jack, trying to rise from the chair. It is you, Paddy!" The comrade in arms he'd long given up for dead, standing, grinning before him.

Paddy turned to introduce An Luc. "My good friend, whose father, a proud Montagnard, you also knew in Vietnam."

An Luc smiled as he shook Jack's hand. "I have heard much about you, Tuan."

Jack introduced Bob Thompson to his visitors. Still feeling the effects of the sedation, he recalled his last handshake with Paddy on the airfield at Tan Son Nhut almost thirty years ago. Yelling the traditional salute, "Gia Sao," little did they guess that their farewells might be their last.

Jack listened, scarcely believing as Paddy told of his reunions with Jean Davost and Victor Perry. "Perry was one of the victims in yesterday's sabotage of the TransAir flight over Scotland."

Through Tom Feely's arrangements they were led by the hospital administrator to a nearby conference room. With obvious reluctance, Thompson excused himself to make some phone calls.

Inside the conference room the initial excitement of the reunion had settled. Jack described the grim events since his arrival, Graham seeming to feature in every one of them. In answer to Roger Moorefield's questions – yes, Thompson had also been present at the meeting at Queen's, where again, Graham had appeared. And no, he had no idea who had fired the subsequent shots.

Jack described the Seanache's account of Ajax; also new evidence of threats from the Middle East. In answer to questioning from both Roger and Paddy, he repeated the Seanache's firm conviction that the Republicans had no role in the murder of Michael and Beth Weatherby, in Madam's assassination, nor any part in the sabotage of the TransAir 747 over Scotland. According to Jack, the old man was a direct speaking Ulsterman; he genuinely felt his own time was short, he had no reason to lie. Jack made no mention of the Seanache's account of the Collins deception, nor of the role of Paddy's family. He wanted to discuss that privately with Paddy later.

Paddy Finucane wondered how Ajax could have been in effect so quickly. As he understood it, the plan had not been authorised. How had the Seanache known about Ajax? Michael and Beth's murders were still unsolved. Jack's story of the Seanache's third nemesis seemed to focus more attention on the Middle East. Once the focus of Beth's fears, now a likely option of terrorist threat. Paddy remembered Michael's warnings of the renegade drift of those in PASS, and the corporate corruption of the China Scheme. With reference to an international criminal drug conspiracy linking the Gibraltar IRA killings to a British undercover agency, Paddy wondered if MI6 or a rogue group was involved. The "Silk Route" revived. Inferences were beyond belief.

Graham, Paddy sensed, was a key figure. What exactly was his role? Who was responsible for his actions? Who, in effect, had sanctioned the killings in the Mournes?

Perhaps with the help of Thompson, an internationally respected journalist, and with Jack – many of these questions could be answered. They could also explore and expose the conspiracy Paddy was sure was responsible for Anna's murder - those he had referred to at the DEA meeting. Knowing he was among friends, Paddy candidly expressed his thoughts.

Sirens of emergency or police transports echoed through the streets. Louder voices from the crowded emergency area arose in a growing human chorus of anger and protest. A gathering crowd outside the hospital chanted and sang, placards waved. Not far from the conference room, blinking shutters of cameras, shouted questions from insatiable news crews, now suddenly in breathless attention.

Jack listened, then nodded toward the windows. "Whoever thought they'd silenced the Seanache made a terrible mistake. His voice, I believe, will be even louder now."

Roger Moorefield paced the floor. "Graham is demanding you face criminal charges, Jack - or, alternatively, expulsion from the U.K. There are grave implications for Anglo-American relations, as I'm sure you all would agree."

Paddy interrupted. "He could bring charges. Obviously some might support this, but for other reasons I don't believe he will."

Tom Feely added, "Since the incident on the plane, we have retained legal counsel and gone surety for Jack's availability. The NIO has complained. They insist that this is equivalent to parole - that parole may already have been forfeit. We have denied the validity of any tenable charges, till today. Yet, in other areas, as you've said Roger, the situation is going to be more difficult."

Roger nodded. "Your situation, Jack, is certainly complicated. There are grounds for caution on both sides. I spoke with the ambassador in London this morning. He expressed concern for your safety. I must return to London tonight. Before leaving, I'll talk with the Northern Ireland Office, then brief Tom here. While I'm still in Belfast, I'll be getting in touch with Central Intelligence and National Security in Washington. Also, I'll have a quick word with the Irish Affairs Liaison team, with Hugh Reilly, spokesperson at the White House. The President has expressed concern. He is looking for a complete report."

Roger Moorefield reached for his briefcase. "I'm sure we can work this out in the next few days." He smiled. "We might persuade the British government and the NIO to hold off on any rash action." Adding a word of caution, "Perhaps both of you can influence Mr. Thompson to exert some discretion - to wait until we have more facts." He looked over at Paddy, "I promised I'd give Geoffrey Gordon a call as soon as I returned to London, Paddy. You'll also be in touch there, no doubt."

Moorefield reached to shake Jack's hand. "You've certainly had an eventful homecoming. Hope your injury gives you no further trouble. Your account has been most helpful - obviously there's work to be done. With Tom and Paddy's help we'll get the story straight, just as you've told us, Jack - for the press, the State Department and the investigation. I would avoid any more confrontations with Graham."

Roger paused. "Jack, Paddy, it's been good to see you again. Sorry it had to be under these circumstances." As he moved to the door, accompanied by Feely, "We'll look into the Seanache's reference to problems from the Middle East. See you later, Paddy. We'll stay in touch."

Feely shook hands with Paddy and Jack. "Take it easy, Jack. I'll be calling you in the morning, at your cousins' house, right?"

Across the hall Bob Thompson was making phone calls, hastily scribbling notes. He adjusted his story to protect his sources, wary of any premature revelations, to conform to censorship restrictions, and within the editorial constraints of *The Times*. Thompson was also wary of giving warning to the real culprits - the extent of the conspiracy still to be learned.

Describing the shooting of the boy and his grandfather, Thompson wrote of the continuing turmoil in Northern Ireland, the heightened tensions following Madam's assassination, evidence of increased undercover operations revealed in the episodes of the past several days. He made no mention of the possible existence of an assassination plot, nor of Graham's link with other events.

Within minutes, his deliberately tailored version of the incidents in Northern Ireland, soon to be carried by Reuters and other international news agencies, was on its way to London.

The world would pause to listen perhaps, for a brief moment of compassion, to bear witness, adding their voice in protest - then quickly turn their attention to other areas of greed, and no doubt, of conflict.

Neither Thompson nor the international news agencies, the British government, the Northern Ireland Administration, nor the world at large - were quite prepared for the reaction that followed the distribution of Thompson's story. TV coverage, along with pictures of the stark beauty of the bleak mountains and misty glens, gave a haunting perspective to the sparse factual report of an old man, his resistance, and now, of his murder. The convenient designation of "terrorist" escaped a curious and sceptical foreign media. Interviews with local historians of previous ethnic cleansings and famines these mountains had once witnessed lent credence, also served to draw attention to facts, long well hidden, of a people, their land and culture vandalised.

To the surprise of many and to the discomfort of some, the world indeed paused and refocused. Paparazzi flooded into the Irish northern province. Some explored the flaws in the traditional, righteous image of the colonial marauder. As the world reacted with an unexpected spirit of outrage, it became a source of surprise, anger and embarrassment to the British government. Britain, once again on stage, its vaunted image of the noble arbiter at odds now with its role as the criminal perpetrator.

Among the foreign journalists arriving on the scene was Paddy's friend, Anton Safarov, of *Paris Match*. Safarov widened the scope, revealing the recent death of the boy's father, Frank, fighting against American colonial oppression and intervention in Nicaragua. Ironically, also a fugitive from the fight for freedom in Northern Ireland. *"History repeats itself, from Afghanistan to the Gulf,"* Safarov wrote. *"The mujahidin, FLN, PLO, Sandanistas, Irish Republicans – all victims of the colonial imperative."*

The boy, his father, and now his grandfather all became brave symbols of resistance, heroes of the oppressed. Letters, cables and cyberspace resounded with messages from remote parts of the hemisphere. Not to be denied, a gathering voice of

253

inquiry rumbled or sang an angry chorus, worldwide.

Thompson knew there would be versions of the story put out by the Northern Irish Administration. A busy disinformation campaign from the British government was a role readily assumed from long practice. Yet, distracted by events elsewhere, they had been "beaten to the post". Thompson well knew Britain's historic compulsion to assume the title role, its personification of the "rule of law", from Magna Carta to the Glorious Revolution. The civil pose and poise more important than the substance, or God forbid, the truth.

Thompson decided he would set up an interview with Wolsey, the appointed leader of the interim government since Madam's assassination. Did Wolsey not realise the impact of this cascade of adverse international opinion? It seemed a good time for compromise.

Thompson's thoughts turned to the expensive information, paid for by himself, obtained the night of Madam's assassination, at no little risk. He knew this made him liable to prosecution under the Emergency Powers Act – transgressing the rules of National Security. He wondered now, had he been given what he'd paid for? What else had been in Madam's briefcase? Who else had seen it? Names were there on the flame-singed paper, Madam's among them. Seen in poor light, was it also De Veere's? In the nervous rush he couldn't recall an authorising signature. He'd focused on the names of the intended victims: McCarton, the woman who'd spoken at Queen's, others. Even now Thompson realised he knew too much.

Another brief series of phone calls - one to British Army HQ in Lisburn, one, to a number in Paris, then to the Europa Hotel in Belfast. All confirmed the significant list of international arrivals for the funeral. The Seanache's shadow had spread far and wide. Checking with contacts in Dublin, Thompson was now surprised to learn of the Seanache's secret meeting with Maloney less than three days ago, of a brewing scandal within the southern government.

Outside the emergency area people now stood, hands joined, voices raised in chorus. No song of defiance or protest, but a popular ballad, remembering the Seanache, a life dedicated to freedom, to human rights. And for the boy perhaps, "We are the children," they sang, "the children of the world."

Closeted in a nearby anteroom Graham told his story, frequently interrupted by a member of Security of the Northern Ireland Administration. His account was under attack. Contrary to standard procedure, neither Northern Ireland Security nor MI5 had been extensively informed by Graham prior to setting out on his urgent mission. His selective "briefing" of the regional RUC office with exclusion of "Northern Government oversight" had aroused suspicions. A veteran of the Regional Civil Service Bureau listened in worried silence to Graham's testimony.

The Northern Ireland government was now the focus of criticism by a jeering press, worldwide. Official resentment was smoothly conveyed by the young Director of Security, as the senior administration representative took notes.

Graham tried to keep attention focused on "the primary goals" of British intelligence, to apprehend Madam's assassins and their secret agenda. Stubbornly, Graham commenced to redirect attention to include the IRA among other suspects in the downing of the TransAir 747. A further diversion focused on the "meddling" intervention of the "disloyal Jewish journalist", as Graham slyly described Thompson, referring to Thompson's frequent criticism of the Northern Ireland Administration. Describing Thompson's unwarranted attack during the exchange of fire with "terrorists", Graham implied that he himself had courageously tried to save the lives of those on the remaining aircraft.

As Graham had surmised, the senior Northern Ireland Security officer, another anti-Semitic, "hard line loyalist", frowned, nodding his head. Though he disliked Graham, he had even less liking for Thompson.

The recurring presence of the American, Jack Edwards, was again deliberately characterised: "Belligerently involving himself twice in less than twenty-four hours." Graham spoke disgustedly of "his treasonous talk" at Queen's, "a typical, ex-pat Irish Nationalist piece of arrogance, interfering in the affairs of Northern Ireland. This time it's worthy of deportation proceedings."

Graham proclaimed, in implausible overreach, "The unfortunate wounding of the boy on a routine reconnaissance could well be ascribed to reckless endangerment by McCarton himself; the result of return fire after the IRA fired the first shots."

The bald distortion of the fatal shootings had not impressed Graham's listeners, the Security official commenting that the boy's involvement was unfortunate in that the Administration and British "anti-terrorist" measures were already the subject of international attention by various human and civil rights organisations concerning similar episodes of "unwarranted assassinations". The SAS, for the "Nemesis revelations" relating to the murder of young IRA recruits in the border counties. And again, the Paras, for shootings in Derry during the Civil Rights marches of the seventies. All would again be up for unfavourable international review.

Graham tried to gain favour in the officials' reception of his story, pretending to reluctantly share a further confidence. The officer accompanying him on the mission, Graham stated, had done the actual shooting, despite Graham's repeated warnings, and had neglected to check with him before engaging the terrorists. His unauthorised response had resulted in the retaliation that had taken down the first flight.

Graham saw the younger official's quick change of expression. "Australian SAS, a Major Tracker," said Graham. He was surprised to hear confirmation of his own suspicions from the Security officer, now looking more worried. Tracker, he was told, was a replacement for Major Grey, originally assigned to Graham's mission. Grey's body had been found earlier this morning - in the Thames.

There was a knock on the door. In response to a word from the Northern Ireland Office official, an SAS NCO peered round the door. "Did Mr. Graham wish to accompany the prisoners to the detention centre? They're ready for takeoff."

Graham nodded, silently shaking hands with the two administration representatives. He had always accepted he was on his own. Increasingly aware of his vulnerability, he felt marginalized, sensed the presence of a different, "other game". An outsider - not one of the Oxbridge fraternity, he would be the scapegoat. He saw the possibility as he moved to the door. At best he would receive an early retirement, at worst, public humiliation and exposure, as in Borstal years, a return to the streets. *No way in hell!*

In the triage unit of the Royal Victoria Hospital, attention was focused on the partially curtained alcove where a busy surgical team worked on young Sean, fighting to stabilise his condition before moving him to the operating room.

The arrival of Sean's mother created another media flurry. Mary hurried from Sean's room, putting her arm around Sheila, waving off the convergenge of reporters and photographers. She led Sheila to the nearby treatment room where Jack waited with Paddy and An Luc.

Sheila had been given the news earlier that morning, just before landing at Heathrow. Her return flight to Belfast had been held up more than an hour by increased "security". Mary held Sheila for a moment, giving details of Sean's condition, trying to reassure her. She then hurried to rejoin the busy team across the annex.

Sheila was startled to see Jack Edwards again. She hadn't seen him since the episode on the plane. Despite her distress, she greeted him warmly, expressing her concern for his injury. Jack introduced Paddy and An Luc, both expressing their support and encouragement.

Sheila stood beside them, her head bent, tears falling as she spoke. "He's just getting over his father's death. Why him? God forbid – he's too young to follow his father, and now his grandfather."

Mary rejoined the team in time to assist in another crisis in their patient's desperate course. Hands and fingers flying, they focused, intent on the mangled anatomy. Eyes on the blinking, beeping monitors, exchanging frustrated glances, they tried to meet the desperate challenge.

Quick demands, "Eight more units! Stay four ahead! It's his pulmonary artery." A head raised momentarily. "Tell them to set up for bypass."

Mary stood by the doorway, waiting for word to notify the operating room they were on the way. She heard the louder voice above the rhythmic professional exchange. "He's into V fib!" A desperate, "Jesus - we're losin' him!"

All heads momentarily raised to glance at the cardiac monitor as the voice called urgently, "Defib, quick - defib - defib!"

Paddles extended to the open chest. The sudden jerk of Sean's body - a circle of upturned faces, eyes on the monitors. Then a relieved, "Sinus rhythm!" From the head of the table, "Pressure's stabilized - we're O.K. for the moment."

Instantly the team resumed the delicate restoration of functional integrity to the torn tissues, flow to the patched vessels, blood and oxygen to brain cells and to other vital organs. Life stubbornly persisted as young Sean, oblivious to his perilous journey, slept unaware.

"Let's get him upstairs." Within seconds the wheels of the table unlocked; the team, Sean in the centre, moved as one unit toward the elevators. Mary led the way, turning to call to Sheila. "Pray for us, Sheila, Jack!"

Sheila ran across, bent to kiss Sean's forehead. She pleaded, "Please take care of him!" The elevator doors closed. "It's in God's hands now," Sheila whispered through her tears.

The emergency area returned to its hectic routine; the distracting pause for some, just another challenging emergency. For others, attention refocused. Cautious words were exchanged, testing political sensibilities before venting personal comments. All ready victims, proponents or opponents of the "colonial myth". For the few, studied ambivalence - affected impartiality.

Sheila was offered a room at the hospital. Jack, ready for discharge, promised to check with her in the morning. Giving Sheila his cousins' phone number, he joined Paddy and An Luc as they made their way toward the exit.

In spite of the tragic circumstances, Jack and Paddy were incredulous at their good fortune in finding one another. The conversation gathered momentum; they scarcely paused to give directions to the cab driver.

Recalling his promise to the Seanache, Jack felt it was time to tell Paddy the more complete story. He left nothing out: the deception, the Granart family papers, the message the old man had passed on less than twenty-four hours before.

"For me, Paddy, the man represented truth and courage - the triumph of the human spirit, the best of men. He was a rare voice in the corrupt times we live in."

Paddy recalled hearing of the Seanache many years before, perhaps during his year with the Brigade of Guards, while on station in Northern Ireland. Startled at this new twist to his past, he seemed relieved.

With Thompson's help, they agreed they could expose the whole, sordid regional conspiracy. "As the Seanache had hoped," said Jack, "to rightly assign the guilt where it belonged – to finally bring British mismanagement to account."

"With this and Saigon '75 déjà vu, there are a lot of answers to be found. You certainly came in good time." Paddy added quietly, "You had better be careful. You pose a distinct threat to some."

The rain fell steadily, the streets nearly empty. On the pavement, street lamps formed a chain of dull, yellow reflections. Lurking in the shadows, cautious figures in battle dress, SLR's at the ready, called nervously to one another - uniformed kids from the slums of Glasgow, Liverpool or London, the British "peacekeepers."

Through the small hours of the night, on the surgical floor of the Royal Victoria Hospital the theatre lights burned brightly. Inside the operating suite, figures in scrub clothes gathered about the draped figure of Sean, on cardiopulmonary bypass now for some hours. Sean's open chest, filled with a purposeful distribution of tubes, was occasionally afloat with blood or other fluids as the surgical team doggedly went from one major repair to another.

259

Beside the team of surgeons, Mary struggled to hold
her composure, professionally following the silent signals. Mary
played her role almost instinctively as the hours wore on. She
knew Sean's chances were slim. Twice, his heart had stopped
before they got him on the pump. She thought he had been on
bypass too long now.

Distracted from the usual, dispassionate posture, no
words were spoken; the traditional hierarchy of the operating
suite abandoned. All members of the team knew Sean's story.
With that extra inspiration, together they fought for his life. Each
prayed in their own quiet way. The complex support systems
served their constant or briefly faltering signals, watched by
vigilant eyes. The surgical team fought the odds, each moment
now, more critical.

CHAPTER TWENTY-EIGHT

The American Admiral Mahan's 'Middle East' – 'Lines in the Sand' a Hundred Years On

Belfast's Europa Hotel, the most frequently bombed hotel west of the Balkans, was besieged with a sudden proliferation of bookings, many for distinguished, internationally known political personalities. The violent events of the previous three days seemed to have focused attention in a most unexpected manner. The management of the Europa, personified in the impressive bulk of Mr. Magennis, stood firmly behind the front desk. His assistant beside him whispered, "I hear they've decided to bury the old rebel tomorrow. The sooner the bugger's underground the sooner forgotten. What do you make of it, Mr. Magennis, sir?"

Magennis made no reply. A staunch Unionist, he could scarcely credit it - but this "terminal event" might explain the sudden increase in bookings. Magennis read the labels on the luggage: Europe, U.S.A., the Middle East, India – one even from China.

Magennis uneasily noted the unsubtle activities of the British and Provincial security and their sniffing dogs in an indiscreet search for explosives. His concern was that this latest incident might trigger off another demonstration against the British "corporate lobby". The senior reservations clerk came hurrying up. Leaning forward, he urgently whispered. The Israeli Embassy in Dublin had booked a suite for a personal representative of the Israeli Prime Minister, who was to attend the funeral of Sean McCarton in the morning.

The late arriving VIP from Israel entered the lobby, a casually dressed man of stocky build, suntanned, carry-all over his shoulder, a briefcase in one hand. He stopped to remove his sunglasses.

Magennis, with a tired smile, hurried forward the length of the lobby, hand extended, followed by the assistant manager.

"*Boruch haba.* Mr. Harrari, is it not?" called Magennis with some difficulty. Harrari, with a puzzled smile, nodded, acknowledging Magennis's earnest if strange sounding words, the intent of his elemental Hebrew greeting. Harrari quietly requested a secured phone for his room, and a bottle of Jameson and soda.

Seating himself in his room, Ben Harrari turned on the television. Describing plans for the funeral of Sean McCarton the following day, the reporter made a brief reference to the role of an American in the events of the past few days, now likely facing charges for security violations. Harrari was startled to hear the name.

The phone rang. With pleasant surprise, Harrari exclaimed, "Bob! Must be all of ten years. I need scarcely ask what you're doing here." Curious, amused, Harrari asked, "How did you know of my arrival?" As the voice replied, Harrari responded with a laugh. "I'm only here for a few days." He paused. "Yes, something's not right. We both have questions to ask." Glancing at his watch, Harrari responded, "Right! See you in thirty minutes, the pub across the street."

The Victoria Pub, once the fashionable meeting place of the Edwardian barons of industry and title to sip and gossip, had been an apt reminder of colonial Belfast. Now the Victoria was a quieter place, almost a retreat. In the dim lit interior, Harrari slowly edged his way past the bar patrons to the inner snug where his friend sat waiting.

A world away, on the embattled west side of the city, beneath the streetlights, the high walls and dark facade of the Royal Victoria Hospital, a group of people stoically huddled together. Some held candles, quietly chatting to one another, sheltering the flickering flames from the rain. On the surgical floor of the Royal Victoria Hospital, through the small hours of the night, the theatre lights still burned brightly.

Early the next morning Bob Thompson picked up Jack Edwards. With Paddy Finucane and An Luc, they were headed for the Seanache's funeral at Kilcoo. Tom Feely had called just before Thompson arrived, suggesting Jack consider foregoing the ceremony: "to save future British American misunderstandings and ill feelings." Jack's response was a curt negative.

As they passed down the Falls road, Jack informed them of Sean's progress. In an earlier call to Sheila, he learned Sean had survived the surgery, but was still critical.

They listened in silence to the morning news while Thompson drove. The reporter gave an account of the growing number of prominent international political figures in attendance for the funeral. Among them, the Irish Taoiseach and, surprisingly, two voices from the Middle East. One from Israel, the other, an Arab from the beleaguered West Bank settlement.

"That will certainly raise the stakes - make the absence of English representation more noticeable," said Paddy. "Few politicians anywhere I know would take the risks the Taoiseach Maloney takes."

"No escaping," Thompson added. "Time for change long past. Pity's that it takes the death of McCarton, or innocent Jewish or Arab settlers to achieve it."

Edging his way through traffic, Thompson casually remarked a friend would be joining them for the funeral. He parked in front of the Europa Hotel, inviting them to come inside. "Think you'll enjoy this. He's got quite a story to tell."

"There he is," said Thompson, waving across the lobby to an indistinct figure silhouetted in the light from the windows. The man returned the wave, moving quickly toward them. "Gentlemen," said Thompson, "an old comrade, Ben Harrari."

Paddy and Jack broke the silence in one voice, "Ben!"

"Jack, Paddy, I don't believe it!" Ben laughed, tears coming to his eyes.

"Veteran's reunion!" Thompson grinned.

"That and a lot more," said Paddy, turning to introduce Ben to An Luc. "Back from the dead - Lazarus returns!"

With mixed emotions, they marvelled at the odd

circumstances of life, the twist of fate that had brought them together again, another friend who had survived.

Ben explained, "Bob and I met years ago in Israel. I had heard your name Jack, in the news. Wondered had I misheard or thought, maybe a different Jack Edwards? I mentioned it to Bob last night. He told me your story, and that Paddy was here too. I scarcely believed it. Told him to say nothing till I was sure."

Thompson reminded them of their engagement in Kilcoo. They headed for the car, each answering the other's questions in rapid succession. Jack remembered Ben Osten, as he was previously known in Spec Force Seven - the serious young man, a perfectionist, whose calm courage had won the respect of all who had worked with him.

Ben described his escape through the swamps of the Mekong Delta, boarding a Dutch freighter to Singapore and on to the United States.

"In the States I discovered we were all listed MIA - our mission didn't exist." Paddy and Jack confirmed a similar response. Ben continued, "I determined to go home, to give my services to my homeland. I always felt a yearning to explore my heritage. As an eager Zionist, I was given a new identity, a new name."

Now Ben Harrari, of Israeli intelligence, and ambassador of Israel. "I lived in a precarious world of undeclared war. Yet I never forgot my parents reminding me that both Arab and Jew were of the same Semitic family."

Shortly after Ben's arrival the Iran-Iraq War commenced. "We now know the scarcely concealed intent." Ben shook his head. "Israel in '81, forced to take matters into its own hands, struck the Iraqi nuclear plant at Osirak, seen as a grave threat. Then in '91, the first Gulf strike, with incalculable collateral damage. The real intent, the continuing colonial supremacy of the Brit/US alliance and their vested interest in the fossil fuel bonanza. Worse again, the chemical, biological, and nuclear weapons of mass destruction, sold indiscriminately to those transiently seen as strategic allies for American or British interests, with a military presence now in over a hundred countries worldwide.

"I knew there must be a better answer." Ben paused, looking to each of them, "This is where I first met Sean McCarton. "For many of us, Sean McCarton seemed timeless, indestructible. His name is legend among the older, former members of Irgun, of Haganah. Another reason I am here today." Ben paused again, glancing over at Thompson.

Thompson, his eyes on the road, spoke quietly. "Ben, whatever passes between us, stays with us." Ben nodded, satisfied.

"As a young man during the late thirties," Ben continued, "the Seanache, like the Jews in Germany, for different reasons, was on the run. He found his way to the Middle East; quickly became fluent in both Hebrew and Arabic. He learned the history and the culture. He shared in the problems of the region, trying to find the common theme of peoples oppressed and exploited. He wanted to bring us together. In times of great difficulty and danger, he earned the respect of those he dealt with."

Ben described the world McCarton had confronted, a decade of economic and moral depression, where supremacy flourished – stumbling from one war to the next. Everywhere, the people, victims of corruption and rising public disorder. A world everywhere, "at war with itself".

"In the Middle East the British mandate of Sykes, Lawrence, Churchill and Bell prevailed, imposing new lines in the sand – the compliance of the newly appointed princes, kings and sheiks ensured in exploiting the world's energy resource. And in Palestine, the Jewish and Arab people were denied their homeland." Ben's words were bitter. "Shiploads of Jewish refugees in the Mediterranean were turned back to the certain death of the holocaust."

As Ben described it, the Middle East after World War II was a world of higher stakes and more dangerous times – of the covert agenda, from MI6 to CIA to the Russians, the GRU and the KGB. In more recent years, their "fronts" for private enterprise, rank opportunists all. Finally to the Syrians, the Al-Kassar brothers and an even more dangerous world of make-believe. For the Seanache, a perilous existence.

Ben shook his head in awe. "The stories of the Seanache's feats grew from myth to legend. He saw the Israelis and the Arabs as one people - saw their common Semitic origins, their common laws - their shared prophets, their single reverence for the holy figures of each tradition. As a member of MATZPEH, an Arab-Israeli conciliation group, he tried to help each understand and survive in Israel's struggle for recognition.

"Among the former members of Irgun and Haganah were the Seanache's friends, Harry Saiko, Yossi Raviv, comrades from the beginning. Even to those regarded as the fathers of the nation state of Israel, Weizmann to Ben-Gurion, the Seanache was among the few non-Israelis whom they came to recognize as national heroes.

"After '73 none of us were sure who the real enemy was. There were other forces at work. In a clandestine world, opposing factions were less obvious - more dangerous. Yet the Seanache continued to help us. Unknown to any of us, we had a new enemy."

Ben's expression was troubled. "For Israel the price of '73 was too high. For the Seanache the price would be even higher. He had blundered, we later learned, into other 'games' of private enterprise. Trading in guns, drugs, terrorism and oil, their battle for supremacy knows no limits. The deal the Seanache had made for weapons for the Irish cause had a higher price than he imagined.

"From his efforts to save Israel, a fatal association had arisen from the Soviet Syrian connection. The link, Abdul Said, member of Syrian intelligence, the Mukhabaret, a friend McCarton had known for many years - a man with little sympathy for the British American alliance, or for the Russians - a man who played both sides. Said's goal was little different from the Seanache's - to rid the Near and Middle East of all colonial intruders.

"Said was also, we later learned, the agent of El Nabi, the 'chosen one'. In dangerous times, not uncommon in the Middle East, proclaiming the Muslim world resurgent. We later learned however, El Nabi posed a different threat."

Jack Edwards remembered the Seanache's urgency to

266

describe those who followed him – his first nemesis, British intelligence; his third nemesis, men from the Middle East, who dealt in weapons, drugs and lives. Ben's words verified the story the Seanache himself never had time to tell.

For Paddy Finucane, Ben's reference to those who traded in weapons and drugs, reminded him of Beth Weatherby's anxious concerns, and of Anton Safarov's reference in Afghanistan many years before of the appearance of another weapons source to the mujahidin.

"It must have been several weeks ago," Ben continued, "the Seanache contacted Harry Saiko and Yossi Raviv at Metsada - top secret Mossad headquarters in Tel Aviv. An impending catastrophe he'd said. Apparently, some months before, Abdul Said had called him. Said was in trouble. El Nabi's crusade was no longer Said's. It was a different El Nabi who had emerged. From the benign, 'chosen one', now to El Algazi, the 'conqueror'. Said spoke with the Seanache again, the same day the Seanache decided to call us. El Nabi's goals, Said had discovered, were not the liberation of the peoples of the Middle East, but of their enslavement to El Algazi's own plans - a new jihad of world conquest.

"We were greatly concerned - knew nothing about this Algazi. According to a vague description from Said, Algazi's location was in a remote region of northern Iraq. The man's deliberately discreet profile was ominous. As a double agent, Said's credibility was always in question. There was no way for us to verify his story. Yet we trusted the Seanache. This did little to reassure those in the Cabinet.

"Said had called us. Following the kidnapping of the French scientist, Senjaye, this held a greater significance. Said's message this time was that the kidnapping was a deliberate ploy. Senjaye, a Kurd, was a willing partner it seemed, in El Algazi's plans. This information, and something else he'd mentioned, Said had planned to pass to a British agent in Paris. The agent never reached the assigned meeting place." Ben turned to look at Paddy. "He was assassinated. The agent's wife," Ben was sadly shaking his head, "worked for us in Paris - she was also assassinated."

To Paddy's startled query, Ben nodded. "Yes, Beth and Michael Weatherby. The same night, Beth Weatherby had called the Israeli Embassy. She was afraid for her husband. Apparently, we were too late." Ben's voice sounded deeply troubled.

"In another urgent communication, the Seanache told us Israel was within immediate strike range of nuclear and biological warfare capabilities. The countdown to a second holocaust, in Said's words, could have already commenced. With little substantive evidence, we now faced a threat not alone to Israel, but to the entire Middle East, and more - to the entire Western civilisation. In Israel, the sceptics were beginning to be convinced."

Said's other message, reference to a top-secret, undercover drug deal, was of transient interest to Ben's distracted listeners then.

"The story seemed preposterous. Yet we who had known the Seanache believed him. In the succeeding weeks," said Ben, "we intensified the search across the region - extended communications with other agents worldwide. We already had the area under surveillance for some time. Nothing unusual was reported.

"Less than a week later, again too late. Abdul Said was found murdered in a village of northern Iraq, bordering Syria. He had been crucified, his body hung on a crude gibbet in the centre of the village. The ritualistic manner of Said's death surely intended to serve as a warning. A fatwa, a sentence of death, we learned, had also been passed on the Seanache himself. He'd scoffed at this."

Crucifixion again. Paddy Finucane began to think of the possible association. Little different from the intended purpose of Deevers' similar execution or indeed, that of Anna. Paddy remembered Michael Weatherby's description of the three IRA members shot in Gibraltar, who had blundered into a major undercover drug plot. Maybe for Said, the same - for Beth and Michael too. The crucifixions, a deliberate symbol, a signature perhaps.

"As I told Bob last night, Ben concluded, "the purpose of my visit is twofold. To represent our sorrow and respect, and to find out who really killed the Seanache, hopefully, to learn more of the threat now posed by this El Algazi."

Bob Thompson slowly approached the village of Kilcoo. The body of the Seanache had arrived at the final resting place of his restless spirit. From north and south they came, borders now irrelevant - and from many parts of the world, to accompany the mortal manifestation, for each of them, of the very spirit of a Universal Freedom. In unspoken agreement, the procession proliferated, feet shuffling the dusty road, voices quietly murmuring in prayer, all religions and none.

They moved through the glens and rugged slopes of McCarton's childhood, pausing above the deep valley, the still sheep on the purple hillside. They listened to the clear, harsh voice of the northern highlands, the skirling of the piper - the high sweet notes of the Cualin. A chorus of voices sang songs of freedom and hope.

An incongruous scene - the rustic, isolated village of low roofed cottages, the narrow roads packed with mourners, the curious, eager paparazzi. Jack Edwards felt a stirring of memories, words from his father, and of his grandfather. In the churchyard they lay, generation to generation, their spirits watching. He felt their presence, seeming to see the face of a returned son.

Above them, white scudding clouds raced eastward, in the infinite blue vault of silent space. About them, an ancient pre-Cambrian landscape, witness to the turmoil of the late arriving, quickly departing human presence.

CHAPTER TWENTY-NINE

Victoria Tower

In the pre-dawn, in the ancient London Palace of Westminster, two men stood in an anteroom off the Royal Gallery beneath the Victoria tower.

"How can we have so completely fucked this one up?" Sir Arthur Wolsey, interim government leader since Madam's assassination, paced restlessly.

Sir Geoffrey Gordon, Director General of MI5, stood uncomfortably; on his face an expression of grim dismay. Since late the previous day Gordon had received a succession of troubling phone calls, the first of which came from the office of Roger Moorefield, at the American Embassy. There was some question about detaining the injured American, Jack Edwards, for a hearing. This, Moorefield suggested, might result in embarrassing international repercussions - perhaps better managed with more discretion. A call from the British Foreign Office relayed the distress of the American Consul in Belfast. The need to defuse the situation was crucial.

The young boy's condition was critical, drawing an increasing gathering of international sympathy and support; every sort of human rights and other humanitarian agency represented.

Wolsey saw the path that must be followed. A word to the British Embassy in Washington and a pre-emptive further word to the American State Department might yet restrain the more dangerous voice of the Irish National Forum. The British-American partnership was at times a fragile union. Sometimes a fickle suitor in the face of the other, "special" American association, the mobilisation of the forty million Irish Diaspora, a powerful constituency when aroused.

Late last night Gordon had received another call from an MI5 officer at Lisburn. MI6, involved in the recent action in the Mournes, the same group involved in the earlier incident at Belfast Airport, had acted independently of regional security, resulting in misunderstandings and resentment. Disputes had arisen between British intelligence, Northern security and the Northern Ireland Office. Gordon doggedly resumed his litany of the week's disasters.

"The extent of the media coverage at the funeral of Sean McCarton was unexpected. Security from the Northern Ireland Office was overdone. Military and police were everywhere, helicopter patrols constantly overhead. The press had a field day."

Pausing momentarily to regard Wolsey's expression, Gordon stammered on, distracted with the larger picture. With the right wing, PASS, resurgent, it seemed Britain would never shake the imperial image. The aggressive, global expression troubled Gordon, not inconsistent with the end of the cold war, the hegemony now of an unopposed United States and Britain. Their unrestrained agenda, their hunt for the "axis of evil", Gordon was convinced, had dictated the trend of the past two decades.

With an expression of grim disbelief Wolsey stood in front of the unhappy messenger as Gordon continued, enumerating the nationalities represented at the obsequies in Kilcoo the day before. It was a significant third world quorum, the calibre of Mandela, the voice of the oppressed.

"No more the world our playground, Arthur. Other forces in charge, I'm thinking."

Arthur Wolsey was appalled. Gordon's attitude and faltering loyalties were revolting. One thing for Great Britain to assist with timely interventions. This, Wolsey ruminated, is Britain's historic, patiently born, lifelong commitment. Quite another, for the emergent third world to presumptuously trespass on the soil of Great Britain for the funeral of an ageing Irish terrorist.

Gordon responded to Wolsey's questions. "Taoiseach Maloney's speech was quite inflammatory. Thompson, the journalist from *The Times* attended. McClean, the Nationalist member of Parliament, and strangely, Mackie, the loyalist." With a pained grimace, glancing at Wolsey's rigid features, Gordon added, "and again, Edwards, the American." An ominous silence descended.

Wolsey was impressed. "All this for an ageing Irish terrorist? McCarton - who was this man?"

More disturbing, Gordon noted, a highly reliable source described a meeting that had taken place between members of the Irish cabinet, Maloney, and Sean McCarton. McCarton had presented confirmation of a purported British plot to assassinate the Republican leadership in the North of Ireland, also provided evidence of deception in the 1921 Anglo-Irish Treaty. McCarton had requested the presentation of this material to the European Human Rights Courts in Brussels, and to the United Nations Security and General Assembly in New York. Maloney, it seemed, had promised his support.

Wolsey had never trusted Maloney - knew the Irish Minister was more than a "Dublin Republican" as far as the North was concerned. Now he was convinced, with his inciteful words at the funeral, less than two days since his cabinet had met with McCarton in Dublin. Probably all lies, thought Wolsey.

The manner in which McCarton died, the timing, Wolsey mused, couldn't have been worse. The old man's death came only days after Madam's ceremonious interment, attended by Presidents and royals. The contrast was striking and unfortunate. Madam's mission had been the restoration of Empire, and the disestablishment of the voice of Labour. Madam's arrogance was in sharp contrast to McCarton's selfless crusade for the oppressed; his funeral only reinforcing the difference. The dignity of McCarton's mission was now enshrined. Another Irish martyr - not what we needed, concluded Wolsey.

This is preposterous, Wolsey thought, as he listened to Gordon's account of Thompson compromising the safety of the SAS mission into the Mournes. As far as Wolsey was concerned, Thompson's loyalties seemed confused; his dangerous polemics were a constant thorn in the side of traditional British government policy. Thompson could be a hostile witness in the hearings that would follow.

"Incredible disloyalty!" Wolsey exploded, interrupting Gordon. "Each of them, this American and Thompson, should be detained under the Emergency Provisions Acts or whatever, charged with obstruction of justice, and interfering with Security Forces in the line of duty." Wolsey was startled to hear Gordon's sudden vehemence.

"The sheer stupidity, and the lies! McCarton was an amazing survivor. His life was almost a century of history."

Gordon returned Wolsey's puzzled stare. "It is hard to know what to believe. The Seanache's grandson was shot by his own people, by mistake, they say. The agent in charge, Graham, claims the IRA fired first, denies giving the order to return fire. Says the SAS 2I/C exceeded orders, firing without permission. He also denies the existence of any assassination plot. If we didn't kill McCarton, who did?"

"The 2I/C, an Australian, was a last minute replacement for another officer, Captain Grey, who was found two days ago. He'd been shot, his body weighted and thrown into the Thames."

Wide eyed, Wolsey asked a quick series of questions.

Gordon's words echoed flatly from the high ceilinged, bookcased walls, to the half open casements of the historic room, witness to countless devious conniving in the affairs of men, excesses or indiscretions manipulated or suppressed.

Gordon quoted from Graham's account. In the incident at Belfast Airport, he was following leads from Paris. It was Graham's contention this IRA unit had a role in the death of the Weatherbys and, not unlikely, in Madam's assassination. They were also suspects in the sabotage of the flight over Kilbrannon Sound. The SAS unit's recce into the Mournes was justified, Graham claimed, in that two members of the terrorist unit who had escaped the shootout at the airport were captured. On both these occasions, the American, Edwards had been involved.

Wolsey was thinking, if the MI6 agent was right, the answer to their problems could be found in their historic protagonist, IRA terrorists. It was appealing, yet unlikely.

The IRA was perhaps marginally involved, with its

limited resources. Not that he'd lose the propaganda advantage, to recruit public antipathy - disengage American support with the excuse for more stringent measures.

Wolsey had recently been warned by Deicey, Director of Security Intelligence, MI6, Middle East, that there was increasing unrest in the Caspian regions of southern Russia. The rebirth of long dormant national identities and other forces were at work. These were peoples with different ethnic traditions, Kurdish and other warring factions. Here, it was said, were Senjaye's kidnappers. More alarming, as states independent of Russia now, was their unique, strategic location, with significant nuclear resources.

Another angle, uncovered during the DEA meetings in Paris, was the new market for drugs and arms. Geoffrey Gordon's final phone call had come from MI5, Belfast, with reference to a planned drug shipment into the Republic from the Middle East. This information alone could cast doubt on the neat conclusions of Graham's convenient MI6 story.

Wolsey couldn't entirely trust the message or the messenger. Neither could he ignore word of a drug shipment to the Republic from the Middle East. More than half of the younger generation were on drugs or had tried them. This would be explosive news in the face of rising unemployment. Wolsey determined to pursue this. He wondered if the drug deal Gordon spoke of included an enabling agency in the UK, or direct shipping from the Continent?

In the week before her death, Madam had angrily described to Wolsey the difficulties she'd encountered in the rejection of Ajax, including Weatherby's attack on government policy. Deicey had suggested that there were grounds to suspect the Weatherbys were assassinated by some agency from the Middle East. Perhaps, Wolsey thought, a drug deal from the Middle East could be tied in with Weatherby's activities, and with the frequent visits of McCarton to both Paris and the Middle East.

Such a story might serve its purpose. Wolsey realised the urgent need to demonise, to "demythologise" the old man. To rewrite history was a convenient strategy. For Wolsey, the old man was a terrorist. Indeed, he deserved his fate.

Geoffrey Gordon's mind was elsewhere. Should he tell Wolsey the curious story of Madam's briefcase, miraculously recovered from the debris by the pub owner, returned for a reward, the day after Madam's demise? More curious, its transient disappearance from the files of Stanfield, DDG MI5, its subsequent reappearance the following day.

Among the scorched papers, Gordon had read the legible pages of the controversial file Ajax, signed by Madam and DeVeere of MI6. Had the plan been rejected, or merely postponed? Gordon wondered, before selling the briefcase to MI5, whom else might the wily pub owner have sold the information to?

Wolsey listened as Gordon's troubled voice described information he'd received of a meeting held shortly after the funeral. Organized at the last minute, it was attended by the same significant, international group that had attended the funeral.

"Among the official or unofficial government representatives was Ghubar, of Lebanon. We know him as the Arab voice for peace in the Middle East. And Harrari, from Israel." Gordon paused.

Arthur Wolsey's focus had been elsewhere, now alert as he listened to Gordon describing the presence of Israel's Mossad.

"The Israeli representative was outspoken, they say, in his criticism of Britain's role in the shooting of McCarton. Referred to it as a murder plot." A curious and insolent intrusion, Wolsey concluded.

Almost reluctant to continue, Gordon chose his words carefully. "It appears there was another remarkable coincidence here. Harrari served in Vietnam with Paddy Finucane and Jack Edwards, the American. They were part of some special forces unit."

Wolsey's expression was suddenly one of total focus. Gordon was hiding something! Wolsey knew of Gordon's acquaintance with the Earl of Clanrickard. Wolsey's suspicions shifted inevitably to Paddy Finucane. Sensing his prey, he watched Gordon gaze distractedly toward the window.

Gordon wished Paddy had called. He had tried to reach him. Paddy was a maverick, like his father. There seemed to be no way out. Gordon continued cautiously, eyes now locked in Wolsey's fierce stare, helplessly sensing his own complicity.

"It was a reunion of sorts. Thompson drove Finucane, Edwards and Harrari to the funeral. Thompson," Gordon reasoned defensively, "could have known Harrari from time spent in the Middle East, or in Vietnam. Perhaps he had even known Paddy – both had spent time in Afghanistan."

Gordon himself sounded unconvinced. He muttered, "Perhaps when I hear from Finucane we'll learn the significance, if any, of these events."

For Wolsey, the whole extraordinary affair was a conspiracy unfolding. In some ways, the replay of a scene - he couldn't quite place it, from times past.

The two men stood in guarded silence. For Wolsey, this reunion Gordon had described was no coincidence. The visitors from Israel, the Arabs; sheiks or itinerant nomads, he didn't trust. As far as Wolsey was concerned, both were still on a warring mission. Thompson, Wolsey concluded, was brilliant but misguided. Finucane's role, Wolsey couldn't imagine. Like others before him, they'd lived too long abroad, no longer Englishmen! Wolsey wasn't slow to give his stern judgment. He stood before Gordon, eyes narrowed, reading a grim indictment.

Gordon desperately intervened. "Paddy Finucane is of a privileged and distinguished English family. As the son of the Earl of Clanrickard he's the successor to the title, and a member of Special Intelligence, MI6. He's recently up for promotion to DDG MI6 SEA. His vetting process was under way before Madam's death – only delayed due to recent events."

Wolsey recalled Madam's comments on her return from Paris, expressing surprise at Finucane's support for Weatherby. She had made it clear to Wolsey then that she would veto the Finucane appointment. Gordon must not have been informed of Madam's decision.

Around the two men rose the stacked, leather bound volumes, sole witness, holding their own historic silence. Hansard's recordings, records of times and crises long gone - of lies and greed - the forgettable words gathering dust.

Seeing Gordon's drawn, haggard expression and listening to his anguished words, suddenly Wolsey remembered the reason for Gordon's fierce defence of Finucane, his desperate attempts to deflect criticism. The scandal from another era; two unexpected deaths, not too far apart in time. Gordon's father, a suicide. Some years later, Finucane's father, dying in a mysterious plane crash.

There was increasing impatience in Wolsey's voice. He began to distance himself from this person before him, someone he'd known for many years. Yet also now, an association Wolsey could ill afford.

"Finucane had some earlier problems, hadn't he? In trouble in Northern Ireland, as I recall - with the Guards, right?"

Gordon stubbornly countered. "At the DEA meeting, Finucane gave a very informative report on the drugs and arms problem in Southeast Asia, receiving personal congratulations from Madam."

Wolsey's mind was elsewhere. As he saw it, an invidious crisis, not alone from the pervasive, festering discord in Asia, from the Gulf, to the Middle East, to the Balkans, and forever, from Ireland – maybe even a sinister conspiracy, aided and abetted from "within our own house". Wolsey leaned forward, his eyes fixed on Gordon.

"Treason afoot wherever you turn."

Gordon agonised. Again, the ultimate embarrassment to Britain. History repeating itself. Bitter memories returned, of the Philbys, Blunt and others of MI6, threatened, enticed or blackmailed to betray their country. Not to forget the untold hundreds of other victims abroad - identities revealed, careers ruined, lives destroyed.

Wolsey erupted, his anger palpable. "Maloney, the third world spokesmen, Finucane and his friends – all traitors to their country! Fucking perverts, all of them!" Gordon paled as he listened to Wolsey's vehemence.

Somewhere a clock ticked loudly. Beyond them, the city of London awoke as it had done for a thousand years; its voice strident, brash or elegant, snobbish or loud and vulgar -

nobs to errand boys, each singing their own peculiar song - all a
dissonant chorus, a cappella.

Wolsey spoke scarcely above a whisper. "That's why
we lost it, Geoffrey. An empire founded on rugged Christianity,
discipline, the indomitable spirit of our great schools, of our
fearless merchant adventurers, explorers, of Livingstone, Milner,
Rhodes and Salisbury. All in a fair trade with the export of
British manners, custom and fair play. We civilised more than
half the world and look at the thanks we get for it! Too little of
the right stuff nowadays, Geoffrey."

Gordon wondered, what "rugged" Christianity? An
exclusive society of the toffs and the yobs. What great school
system? Condoned traditions of bullying and buggery and
their reinforced elitist goals. What heroes? Kitchener of the
Boer War - his, the first concentration camps with over 150,000
detainees, Boer women and children and more than 3,000
deaths a month from neglect and disease. And for such victories
awarded a viscountancy! And Dwyer, the Butcher of Amritsar,
murdering over a thousand Indian men, women and children in
peaceful protest. Gordon was losing faith in Wolsey's fantasies,
everything Gordon himself had once believed in.

Wolsey turned a quizzical glance to a distracted
Gordon. "Finucane isn't one of those damn homosexuals, is he?"

Gordon, appalled, shook his head. "His wife was just
recently murdered."

Gordon stood, gaze uncertain, the guilty schoolboy.
Again he felt he'd failed as Paddy's guardian, something he'd
promised Paddy's father shortly before his death. Sure now
there'd be a hearing - there was a good chance he was going to
have to share in Paddy's judgment - surely not in his disgrace,
and so soon after his wife's cruel death!

Gordon found himself thinking of the destruction of
his own father's career. He sensed again the recriminations -
felt desolate, alone. Wolsey's harsh words had brought back
memories of false accusations, eroding insinuations arising
from the Golitsin defection, the Winona code break - both
triumphs for Western intelligence. Yet, the source of some of
the most consuming personal tragedies and betrayals. It was

Star Chamber and the McCarthy hearings in Washington all in one. All long gone now. For some, the memories lived on, their innocence passionately defended. For others, exile, their role bitterly denounced. For Gordon's father, it was a tragic, if merciful death.

Wolsey stood before Gordon with an impatient stirring of the feet, eyes narrowed.

"Geoffrey, you said you have no idea who authorised the shooting of McCarton - the implementation, perhaps, of Madam's unapproved plan?" Gordon nodded. Wolsey continued, closely watching his response.

"Madam acquainted me with the accusations by Weatherby, supported by Finucane; harsh criticism of Britain First, questioning their involvement in a commercial venture, the so called China Scheme."

Gordon carefully listened. Was Wolsey wondering if he supported Weatherby and Finucane's views?

"Geoffrey, the mystery deepens, with the loss of the American aircraft over Scotland." Wolsey commenced pacing. "There has been no word confirming sabotage?"

Gordon shook his head helplessly.

"Yet I learn, on that flight was an American who had attended the DEA meetings in Paris, on his way to testify in Congress on the international trade in drugs and arms." Wolsey turned to face Gordon.

"No answers yet on any of these issues. Embarrassing – very frustrating. No word on the identity of those responsible for the deaths of the Weatherbys, or of Madam either. And now, you tell me, in the shooting of McCarton, the facts are again uncertain. And Grey, murdered, his replacement, the Australian, supposed to have shot McCarton, he goes down with his aircraft. The only other witnesses - this American, and Thompson, the journalist."

Wolsey again paced. "Who was this Australian? Not to forget the MI6 agent in charge of this damn fiasco! Graham, you said, who had also been in Paris, following the IRA he claims are responsible for all of it. No one else has managed to reach the same conclusions. Yet there are those who might welcome this simple solution. But, Geoffrey, it makes little sense."

Gordon appeared puzzled, wary.

"We're looking in the wrong direction Geoffrey. I'm convinced there's more at stake here."

Wolsey paused, cautious to express his thoughts. "In Paris, Madam's speech threatened other groups. The Weatherby deaths were perhaps an internal affair, the issues confused in an international setting." Again he commenced pacing. "Madam mentioned a disruption at the meeting." Wolsey turned to look at Gordon. "Graham, was he there?"

Gordon nodded, remembering the altercation developing after Weatherby's accusations.

"This Graham - a reliable man you say?"

"Yes, an unusual record - much decorated."

Wolsey continued. "I realise this is scarcely within the realms of MI5 alone, but," He stopped, staring straight at Gordon. "Britain First has been promoting a more positive stance in Northern Ireland. Would this aggressive policy be more of the same? This, Madam sympathised with - not my game. But strongly pushed, we hear, by those in PASS."

Gordon could see Wolsey had found a target. Wolsey's focus was now on PASS and its extension to MI6; indeed, the possible source of Graham's authority. Before realising their extreme goals, Gordon had signed up with PASS; what some had seen as the only recourse following Britain's diminishing image on the international scene. He saw now that he had been misled. It was, Gordon realised, a return to the suspicion and mistrust of bygone times. Not revealing his membership to Wolsey, Gordon silently confessed to himself, could now be an inevitable trap.

"Sir Geoffrey," the conclusive tones introduced the topic Gordon had been dreading, of a gathering retribution for PASS.

"Word again from the British representative in Beijing, and the governor of Hong Kong, conveying the anger of the Chinese government. They accuse the Hong Kong administration of non-compliance with Chinese law and custom – of avoiding tariffs and taxes, money laundering and worse.

"As Madam intended, Geoffrey, be assured it will be among my immediate priorities to investigate this China scheme, hopefully in time to prevent another royal cock-up!" Arms folded, on a favourite subject of contempt, "To fearlessly expose criminal activities in government on a scale only equalled by the successive American Presidential scandals and dalliances with an unrestrained military corporate mandate."

Gordon was only half listening. He had been worrying about the China venture since the meeting in Paris. Formerly pronounced as a sure investment, he realised he should have looked closer into the source. The scandal was spreading quickly it seemed - to Australia now, he'd heard.

Gordon shuddered. He couldn't stem the welling uncertainty. Had he inadvertently lent his name to what was now little better than a criminal enterprise of international dimensions, bringing further shame to his country and to his family? It had seemed harmless at the time. The eager young Turks of Britain First, to win friends, and a vote of confidence for a new Britain.

Wolsey was talking of his increasing suspicions of PASS, the conspiracy both men feared. Gordon wondered desperately, was Wolsey deliberately criminalizing PASS to enhance his own status?

On hearing Gordon's audible sigh, Wolsey glanced at his watch. He was due in the House shortly for the verbal sparring of question time. Wolsey shook Gordon's hand, thanked him vaguely for his assistance. Gordon could feel the cool withdrawal as Wolsey assured him, "I'll inform you of any developments. Keep me appraised of any further word on this drug shipment you spoke of - perhaps Deicey of Middle East station should be in on these discussions."

Wolsey headed toward the House of Commons, feeling a growing sense of resolution. In the first few days of his appointment, the opposition had almost convinced him his interim government would merely be the transition to an early election – an inglorious defeat at the polls. In sudden revelation he saw his redemption in the challenge before him.

Wolsey's turn now to reach his place in history. A new social agenda - devolution of the Irish entanglement, increasing attention to the domestic focus, rebuilding the northern cities and slums. This would ensure his triumph, a source of hope and inspiration for the increasingly disemployed constituency.

Passing the galleries of the House of Lords, he suppressed a brief sense of foreboding. Walking slowly up the Commons corridor to the House, Wolsey muttered tensely to himself. Free Ireland they said, and you would dismember the Empire. Rubbish! The Empire, already gone! A new and different empire now in the making. No warships or armies needed here. With the savings, build an empire of economic allegiances, recruiting the support of Labour.

Wolsey felt sure he could seize the helm, restore the good name of England, with a new era of reason and moderation. A new play on democracy. Proclaim the spirit of Mandela abroad. Reset the stage, generations of ignominy transformed to a time of conciliation. Wolsey could scarcely contain himself.

He would need a tremendous media campaign, brilliant political strategists. He thought of Thompson. Thompson's energy and talents could be a great asset. Perhaps he could create a role for him in the "new voice of change". There would be no need to head off Thompson's handling of the Irish situation, just include and enlist his vision and energies. Wolsey made a mental note to call his friend Harbison, owner of *The Times*. Harbison owed him one.

He heard the booming authoritative notes as Big Ben sounded the hour. Entering the crowded chamber, Wolsey thought to himself, just in time!

In the anteroom below the Victoria Tower, Gordon still stood, staring out across the gardens to the river beyond. The bent figure by the window stood a moment longer, then turned away from the sunlight and sounds of the new day.

Passing the Robing Room, Gordon was remembering the story he hadn't told Wolsey. Something continued to haunt him. The papers from Madam's briefcase. Who else might have seen them?

Reaching the dark shadows of the Norman Porch, the ornate stone faces of medieval England, Gordon turned to the nearby Royal Staircase. Suddenly feeling very tired, he slowly descended, heading for the visitors' entrance, the Old Yard and the streets.

Soon the world would read Thompson's story. As Gordon had heard it, Thompson was the consummate journalist. If he had been aware of Madam's plan, Thompson could be a very dangerous adversary. Gordon stumbled, missing his step.

Emerging from the visitors' entrance, Gordon passed alone up the crowded street. With Wolsey he felt they'd been able to reach few conclusions. Worse, he was unable to rescue Paddy from Wolsey's suspicions, or to salvage Paddy's career. He dreaded the inevitable meeting with Paddy - knew he could be expecting a call from DeVeere. His own innocent association with the China Scheme, Gordon felt sure, would finally exclude himself from any course of honour.

Gordon slowly headed up the broad reaches of Parliament Street, a stoutish figure in Burberry and Homburg, hands in his pockets, unseeing and unseen by the bustling world around him. Waiting for the lights to change, he started at the sonorous clamour of Big Ben. "Too late now," he muttered, "too late."

CHAPTER THIRTY

The Commons

"The Commons", so deceptively, felicitously misnamed, where till less than a hundred years before the common voice had never been heard, only the rantings of those of title and heritage. Winston Churchill once described the historic premises as, designed to instil "a sense of crowd and urgency."

The august body of over six hundred fifty members and their supporting staff were striving to find room among the packed benches. Visitors filled the galleries above the chamber. In the Press section crowded news media, all agog, TV cameras focused.

From her "bully pulpit" the Speaker endeavoured to impose silence, her bewigged head shaking as she vigorously gavelled the desk calling, "Order!" Before her the babbling throng ignored her.

The interim prime minister hurried through the entranceway, escorted by the Sergeant at Arms. Wolsey paused for a theatrical moment, staring defiantly toward the Opposition benches. Taking his seat, he consulted his notes, still breathing heavily from the short sprint he had been obliged to make from the nearest secured phone.

Some moments before, the Sergeant at Arms had informed Wolsey of two urgent phone calls - one from Lord Mays, British representative to the United Nations, the other, from DeVeere, Director General of MI6. With some misgivings, Wolsey had taken the calls.

Mays' voice was agitated as he described the situation at the UN.

"Couldn't be worse timing, Arthur, coinciding with the allegations and investigations of corruption taking place in Hong

Kong. Rumours among the departing British Administration of links with the Middle East don't help. Worse now, rumours of the involvement of prominent public figures here in America, in the Australian government, and others nearer home."

Mays' voice disappeared in a sudden increase in static, returning in mid-sentence. Wolsey felt a chill. Was someone listening on the secured phone? Mays seemed unaware of the interruption.

"There seems to be a deliberate, organised response among several prominent figures in the UN assembly regarding the Irish situation, an attempt to bring attention to the role McCarton played in their own battles for independence. A dangerous and disruptive group," Mays said, "exploiting every opportunity to recruit a quick consensus. They have received support from as far afield as the Muslim Russian Republics. More troubling, from a dissident group exerting a strong influence in China, their voices now regarded, like McCarton, as an emerging symbol of emancipation worldwide; a voice difficult to confront."

Describing widely existing insinuations of Madam's plan to assassinate the IRA leaders, Mays had received word of a strategy requesting a vote in the Security Council to investigate the role of Great Britain in Northern Ireland. The events of the past few days, they claimed, disqualified Britain from her position as an impartial arbitrator, already the subject of allegations of multiple transgressions against human rights.

"Only yesterday members of the Human Rights Committee, of Amnesty International, voted for an investigation of the legality of Britain's position in Northern Ireland. They're trying to push through a vote today for a preliminary hearing.

"They are assigning us an embarrassing image, Arthur. Again, we are placed in a defensive role. Demands are being made for a prompt withdrawal. They suggest the introduction of a NATO peacekeeping force, if you please. Some kind of all island referendum - a shared autonomy for the people of Ireland, including the separatists, the Unionists - independent of our presence!

"On this short notice, we're not prepared. The Irish

Premier, it seems, has made some reckless comments. The Irish-American lobby has impelled Congress to join this rabble. This is madness, Arthur!" Mays sounded desperate.

Wolsey was growing impatient. Time, he could see, was a problem. He made a mental note to call the American President, to recruit his support. He also determined to call in Higgins, the Irish Ambassador, to ask what was Maloney about - first at the funeral, now his critical voice at the UN.

Mays stammered on, "I need an update on the situation in Northern Ireland, to adopt a position which we will later find tenable, if you understand me?" He gave a nervous cough. "They will be voting later this morning." He paused. "You are five hours ahead of us," his voice trailed off, "both in news and in time, it seems."

After briefly reassuring Mays, Wolsey ended the call on an uncertain note. Wolsey made a brief call to the Foreign Office, enabling a quick conduit of information and consultation for Mays. Wolsey hoped Mays could take a proper stand at the UN, facilitating the conciliatory position he was planning for himself.

Wolsey then made a quick call to MI6.

"Paddy Finucane," DeVeere informed him, "has exceeded his warrant, with actions in excess of his assignment. He will be facing a hearing this afternoon. Graham's account of the shootings in Northern Ireland is also being investigated."

Trusting no one, Wolsey made no mention to DeVeere of the message from Mays. He was still troubled by the interruption in the earlier phone call.

Re-entering the historic chambers, distracted as he was, he paused. Home for centuries to the members of this private, entitled club, the great hall resounded to recurring shouts for, "Order!" The Speaker, gavelling the rostrum before her, finally succeeded in gaining control.

From the Opposition benches, a representative of disempowered Labour rose, cap in hand. A foot shifting, uneasy fellow, he spoke with a strong north of England accent.

"Television stations are full of the affairs in Northern Ireland, and the recent demonstrations taking place. The press 'ave been carryin' the story worldwide. Now we've got very little word on all this, an' we want some answers!" Overawed by the occasion and size of his audience, he sat down with a sheepish expression on his face.

There were several shouts and further questions, one obscure comment from the back benches, a languid, pretty voice, "Terrorist bullying - blackmail!" greeted with titters from the Opposition. Wolsey rose to respond, with contrast in tone and deliberately mellifluous prose, once more the Establishment voice.

"As the honourable member records, there have, indeed, been lengthy stories, crass tabloid nonsense on these tragic events and their exploitation by some unfriendly, irresponsible foreign press. The unfortunate boy, his condition uncertain, and his grandfather, a notorious IRA terrorist, now deceased. Most of the comments are coming from unauthorised elements of the so called, free press, or from even less restrained sources, trying to portray the man as some sort of heroic figure, in his war against the majority elected British administration in Northern Ireland."

A voice shouted, "By a gerrymandered electorate!" Heads turned, eyes focused toward the Gallery.

Wolsey continued as other voices rose in protest. "We came in peace, to enforce the law, to arrest a man wanted for international acts of terrorism. We were met with murder and mayhem. The tragic events the honourable member refers to demand resolute action. Justice must prevail. There is an unalterable maxim in this violent world we live in. Simply, that those who live by the sword, die by the sword!"

Again an intrusive, harsh Irish accent, "Right ye' are, an' don't forget it!" Security moved quickly toward the Visitors' Gallery.

A single voice rose above the chorus of interruptions. "Who shot Sean McCarton? Who shot the boy?"

Wolsey shuddered, his mouth suddenly dry as the accompanying shouts drowned out any attempt at a response. The Speaker regained control as the voices subsided.

"The boy's shooting was an unfortunate tragedy, caused by unwarranted and callous gunfire from the terrorists. Their savage and indiscriminate response, I remind you, also caused the loss of several members of our Special Patrol."

The Chamber was bound in the sudden spell of horror and anger. Wolsey again had their attention.

"We are conducting an extensive investigation. Two IRA terrorists have been detained. We suspect they may also have had some role in other recent incidents."

Suddenly aware of the winking eyes of the recording cameras above him, and in response to increased shouts for further information, Wolsey added more prudently, "In the interest of national security, we are not prepared to say more at this time." He resumed his seat.

In the Visitors' Gallery, an elderly couple sat, hand in hand. Occasionally they would smile to one another. Her head nodding, she listened to his whispered words. "This charade's a pitiful burlesque. Before Rome fell, the Barbarians were at the gates. Their time has come an' gone."

In the Chambers below, Wolsey admonished the news media to exert restraint, in the interests of National Security. His comments were vocally derided from the Opposition calling for, "freedom of the press!" Another voice from the Gallery shrilled, "Fascism reborn!" The Speaker's cries for order went unheeded.

Wolsey ignored the last remark, skilfully and eloquently deflecting questions, deferring any substantive answers. Calmly gazing before him, his words deliberate digressions, the righteous voice slyly slid to its target.

"With the intrusion of the criminal Diaspora of Southeast Asia, this is indeed a time for closer international surveillance, and more strict home security measures.

"A decline in moral values is leading to the rise in the use of drugs in the neighbouring Republic, likely origins from the European littoral also a threat to British youth, and this at a time of a rising spirit of unrest, in Ireland and elsewhere."

Even as he spoke, Wolsey's mind was elsewhere. Whatever games he played, he knew the traditional response would no longer hold. It was a different world. For the continuous "Irish problem", plaguing every British government for the past four hundred years - in too many ways now, the game was up. And for Wolsey, not a moment too soon. He continued to mouth the well-worn platitudes.

This was surely his moment of destiny. The countries of the old world regimes were again in disarray. No time to "waffle", as the now sly images of Imperialism were reborn.

For the rustic, urban drones of the dependent voting majority, the unemployable and other lower class yobs, Wolsey would present himself as misled by Britain First and its motives, by the PASS conspiracy. Britain First, the more he learned of it, was undeserving of public trust. Wolsey, a victim of his misplaced trust of the establishment, would be seen as a decent man of the people - trusting and trustworthy.

Wolsey perceived himself truly a patriot, fearlessly defending his fellow countrymen with a vigilant, discerning eye. His suspicions confirmed from the earlier discussions with Gordon, Wolsey now clearly saw the villains in PASS, and likely others in MI6. He was planning to place the blame where it would best be absorbed, with the recently dead, the innocent and their executioners. He would wait till all the evidence was in. With some well-chosen public censure, he would negotiate the replacement of the more visible opponents with some suitably chosen colleagues. Geoffrey Gordon, once a timely candidate, was now more a liability, a convenient victim. Wolsey concluded, Gordon must go.

The recent mission to Northern Ireland would serve up a widening array of suspects and victims. And as he had concluded listening to Gordon, and from Mays' phone call, there was evidence of real problems developing from the Middle East. Among the suspects was Finucane. The curious gathering of Finucane's friends was a dangerous association for a member of British Intelligence. Indeed, Wolsey cautiously concluded, DeVeere himself was not above suspicion.

Wolsey suspected the allegations of the Chinese government and Madam's suspicions of the so-called China Scheme might well be correct. He wondered to what extent such a fraud had been subscribed to, not alone by members of the Hong Kong administration, but also by some in the Australian government and, undoubtedly now, by others within the home government. He realised his good fortune in not associating too closely with those in Britain First, despite their frequent overtures. The final word here could be a vehicle toward his certain progress to elected Prime Minister.

Wolsey had already determined his critical relationship within the European Community. His leadership in such a body, less the traditional confrontation, more a cooperative member of the new European family, could restore Britain's historic leadership in the West. Emancipation of the English people from the Northern Irish economic yoke. No doubt this would be seen as a liberation for the Irish people – even the redundant "colon separatists". Ireland, a single socio-economic unit, no longer "beggar-nanny", more than able to support itself. The savings from the subvention monies would be used to create new jobs in the high unemployment reaches of northern England, for housing, education and for other improved dependency support.

Warming to his theme, Wolsey saw the harvest of peace on the outer islands of Europe as, the "Wolsey Restorations". More important, he saw the real goal, the restoration of the lost spirit of England; the mother country - her children grown now, the mother able and willing to let them go it alone in a community of nations.

Whatever developed from the hearings at the United Nations, he would plan his agenda in a series of cautious concessions, yet with a firm stand against terrorism. Arthur Wolsey, descendant of generations of the Imperial establishment, masters of survival, of astute prevarication, obfuscation and sly divergences, would seek all alternatives to confrontation for which today's Britain was less equipped.

Quickly refocusing, Wolsey heard a voice from the Opposition benches requesting the Prime Minister's further comments on the unjustified use of excessive force in the past seventy-two hours.

Wolsey rose to stand before the Table of the House, sensing the trap, his gaze fixed defiantly on his questioner. He paused, then, somewhat abstrusely, commented,

"Just as Madam herself, recently so brutally assassinated, quoted the words of Santayana, 'to forget history is to repeat its mistakes.'

"As with many of my illustrious predecessors, we are obliged, yet again, to resort to stern counter measures against another generation of terrorists - to protect law abiding citizens. The boy was the sad victim of one of their own indiscriminate, terrorist excesses. These are the people to whom justice, with a firm, fair hand, is being administered in Northern Ireland."

His focus re-fixed on his questioner, the paternal tone prevailed. "This generation of terrorists will find the hand of British justice equally implacable. Peaceful resolution is their only recourse." As if on cue, a burst of cheering erupted from the Government benches.

Wolsey's inspired moment quickly passed. His questioner had risen, with a curt shout, "Would the Prime Minister like to answer the question? The request was for information - not this rambling digression!"

The cheers were quickly drowned out by jeering and laughter from across the aisle. Questioners stood, waving their hands. Among them, the Opposition's eloquent Northern Irish voice, waiting to play the part Wolsey had in mind. Glancing at the Speaker who was gavelling furiously for silence, Wolsey faced his opponents, arms folded, chin pugnacious. Churchillian, he stood, waiting for the demonstration to cease.

Wolsey then seated himself, his gaze drawn to an elderly couple in the Visitors' Gallery. Expressionless, they returned his stare. As the shouts and questions resumed, Wolsey was startled to see Geoffrey Gordon enter the Gallery. He took a seat, shoulders hunched, his face in the shadows.

Again, calls for questions. Wolsey stared toward the Opposition benches. He sensed the unwavering gaze from Gordon, and from the couple seated nearby. The Speaker, her wig askew, continued calling for order.

The moment's silence was interrupted by a penetrating north of Ireland accent. "Civil Rights suppressed in Northern Ireland. No free speech in Northern Ireland." There was some booing, some shouts of support. Again from the Speaker, "Order! Order!"

Wolsey waited, then replied, "It seems you sir, must have enough of both in Britain to be able to utter such

291

words in this House, birthplace of free expression for all men everywhere."

"And mother of oppression", continued the implacable voice. Wolsey couldn't quite see where the comments were coming from. The same voice spoke again. "The American colonies only succeeded in freeing themselves from the mother of freedom by kicking her out." This brought snickers and laughter.

Wolsey rose and responded angrily, "There are some radical elements within the House whose aim seems to be directed to subverting the responsible government of the country." There were cries of, "Hear, hear!" from the government benches behind him.

A Unionist member rose to speak. He was a notably hard core Loyalist, Protestant clergyman, whose presence Wolsey considered an embarrassing but necessary burden. Staring about with a surly expression, his curious accent rendered his words nearly unintelligible. It was a typical if inauspicious beginning, well suited to Wolsey's purpose.

"As a loyal subject of Great Britain, I will not be deterred from defending the lawful rule of the Unionist government of Northern Ireland."

There was suppressed laughter from both sides of the House. Stop while you're ahead, Wolsey was thinking, his senses offended by the crude, historic redundancy of the man. With luck, he thought, the need for such a vote will soon be equally redundant.

Red faced and defiant, the man glared angrily around the room. The short, stout figure cleared his throat, blew his nose loudly. He ignored the taunt, "Is that all ye' have to say, Reverend?" Amid further giggles and hoots, the Speaker rose from behind the dais, her voice shrill, wig trembling, robes billowing.

"Sergeant-at-Arms! We will not tolerate this hooliganism! Give the man 'is chance!" Voice shaking with indignation, now in more proper Oxbridge tones, "Attention please for the Honourable Unionist member from Belfast."

Seeming oblivious to the subdued titters, he began, "The

world, and indeed, a large section of the British public have again been misled, in sympathy for the young victim of another terrorist act."

To Wolsey's dismay, he added, "As the Prime Minister has said, the killing, the bombings, the shooting, the sabotage, the assassinations are all droppings of the same sheep." The last observation brought bursts of laughter, gavelled to silence. The little man plodded doggedly onward, only to be again interrupted.

"Reverend, ye're a lying, bitter wee man! Your days are over."

In stunned silence members stood, peering about. Muffled shouts sounded from below the Gallery as several CID officers lead a struggling figure toward the exit.

Wolsey raised his voice to be heard. "I will be happy to answer your questions, civilly phrased, even from those not according the same courtesy to their fellow members - who seem to think that force and hooliganism will replace the rule of law and order."

Again the hard voice, penetrating the raucous exchange. "We've just listened to that." Scarcely a pause and the earnest pas de deux, the contrived appearance of "democracy at work" continued. From the Visitors' Gallery, the elderly couple listened in amusement. The disordered mockery prevailed.

A surge of requests calling for "Questions" subsided as the stout clergyman rose again. Christian humility forgotten, defiant now, he shouted to be heard. Members on both sides of the House waved their arms toward the preacher and the Speaker, deliberately pointing to their watches; some blatantly yawning or rudely gazing at one another with raised brows.

The little man angrily shook his notes toward the Opposition benches. "We all know the forces of evil that are being unleashed abroad: heathen forces of the devil the Prime Minister referred to, giving money, arms, drugs, bombs an' the like to those who've never known what Democracy's about. Never known the meaning of freedom!"

Another voice, "As in Northern Ireland, right?"

Visibly agitated, the minister of God continued, "It's

time they accepted that the word of God comes first! One of the
responsibilities of those living in a Godly, free society," he went
on, more comfortable in his assumed role, "is to be tolerant of the
rights of others. And," he added smugly, "to respect the law."

Renewed acclaim was shouted from the government
benches, "Hear, Hear!" Again a different voice, clear,
penetrating, spoke out. "In northern Ireland? Whose law? Whose
freedom? Whose rights?" The other intransigent voice was about
to be heard, Wolsey's plans now being realised.

The clergyman stood, hands on his hips, a man and a
tradition at bay, glaring around the chamber. His glares met with
hoots, laughter from the Opposition benches - a call, "Answer
the question!" Flushed and defiant, he shouted, "Make your
questions then! I'm not beholden' to any of you. We're part of
the U.K., the voice of an independent people, an' with or without
your help we'll stay that way!"

With a deep, gruff resonance another voice spoke, the
accent more Scottish, with rolled, definitive consonants.

"There ye stand, wee man, the last Roundhead,
disowned descendant of the conqueror's mercenaries. Cherishing
your differences - only sustained by your contrived ancient
religious hatreds nobody else cares about."

All heads turned toward the backbenches. Straining
faces peered from the balcony. A tall, sedate figure emerged
from the shadows below. Jim McClean, Nationalist member of
Parliament, slowly stepped toward the front. With a smile on his
face he pointed toward the Government benches.

"Wee man, do you not see it? Your differences are a
fantasy, all tight in your mind. You're just another one of us,
sharing the same island. Your fears and mistrust, man, are
nurtured and exploited by the criminal doctrine of separatism, of
discrimination and partition. Come out of your corner and let us
share your fears - share the soil all of us and none of us own."

Wolsey hadn't counted on this. Things were not going
according to plan. Wolsey again noticed Gordon, face still
invisible, and the elderly couple, returning his stare. He found
himself wishing Security would clear the Gallery. Those staring
eyes had begun to disturb him far more than the rowdiness in

the Chamber.

McClean, arms folded, one hand to his chin, considered, then slowly continued, "As Mandela, jailed as a terrorist, has shown us, and the dream Martin Luther King spoke of. If bitter recriminations are no answer, a wee bit of honest disclosure helps. When you preach violence or vengeance, you've forgotten the purpose of your religion."

McClean gazed at the little preacher, now stirring uncomfortably. Among shouts from the Government benches and from the Speaker, Wolsey sat silent. McClean, oblivious to the objections, turned to face Wolsey.

"The stink of your theft and exploitation, your doctrine of separatism and class distinction, your deliberate speech and mockery of justice, your titles and your vestments - all false trappings of supremacy, marks of illegal possession - of your mislabelled monarchy now retired. This is the only heritage you're remembered for."

McClean gazed at the faces. The Chamber silently waited. The very presence of the man, his speech and confidence seemed to command the audience.

"In the words of the American President Lincoln, reluctantly compelled to fight a civil war to sustain the integrity of the United States, 'A country divided against itself will not endure.'"

Shouted objections were followed by an angry cry from the Speaker.

McClean continued. "The key issue, economic inequity - a vision of things to come. At a time of worsening global unemployment, all of us share the guilt. Labour the victim, my friends, of universal corruption, of corporate greed. In the UK alone, more than twenty percent of the population live in poverty."

In an uncomfortable silence, McClean turned to look at his Unionist countryman. "And my friend, no better in Northern Ireland. The separated fiefdom flounders along as a dependent, branch plant, civil service economy. A six billion deficit, while its southern brothers have a six billion surplus. And that's your separatist Union party, my reverend friend!"

McClean faced the preacher across the aisle. "Don't you realise in a United Ireland you'll exert more influence among your own, more voice among your own than you'll ever have among these strangers, who care nothing for you?"

"With Ireland viewed as a whole community, whatever the cultural affinities cherished, the achievements of a shared economy will have the final impact - the voice of the community."

There was a burst of cheers and clapping. Wolsey sat, strangely silent. McClean was expressing much of Wolsey's own goals. Turning again to confront Wolsey across the floor of the chamber, McClean's voice rose.

"Prime Minister, this is your unique opportunity to be remembered in history as the man who courageously undid a great wrong, who attained greatness by helping us all in reconciling our differences."

Suddenly a member of the Opposition hurried from the benches to McClean's side, handing him a note. McClean read the message, looking momentarily startled. He stared hard at Wolsey. "Is there no end to your great games?"

Angry voices rose in protest, members on the government benches called, "Sergeant-at-arms! Madam Speaker!" Unfazed, McClean raised his own voice, the resonant Scottish consonant penetrating the discordance of unintelligible Tyneside or deliberate and mellifluent Oxbridge drawl.

"We have just received word from the United Nations calling for a meeting of the Security Council on Article 2(7), issues of Domestic Sovereignty in Northern Ireland and areas of persistent and unresolved sectarian conflict. Threats of the legality of Britain's qualifications as a member of NATO." In the uneasy silence, McClean's gaze never faltered. "More secrets to be revealed, more to tell, Prime Minister? Or more lies? I call for a vote of no confidence in this government."

From the Opposition benches some called, "Hear him out."

Among a renewed outburst of shouts, the Speaker's voice was just short of a shriek. "Your time is up Sir! Yield the floor! You are out of order!"

McClean spoke forcefully as Security made their way along the Galleries. "The Seanache was a victim of your meddling and your lies. Before the House I would ask the leader of this Interim Government - was this mission an attempt to carry out the deceased Prime Minister's unapproved plan Ajax - to assassinate the Irish Republican leaders?"

Security officers approached McClean, uncertain, deferential. They stood by, reluctant to physically intervene in this Sanctum Sanctorum of the Establishment.

McClean called out, "I demand the arrest of those responsible for this terrorist campaign by British Intelligence. The only resolution is for Britain's withdrawal of her troops from Ireland, withdrawal of her administration, subvention, her bribe. Then you'll see them all at the table! No bribe - no enforcers! No money - no war!"

The whole chamber stared toward the pale, Patrician features of the interim Prime Minister. Summoning stubborn resources, Wolsey rose, glared across the aisle. Agonising, he wondered, was this a blunder of historic finality? The remnants of Empire, resonant of the glory of Rome reborn, now a miscarriage - conspiracy revealed in all its ugliness. Perhaps his time had indeed come, and gone.

Briefly he glanced toward the Gallery. The elderly couple had risen. Returning his stare, the old man smiled, then they were gone.

At the rear of the chambers, the constant, rhythmic sound of television cameras presided over an era stumbling to its tawdry close.

CHAPTER THIRTY-ONE

The Deception

In leather lined, oak bound comfort in the reception room of the legal chambers of Stokes and Stokes, An Luc sat, patiently awaiting Paddy's return. His mind was filled with wonder at the strange path he seemed destined to follow since leaving Muong Sing. He thought of Terri Sai, supposedly in Hong Kong. He wondered if she was in danger.

One floor below and a world away, in the dusty vaults of the prestigious firm of legal consultants, Paddy Finucane confronted a stack of deeds and records. Among them, an accounting of the "stolen acres" of conquest - land grants bestowed on The Earls of Clanrickard, to ensure their loyalty to the royal succession. Early parchment contracts told of decades of possession and callous repossession - the eccentric priorities of an era long gone. Among the papers rested a family's secrets of once titled baronies, the tragedies of yesterday, its reality now harshly manifest.

Sir Reginald Stokes had personally attended to Paddy's urgent demand for the Granart papers. The old man located the dusty metal boxes containing a substantial collection of files, folders and ledgers.

Paddy spread the material before him, hesitant at first to explore what would surely be a Pandora's box. He hoped to find some answers, verification of the story revealed to him in the past few days by Jack Edwards; the Seanache's account leading to the subsequent, "accidental death" of Paddy's father.

Untying the cords that bound the dusty ledgers, he reverently withdrew the age-browned papers and began to read; as time passed, to listen. Eager whispers filled the room. Insidiously, Paddy found himself drawn back in time as his eyes

298

raced across the brittle pages.

Paddy wondered what Geoffrey Gordon had known about his father, and had never told him. He was reminded of the summons he received, requesting his urgent attendance at Whitehall later today. MI6 Deputy Director General Blount had sounded distinctly uncomfortable, alluding to questions relating to his actions in Northern Ireland. Paddy glanced at his watch. He was still in good time.

Paddy sat back as his thoughts turned to memories of his father. On vacation from Harrow, his father stood beside him on the stone jetties of Newcastle harbour. Before them, the beaches of Dundrum Bay swept to the north. His father, seeming sad and pensive, reminded Paddy, "On such a day almost four hundred years ago, our ancestors sailed from the barren moors, the southern Uplands of Scotland, to these same silent beaches. Stern and forbidding mercenaries, fierce conquerors, hard eyed Calvinists - seeing themselves as righteous missionaries, men of God, the Bible and Lord Cromwell. And that, Paddy, is our heritage."

Paddy's thoughts turned to the voices of the mourners at the Seanache's funeral. The timing of the Seanache's death made the impact inevitable. An Anglican bishop, former Chaplain to the House of Commons, had introduced himself as a "privileged friend of Sean McCarton." Describing his shame and grief, he called, "When will it be enough?"

An elderly speaker from South Africa described his people's similar struggle with Apartheid, emerging as victims of a beleaguered and partitioned continent. The South African had met the Seanache many years before. His goals were similar to McCarton's. He quoted from a young American, Robert Kennedy, in South Africa in 1966, in support of their struggle for freedom.

"'Each time a man stands up for an ideal, or acts to improve the lot of others, or speaks out against injustice, he sends forth a tiny ripple of hope.' These words, as easily applied to the Irish struggle," the South African told them, "gave courage to those like Steven Biko and many others who fought Apartheid and discrimination in South Africa."

A young fugitive from China, Liu Xiabo, founder of the dissident "New China Group", who now lived and worked in Hong Kong to restore freedom for his fellow countrymen, told them the story of a young Chinese woman, a student at Beijing University. "In her writings she conveyed a new philosophy of wisdom, truth and tolerance - of faith and love and sharing. From her we came to know the patient courage and humour we needed to prevail. Aija Tsi, her name, like the Seanache's, will live long after we are gone."

The remote sounds of the tocsin of Big Ben, the traffic from the nearby streets, drew Paddy's thoughts back to the circle of light about the sheltered annex. He sat reading to the last page, occasionally making notes. He looked up then to see the silent figure of Sir Reginald Stokes regarding him from the stairwell. Without comment, Paddy gathered the pages of Edwina Granart's journal, and two chosen letters, the precious envelope with its fragmented seal, and the long concealed original copy of the Treaty, placing all carefully in his briefcase. Paddy rose, latched his briefcase and joined the elderly barrister.

"Hope you found what you sought, Paddy."

Paddy nodded, handing Stokes a list of the letters he had removed from the files. He wondered if Stokes was aware of the material in Lady Granart's journals.

"Do you recall Sean McCarton's visit seeking to read the Granart files?"

Shaking his head, Stokes stared perplexedly at Paddy. Preceding Paddy up the stairs, Stokes replied,

"In a way Paddy, necessary as it was for so many reasons, I was sorry to see your return to England. It seems to reopen old wounds."

They stared at one another, Paddy at a loss for words. How much did Sir Reginald know about his past? Stokes almost whispered, his eyes gazing across the room with a far-away expression, "On the occasion of your father's last visit, I felt he knew his life was in danger."

Rejoining An Luc, Paddy revealed to Stokes their intention to leave for Hong Kong the following day, to attend to urgent business. Stokes murmured, "In the words of Mao

Tse Tung, 'So many deeds cry out to be done - and always urgently.'" They shook hands, the older man gazing almost enviously, sadly even, at Paddy and An Luc as they crossed the park beneath the trees of Grey's Inns Gardens.

As the cab threaded its way toward Whitehall through the late afternoon traffic, Paddy stared ahead, distracted. He reached to the inner pocket of his jacket, reassured by the small, hard packet of keys. After Sean McCarton's funeral, they had made an unscheduled stop in Castlewellan, not far from Kilcoo, where Maloney, his political role and discretion forgotten, told them stories of the Seanache, and of their meeting in Dublin less than forty-eight hours before his death. Paddy remembered the different faces, a cross section from the graveside, an international presence.

Arriving back at the Europa from Castlewellan, Paddy, An Luc and Ben Harrari were joined by Jack Edwards, who had gone to visit Theresa at the women's jail in Armagh, then to visit Dan at the Maze in Belfast. Jack had decided to postpone his return to the US; his evidence was now being requested by Theresa and Dan's counsel to assist with their defence.

Jack had also stopped at the Royal Victoria Hospital to check on Sean. Only Sheila was permitted to see her son, still listed as critical. The news was not good. During a time of consciousness Sean had asked his mother to give Jack a "wee trophy", for trying to help his granddad. Reaching inside his pocket, Jack brought forth a crumpled envelope. There were exclamations of surprise from both Paddy and Ben when Jack withdrew a dully-glinting little key.

"Dan gave this to Sean as we waited to take him to the Royal Vic," Jack explained. "It had been given to Dan in Nicaragua." Jack laid the key on the table.

"Dan told me the incredible story. In Nicaragua, Frank and Dan's commandant, El Negro, a Black American veteran from Vietnam, had given the key to Dan. The commandant told Dan a brave lady had given the key to him during a bloody firefight in Cambodia, shortly before the Americans left Vietnam."

301

"Buddy Johnson!" Ben and Paddy exclaimed together. It could only be the great master sergeant who had served with them at Phnom Penh. Another member of Spec Force Seven, alive!

Reaching inside the envelope Jack revealed a second key, an exact copy of the first. He described his own harrowing escape. Jack was in Saigon awaiting word from Spec Force Seven's mission. Word of the disaster had finally come from An Luc's father, Y Jhon. An Luc listened, sad but proud to hear how his father, wounded in the streets of Saigon, had delivered the message and the key from Paddy and Anna, before he died.

Paddy reached to add his, and the one from Jean Claude Davost to the collection. Ben Harrari laid his own key next to the others.

"I carried this as a memento from my time with Spec Force Seven, an inspiration in later conflicts."

Paddy's last conversation with Perry confirmed for all of them the continuing significance of the keys, Perry's confession now lost.

Jack gathered the five keys lying before him and pushed them toward Paddy. "We're with you, Paddy," he promised, "wherever they lead us."

Ben nodded. "There are others looking for these keys, he warned. "It's whoever gets there first."

Shortly before midnight, Bob Thompson joined them. He had been held up, interviewing the international visitors at Castlewellan. Thompson invited them to join him in meeting someone of special significance to all of them. Smiling broadly to Paddy, "Someone you've met before, I believe."

Paddy, An Luc, Jack and Ben followed Thompson through the doors of the old pub across the street. Paddy was genuinely surprised to see the smiling face of Rashid Safarov.

With a shared sense of trust, Safarov and Ben Harrari found instant common ground. Each recognised growing concern for Abdul Said's identification of El Algazi as a possible link to the continuing mystery of Professor Senjaye.

Safarov chose his words carefully.

"My sources are reliable, and time is short. The role here

Paddy, we suspect, is being played by a British Intelligence link with a major drug cartel. The reason perhaps, for the ultimate strike in Gibraltar, to guard other secrets. Who knows," Safarov remarked. "A different link, other executioners perhaps."

Paddy began to see a common thread, a possible drug connection further east to Hong Kong. For Paddy, still feeling the pain following the loss of Anna, an even wider threat was emerging. The manner of her death, the Weatherbys' brutal assassinations, Victor Perry's "confession" and demise, the Seanache's "third nemesis", and Safarov's story, confirmed the presence of a more sinister agenda. Recent suspicions of an even more militant role stirring possible nuclear confrontation or worse, in "middle Asia" – were given very real credibility.

As they'd left the pub, everyone promised to stay in touch. Paddy told Jack of the summary order he'd received for his immediate return to London, for an urgent meeting with the Directors of Intelligence at Horse Guards. The tone of the summons left little doubt in Paddy's mind of trouble ahead. Jack revealed his decision to resign from his role with the National Security Agency, and US intelligence.

"Both of us out of a job," Jack joked, smiling at Paddy as they shook hands on the steps of the Europa.

CHAPTER THIRTY-TWO

The Hearing

On arrival at Horse Guards, Paddy paid the cab driver. An Luc nudged his arm. "Tuan, look! Again they watch us." Paddy turned in the direction An Luc was staring. For a brief instant, the old couple from Paris stared back at them from across the street. Then as quickly they were gone.

Inside the reception area of Horse Guards, the unsmiling secretary acknowledged "Lord Finucane", with a curt nod to An Luc.

"The committee will see you shortly." Primly she added, "Mr Bill Whitcombe, in Hong Kong, has left a message for you to call."

An Luc took a seat as Paddy walked over to the tall Georgian windows. He gazed out past the wrought iron fences to the gardens of St James' Park. Beneath the trees, children played, giddily chasing one another across the bridges and around the lake. Paddy saw none of these things; his thoughts were of Anna. Firmly grasping the briefcase where the precious papers reposed, he reached inside his jacket to touch again the small packet of keys.

"Lord Finucane, the committee will see you now."

With a quick nod to An Luc, Paddy passed into the large inner office. A formal row of people sat at a long table before which a single chair was placed. There were no greetings; the committee seemed oblivious to his entrance, talking in quiet undertones to one another.

At the centre of the table Paddy recognised DeVeere, Director General of MI6, and his assistant, Deputy Director General Blount; others were unknown to him. To one side, he saw Geoffrey Gordon, who barely acknowledged Paddy's gaze.

Beside Gordon, the DDG of MI5, Maurice Stanfield, returned his look with a more friendly nod.

"Lord Finucane, will you please take a seat?" DeVeere asked. "This hearing today has been requested by the Prime Minister, Sir Arthur Wolsey."

DeVeere made brief introductions. Some of the names, Paddy remembered, Michael Weatherby had mentioned, including Deicey, from Security Intelligence, Middle East. Only Southeast Asia station, it seemed, was not represented.

"Lord Finucane, it is our understanding that you attended the funeral and subsequent rituals of the known Irish Republican terrorist, Sean McCarton, and that your role contradicts the purpose of your assignment, and is contrary to the interests of the intelligence community. Completely without our authorisation."

DeVeere glanced at the notes before him, then toward Gordon, as if specifically seeking his concurrence. Gordon, his gaze fixed rigorously before him, sat silent, immovable. Irritated, DeVeere continued.

"Lord Finucane - we were concerned to learn these meetings were also attended by some persons of international political stature." His voice rose slightly. "Some of these members were heard to express critical comments regarding Britain's role in Northern Ireland, using the occasion, I might say, as an opportunity to express terrorist sympathies and support. All of which your comments seemed to support."

His tone became harsh. "This, from a member of British intelligence - of a distinguished heritage, recently short listed for a responsible appointment in the Service. Your indiscretions, Lord Finucane, I would suggest, scarcely reflect this background." Paddy listened to the man's insensitive arrogance.

DeVeere stared grimly at Paddy. "These inappropriate demonstrations occurred in the presence of, and with the apparent collusion of a member of the American intelligence community, whose actions have yet to be explained. More indiscreet, and scarcely in your favour, in the curious company of a member of Mossad, witnessed in the presence of a widely read political columnist, not noted for his sympathy with British policy."

In response to a query directed to him by a committee member, Geoffrey Gordon commented, "Jack Edwards, I am told, has resigned his role with American intelligence, and is extending his stay in Northern Ireland." Gordon glanced uneasily at Paddy as Blount quickly interrupted.

"To give evidence at his own hearings, brought up by the Northern Ireland Office at the request of a British intelligence representative on the scene."

DeVeere hastily interjected, "Choosing to testify in the defence of the arrested terrorists. And today, news from our team in the United States," DeVeere's voice sounded incredulous, "the American is offering his services as a witness for the case being made by Human Rights Representatives at the UN. And again, we learn from our representative in Brussels, by Amnesty International at the European Courts at the Hague. Both complaints, on the conduct of British Security Forces in Northern Ireland, challenging the eligibility of British membership in the United Nations, on the basis of the ongoing sectarian conflict." DeVeere paused, grimly glancing up and down the table. "The situation, gentlemen, is out of control." DeVeere's anger was barely concealed.

Geoffrey Gordon gazed unhappily toward the windows. Jack Edwards had not wasted time in carrying out his intentions, nor had Graham, in contacting the home office.

For many seated before him, Paddy realised his role sent mixed signals. For some, a transiently useful pawn in the farcical "games", seeing their own role magnified in the fight for centre stage. For others, Paddy's evident defection was a dangerous nemesis. Paddy remembered Weatherby's warnings, how in the "intelligence community", old traditions die hard - DeVeere their suave prototype. In former days, Reilly, ace of spies, to Lawrence and Bell, to the later Philbys.

Paddy looked into the hard faces before him, wondering what their game was now. The devious arrogance of the elders, of SIS, of MI6, watched now by the untrusting colleagues of MI5 and their ancillary services. Paddy saw a mixed jury before him. For some in MI5, Paddy's family heritage placed him as a member of the establishment, of the favoured few. For those in MI6, his unconventional history, his prior service with the Americans in foreign fields and the uncertain story of his father's death all placed him in a realm of mistrust. Yet for the decent few, the moral sceptics, successors to Weatherby - wondering if Paddy's political apostasy reflected his own peculiar non-conformity - they listened.

"We are curious," DeVeere said, carefully watching Paddy, "as to who might have organised these meetings following the funeral." It was not a question, but more of a statement from one who already knew, thought Paddy as he stared back at DeVeere. He quickly saw the other struggle here. Could Arthur Wolsey have set the stakes, or was it DeVeere, waiting in the wings, ready and eager to take advantage of Wolsey's errors?

There was a moment's silence. For some, weighing the issues; choosing sides perhaps. With cautious glances, papers were shuffled; each member of the committee refocused, their attitudes now more predatory.

Morris Stanfield, a veteran officer of MI5, asked almost deferentially, "How did you perceive your role in the events in Northern Ireland?" Plainly designed to offer Paddy some mitigating circumstances, Stanfield proffered, "Perhaps in your zeal to extricate the American, your long time friend, might you have overstepped your assignment? The meeting referred to was merely a spontaneous gathering of international observers?"

Looking to other members of the panel, Stanfield continued, "And, in Lord Finucane's own case and that of his former comrades, it was indeed an unexpected reunion. To be noted," Stanfield gazed along the table to each member of the panel, "well recognised - Lord Finucane's very distinguished record here, and in the later campaign in Afghanistan against the forces of terrorism."

Some still regarded "Lord Finucane" as one of the favoured few, yet one who seemed to have spent as little of his life as possible in England. As a further reminder of his unconventional "colonial ways", he had an Asian bodyguard, who rarely left his side.

The hearing was briefly interrupted by a knock at the door. The secretary motioned to Stanfield, who hurried from the room.

Blount, DDG MI6, another Cambridge prodigy, leaned across the table, gazing toward Geoffrey Gordon. "We are aware that Lord Finucane," he deliberately stressed the title, "and the late Mr. Weatherby were present when Madam's plan Ajax was first discussed. We have learned of the government of Israel's knowledge of this supposedly classified plan. Now we note their presence at the eulogies for McCarton. Indeed, represented, we're told, by a close friend of Lord Finucane. I would suggest that the leak of plan Ajax was, in fact, the responsibility of Lord Finucane or his late friend, Michael Weatherby."

There was an uncomfortable silence. Paddy saw DeVeere glance at the ceiling, imperceptibly shake his head at his Deputy's casual indiscretion. In trying to implicate Paddy or Weatherby as the source of the leak to the Israelis, Blount had only succeeded in further focusing attention on the possibility that the recent shootings were indeed the result of an unauthorised execution of plan Ajax.

As Paddy anticipated, his response was unnecessary. Another member of MI6, Richards, hurriedly changed topics. He reminded his listeners of Paddy's disciplinary problems in the Irish Guards. Reviewing Paddy's records, Richards paused, obliquely adding, "Following the conclusion of the Vietnam conflict, Lord Finucane, you elected to remain in Northern Laos. Am I right?" Paddy nodded, knowing well where this was leading.

Cautiously then, the questions became more personal. Lord Finucane's wife was Chinese? Their home near the Chinese border, a refuge for dissident Chinese, in the epicentre of the Golden Triangle, involved in the manufacture and transport of drugs from southern Asia to the rest of the world. "This," commented Richards, slyly pursuing his path, "was some time before your independent assignment to Afghanistan. Both areas are the largest producers of opium and heroin in the world."

There was a palpable silence. Paddy's eyes were fixed on Richards as he consulted his notes.

"What was the extent of your own involvement, Lord Finucane, in the Chinese dissident movement? And, as with the mujahidin, what was their concurrent involvement in the drug trade into China?" Then, incautiously, "Were you yourself involved in the active drugs for arms trade, the threat you referred to in the DEA meetings? Did this play a role in the circumstances of your wife's death?"

Seeing Paddy's menacing stare, and hearing the cough and shuffle of some of those at the table, Richards falteringly withdrew his question, adding that he would wait to see the evidence.

DeVeere, suddenly leaning forward, directed his gaze toward Gordon. "Any further word, Sir Geoffrey, on the murder of Captain Grey?" It was a startling change of direction. Staring uncomfortably at the papers before him, Gordon shook his head.

Gordon was not being completely candid. His thoughts immediately reverted to Graham's story, that the Australian who volunteered to take Grey's place had been unauthorised. Gordon had wondered about this. After the meeting with Wolsey earlier, Gordon had called a friend at the Australian Embassy, who confirmed that Tracker was indeed a highly decorated member of Australian SAS.

Gordon had listened with growing distress as his friend referred to, "a bloody great scandal in Hong Kong. Some sort of illegal investment scheme that's causing a lot of stir 'round here. Some of our chaps, they say, are involved. Sorry about Tracker, but the chap who arranged his assignment over here is now facing charges - conspiracy to defraud is all I can say at this time."

The words had left Gordon stunned. With some excuse, he abruptly hung up. Everywhere he looked impending disaster loomed. The China Scheme was proving a disaster. He could only imagine the disgrace. The ultimate personal humiliation was more than he could bear.

Gordon had received a call then, from DeVeere, of the impending interrogation of Paddy Finucane, apparently arranged with Wolsey's support. He felt betrayed. Why had Wolsey not mentioned his intention to have Paddy up before the

Directorate?

The one sided exchange continued, with Paddy's occasional, monosyllabic response, silent nod or shake of the head. Paddy's actions seemed puzzling, even to Gordon. Deeply troubled, Gordon saw the division between MI5 and MI6, the tricks and games in arrogant replay. Gordon only hoped the result would not be the same as the Weatherbys', or Paddy's own father - an "accident" conveniently arranged.

Again the secretary entered, delivering a note to Gordon. Gordon, reading the note, frowned. He excused himself and followed her from the room.

In the room above Horse Guards, across from St. James' Park, where the evening shadows lengthened, the moment of truth was being dexterously circumvented. Many now avoided Paddy's stare, shuffling papers or gazing elsewhere as Blount blithely invited Lord Finucane's response, "that we might decide which way to proceed in this unfortunate affair."

"There isn't enough time," Paddy finally began, "to undo the rumours you've spread, to expose the lies you've spoken. Sean McCarton was a man belonging to every country where freedom is cherished. He shared his life and support for the cause of oppressed peoples everywhere. Likely he's now a hero, and as large in stature to all those struggling for freedom in other areas of the world. It was my privilege to attend his funeral." Paddy looked at the faces before him; some stone eyed, unmoved, some listening.

Gordon returned. As he took his seat, he glanced about, immediately sensing the restless hostility. Paddy continued.

"In response to some of your questions, your misguided, ill informed or pedantic observations don't do you credit. We're all victims here. Deliberate products of misconceived prejudice, the distortions of British history. The interment of an old man," said Paddy almost reverently, "was an enshrinement of a legend for some. For me, the fall of another empire - finally thankfully, evanescent."

Gordon stared at Paddy. Chairs shifted in resentful expression, yet a modicum of restraint was evident; Paddy's words, or their own reservations, now dividing his listeners.

Blount and Deicey scribbled an occasional note. As Paddy described it, it was a clear denunciation of the creed of Britain First and PASS, of the very tradition they stood for, all that DeVeere and many on the panel had been raised to. For them, Paddy's words were the substance of his own convictions.

Across the parade ground, in the park and along the Mall streetlights flickered on. In a light rain, pale reflections were strewn on the wet pavements or floated among the trees. Everywhere, the pedestrian surge, across city streets, by Marble Arch, at Speakers Corner.

Paddy's testimony continued. "I recently read the uncensored version of history - learned the deception. The tragedy and shame may well have played a role in the unexplained disappearance of my father so many years ago.

"I came here today, to listen to the confusion and complaints of some, the self doubts, the lies of others, to tell the story, and to tender my resignation to Sir Geoffrey Gordon. I am ashamed of any part my family has played and want no further part in it, only to enable decent, English people to confront the truth."

Paddy concluded, speaking to each uneasy face before him - there would be no misunderstanding. "I will expose those responsible for the death of Sean McCarton, of the Weatherbys, and yes, unravel the mystery of my father's death. And surely, that of my wife. It is certainly a fact of history that only the submissive silence of the rest of us permits such evil to endure and recur. Perhaps we will learn now who the real enemy has been. Whatever the next historic catastrophe, we must now put our own house in order. And indeed we may discover then, we have been our own worst enemy."

Arms folded on the table in front of him, peering grimly from his notes, DeVeere slowly, pontifically responded.

"Lord Finucane, it is our conclusion, indeed in your own words, you don't fit, are not fit to be in her Majesty's service, which you seem to despise. Your words and actions convict you of disloyalty. Your unauthorised presence at the funeral of the terrorist, McCarton - your further attendance and indiscreet comments at the subsequent illicit gatherings - your earlier indiscretions in Paris are all an embarrassment to the British Government and to the Service."

The Director General concluded, glancing up and down the table, "I must inform you your proposed appointment to Southeast Asia has been rejected. Further than that," DeVeere was breathing heavily, frowning angrily, "since it seems you have offered your resignation, perhaps that is the best resolution of the whole matter."

Gordon could see the arrogance of some on the panel who had sealed Paddy's estrangement, confirming his mission to expose them. Uneasily, he knew there would be those who would make sure Paddy failed to reach his goals. Answers would come, yet all too late for the victims. Surely now too late for me, Gordon thought, sombrely glancing to either side.

No more to be said, DeVeere angrily gathered his papers. The hearing had raised more questions than it had answered. Blount's callous slip and other more immediate threats were now evident. Since Paddy had withdrawn from the Service, it seemed there were no other punitive or restraining measures he could impose. DeVeere was not reassured, saw another scandal imminent. Paddy's research into his father's death would be unhelpful to his own plans. Whom could he trust? Too many players, too many games. The greater threat now lay at home. Finucane's views could not be taken lightly. DeVeere looked about furtively. Guarded expressions avoided his glance. Two can play at that game.

Paddy rose, walked to the door, his eyes momentarily meeting Gordon's. How old and worn the man looked, his troubled expression and distant distraction. Gordon looked away as Paddy turned to leave. The other members of the Directorate had little to say to one another, some with a perfunctory nod to Gordon as they left the room.

Gordon stood, stared unseeing toward the distant street lamps. Moments later, his secretary stood by the door. He hadn't heard her knock; her quiet words repeated, "A phone call." Gordon, startled, quickly turned, apologising.

"From Morris Stanfield." With the incurious aplomb of long experience, she closed the door behind her. Gordon reached for the phone.

"Geoffrey. This is Morris Stanfield." In the silence that followed the quiet acknowledgment, Stanfield continued. "I'm at the Noah's Ark, the pub in Surrey owned by Lavery, the man who gave us the briefcase." The words hurried on, "I had a call from Security. They told me Lavery had disappeared." Still somewhat distracted, Gordon remained silent.

"I talked to Lavery's wife. She's hysterical, Geoffrey. She spoke of her husband's growing fears since the assassination. She mentioned something about different people questioning him. He didn't seem to know who they were."

Gordon said nothing. He was thinking again of the transient disappearance of Madam's briefcase, the delay in its original transfer from the pub owner, or from MI6 – he wasn't sure which!

Stanfield continued. "After the accident, one of her husband's first calls was to Security." Gordon sprang suddenly alert. "Another was to the newspaper man, Thompson, the same one who came down the night of Madam's assassination."

There was a pause. "Are you there, Geoffrey?"

Momentarily surprised by the casual reference to the journalist, Gordon had found the answer to a number of questions. Thompson's early presence in Northern Ireland was in many ways to be expected. Yet to be at the airport, as Gordon had heard it, in time to interview the American and British agents involved – he must have had prior information. Suddenly now, Gordon recalled Thompson's presence in Paris the night Madam had presented her plan Ajax. So Thompson had been at the Noah's Ark, possibly, even before MI6!

Gordon grunted some acknowledgment, scarcely listening as Stanfield concluded. "I've asked Westcott to send someone down to look into things. He's sending Colin Stene from Watchers, Internal Security." Stanfield then asked how the hearing had proceeded. Gordon answered with a brief negative summary. "What a shame," Stanfield sympathised. "A good man - like his father, a victim of circumstances, eh?"

Muttering some quiet assent, Gordon ended the call. Replacing the phone, he sat for a moment. Then, pressing the intercom to his secretary, he requested that he not be disturbed. She reminded him that Whitcombe was awaiting his call in Hong Kong.

Gordon walked to the window. What else had Thompson seen in Madam's briefcase? Then cynically, how much had he paid for it? If true, Thompson and Lavery were both now subject to charges for transgressions against National Security. Gordon suddenly recalled Stanfield's parting comment. He wished he had checked with him before calling Westcott. Westcott was one of "theirs" and, he recalled, an enthusiastic member of Britain First, likely of PASS.

Peering out the window, he stared into the gathering shadows. A misty rain fell in the flicker of the street lamps. Incredible, for a moment he thought he could see them clearly - the elderly couple he had sat next to in the Commons. Hands to the glass, he peered out across the parade ground below. He was unaware of the door opening quietly behind him, oblivious to the murmured solicitation by his secretary. She gazed, concerned, toward the bent figure - a motionless, muttering silhouette. Turning, she left the room, softly closing the door behind her.

Gordon was sure now, watching the couple as they made their way toward the darker shadows of St. James' Park. For a moment he thought he saw them turn, hand in hand, stare toward him, watching him. Could they really see him?

He pressed his face against the cool surface of the rain-misted pane. He rubbed his sleeve across the glass, peering intently toward the distant shadows. The streetlights were glowing now, transforming the shadows, creating new ones. He pressed harder to the glass. Where had they gone? He shivered. Who were they?

Suddenly he felt very old, very tired. He decided not to return Whitcombe's call. What was the point? The room grew darker. Lights flickered across the city, misty beacons among the trees of the distant St. James' Park.

CHAPTER THIRTY-THREE

"Western banks concentrate on the visible - whereas we stress the invisible." Comment of Agha Hassan Abedi, co-founder, with the help of British MI6 etc., of the Bank of Commerce and Credit International - at the BCCI corruption trials, 1988.

Paddy awoke to the phone ringing. It was near midnight.

"Sorry so late, Paddy, I tried to call earlier." Thompson sounded out of breath. "Remember Lavery, the pub owner who gave me the lead on Ajax? He called me. He was scared; felt he was in great danger. He couldn't tell me on the phone, something about a foreign lot, a possible link to Madam's assassination. And something about Grey's murder, the original C/O of the mission to the Mournes."

Thompson raced on. "I just got back from the Noah's Ark. Lavery wasn't there. His wife told me he panicked. She said he talked to someone in British Security by the name of Stanfield. We waited till evening; still no sign of him. He's disappeared, Paddy."

Paddy remembered Stanfield leaving the room during the interrogation at Horse Guards.

"Geoffrey Gordon mentioned Lavery the other day," said Paddy. "He doesn't trust him, said his story's always changing. A witness, perhaps, of more than he'd revealed, likely a victim now."

Paddy told Thompson of his departure to Hong Kong later today, to follow up on leads connected to the China Scheme. And, to locate Terri Sai, who probably held clues to Anna's murder. An Luc had been pleased to hear of Paddy's decision to follow Terri's path to Hong Kong. "It is the way, Tuan. The path back to Hong Kong will lead us to those who killed the lady Anna." For An Luc, it was a calm acceptance of *Kan Khat*, their destiny.

Checking the time of Paddy's departure, Thompson replied, "I've some calls to make; I'll meet you over there sometime after ten - that should give us a few hours sleep. See you then."

The curtains stirred in the night breeze from the river. Traffic sounds were muted as Paddy sat, wide-awake now. The news about Lavery had made him uneasy. He thought of the successive assassinations. The Weatherbys, Victor Perry, Abdul Said, even Madam, victims perhaps, of the same predator? And Sean McCarton? From the questionable motivation in the kidnapping of the Kurdish Scientist, Senjaye, to the now increasingly more significant international developments of the China Scheme, Paddy believed he had begun to unravel a chain of increasing international threat. Paddy was appalled at the enduring impact of Deevers' influence – the keys, their immutable, bizarre role. He remembered Victor's comment, that he would "tell all" in Washington - before it was too late.

A little after ten a.m. Paddy and An Luc greeted Bob Thompson in the hotel lobby. Seated in a corner of an otherwise empty restaurant, Paddy described the tense interrogation at Horse Guards the previous day.

"I gave them my resignation, Bob. I really didn't have much choice. It was a farce."

"You're well rid of them, Paddy," Thompson offered, with a cynical smile. He then mentioned there was still no clue to the whereabouts of Lavery.

Acting on a hunch earlier that morning, Thompson had managed to arrange a meeting with the C/O of Tracker's SAS Base at Aldershot. By a stroke of luck the colonel knew Thompson, had attended a course of lectures Thompson had given during the war in Afghanistan. The colonel spoke freely of Tracker, "The ultimate professional". Tracker's experience, special skills, fluency in Indo-Asian languages, expertise in hi-velocity missile technology had gained his C/O's admiration.

"The colonel," Thompson recalled, "described Tracker as 'quite keen' to volunteer to take his friend Grey's place." Thompson reminded them, "The Noah's Ark is less than twelve miles from Madam's residence. Madam's flight was on landing approach above the pub when struck by what was believed to be a ground to air missile. Grey's body was discovered at the bottom of the Thames, not far from the Noah's Ark. Tracker," said Thompson quietly, "I think we agree, though assigned to the SAS in Northern Ireland, was his own person, on his own mission." Paddy and An Luc shared the same conclusion.

"Maybe my imagination, Paddy, but since Heathrow I've had the feeling I'm being followed. As my cab left the airport a car pulled out beside us, then dropped immediately behind. Nothing subtle, as if they didn't care who noticed. Don't know what to make of it." Thompson added, "This makes me even more concerned about Lavery."

Paddy remembered his own experiences in Paris, where An Luc had first mentioned the older couple watching them. Paddy told Thompson he had watched a brief view of activities in the House of Commons on the news last night. As the cameras panned the Gallery, for a moment he recognised Geoffrey Gordon. More startling, just apart from Gordon, an elderly couple sat staring toward the camera. In that brief instant Paddy recognised the pair they'd seen in Paris, the same couple An Luc had seen in London. Could they also be watching Thompson? Not even this prominent, internationally known journalist, Paddy felt, could be safe.

Paddy then recalled a phone conversation with Jack Edwards the previous evening. "Jack said Maloney's attendance at McCarton's funeral and at the wake apparently did not have the wider support of his own government. His opponents called his journey to Northern Ireland a 'pilgrimage to terrorism'. Jack also heard, from others, admiration for Maloney's personal courage, for the considerable risks he had taken in his decision to be present at the funeral."

Thompson quickly commented, "The response to Maloney's actions might have been too soon. If Maloney recruits sufficient support at the United Nations, the European Union in Brussels, and the Irish-American Diaspora, not forgetting the wider influence of the others who attended the meeting, we might well see him and his government survive – figures even, of some international stature.

"More significantly," Thompson added, "In deciding to speak at the funeral, perhaps Maloney felt it was a chance to redress the wrongs they'd done McCarton and other incidents in previous years - the suppliant role of the Irish government in their shameful cooperation with British Security.

"That's surely something the Northern Ireland Administration and the British Government would wish to prevent. In fact," Thompson added, "that is probably the first time the topic of Northern Ireland, the uncensored version, has been on worldwide television, reaching an international audience.

"Has Jack heard anything about Dan and Theresa?" Thompson was well aware the decision of the judiciary in Northern Ireland follows the British path of arrest without warrant, detention without trial, and more recently, torture or termination.

"Jack told me Theresa and Dan are holding up well, with great courage," Paddy said, "Both are anticipating a significant international impact from Jack's testimony."

Paddy told Bob of the discovery of the legal documents among his family papers. "Perhaps now, with the evidence supporting McCarton's 1921 Treaty deception and Lavery's unwitting gift from the debris, authorising Ajax, there will be enough evidence to dismiss any charges. Not to forget the support generated from your own and other critical editorial comments, Bob."

Thompson nodded in agreement. He readily accepted Paddy's suggestion to copy the Granart papers, to deliver them to Belfast as soon as possible.

"Even now Bob, shadowed as both of us seem to be, these papers may be safer with you, and available where they're needed."

Paddy then told Thompson about a call he had made to Bill Whitcombe in Hong Kong. Whitcombe had described his

318

concern that McCarton's death was causing widespread criticism of British and American policy in Asia and the Middle East, inciting a more desperate response everywhere.

As Whitcombe had revealed, the repercussions of the China Investment Scheme were indeed global, unveiling a latter day Enron or Ponzi scheme, involving members of the outgoing administration in Hong Kong. There were also implications that those invested in the scheme nearer home were unaware of its criminal connections. Questions were being asked in the House, allegations of possible involvement of key Government figures, as well as in Australia.

As Paddy knew, Roger Moorefield was well aware of the scheme's wider scale, now under investigation. Could Geoffrey Gordon have inadvertently become involved?

Despite repeated efforts in the past few days, Whitcombe had been unable to reach Geoffrey Gordon. More worrying, he had received no return call, despite leaving messages with his secretary.

Whitcombe had heard no further word of Terri Sai, commenting that she may have gone underground with her friends in the dissident group. Before hanging up, Whitcombe promised to be at Kai Tek to meet them. He assured Paddy they would be continuing the search for Terri Sai.

As the early lunch crowd began to drift in, Thompson received a call from Lavery's wife. He left quickly, wishing Paddy and An Luc a safe return. One of the hotel managers approached their table. He bent low, murmuring to Paddy in a low voice, "Sir, there is a call for you. A Mr Stanfield – decribed as urgent."

Paddy picked up the phone in the manager's office, identifying himself. There was a pause, an audible grunt, a clearing of the throat, a sigh – then the voice of Morris Stanfield.

"Paddy I've got some bad news." Stanfield spoke reluctantly, his voice hoarse, "Sorry Paddy, but they found Geoffrey in his office at Horse Guards." The final words were choked. "He's dead – he shot himself."

CHAPTER THIRTY-FOUR

"Greed is good - greed works - greed is right - greed clarifies, cuts through and captures the essence of the evolutionary spirit." Gordon Gekko, from the movie *Wall Street,* 1991.

Above the rolling green fens, yellow with cowslips, the sleek sparrow hawks circled in uneasy flight, their fierce yellow eyes peering toward the furtive prey below. And the brown, slick rabbit, the bounding hare, the tiny field mouse - each momentarily paused, ever aware of their watchful nemesis.

At Gatwick airport outside London, British Airways flight 104 for Hong Kong prepared for takeoff. Two men and a woman stood by the rain streaked windows of the departure lounge, watching in silence as the DC 10, in turn, thundered down the runway. Climbing steeply, flight 104 disappeared into the mist.

The three people moved from the window, walking quickly to the main terminal building. The woman, tall, dark-eyed and handsome, picked up the wall phone. Speaking in French, she made a brief call to a number in La Villette district of Paris.

Flight 104 turned eastward, soaring serene, its presence in the cosmos, infinitesimal. Its passing went unseen by the fishermen of Gascony as they laboured far below in the choppy seas of the Bay of Biscay - unheard by the fishermen of Catalonia, hauling their nets off the Balearic Isles, or by herdsmen in silent watch on the slopes of the Pyrenees. A blink in the eye of time, its silver reflection winked blindly in the setting sun; momentary distant thunder the only indication of its passing.

Only hours since receiving the news from Stanfield of Gordon's death, Paddy anguished; if he had tried to reach

Gordon last night, maybe he could have said something to make a difference.

Stanfield had been willing to confide in Paddy, seeming to share a similar troubled hindsight. Called away during Paddy's hearing to the pub near Aldershot, he had later called Gordon, telling him the pub owner was missing. Not realising the extent of Paddy's knowledge, Stanfield explained, "the one who found Madam's briefcase. A sensitive issue Paddy.

"Gordon had sounded depressed. the hearing was trying for him. But there was much more to this whole issue.

"He left a note. It was quite rambling – how he'd let his father down, that he'd failed the trust your father placed in him. He blamed himself for everything that had gone wrong. 'Government espousing all the wrong principles', he wrote."

Paddy had sensed the drastic change in Gordon's attitude - his distracted posture during the proceedings at Horse Guards, his dejected demeanour, indifferent responses. The blame for Paddy's transgressions likely had implications, not alone for Paddy, but also for Gordon's future. Paddy thought of Geoffrey Gordon's lifelong efforts - selfless, dedicated, to have his father's name and his reputation restored - tragically incomplete.

Prior to Paddy and An Luc's departure for the airport, Thompson had left a note for Paddy.

Lavery's wife believes he's dead. Someone promised a follow up from Security Services - never showed. Wife has letter to me in event of husband's death. Will call you. Safe journey."

Paddy realised Bob was in a race with MI6. Stanfield had indicated Stene, of Watchers, was likely also on his way out to Aldershot. Stene, as Paddy recalled, was a member of PASS.

Before take off, the flight attendant had handed Paddy another message. *"Letter confirms Ajax authorised. Bob."* At least one of Weatherby's suspicions was now confirmed.

A tall, slight Chinese man threaded his way up the aisle, checking seat numbers. Paddy recognised him from the Seanache's funeral. "Liu Xiabo," Paddy exclaimed. Shifting his briefcase, Liu reached over to shake his hand.

"I thought you had left for Hong Kong from Belfast,"

321

said Paddy. Liu explained he had been delayed in London. Promising to talk later, Liu Xiabo continued up the aisle.

Flight 104 ran from the night, drifting across the Zagros Mountains of Turkey far below, across historic remnants of bygone empires. Across the wilderness, home to the nomadic peoples, too many toiling in ignorance and poverty - the eye of God perhaps, watching over them from on high.

As they passed south of the forests and jungles of Myanmar, Paddy and An Luc grew restless, sharing some instinctive awareness. Far below lay the gardens of frangipani and the tropical scented, once French colonial settlement of Muong Sing – distant site and silence of Anna's grave.

Some hours later, the pilot announced their passage over the tiny island of Macao. Paddy remembered his visit there with Anna. Now before them, the Chinese mainland, the New Territories. Ahead, Hong Kong and the Victoria Peak. Paddy recalled the words of England's Queen Victoria, of her husband, Albert of Sax-Coburg, in the winter of 1841,

"Albert is so amused at my having got the island of Hong Kong!" The remote, four hundred square mile territory, then inhabited by some five thousand peasants and fishermen, was referred to by her foreign Secretary, Lord Palmerston, as a "barren island."

The DC 10 drew up before the main arrivals buildings. Paddy and An Luc preceded Liu Xiabo, all three slowly funnelling their way up the narrow aisle into the wider corridor of the air bridge.

Catching up with them, Liu gave Paddy his card, telling him to call if he could be of any assistance during their stay in Hong Kong. Paddy assured Liu they would be calling on him, in turn giving him his card with Whitcombe's number. They joined the throng, each going to a different custom gate - Liu to those with temporary cards - Paddy, with a British passport and An Luc with a special pass arranged by Whitcombe.

Emerging into the arrivals area, Paddy rejoined An Luc and proceeded toward the barriers. Confusion quickly followed. A woman's piercing scream, repeated cries. Paddy saw a blur of action. People gathered like frightened children, cringing, looking about in fear. Close by, a great shout. Just ahead, An Luc dropped his hand-case and crouched, pointing ahead. "It's him, Tuan!" An Luc began to run. From beyond the scattering crowds, Paddy heard again the woman's repeated cries.

Paddy watched helplessly as An Luc leapt the barrier and ran straight into the fleeing, terror stricken crowd. A Chinese girl stood apart, eyes staring, one hand to her mouth, pointing to the running figure of An Luc, who now disappeared. Suddenly Paddy saw Liu Xiabo jump over the barrier, moving quickly toward the Chinese girl. She turned to Liu, plainly relieved to see him. At that moment, Bill Whitcombe appeared. He ran over to where Paddy stood. "My God, Paddy, what was that all about?"

"Some reception," said Paddy, staring around the arrivals building, trying to locate An Luc. Turning back toward Liu Xiabo and the Chinese girl, he was relieved to see An Luc emerging from the throng of passengers. Paddy saw Liu and the girl in animated conversation. To his astonishment the girl, seeing An Luc, ran excitedly toward him. Like long lost brother and sister, they embraced. An Luc spoke, pointing from Liu to Paddy and Whitcombe. The girl, now uncertain, gazed toward them. The men approached, expressions somewhat puzzled.

"Tuan, no longer missing - this is Terri Sai." An Luc murmured quietly, "Destiny not fail us, Tuan."

Paddy was stunned. Staring at the Chinese girl with long dark hair, he sensed Anna standing beside her. Paddy reached for Terri's hand. Tears running from her eyes, Terri greeted Paddy and Whitcombe. Her eyes on Paddy, softly she said, "Lady Anna was my friend."

First An Luc, then Terri tried to explain to their bewildered friends what had just happened. Terri was there to meet Liu Xiabo. Her eyes grew wide.

"I saw the man clearly!" She shivered. "He was there the night lady Anna died." Startling words for Paddy. "The same one who killed Peter Ramaiah, the day I landed here." Terri's voice trembled. A shadow crossed her face. "I couldn't believe it. The man was staring toward An Luc. He reached into his jacket, and I started screaming."

Paddy turned to address his longtime friend. "Maybe just as well, An Luc, that you didn't catch him - no one hurt."

Bill Whitcombe smiled at Terri. "My wife will be especially happy to hear you've been found. She's been very worried since you left."

"I'm sorry I didn't contact you," Terri said. "I didn't even dare to possess a visa until recently. I trusted no one; I was afraid."

"You must do what you feel is right, Whitcombe reassured her. "Your reappearance today might have cost your life."

Whitcombe's classic English Bentley arrived at the curb. As they pulled into the busy traffic, Terri described her terrifying escape to Hong Kong. Wheeled in the cleaning cart by the courageous Mrs. Tsieng to a remote part of the airport, she had been taken to the old lady's home in Mong Kok. From there Mrs. Tsieng helped her search for Liu Xiabo.

"With the message of my friend, Aija, attracting a dedicated following among Liu and his friends, I found her way increasingly the accepted path to a new China. We published a paper, circulated to the mainland, and more widely throughout Southeast Asia. And as we've recently learned, universally popular even in America. We have come a long way since the days of resistance and rioting in Beijing."

Terri described the preparations for the coming handover of Heung Gong, the "fragrant harbour".

"Hong Kong to China is now a complex conflict of interests," said Terri, glancing from Paddy to Whitcombe. "Democracy, even in its western form, has never ruled here. The Taipans," Terri explained, "the greedy colon fraternity, unless restrained, Mammon could still prevail. With minimal interference from the new Chinese Administration, the money harvest, the feeding frenzy Hong Kong is known for, will surely thrive for the coming century."

Bill Whitcombe readily agreed. "Hong Kong's moment in history. As in South Africa, anything's possible now. Change is urgently needed, but not an easy task. In some respects it's indeed a challenge, sustaining markets while teaching restraint."

Realising the enormity of the challenge, Liu Xiabo added, "Setting goals for all of us. Yet a point in our favour perhaps, inextricably tied in the island's future - the investments of the wealthiest nations will be compelled to accept an equal liability. You stay, you pay. Now a two way street. Also perhaps, a lure. Capitalist investment and public ownership."

"You are right, Liu," said Whitcombe, "but it depends on who exerts hegemony - who controls the future of the New China - the Taipans of Mammon. Freed from a radical version of socialism, economically and humanly flawed, what political expression will finally evolve? Freed from colonialism, who will take charge? Another dictatorship or the peoples' voice? Here, in Hong Kong, China's gateway to the world, a model for all China may arise."

Terri quickly added, "What you say is true. Not all, but many like us – we look for other goals besides money. Hopefully the new principles we preach and practice might be the answer. Once a dream, all our goals are now attainable in this new and ancient Heung Gong."

Turning into a different world, the real Chinese village of Kowloon, the driver crawled through the narrow side streets, skilfully avoiding hawkers and vendors in the open markets, a familiar memory to An Luc. Whitcombe requested Terri and Liu join them later that evening, insisting on sending a car for them. Liu and Terri accepted.

"It is such remarkable good fortune we are finally together again," said Terri, "with Aija's and Anna's spirit very much amongst us. I feel sure only good things will now happen."

An Luc's thoughts returned to the scene at the airport. What had he come for this time? Who had he come for?

Later that evening Paddy, An Luc and Bill Whitcombe stood on the terrace on the top suite of the Royal Hong Kong Yacht Club, assigned to Whitcombe as DG, MI6 Far East Station, by the Hong Kong Administration's Intelligence Office. Directly beneath were smooth lawns, palm trees, docks and terraces. The beleaguered ostentation, the opulence, symbols of borrowed luxury shortly to be unavailable.

Paddy brought Whitcombe up to date on the developments in England and Northern Ireland. Whitcombe agreed Wolsey was in for a difficult election.

"More recently, said Paddy, "dangerous allusions to your area of interest, Bill - the involvement of some in the Hong Kong administration in the China Scheme. With these ongoing investigations, everyone is running for cover."

Expressing his own mistrust of the PASS agenda, Whitcombe was troubled by the circumstances surrounding Gordon's death. For the first time, he reluctantly recognised good reason for Stanfield's scepticism of DeVeere's credibility.

"What happened at Kai Tek," said Paddy, moving on, "I suspect, was a foiled assassination plan." Paddy's gaze was directed to An Luc.

"Yes, Tuan. Perhaps he was waiting for one or both of us. Who knows? What troubles me, is how did he know any of us would be there?"

Distracted by the changing scene before them Whitcombe and Paddy sipped their drinks, savouring a rare moment of tranquillity.

"As night falls," said Whitcombe, "high powered speed boats prepare for the smugglers run of drugs and people to any one of the hundred islands off the Pearl River estuary. They say more than nine hundred a day."

Before them, towering skyscrapers, lights winking in the evening sky like giant Christmas trees, ascended in glittering procession to the darker reaches of Victoria Peak. Below the Peak, once exclusive, residential, "for Whites only" lay the Central district of the island shoreline. Behind the elaborate typhoon shelters, expensive yachts were moored to either side of the "royal" Yacht Club. There was little sign of the soon to be gone British naval vessels, their presence now reduced to several inflatables.

Liu and Terri arrived, Terri radiant in a pale silk Ao dai, her long dark hair billowing around her shoulders, her eyes shining. It was a quiet, happy reunion of survival, of warm, if sometimes sad remembrance. In the instant darkness of a tropical summer night the scene about them became more spectacular. Before them, the broad channel occasionally lit up with the brilliant explosion of a distant firework display. For Paddy, it was an evening of revelations and renewal.

After dinner, a cool breeze from the bay stirred the trees. Whitcombe found a wrap for Terri's shoulders as they sat listening to her story from that night in Tiananmen Square. At times struggling to control her voice, Aija's loss was still so personal and painful. Paddy could only agonise at the obvious pain of someone who had shared a loss as great as his own.

"I first saw El Braderakan, they called them, at the market in Peshawar. Rarely apart, they said. The one they sometimes called El Sadar, or the Imam Zaman, is a frightening figure, who trades in drugs and lives. I only caught a brief glimpse of him. The one who reappeared today at Kai Tek is his shadow, the one with the gold teeth. When I thought I had forgotten them, they would reappear, as in a nightmare."

On Whitcombe's further questioning, Terri described the Imam Zaman. Ibrahim had told her, the biggest arms dealer in Pakistan and across the border. His sources were everywhere, Russian, Chinese and yes, even British and American. Here, Whitcombe, Paddy and An Luc glanced at one another. Paddy nodded, recalling the new supply source for the mujahidin, through the BCCI from China. Weapons for drugs, and drugs for money. All the deadly harvest from the poppy fields of the Kunar province of northern Afghanistan.

Terri spoke, her voice quiet. "Three features I remember. He was a very powerful looking man, short, thick set, like a wrestler - his voice, deep. And, rare in that part of the world, fair hair, long as I recall - tied back. As I later heard it said, a Russian maybe. Ibrahim's family spoke of many Russian deserters who tried to survive in the region, who could have developed such a business in drugs and arms."

Terri paused a moment. "Some said, in that region there were a fair skinned people, blond haired descendants of early Mediterranean people - the long ago conquerors from Greece. Possibly others, more recent Europeans or Australians. During the Vietnam war, the area was full of them." Paddy was nodding in agreement, remembering the Australian detachments he had come across in Vietnam.

Terri continued, her words now confirming Ben's story of the Seanache's third nemesis - repeating the words of Abdul Said and again, of Safarov - "This one of many names, formerly, El Banau. Later now, El Algazi." Paddy and An Luc gazed at one another.

"Better known as the 'nameless one'," Terri wondered, "yet, of so many names." Then, quietly, looking to each of them, "This man and his shadow, El Braderakan - the men that all men fear."

As Terri told of her weeks with Anna, she rose and came to sit by Paddy. Seeing Terri's difficulty as she struggled with her emotions, Paddy reached for her hand.

Glancing to An Luc for confirmation, Terri recalled the warnings by the Chao Keung, of the appearance of the Farang Dang Mo, the long nose stranger - likely, a Caucasian - and his shadow, they said.

Trying then to share happier memories, Terri recalled, "Being with Anna was the first real happiness I had known since leaving China. Like the wanderings of the Buddhist Goddess, A-Ma, sailing and surviving many storms - to finally reach sheltered harbours. From where, as legend has it, she ascended into heaven." Smiling as if to reassure her friends, "It is an old legend. And, as you can see, I am still here."

Immediately overwhelmed with sadness and guilt, she cried. "But Aija and Anna are gone." Even as she spoke, Terri sensed her presence, could almost hear Anna's voice, "The key, Terri - see that he gets the key!"

With tears in her eyes, Terri looked at Paddy. Reaching beneath her long hair, she undid the clasp and removed a gold chain from around her neck. Gathering the chain and its stubby pendant in her hand, she held it for a moment, then handed it to Paddy.

Paddy took it from her almost reverently. He sat staring at the tiny brass key.

Her voice just above a whisper, her eyes on Paddy, Terri said,

"Anna told me to be sure to deliver this into your hands." She looked into the shadows where Paddy had retreated. "Anna told me the story of the keys, Paddy," she said gently, "what they might mean. Innocent souvenirs, or symbols of hatred, blackmail, greed and revenge. Yet, perhaps, appropriate now, the key to the identity of others."

Terri struggled painfully on. "I promised I would give you her message." Tears fell down her cheeks as she cautiously repeated Anna's final words, carefully memorised.

"'Tell my Lord, that I love him. They came for me - and, without him, I am not ready to go.' Then, Paddy, with great difficulty, she spoke the words repeatedly, 'Phnom Penh'. A name, Deevers, I believe. And again, 'Force Seven'. Then, 'they came for the keys!'" Terri lowered her head, crying quietly.

Paddy squeezed her hand as she continued. "Those who came that night, I recognised from Peshawar. Anna recognized them too, Paddy. She couldn't seem to remember their names, kept repeating words, as if reaching for what would help. She kept repeating, 'friend', in different dialects - in Vietnamese, 'ban'. Then, in Chinese, 'pung yao'. Then again, 'shung de' and, again in Vietnamese, 'ban dong hanh'. She said, 'my Lord will know!' Then, again, 'Crazy, but it was his way'. Terri stared at Paddy, silently pleading that he would understand. Her eyes studied his anguished expression.

Had it made any sense? Had she failed Anna? Terri covered her face with her hands.

Paddy rose and knelt beside her. An Luc, head bowed, leaned forward, also trying to comfort her. With a deep breath, Terri regained control. She gritted her teeth in her resolve to bring Anna's killers to justice.

"For many days after I was in shock. Yet Anna's words stayed with me. The other thing I will never forget," said Terri, "that deep, booming voice. I saw them, Paddy. They passed only feet from where I stood." Fiercely Terri went on. "The flash of gold teeth. They wore hats, yet I can still see the flying blond hair of the shorter, muscular one. Just as I saw them in Peshawar. The tall one, just as we saw him today - just as An Luc also recognised him." An Luc nodded.

Terri stared across the harbour, toward Kowloon and the Territories. The ruffled waters stirred, the all night firework display still arching above the far shore.

An Luc nodded in agreement as Terri concluded, "I believe, in each, his destiny, his Samsara. At whatever price. Just as I helped Aija spread her beliefs of compassion and sharing, so also, with Anna. I feel we were destined to help one another, as Anna helped the refugees and so many others."

Paddy rose. He slowly paced about the deck. "An Luc and I came to Hong Kong to find you, to listen to your message from Anna and to find those who pursue the keys. As you've said Terri, no doubt about it, our Samsara, a miraculous or perhaps, an inevitable happening. The further the story progresses, the nearer I feel the disturbing sense of a growing threat. Yet also, a sense of resolution."

Paddy glanced at An Luc. "The keys may not be the final answer. Other forces are at work here. A collection of such unlikely circumstances could never happen twice in any lifetime. Yet, as Anna predicted, they are a recurring lead to events we learned of in Paris and again in Northern Ireland. And now, in Hong Kong."

He looked at the harbour before him. "What is the link to Anna's killing? What role has the China Scheme with Deevers' continuing operation in Southeast Asia – perhaps, what Perry and many others died for? Why the Weatherbys, the Seanache,? I wonder, what role has Graham with MI6? And Tracker, from Australia – seems to be part of another agenda. Where do they fit in? And again, why Madam's assassination? Too many questions - too few answers."

Bill Whitcombe asked Terri, "What more can you tell us about the Indian boy, Peter?"

Terri told them she had only really spoken to Peter Ramaiah in the few minutes before landing. "Peter told me the name of his master was Kuhn Sa, the local drug lord in northern Laos," said Terri. "As Anna told me, better known to you, Paddy, as Tung Giang during the Vietnam war. Kuhn Sa had been surprised to learn that you and Anna were living in the region. Kuhn Sa was hunting the lost gold reserves, the Vietnam treasure, he called it. He suspected the gold still lay hidden in the region. He learned of your presence in Muong Sing. Suspicious then, this reinforced his commitment to the search, watching you both, wondering whether either of you could lead him to the gold."

Carefully Terri recalled Peter's words. "Kuhn Sa suspected the gold was stolen by an American he'd once worked with. This American had been assigned, Kuhn Sa believed, to assist in some manner in the transport of the gold. The American disappeared the same time the treasure was lost. Khun Sa, Peter told me, was obsessed with finding out what happened to this former partner. Perhaps the unclaimed treasure was in this man's possession."

Tung Giang, Paddy recalled, had played a major role in stolen U.S. supplies and weapons. Once he'd been Victor Perry's, then Colonel Deevers' partner. Paddy had heard rumours of Giang's brigand activities in the region in the last months before Paddy left for London.

Paddy wondered if Giang concluded Deevers' had been involved with the missing gold? Could Giang lead them to whoever had crucified Deevers and Anna? Perhaps to those still hunting the keys?

Terri continued. "Peter believed that Deevers' disappearance troubled Kuhn Sa greatly. Peter had also known of the Farang Dang Mo moving into northern Laos. Kuhn Sa was convinced this man had been responsible for your disappearance, Peter said - likely Paddy, when you went to London, and later, for the death of Anna.

"Kuhn Sa was enraged on learning of Anna's death, because he thought it meant the loss of the lead to finding the missing gold. It was then that he commissioned Peter to follow me from Bangkok."

Gazing toward the glittering rim of lights from Kowloon, Terri shivered. "What Peter said could have been true."

Terri paused, sipping the coffee Whitcombe had placed before her. It was past midnight. The firework display had faded into the humid, tropic night. A drunken chorus wafted from the distant gweilo bars off Causeway Bay. The only other sound was the call of the night herons.

In response to Paddy's further question, Terri shook her head, "No. Peter never mentioned keys."

Peter Ramaiah's information effectively excluded Giang himself as a suspect either in Deevers' or in Anna's killing. In either case, for Giang, their deaths would effectively block his access to the gold.

Paddy recalled Roger Moorefield's comment, "No survivors from Special Forces Seven, the ill fated gold transfer mission." This conclusion Paddy had accepted until meeting Jean Davost in Paris, Ben, then Jack in Belfast. Paddy suddenly wondered, could it be possible? Was there another survivor of the gold assignment they'd yet to meet? If so, he might well be the one who'd outfoxed them all. The one who'd likely crucified Deevers.

Whitcombe had risen. Walking a few paces, he leaned against the terrace rail. "Terri, what you and An Luc have told us has given me a clearer sense of direction. This extraordinary obsession for anonymity only adds to the menace - a truly terrifying picture.

"Tomorrow's handover may be premature for some, in the face of the hearings on the extent of criminal penetration into the Asian corporate mantle. The China Scheme is now a worldwide consortium, vigorously recruiting political support and wide international investment."

Whitcombe turned to face them. "These are dangerous stakes. The China Scheme is under investigation. Hong Kong will be restored to Chinese administration in the next twenty-four hours. It is urgent," Whitcombe concluded, "to resolve this as soon as possible.

"Today," Whitcombe continued, "Hong Kong is China's largest trading partner and is now being run from abroad by the great mercantile corporations of the 'Rentier' system of every nation, and by the Chinese Diaspora. Hong Kong, the major port for trans-shipment of Chinese exports, is more important to China than New York to the United States. And is surely the world's largest trader for the next millennium. Hong Kong is also headquarters for money laundering and other profitable international activities of the Triad criminal groups of Southeast Asia."

Turning to Terri, Whitcombe continued, "Presently, we've also learned, Hong Kong is competing, or cooperating with those Peter Ramaiah described, in heroin trans-shipments to Europe and the United States. Also, some working with the Golden Triangle, Afghanistan, and where you first met the strangers, Terri, from Pakistan. All largely controlled till now by the Triad. Here, I believe, is another reason for the recurring appearances of this 'Braderakan'. Now as we see it, there are increasing reflections of internal conflict. For the Triad, this new enterprise, the China Scheme, with its growing international extensions now competes for control. In Hong Kong, the Triad itself is a force to be reckoned with. Indeed, an empire on its own."

Turning to Liu Xiabo, Whitcombe asked, "As members of the New China group, could you have seen Anna's murder as a deliberate or vengeful act of the Chinese Secret Police, the P.L.A. or some renegade group?"

Both Terri and Liu shook their heads. Terri replied, "Before the warning from the Chao Keung in Muong Sing, I spoke with Anna about this. Chinese fugitives had been passing through Muong Sing for some time. If they had wished to silence Anna I believe they could have done so years before."

His expression grim, Liu added, "With what is at stake Paddy, I believe all somehow play a role. If, as you suggested Bill, they see their path threatened they will not hesitate to kill, and will do so again to protect their supremacy, their profits, their identity - whatever the extent of their globe embracing plans they may share. The damage may be irreversible. We don't have much time. It could be worthwhile to contact friends in the Chinese government, perhaps even in the Triad. Realising the stakes, I see possible cooperation with our own efforts."

His expression more serious, Liu thoughtfully commented, "A shared intelligence source is where we have many friends. Among them I feel is the link we seek to those working with the Triad. Here, I believe, I can be of further help."

Liu glanced at his watch. "Sorry, very late!" Rising, he

thanked Whitcombe for his hospitality.

"Thank you for a very memorable day," remarked Terri. Terri and Liu promised to be in touch. Anna's presence, at peace, was among them, in the still morning air.

CHAPTER THIRTY-FIVE

Where is Great Alexander? Great Alexander lives
and reigns.
Medieval Greek proverb

In Hong Kong it was a day of celebration for some,
of humiliation for others. For the "colons", the ruling classes,
their governor in tears, a day of denial and defiance, the
colourful unravelling of Empire. Renewal, re-empowerment
was everywhere; cranes and drills drowning sibilant tones of
repetitive speeches. Goodbye and good riddance!

Paddy awoke shortly before noon. He found himself
going over the conversation from the previous evening.
Suddenly he had a revelation. He called Terri Sai. Mrs. Tsieng
answered; Terri would be back within the hour.

Impatiently awaiting Terri's call, Paddy once more
questioned An Luc, painful as it still was, about Anna's last
words. Terri and An Luc's accounts differed only in some
possibly significant detail - yet were consistent in description of
the men who killed Anna.

"Anna's words," said Paddy, "were her desperate efforts
to identify these men who'd come for the keys - searching for
some word to help us recognise them - that once, however long
ago, we had known them. Unable to remember their names, she
tried to identify them by remembering the place and the time
when one or both of them were with us, as she told Terri, in
Phnom Penh. The same, An Luc, as you had told me in London.
Last night there was other information I hadn't heard before."

Paddy could scarcely contain his excitement. "These
men, Russians perhaps, may be the same as Kuhn Sa and Peter
said. There are inconsistencies in the names and descriptions.
To some, they suggest El Braderakan. The Imam Zaman, the

'nameless one.' Or remember, An Luc, in the Seanache's, Abdul Said's, and Ben's accounts, the name Algazi, the conqueror. Or maybe, it was Safarov's man in Kabul. Each story told of a man, a name - with its deliberate, evasive ambiguities."

Paddy greeted Bill Whitcombe, who had just joined them in the lobby, then earnestly continued his line of thought. "They are possibly one and the same individual. Clear and unequivocal, these men are international dealers in drugs and arms. And now, as we considered last night, they may have some role in this international investment scheme.

"In my dream, An Luc, I kept hearing Anna repeating those words. This morning as I awoke, I believe I began to understand what she was trying to say. I recall 'shung de'. What does 'shung de' mean, An Luc?"

An Luc, perplexed, could only shake his head. "Shung de is not a dialect, an expression I am familiar with, Tuan." Despite knowledge of Mandarin Chinese, Bill Whitcombe was also puzzled.

The phone rang. Whitcombe answered, exchanged a greeting with Terri, then handed the phone to Paddy.

Terri listened as Paddy told her his dream.

"When An Luc first saw you, Paddy, he would only have told you what he heard me say. As you know, he speaks little Chinese." Terri thought a minute. "Anna, as you know, was from Guangxi in southern China and of the Meo people. There are more than a hundred different dialects. There are even more dialects and colloquial translations in Laos, Vietnam and Cambodia than in all of southern China. Knowing I was from northern China, perhaps she thought I might better understand if she expressed some special nuance."

Terri paused. "Her repeated reference in Vietnamese, 'ban', 'ban dong'. Then, in Chinese, 'pung yao' - each referring, as I understand it, to friend, or friends. Anna used the words, 'shung de', and once she whispered 'hing tai'.

Terri carefully considered. "In the Mandarin, then the Cantonese dialects, each phrase meaning perhaps, something more than friends? Paddy, with these expressions, was Anna referring to a special group of friends? More like an association with a secret society, or a terrorist group, like a fraternity, a band of brothers, a special and loyal group? I just don't know."

Paddy, his voice hoarse with suppressed excitement, almost whispered, "Terri, I believe I do know him - the Imam Zaman, the Algazi, who he might be! Incredible, I'm convinced Anna was trying to remember him from Phnom Penh. And no, the expression is not brothers, or Braderakan, as your friends called them in Peshawar, but is more like shung de. Indeed, a close band, 'the Companions', he called us!"

Paddy looked excitedly at Whitcombe and An Luc, scarcely daring to believe his conclusions. "Another one of us reported missing in action. Alex Kerkorian. A Greek-American, up for anything. We thought he'd been hit by a ground-to-air missile. Incredible! Now the Algazi, the Conqueror?" Paddy was nodding, remembering, and accepting.

"The Braderakan, Terri. One you described as short and muscular. The other, the one you said with fair hair, a deep voice, so desperate to hide his identity. It's got to be him! As the Chao Keung described him, the long nose Caucasian. Not Russian, but Greek."

Paddy whispered, "Alex Kerkorian." This time it brought a clear flood of memories. "Iskander, he liked to be called - once conqueror of the world. And now he aspires to bring his dream to reality, what we thought then were his crazy fantasies." Paddy was stunned at his own conclusions.

Reluctant to divert Paddy's thoughts, Terri said in a quiet voice, "Liu is with me. He has something to tell you."

In a moment Liu was on the phone. "One of the wolves with whom we are sometimes forced to run, has indicated his willingness to help. He will see us this evening in Macao."

Liu suggested he and Terri meet them at the Ferry Terminal at six. Quickly conferring with Bill and An Luc, Paddy agreed.

Bill Whitcombe then made several calls, recruiting the assistance of the American CIA representative in Hong Kong, a long time friend. They met nearby at the American Embassy. Paddy briefed him on the details of the ill-fated operation to salvage the Vietnamese gold, and of his recent discovery that some previously listed MIA had survived the action. In response to Paddy's urgent request to check the records of Captain Alex Kerkorian, the agent assured Paddy he would fax his request to the Pentagon within the hour. Allowing for the time differential, they might receive a reply later the same day.

About to leave for Kowloon and the Ferry Terminal, Paddy was relieved to get the call, and not surprised to learn that Captain Alex Kerkorian had indeed been reported missing in action in April of '75. All others on that mission were also still designated MIA.

Propelled by dual gas turbines, the twin jet foil skimmed the opaque waters with the grace and speed of some prehistoric pterygoid species. On the observation deck, as the little group squinted toward the setting sun, powerful engines thrusting a subdued tremor beneath their feet, Liu familiarised them with their host.

"Senhor Da Dias is legendary. His mother is from China. His father, descended from the first Portuguese explorers. After the war, Da Dias became a successful dealer in the gold market. His business is centred here in Macao. He is a controversial figure. To some he is an emperor from a different era, yet with extensive interests and influence, east to west." Liu went on, "Da Dias is widely respected throughout Southeast Asia. His word is discreetly sought on any major decision in the political spectrum affecting this region."

His voice lowered, Liu added, "His rumoured assumption of the presidency of the powerful 14K Triad is less well known outside this region. Better known in Hong Kong as the Sun Yee On, coming into prominence after the Vietnam War – the branch is a true 'Mafiosa of the East'. It is reputed to control the drug business throughout Southeast Asia – and to supply more than half the heroin shipment to the United States.

"It is my belief, Da Dias is dealing with increased competition from northern Laos, and perhaps with the group you described last night, the Braderakan. This might motivate him to provide assistance in our search."

"Look! Over there - see?" Terri pointed excitedly. "The

pinnacle - that's the Ma Kok Miu, a Buddhist temple - the shrine of the Goddess A-Ma. The early settlers had first called Macao A-ma-gao, bay of A-Ma. The temple, it is said, is the site from which the orphan girl of ancient legend, spared from the storms, ascended as a goddess into heaven."

Approaching Macao, the hydrofoil slowed, quietly settling into its own wake, its lights reflecting wavering beads across the tide. Engines rumbling, lines were thrown, the hydrofoil docked. Following a perfunctory Customs check, they emerged into a colourful, noisy throng.

Liu pointed to a distinctive Bentley touring car and an equally distinctive figure, quaint in an elegant uniform, standing beside it. "Senhor Da Dias' chauffeur, they told me, would be meeting us."

A lovely cool evening surrounded them as the chauffeur drove through the crowded thoroughfares of the city. Above the harbour was a different celebration, Hong Kong forgotten in the first night of the Macaun Mardi Gras. To either side the towering glass and brash lights reflected crude monuments of trade and commerce, McDonalds to Dunkin Donuts. Among the darker side streets of the old town huddled the more discreet regional restaurants, cafés and bazaars.

Paddy saw the old A-Ma-gao, the same Macao he had seen with Anna almost twenty years ago. As the car moved slowly forward, they listened to the tinkering dissonance of viols and lutes, the quavering notes of flute, of musical gourd, cymbal and gong, sight, sound and song of China.

A glowing lantern above a pillared entrance illuminated the driveway to a stately old colonial home, barely visible above high walls. Gates slowly opened, then slowly closed behind them.

The chauffer drove a short distance. Stopping the car, he opened the passenger door. Before them stood a great terraced mansion. Through the pillared doorway came a slight, lean, grey-haired man, with two formally cloaked attendants at his side. Smiling, his hand extended in welcome.

The chauffeur ushered his guests forward, introducing them to their host, Senhor Jose Da Dias. Da Dias, gallantly solicitous to Terri, greeted each of them warmly. The slow and gentle manner belied the extraordinary achievements of this great Mandarin. Liu Xiabo humbly expressed his gratitude to Da Dias for agreeing to meet under such short notice.

Glancing into the man's eyes as he was introduced, Paddy realised something Liu had obviously not known - the great Taipan was blind.

Their host, attendants at his side, led them from the reception area to a high-arched marble hallway. Above them rose an ancient, oak-beamed roof, its great chandelier glowing above the marbled stairways. They passed into the reception room. Da Dias' attendants stood by as their host offered his guests aperitifs - then, after filling the requests, they quietly left the room.

As they sat in the warm half light, Da Dias asked An Luc where his people were from. Pleased with his reply, Da Dias pointed out their common Meo heritage. Nodding toward Liu and Terri, Da Dias gallantly expressed his admiration for, "the efforts you and your friends are making to resolve differences with the Chinese government, assisting in the rebirth, embracing the ancient Confucian values advocated by your friend, the courageous young lady, Aija. Some in the government," said Da Dias, "are persuaded by their old views, mistrust of our people's tendency to premature misjudgment, our own civil strife."

Da Dias, evidently enjoying himself, addressed Bill Whitcombe on the Hong Kong restoration, tactfully describing, "the welcome resolution, the clear path for a new China." Paddy and Whitcombe nodded in acknowledgement as Da Dias continued, "The urge for every form of blatant misrule is upon us, misconceived ideologies with deliberate intent to mislead everywhere - the same devils dressed in different clothes." Paddy was impressed, saw the significance of Da Dias' description of the political impact as an oblique reference to the China Scheme.

"Alternatives must be devised," said Da Dias quietly, turning in the direction of Liu and Terri. "The responsibility, to listen to the voice of the people. Here I agree, with caution, the principles Aija described - returning to the only viable unit we have. The voice of the family, among other priorities, must be given fair and careful interpretation."

Impressed by the obvious sincerity and wider commitment of the distinguished Taipan, Paddy realised the extensive work both Liu and Terri had done to influence the opinions of such an exalted and remote figure.

Da Dias' expression was serious as his sightless gaze rested on his audience. "The true resurrection of these values, will be, in time, a reclamation of the new principles to which the Chinese people aspire.

"As I am told, the peaceful revolution promoted by the followers of Aija is already achieving this goal." Da Dias smiled. "And successful they have been. As we know, the Chinese economy defies description. Now the most rapidly growing economy in world history - yet this itself brooks caution."

Paddy and his friends were startled to hear the clamour of a gong, sonorous, subdued, reverberating throughout the house. Perpetuating the legendary allusion, the days of the Mandarins, the door opened to admit Da Dias' two menservants, now in long gowns, with suitably inscrutable expressions. Together bowing, one quietly announced, "Dinner will now be served."

Preceded by the majestic trio of Da Dias and his attendants, Paddy and his friends followed the procession to the opulent and elegant dining room. Da Dias took his seat at the head of the table. Discreetly the attendants removed or replaced the dishes and served the wines as Da Dias engaged his guests in a humorous and entertaining exchange. As he listened, Paddy surmised they were seeing only one facet of an extremely complex personality.

After dinner, the guests retired to the library, another tastefully furnished room containing a striking collection of antiques, walls lined with books. Among the opulent symbols of past centuries, Paddy found himself wondering, where does this gentle spoken connoisseur, archetype of traditional Svengalian shrewdness, master of the Chinese art of Guanxi, fit in?

Comfortably seated before the fireplace, Da Dias continued in pleasant conversation with his guests. Paddy was impressed with their host's entertaining, yet seeming deliberate digressions, his cautious restraint in broaching the purpose of their meeting. It was clear to Paddy that Da Dias knew more about his guests than they would ever know about him. Da Dias' sightless gaze now fixed ahead, his expression serious. He drew on his cigar, slowly exhaling.

"Lord Finucane, Senhor Whitcombe, I have considered, and I believe, understand the compelling and urgent reasons for your visit." Da Dias paused reflectively, again slowly drawing on his cigar. "An interesting and disturbing story. Not alone of your own personal loss, Lord Finucane - but for all of us." Paddy was surprised by the sudden change of tone.

Da Dias turned in Paddy's direction. "For you, Lord Finucane, it is a matter of honour to find the man who killed your wife." His head moved slowly side to side.

"Indeed it is, Senhor," Paddy quietly interjected.

"In this investment scheme," Da Dias, more cautious, stared straight ahead. "Your concerns as conveyed to me are of an unfortunate association, designed perhaps, to assume control of the Chinese economy. Recent associations of this organization you seek to identify also involve a specific threat to world peace."

Da Dias nodded abruptly, seeming to have made up his mind. "My friends, in some respects we share a common interest. Though many of these concerns are now history, some of the events remain sensitive issues, and here, we must trust one another's discretion. Also, I feel, I must clarify my point of view and that of my people."

Head slowly swinging side to side, Da Dias continued. "I sympathise, yet I cannot share your own personal vendettas. Less even, Senhors, with your affinities for the alleged areas of threatened conflict. It is up to each of us to decide who are our real friends - or enemies."

Da Dias continued, "It has been a history of an unequal exchange. From the West, forced administration of a harsh form of Christianity, for the right to enslave people everywhere. Today, in Hong Kong - a mockery! The ceremony, a burlesque I am thankfully unable to observe. As we now know, the profits went elsewhere.

"As I first heard your story, my decision was a rejection of any element of a national territorial dispute, some sanctimonious witch hunt. That is, until I was informed of the gracious lady, Ms Sai and Senhor Xiabo, with all that was implied in their new China crusade."

Da Dias paused again. "My decision was influenced by information I have received in the past few days, the impact of which transcends the significance of the investment misadventures you described." There was an expectant pause.

"I have been recently informed through reliable sources in Bangkok that a group, well known in northern Laos and Pakistan, has recently become involved in the purchase of large quantities of high grade plutonium from the former Russian republics. As you have likely heard, the oil beds of the Caspian are now the focus of imperial appetites. For this reason alone, and for the cause of a new China, I am willing to participate in your quest." Paddy felt a great sense of relief.

Da Dias continued, "Our task, my friends, is not easy. This man you describe - he inspires much fear, is well protected, is indeed elusive, a man of great power and wealth." He paused. "For obvious reasons, it is also in our interests to find him soon." Da Dias, drawing reflectively on his cigar, exhaled, smoke obscuring his expression.

Da Dias turned his head, facing toward Paddy now, his expression curious. "Senhor Xiabo tells us, Lord Finucane, that you yourself might have known this man we seek. You may even have served with him during the Vietnam War. An American? A man you have described as fanatical in preserving his anonymity."

Paddy found himself nodding without comment. Rising with his back to the fireplace, Da Dias spoke gravely now.

"During the war in Vietnam, there was an American colonel with whom some acquaintances in Hong Kong were in business, trading in weapons and other commodities, making significant profits. The American, Deevers was his name, came to me, seeking to purchase gold in large quantities. We worked well together." They listened to the story Paddy knew well, from a different perspective now.

"We completed our business with the assistance of a number of foreign banks and other off shore agencies, as well as those in Hong Kong and in Macao - Chinese, Portuguese or British owned. It was, as you can imagine, a very profitable business for a world in recession.

"To safely arrange the gold exchange," Da Dias continued, "we were obliged to seek the good will and cooperation of the Chinese government, the provincial commissars of Kwantung Province, as well as the Portuguese administration in Macao. When the American colonel learned of this extending network, as well as the cost of doing business, he became more suspicious, fearful that the Chinese government would expose him."

Paddy could only shake his head in wonder - Deevers, afraid of the very fate he'd chosen for those who'd worked for him.

"On one visit, Deevers spoke of an American investigation into the Black Market business in Saigon, causing him great anxiety. He told me the Chinese had agents in Vietnam. The South Vietnamese government soon joined the investigation. He seemed less afraid then - had friends there, he told us.

"As time went on," Da Dias continued, "he was growing increasingly fearful, trusting no one. The American position soon deteriorated," said Da Dias, smiling. "Deevers became more reassured, purchasing more gold, increasing his holdings. Just before the American withdrawal, the colonel confided to me that he had outwitted his enemies."

Da Dias recalled Deevers' exultant description of his plan to foil his would-be betrayers. He had informed everyone that he kept a file of their dealings, the record of their duplicity under lock and key, at his pleasure, in banks in Hong Kong. It was a foolish indiscretion - misguided, arrogant - surely not lost on Da Dias, only strengthening the hand, inciting the further curiosity of those he dealt with.

Paddy, An Luc and Terri gazed at one another. They were listening to the story of the keys, just as Anna had told it. In effect, Paddy guessed, Deevers had slyly felt he was also warning Da Dias, not knowing the power of the great Taipan. Anna and Victor Perry were among those blackmailed by Deevers, thought Paddy, and finally, Kerkorian, who chose to challenge Deevers, who'd killed him, yet never found the keys.

"Among the last moves Deevers made," said Da Dias, "was a change in his banking practices, transferring his possessions to Macao and other off shore repositories.

"Suddenly," Da Dias continued, "early in seventy-five, the colonel's visits ceased. I thought this might have been due to the difficulties during the American evacuation from Vietnam. It occurred to me that the colonel might have lost his life, despite his plans."

Placing his brandy glass on the mantel, Da Dias drew on his cigar. "Some weeks later, to my surprise, I had a visit from a young American. A commanding personality - a sense of vigour and urgency. He told me that he was one of the colonel's partners. He told me Deevers had been badly wounded, obliged to return to the United States, that he was recovering but unable to speak. This young man seemed very anxious to avoid identification. Curiously, I recall him showing me a small, bronze key, saying the colonel had given it to him as a token of good faith. The key would be access, with my assistance, to Deevers' bank vault in Hong Kong."

Da Dias recalled his growing doubts about this man. "He said the colonel would be obliged if I could help him - and here the lure, I guessed - in negotiating the sale of a large quantity of gold that had come into their hands."

Da Dias paused, turned toward them, as if wishing to sense their response. "I didn't believe the young man - he didn't seem to know that Deevers had transferred all his possessions out of Hong Kong. I deferred an intrusion into Deevers' vaults and, with some difficulty, my friends and I agreed to arrange the gold transaction."

Da Dias seemed hesitant, the circumspection of a prudent man, measuring the risks and benefits of disclosure. His decision made, he continued.

"The sum of the gold bullion involved was considerably

more than we'd previously dealt with in any one negotiation, larger than any previous single gold transaction for Macao in any entire single year. The transaction took some time. There were a number of meetings." Da Dias paused again.

"Everything he did seemed to be on an imposing scale. My curiosity about him was later rewarded, my suspicions more than confirmed. In view of the circumstances, his desire for anonymity was understandable." His brow furrowed then, trying to recall the face he'd seen, the name he hadn't spoken in so many years. As it came to him, he pronounced the unfamiliar name with some difficulty. "Iskander, I believe." Then with more conviction, "Yes, Iskander. Not a man, nor a name I could easily forget."

Paddy, Liu, Bill Whitcombe and Terri quickly exchanged glances. Da Dias continued his extraordinary tale, confirming the conclusions Paddy had reached only that morning.

"I soon learned that the gold had been stolen, hijacked through some incredible act of piracy in the South China Seas. Apparently this man managed to navigate a course to the Ladrones with the assistance of some members of the crew. The others, I was informed, had been killed during seizure of the vessel. Fortunately for us, one of the crew, fearing for his life, told the story to a friend on Lantau island, before he too, disappeared."

Paddy recalled the formidable mercenary he had once known, outstanding even then. Alex Kerkorian had joined Special Forces late in seventy-four. His transfer to Spec Force Seven had been arranged, one step ahead of an investigation into Kerkorian's activities in Burma and Northern Laos. As a pilot with Air America, he had spent three tours in Vietnam and Cambodia, flying either helicopter or fixed wing aircraft on special missions. A Tin Jockey, transporting Meo insurgents or similar CIA recruited guerrillas, weapons and supplies, and, not uncommonly, flying opium to the markets in Bangkok and Saigon; supposedly to help pay for the CIA's clandestine wars and their warriors. Paddy remembered Kerkorian's evasion of any questions about his personal life. Kerkorian had taken to calling their group the "Companions", the name of the bodyguard accompanying Alexander the Great. It was at about this time Kerkorian had decided he wished to be known as Iskander. Paddy never recalled anyone confronting or ridiculing the man.

It was clear now to Paddy where Kerkorian had played a useful role in helping establish Deevers' trade throughout Cambodia, northern Laos and the Golden Triangle. Kerkorian's immediate assumption of control was the only inevitable response to a logical criminal legacy. Also, Paddy saw, the American government's decision to deny his previous mission to Phnom Penh - denying even, his existence, at best "MIA", was an unexpected bonus for Kerkorian. His anonymity established, the Vietnamese gold, never existing. Senhor Da Dias was speaking as Paddy's mind returned to the present.

"Iskander again asked for my assistance in obtaining access to the vault in Hong Kong, willing to pay generously for my troubles. I told him he would need more than the single key, and that this would require re-establishing contact with those who had set up the system. When he heard they would likely look for permission from Deevers and significant identification to access the vaults, finally that the vaults were no longer in Hong Kong but in Macao - Iskander disappeared.

"It has been said that a man fitting Iskander's description has emerged in these regions from time to time. If indeed it is the same man, he has shrewdly and discreetly created a very successful trading conglomerate throughout Southeast Asia. And it is noted, as with Iskander, always ensuring his role is concealed."

Thoughtfully, Da Dias went on, "His most successful business venture is the enterprise today known as the Southeast Asia Corporation - SEACO, with extensive interests worldwide. SEACO competes successfully in the American and Japanese markets through many subsidiary companies - a hi-tech investment enterprise in laser, chemical and computer technology. From this, perhaps as a silent partner, Iskander, anonymous, invisible, directs the multiple investment interests this global corporation now controls."

Da Dias turned slightly toward Paddy. "Perhaps, Lord

Finucane, as you and Senhor Whitcombe have implied, Iskander even plays a role in the China investment scheme you refer to." Da Dias sat now as Whitcombe spoke, also requesting the discretion of their host, both revealing information that made their course and trust in one another irrevocable - dangerous priorities established.

"In my own investigations into this China scheme," Whitcombe began, "I have learned SEACO, as you have said, is an international corporation whose size compares favourably with the largest anywhere. Its securities and stock holdings are indeed well diversified. I have also been informed that SEACO has been the focus of several recent investigations by the Financial Action Task Force and other regulation agencies - from Hong Kong and elsewhere." His eyes on Da Dias, Whitcombe added, "Today's ceremonies are well timed for some."

Paddy watched Da Dias' expression, wondering just how much of this information their host already knew. Da Dias face remained unchanged.

"Further," continued Whitcombe, also closely watching Da Dias, "since we are committed, for different reasons perhaps, to helping one another - a confidential revelation. FATF is investigating the China scheme's monies, they allege, improperly transferred under the guise of Chinese national ownership. The investigation agencies are looking into the role of SEACO in clandestine stock transfers and unregistered buyouts." Whitcombe added frankly and ruefully, "In all these investigations we have received little cooperation from the Hong Kong administration, the governor's office, or their Australian counterparts."

Paddy remembered Whitcombe's description of similar methods used by the Triad in transferring profits worldwide. Da Dias, his expression inscrutable, remained silent. Each wondered the extent of the other's role, Whitcombe knowing, and Da Dias acknowledging that other, more immediate priorities were the urgent focus.

Paddy saw the dangerous path. Maybe still at odds, ultimately Whitcombe and Da Dias had to trust one another. For Paddy, there was no option. Without Da Dias' regional authority and influence they would never have a chance to locate Kerkorian, or indeed, to prevent him achieving his plans. Paddy listened as Whitcombe described his fateful conjectures.

"Massive infusions of capital, handled discreetly by SEACO, were transferred to fantasy corporations, overseas funds without tax, tariff or any loss to SEACO, then reinvested across the world at exorbitant interest, through invisible money changers. A complex but ingenious Ponzi scheme. The ultimate victims, the investors. No loss to the invisible, inaccessible empire of Iskander."

Suddenly, unaccountably, Da Dias quietly took up the story. "Perhaps indeed now, Iskander is the brilliant fiscal strategist who conceived this idea. Perhaps sure he remains anonymous, his own resources untraceable, just as the American colonel boasted for himself, so many years ago.

"My friends, if so, then it is not unlikely that this is an essential role in the man's total strategy. To deliberately destabilise world currencies, contrived to coincide with, to distract from the final, ultimate use of selective nuclear or other aggression. Simultaneous economic and military intervention on a cosmic scale never before equalled, throwing governments into international chaos and conflict - the victims of Iskander's whims." The old Taipan was grimly shaking his head.

Whitcombe commented, "If your information, Senhor, and Lord Finucane's conclusions about the coincidental role of Iskander are correct - then, though he may well suffer the inevitable exposure, in the economic sphere the damage will already have been done. Whatever military ventures he planned will surely follow."

He paused. "It seems all the more urgent that we discover the affairs of the China Scheme, and of SEACO, with or without the help of the Hong Kong administration, or the Chinese government. Track the man down as soon as possible. Hopefully with your help, Senhor Da Dias."

Da Dias turned to Paddy. Gravely, he asked, "Lord Finucane, you are quite sure the men I have told you about are the ones you knew in Vietnam? Iskander is the man we must find?"

His own tentative conclusions now confirmed, Paddy
assured Da Dias that Iskander and Kerkorian were one and the
same. For a brief moment Paddy sensed Anna's presence, warm
and vivid, before him. He raised his eyes, startled, then strangely
comforted, to find Terri's eyes on his.

"Alex Kerkorian," mused Paddy, "Iskander, a man of
many names, Imam Zaman, Braderakan, Farang Dang Mo, and
another - Algazi, the conqueror." Paddy recalled Kerkorian's
comments about their final assignment with Special Force Seven,
"The number seven, to the Greeks, is a lucky number. All will be well."
Kerkorian's plans at that point, Paddy surmised, of a broader
scope than anyone suspected.

Da Dias rose to pace the measured distance familiar
to him, hands folded behind his back. "This morning I learned
that the 'Braderakan' you have just mentioned are no longer
in northern Laos. They have returned to Pakistan, dealing
in weapons grade plutonium from Kazakhstan - a nuclear
resource, I am told, greater than that of the Ukraine."

Based on what he learned from Thompson, Paddy told
Da Dias of the presence, in England, of a team of professional
assassins from the Middle East at the time of Madam's
assassination. He described Ben's suggestions, based on Israeli
Intelligence, that the obscure figure from the Middle East, Algazi,
could have been responsible for both Madam and the Seanache's
assassinations, for a similar purpose. "Ben was convinced," said
Paddy, "that the man posed a major threat not only to Israel, but
also to the world at large."

In answer to Da Dias' immediate question, Paddy
shook his head. "The exact location of Algazi has not yet
been determined. From all information, it is estimated to be
somewhere in northern Iraq."

Da Dias, feeling for the chair beside him, slowly
resumed his seat. "The Chinese resumption of sovereignty has
no doubt added a sense of urgency to the plans of this man, risk
to premature disclosure - to seizure of the colonel's resources he
is still striving to acquire."

Silence and shadows seemed to gather about the old
house. In the gardens, the night winds were still. From the

marshes of Kwantung Province wafted the thin cry of the night birds. From the old town, distant, dissonant notes of laughter, thin reedy sounds of music, from the casinos, the resonant beat of the late night disco.

Glancing at Terri, Paddy remembered another night, long ago. The party in Saigon, when he'd first met Anna, when their world was young. A world of dreams, all too soon to disappear. Terri caught his glance. They smiled at one another.

As they left the great mansion, Paddy guided Terri along the uneven pathway, closely followed by An Luc, ever watchful. An Luc's heart sang. He sensed a rebirth, resolution for his lady Anna, for his Tuan, and for Terri, alone no longer. Confirming his belief in a happy outcome for each of them, for An Luc it was fulfilment of his commitment; his promise to the lady Anna realised.

CHAPTER THIRTY-SIX

Pottinger's farewell

Twenty-four hours later Hong Kong still celebrated, as a Greater China watched the final colonial departure. Few traces remained of one hundred fifty years of colonial rule, British presence, no longer discernible. Victoria Harbour, busily indifferent, bustled about its frantic daily activities, the great yellow and red flags of the Peoples Republic hanging limply from the main masts above the city.

First word from the west, a phone call from Bob Thompson. Lavery's body had been recovered from the Thames near Henley, near where Grey had been found. The link was growing stronger between Tracker and his foreign friends Lavery had described at the pub near Aldershot.

Thompson learned that the main figure indicted in the Australian government's investigations, the Deputy Director of the Department of Defence, was indeed the one who had sponsored Tracker's appointment to SAS at Aldershot. As a news hungry international press reported the hearings in Australia, speculation commenced on the extent of involvement of members of the home government. Gordon's ill explained suicide had directed public attention to the China Scheme. The hunt for a scandal was on.

Paddy gave Thompson a detailed account of his evening with Da Dias. With the help offered by Da Dias, they planned to contact Kerkorian.

Paddy described the plan, as Da Dias had suggested, to offer Kerkorian secure access to Deevers' vaults, through the holders of the keys. "The intent is to draw Kerkorian from his lair, to stop him before he pulls the trigger on a nuclear or chemical disaster of possibly universal proportions. For

Kerkorian, it would also be a chance to silence those who once knew him." Paris, the location of SEACO and the China Scheme's European headquarters, was deliberately chosen, an area of activity well used by the Kerkorian connection.

As Paddy, Terri and An Luc prepared to depart from Kai Tek Airport, joining the exodus in a sombre outflow, the predatory shapes of helicopters, red striped fuselage of the Peoples Republic flew west to east, their canopies winking boldly in the sun - the clatter of rotors echoing flatly across the waterfront. Their unsubtle strut was a final teasing reminder that it was all over - for some. Victoria's once "barren island", reinvented and restored.

Observing the scene, Paddy remembered the colonial link to Ireland, Pottinger Street in Belfast – the name of the first Governor of Hong Kong - now indeed, Pottinger's farewell. For Paddy, the airborne message confirmed it was time to be gone.

Some hours later, flight 107 and its passengers bore steadily westward. Its progress was monitored closely through international air traffic tracking procedures, also closely followed by Chinese aerial reconnaissance at Chan Chiang, perhaps reflecting a growing sensitivity of the suzerainty of the Chinese government over its expanding Pacific littoral.

From Chan Chiang, information on the estimated arrival time of flight 107 in Bombay was also transmitted, along with departure times on its continuing path to Tel Aviv, and final leg to Paris. This and other data were conveyed to interested parties even further afield, their world still in darkness, to a remote region in the foothills of the Zagros Mountains of northern Iraq.

From the South China Sea to the east, the rising sun seemed to pause, momentarily suspended. Its eye cautiously squinted westward, across the dense, green slopes of Vietnam far below. Deftly etched, like a Japanese watercolour, the figures of the early morning fishermen in their slim pirogues stood in silhouette between the invisible shorelines of the mighty Mekong. Creeping across the rice fields of Cambodia, the risen sun groped, perhaps in momentary, sad reflection, amid the ruins of Muong Sing, the mountains of memory of northern Laos. Here, where Anna and Terri once shared their dreams, where Terri and An Luc fled from its nightmares.

Scarcely daring to believe what he'd learned in Macao, Paddy was engrossed in the reality of Kerkorian's dangerous delusions. Slowly turning the pages of the book Whitcombe had given him, he read of a long dead king of the remote Greek province of Macedonia, obsessed with the spirit of arête, of pothos – of daring to try the impossible. World conquest his goal, he marched to doom and destruction. Following Alexander's path, Paddy recognised why this ancient tale of war and deception had inspired Kerkorian to follow in his footsteps.

Across from Paddy, Terri Sai slept fitfully. In the world of dreams she relived the terrifying apparition from Peshawar, the Braderakan. Stirring with occasional restless muttering, she returned to the mountains, the silent valleys of Afghanistan, to a simple cairn of rocks where Aija lay.

They now passed far above the Ganges, in union with the rivers of reincarnation, ever drifting in a ceaseless flow of time and life, from the incipient first, clear, trickle from the ice capped peaks of the mighty Himalayas. Gathering to thunder through dark, echoing gorges, the clear mountain silt emerges, swollen with carcass and carrion, sacrificial, funereal, of man and beast.

Mother Ganges' sacred and profane effluvia, its miasma of old death, of young love, of spiritual repletion. The plundered human heritage of four thousand years - of the British East India Company, of the days of the Raj. All the enduring spirits in their endless cycle of redemption and reincarnation. Drifting flowers and holy men, floating on the rivers of time - the spirit of India in the land of the Jains. Floods of unclear mystical majesty drifted in vast tides of human and natural debris to the sultry delta; east, to the Gulf of Anaman and west, in a mighty surge, to the torrid sweep of the Bay of Bengal.

As An Luc followed the sun's light, gazing in wonder, surely he sensed their Kan Khat. Listening to the story unfolding in Macao, An Luc had concluded the evil forces were even now watching, following their path. An Luc, a Khon Kong - did he believe it, defying death itself? Guided by the Buddha, he must follow the path ordained. He must be ever watchful for the sly presence. His only concern, like his father, was to be ready.

As Terri muttered in restless sleep, beside her Paddy gazed out toward an opalescent sky. He recalled both An Luc and Terri's comment when An Luc had asked Paddy how he would recognise Kerkorian, if Kerkorian were to accept their invitation to meet in Paris. It had been almost thirty years since Paddy had seen him.

Terri had assured him that she and An Luc also had a commitment, not alone to Anna or to Paddy, but to each other. "We will face Anna's killer together," she said. "The Goddess A-ma, finally able to return home, at peace."

Paddy had silently taken her hand. No more was said.

CHAPTER THIRTY-SEVEN

"One day shall come to Asia's wealthy land an unbelieving man, wild, despotic, fiery... and all Asia shall have an evil yoke." The Greek Sibylline Oracles

At the Bombay terminal Paddy, Terri and An Luc transferred to their connecting flight for Tel Aviv. The El Al flight rose sharply, turning south above the historic, deep-sea port.

Terri Sai sat, pensive. Drawn to the vanishing view below, Paddy was describing the colourful history of Bombay, its thriving boulevards and beaches. Once the least attractive of Britain's colonial assignments, the squalid, pestilential city was annually ravaged by torrential monsoon floods. Yet, curiously, it was among the first of the British established, so called permanent settlements.

"The conception then, of the new global village, from India to Egypt to Africa to Ireland, to the American colonies and elsewhere," said Paddy. "As elsewhere now, you give your freedom, in exchange for the three C's - Commerce, Christianity and Civilisation - colonial style. The irony is, while we were in skins with no common language and a pantheon of primitive gods, from India came the precedent to Christianity, the Monism of Buddha, of Shankara to the Upanishads. The first colonial governors here, Clive and Hastings, impoverished the people, stealing millions. Both were later tried by Parliament for theft and acquitted - Clive committing suicide."

As the El Al flight headed toward the distant Gulf of Oman, Terri told Paddy of the strange dreams she'd had. "As Aija once described it, from the age of the fearless Mongolian horsemen, of Alexander the Macedonian; the path of conquest Whitcombe says Kerkorian now seeks to follow." Terri clasped her hands, closing her eyes briefly. "It was a frightening dream – so real!

"And to realise," Terri added, looking now at Paddy, "at the same time Alexander the Conqueror stood in the Wakham Corridor, staring across the empty deserts - beyond his gaze lay another world. From transient conquest, to the world of Confucian China. And he made his choice. He turned away.

"Something else I remember now. In Peshawar, Jalad Khan told me the Braderakan had been seen in the same Wakham region during the war in Afghanistan."

Terri looked from Paddy to An Luc. "The links between events and people are sometimes more than a coincidence. It's stranger now that the dreams and memories should return so vividly; the legend of Alexander, and his reincarnation reborn in the dreams of Kerkorian. And always now, I have the feeling that Aija, like Anna, is guiding us."

Paddy nodded in agreement, adding, "Sometimes there lies a fine line between dreams and reality. Your dream and recollections, Terri, are part of a series of remarkable coincidences. What Aija told you is true. Alexander did pass that way on his return from what are now the former Soviet Islamic republics. All these regions are now a nuclear tinderbox. And," Paddy continued, "with Tadzhikstan bordering China, it provides a busy site for drugs and arms exchange, another likely scene for Kerkorian's activities. It's no coincidence that he and the Braderakan have been seen in that region during and after the Russian war in Afghanistan."

Paddy read from the book, *Alexander of Macedon,* Whitcombe had given him. "Below us, the Arabian Sea, the desert, Alexander's final and reluctant road to more conquest, to his limits and, finally, his death."

Irresistibly Paddy, An Luc and Terri found themselves drawn back in time as the figure from legend quickly came to life. Paddy compared the extraordinary odyssey of Alexander to the Kerkorian he remembered. Momentarily sharing the myth of Alexander – Kerkorian's replay, the nightmare, became a more harsh reality.

Flight 125 bore steadily toward the Gulf of Oman as

Paddy occasionally checked some detail, turning the pages of the book. What was it that this legendary figure from two thousand years passed and Kerkorian could now share? Kerkorian's goals little different it seemed, achieving conquest, "arête", always daring to go the further step.

From the Pamirs of Northern Afghanistan, Paddy told how Alexander had made his way south into Pakistan, just as Terri and Aija had done.

An Luc nodded as Paddy went on, "An Luc and I might have been in those regions at the same time as Kerkorian. We were obtaining weapons, recruiting and training fighters for the mujahidin. We too saw the extent of the drug market, traders from all over the world. Possibly Kerkorian and his companion were among them. Yet I now believe Kerkorian's trade in drugs and arms was not the only reason for his presence in northern Afghanistan."

Paddy continued the ancient saga of the young Alexander, whose adventures Kerkorian had become so strangely obsessed with. Striving to separate fact from myth or fantasy, they tried to understand the extraordinary, elusive character. Like Kerkorian now, an enigma to those who thought they knew him. Both, blood thirsty, vindictive, vengeful and ruthless.

"As I recall," said Paddy grimly, "Kerkorian had few real friends, yet none ever challenged his courage. And throughout history, Alexander's record of conquest and tactical brilliance has never been equalled. Perhaps this is what Kerkorian seeks to emulate – what we most fear." Paddy recalled the words of the prophet in Alexander's time, that one day he'd become "lord of Asia". He saw more clearly now the similarity of Kerkorian, or Iskander, as he would be called, and Alexander - centuries apart.

"Some things Da Dias told us arouse my curiosity," Paddy mused. "What might have compelled this man that I once thought I knew, on this incredible path? Alexander's life, like Kerkorian's, was very complex. "What was Kerkorian's story? Among Alexander's goals," Paddy read, "to be the best, regarding himself as the reincarnation of the warrior hero, Achilles, invincible. Kerkorian referred to Spec Force 7 as 'The

Companions' – the name of Alexander's fighting elite from history. Kerkorian, in a remote time warp. Two 'boy men'; Iskander, following Alexander's Achillean legend, their stories two thousand years apart."

Paddy turned the pages, "In the words of the oracle at Delphi to the twenty-four year old Alexander, 'My lord, thou art invincible - aniketos! Alexander's only remaining goal, his immortality ensured." They marvelled at the brash audacity of the young Alexander on his embattled path to an early death, also to his own eagerly sought, everlasting immortality. For Paddy, the faces of Alexander and Kerkorian were now merging. The uncanny similarity of two personalities, existing eons apart, was becoming eerily very real.

"Soon now," said Paddy, looking out the window and downward, his voice hushed as if witnessing the scene, "we will be passing over the site of Alexander's final tribulations, and likely now, Kerkorian's."

Paddy's hushed words evoked a colourful and tragic era. "The unchanging quandary. For Kerkorian, the seismic shift, from terrestrial conquest to a different world, no economic borders, more invisible spoils, of currencies and energy resources – all the same, the hunt for wealth and power. The paradox of our most dangerous dilemma."

"The challenge," added Terri, slightly perplexed, "with all we have learned, Paddy, it gets no easier. From Genghis Khan, to Tamerlane, from Alexander to Kerkorian - the world we live in is a recurring scene of killing and conquest. And now, the Brit/US crusade - a mission of bombs and sanctions versus the designated 'rogue states' – the non-compliant effectively silenced. Democracy everywhere, I believe, is a dwindling fantasy."

Paddy slowly nodded. "Our basic indifference unchanged. In Acton's words, 'power corrupts - absolute power corrupts absolutely.'"

Paddy described how Kerkorian's decision to volunteer for the Spec. Force Seven assignment now seemed to indicate well laid plans. Perhaps Kerkorian's warped genius had been greatly underestimated. The limitless potential of the international trade in drugs and arms appeared now as only a first step in his complex plans to "seize the hour", to realise his dreams of world conquest. Kerkorian, as Iskander, determined to achieve his own megalomanic fantasies. Like Alexander, his mentor, every option a challenge! Terri described the Chinese expression, weiji – the challenge meaning both crisis and opportunity.

Alexander of Macedon, Iskander, Kerkorian, AlGazi, El Banau, the nameless one - Paddy found himself with an undeniable concern, not alone for the plans of Kerkorian as he thought he knew them, but more evident now - the ability of the Kerkorian he didn't know, to accomplish them.

Paddy quoted the final words of the ancient oracle, "And all Asia shall have an evil yoke, and the drenched earth shall drink in great slaughter". No change there. Paddy was remembering the world Terri and An Luc had grown up in, his own years in Vietnam, the unending struggle in the Middle East, Northern Ireland and beyond.

Paddy was silent, remembering Kerkorian's joking comments about claiming his reward, never betraying himself, when Anna had given him the key at Phnom Penh - watching as she'd distributed the others to herself and Paddy, to Davost and Harrari, to Buddy Johnson and An Luc's father. Perhaps Kerkorian hadn't realised at first. These, the very keys he'd killed Deevers and Anna for, yet never found.

Paddy listed the victims of Kerkorian's brutality - Deevers, Anna, Peter Ramaiah - likely now, Perry and the two hundred fifty innocent passengers of the flight sabotaged over Scotland. Even, he suspected, the Seanache and his Syrian friend, Abdul Said among his victims. Perhaps, even of those less innocent, Madam Prime Minister and others. Where was Iskander now? What was his next step? Terri remarked on the millions who would surely die should Kerkorian's cunningly contrived jihad continue to spread to a worldwide conflagration.

The pilot announced their course, now off the coast of Iran. Giving them the expected ETA, he requested them to fasten their seat belts, expecting mild turbulence. Infinitely fragile in the scope of an immeasurable universe of measurable response, the

767 and its passengers held its precarious course, in the far less predictable constellation of human aspirations and conflicts.

Passengers nervously glanced beyond the wingtip to the still, amorphous clouds beneath - the sun an almost reluctant witness, commencing its long journey westward. To the east, the dry, barren reaches, the khamsin, hot winds of the Dasht-e Kavir, the vast, salt deserts of central Persia – graveyard of Alexander's dreams.

Far beneath El Al flight 125, the sun's fading light stealthily fingered the shadowed gorges, the deep valleys. Above the valleys echoed the scream of the highflying falcons, the eagles, eager hunters peering earthward, searching for their prey.

CHAPTER THIRTY-EIGHT

For many shall come in my name, saying, I am Christ; and shall deceive many. And ye shall hear of wars and rumours of wars: see that ye be not troubled: for all these things must come to pass... Matthew 24: 5-6

Casting a distant purple shadow, the brooding granite shoulders of the ancient mountains of Judah peered across the plains of Sharon. At their feet lay green valleys, rolling sand dunes, silent deserts - east, to the Jordan, and west, to the farms, the settlements and the kibbutz of the embattled "promised land." Israel, greeting successive waves of the returning *alyot* to this Holy Land of war and peace. The once primal, prehistoric crossroads of the Near East, of the massacres of the Christian crusades, was now a glutted space in inharmonious dissonance. A devil's chorus in God's garden.

Beyond the dunes rose the ancient port city of Tel Aviv-*Yafo*. Further westward, the endless blue depths of the Mediterranean, its still surface deflecting the brilliance of the noonday heat. Eastward, in the haze beyond the Jordan, a mirage land of legend and unravelling dreams.

From Israel and across the world the Jewish Diaspora return home - curious tourists, students of history, Jewish or Christian missionaries, Biblical scholars, or others, fugitives, spies, terrorists. All the cosmopolitan nuance of the great city of Tel Aviv, Israel's glittering cultural and commercial centre.

Above the babbling font of Babel, just a block from the city centre - the wary, watchful eye and ear of Israel's superlative intelligence service, Mossad. Within the grim, featureless building, an urgent phone call was passed through to Ben Harrari's office.

Ben picked up the phone. The distraught, uneven tones

sounded distant, worried, frightened.

"*Baruch Hashem* - blessed be God!"

It took Ben a few seconds to recognise the voice he had listened to in Northern Ireland just over a week ago. These were not the tones Ben had heard at the funeral - not the calm, reasoned voice of one of the most respected peacemakers among the few moderate Arab spokesmen, but uncertain, anguished notes of desperate urgency.

Accepting Ghubar's quick request to avoid identification, Ben listened to a nervous monologue.

"I have little time, my friend. All of us are in great danger. My efforts have failed. I will try to leave here tonight or in the morning." Ghubar made a quick reference, incautiously revealing a possible avenue of flight.

Trying not to detain him, Ben did not interrupt. He listened to Ghubar's frightened words. Apparently, he had been on some sort of diplomatic peace negotiation in an effort to contain the fighting that now spread from the Caspian.

Ghubar spoke of a "third party", bringing Ben's mind back to Paddy's news only that morning. Ben had just received an earlier call from Deicey, British Security Intelligence, Middle East. Deicey had seemed anxious to meet with Ben to assess Israel's position on Mid-East developments. Deicey was also following up on links to the still unresolved Weatherby assassinations. There were many unanswered questions. Since after the Seanache's funeral and with Safarov in Belfast, Ben was convinced both Graham and Tracker were part of a renegade operation – possibly, of MI6.

Ghubar barely paused, "Abdul Said's assassin, the one Safarov spoke of, the one of many names, is behind this devious strategy. As soon as the US and Britain are involved in this region - Iraq, the trap - the word is, he will move. And Ben, someone from British intelligence was seen in this area in the past few days."

Ben waited. He heard the ID system lock in. Unable to resist, he found himself asking Ghubar of any further word on Senjaye, the French scientist.

"I know him. A strong advocate of Kurdish sovereignty.

I have heard he is perhaps working with them now - I don't know. El Ze'im, they tell me, employs a strong team of scientists. El Ze'im's chemical and biological warfare arsenals have been building for years - not easily detectable.

"El Algazi, or El Ze'im, as they call him. The 'Anointed One'. An elusive enemy. Some claim to have met him in northern Iraq, in the mountains above Al Mawsil. The site, I am told, is well protected from aerial surveillance."

Occasionally Ghubar's voice became distorted or disappeared in a storm of static. Ben heard "China Scheme", and "Beckaa Valley". Suddenly Ben heard the sounds of an outside "lock in". He signalled for assistance in monitoring the call, a sophisticated linkup with Mossad international trace agencies.

Ghubar's voice grew more urgent. "I believe they're onto us." After a moment's pause, Ghubar murmured quietly, "Baruch hashem." His voice disappeared in a storm of static. Suddenly Ben heard a distant shout. He heard fumbling at the other end of the line, a remote click, then as suddenly, silence.

Alarmed, Ben connected to an agent in Shiklut. Personnel confirmed they were working on location ID. "Contact me as soon as you have information," Ben directed.

Ben held the phone a moment, remembering Ghubar's bitter words after the Seanache's funeral - the fate and history of the Middle East, the running conflict with its divided identity. Ben knew why Ghubar had chosen the path of peace and compromise. Ghubar, a single voice against war as an instrument of political policy; a dangerous role to play. Ben glanced at his watch. He needed to leave shortly to meet Paddy's flight. He quickly listed a series of calls to be made. He spoke to Special Operations headquarters. Sayret Matcal, those that carried out the Entebbe affair, would handle the rescue operation.

As he waited for the call from the Prime Minister's office, Ben rose, looking through the windows at the children at play. The children lived their lives, hostages to the constant threat of war, in constant range of terrorist attacks, random shootings.

Sadly, Ben thought of the words of Abraham, "From the Wadhis of Egypt to the Greater Euphrates, all is yours." A promise still not realised. Even now, despite the unending cost,

Ben only knew gratitude for the more restricted domain - the jealously coveted, embattled oasis. Finally their homeland, this fertile sliver between mountain, desert and sea.

Ben placed a secure call to the Israeli Embassy in Washington. He then placed a call to Yossi Raviv, head of Metsada, arranging a meeting for later that evening.

Ben called Arik Cohen, head of Shaback, asking him to set up a "total security situation" for incoming El Al flight 125 from Bombay. He made another call, confirming a later meeting to include the head of Mossad and the Prime Minister, moved to the following morning. He instructed his secretary to put all calls through, at any time. It was going to be a long night.

As Ben was driven to the airport there was a hurried exchange, bringing Harry Shaiko, Assistant Director of Aman, Military Intelligence, up to date on Ghubar's situation, answering calls from the Prime Minister's office, from Shiklut - still trying to trace Ghubar's call. As Ben and Harry Shaiko arrived, Ben's phone rang again. Arik Cohen was already at the airport.

"They're landing now. We've covered the airport. We're in Security Building B. Where are you?"

Ben quickly responded. "Be right there!" They were out before the car had stopped, pushing past emerging passengers.

Ben Harrari, Harry Shaiko and Arik Cohen met the contingent of Security as they emerged from the passageway. A moment of hasty greetings, then with Cohen's assistance Paddy, An Luc and Terri were unceremoniously hustled from the terminal. Closely guarded by Shaback, they boarded a waiting car. In a second car, Cohen's people followed them from the airport. Shaback had already surveilled Ben's house and would cover Paddy and his friends for the rest of their stay in Israel, and on the further flight to Paris.

Ben's wife, Sara, a vivacious lady, recently elected to the Knesset and the new Madam of Israel's Labour Party, warmly welcomed them. Their home was situated above the beaches of Herzlyya Pituach in the northern suburbs of Tel Aviv. Sheltered by wind bent pines and palm trees behind the sand dunes, the green lawns and gardens provided a sense of tranquillity and seclusion.

Having a short time to relax, they gathered on the deck above the gardens. Despite the more ominous aspects of their visit, there was a genuine spirit of celebration and reunion. Soon Terri and Sara were in quiet conversation; Paddy, Ben and An Luc catching up on each other's news. Harry Shaiko soon joined them.

As Ben had arranged, they were quickly joined by Yossi Raviv and Arik Cohen. Ben relayed Ghubar's communication, and the developing plans to locate and bring him out. He repeated Ghubar's description of events, naming again the mysterious character, El Algazi, El Ze'im, his sometime location in northern Iraq.

Sara and Terri crossed the gardens to the quiet beach. They walked barefoot in the cool sand, sharing the solitude. Discreetly guarded by security, they talked of friends and family, feeling a warm sense of trust.

Her voice almost a whisper, Terri spoke of her growing concern for Paddy in his efforts to confront Kerkorian. Sara noticed Terri was barely able to control her shivering, her eyes wide with fear as she spoke of Kerkorian's actions. Sara felt it too, like a sudden chill in the late morning air.

Sara shared many of Terri's fears, expressing her immediate concerns for her family, the impact of recent events on the people of Israel. A Sabra, born in Israel, Sara was a member of the New Force movement, seeking a policy of conciliation, a viable future.

"The decline in Western cultural values, self-destruction of Communism, the moral vacuum, escalating violence, all finally propelled me into politics," Sara told Terri. "So many had given their lives, I felt convinced that a new perspective, transcending national boundaries, the voice of women - wives, mothers - was sorely needed. In a world where men's voices predominate, there is an inclination to the aggressive response. On the contrary, women's tendency, psychologically and biologically, is to commit to the future, to protect and nurture the family."

Sara glanced at Terri, smiling. "Hostile attacks are something we try to live with. The turmoil is seen by some as a fratricidal war of biblical origins, the Arabs, our Moslem brothers and sisters. But most of us now realise this is a deliberate distortion of the facts. The roots of the present conflicts here and in many other parts of the world, as you will see in Ireland, lie in a more recent history."

Sara stood gazing across the beaches. "Both our peoples were victims of the Western intrusion, the marauding Crusaders scarcely bothering to portray themselves as Christian missionaries. In reality, murderous zealots, driven out by the Ottoman Turks. Most people Terri, don't know that the Golden Age of Jewry occurred during the apex of Arab power in Moslem Spain. When the Spanish Christians under Ferdinand and Isabella replaced them, they brought the horrors of the Inquisition.

"The British came, fresh from the reckless, human expenditure of the 'War to End All Wars', further dividing us. They came with their lies, promising a homeland to the Arabs, to the Jews. None of their promises were kept, the so-called Middle East finally partitioned into dependent oil sheikdoms – zones of continuing political influence.

"Until the establishment of the Jewish State the British imprisoned, hanged or deported to Africa hundreds of Jewish freedom fighters. The Arabs also fought the Mandate – inevitably, sadly then, we fought each other. So it has been - and now to the American's Middle East and their new Imperial agenda."

Sara occasionally glanced at Terri as if to measure the effect of her words.

"Ghubar is not the only one – there are other Arabs and Jews who see sharing our land as the only path. There are those of us who are learning to trust one another, who seek to rid ourselves of British and American sovereignty – till now, our only source of oil and nuclear weapons, indeed, of our survival.

"Yet again, Terri, it seems the passion of Islamic resurgence is being used. From the Russian Republics it is a deliberate political manipulation. The extinction of the State of

Israel, under pretext of the restoration of a Pan-Islamic empire, a jihad from Afghanistan to the Caucasus. For the Anglo-American Svengali this is an open market in an endless war, their excuse, to restore their version of democracy and freedom. Arab and Jew being reduced to colonial dependency."

"This is indeed the time for a different harvest," Terri replied, "one that my friend Aija Tsi has so briefly sown. A new beginning. Ahimsa, without violence, as Gandhi had shown. Time to encourage women to extend their natural role."

Sara nodded. "Perhaps, with Aija's inspiration, those of the New China Movement and women in similar groups everywhere will communicate on an international level. Devise a universal response to the callous depletion of the natural human resource, our children."

They stood in silence, thinking of the uncertainty of the future. They listened to the beach sounds, of the rising tide, the occasional distant cry of the seabirds.

CHAPTER THIRTY-NINE

The Plains of Sharon

Back at the house, as the sun fell across the silent beaches of Herzlyya Pituach, there was a succession of phone calls. They had traced Ghubar to an area in northern Syria, close to the Iraq border. They would be sending a unit in.

A call from Deicey was passed through. Sounding strangely curt, nervous, Deicey uncharacteristically apologized; he wouldn't be able to make the meeting he'd scheduled for the following day. Something urgent had come up, requiring his immediate attention.

As they discussed the implications of Deicey's communication, Ben suggested to Paddy that the situation in London might have drastically altered Deicey's priorities. Both Ben and Paddy had little doubt those in MI6, in PASS, under considerable pressure from events in Australia and Northern Ireland, were eager to know more about the changing situation in Hong Kong and the 'new China'. Paddy couldn't think of another reason for MI6's unusual request for a meeting with Ben, especially so soon after his controversial appearance at the Seanache's funeral.

Ben couldn't help linking Deicey's distress with Ghubar's earlier message. Perhaps Ghubar had identified Deicey's presence. Perhaps Deicey and Ghubar shared similar information, with now similar concerns, yet for different reasons.

Yossi Raviv agreed with Ben. Deicey's motives were easily questionable. Was Britain again acting its traditional inciteful role between the Russians and this new evolving "Muslim Army of God"?

There was another phone call for Ben. He nodded to Paddy as he switched the phone to speaker. "It's Jack, from

Belfast, returning my call." Ben assured Jack that he was on a secure line.

Greeting each of his listeners as Ben introduced them, Jack told them he had heard from Bob Thompson the previous evening. Jack was incredulous at the news of Kerkorian's reappearance. He had called Roger Moorefield in London, asking for an urgent background check on Kerkorian. "I'm expecting to get word within the next twenty-four hours. Your visit to Macao, Paddy, was a great stroke of luck!"

In response to Paddy's question, sadly Jack replied, "Sean's condition is worsening. Infection is just overwhelming him. But whatever the outcome for Sean, his story has generated a cause of its own."

Quickly Jack told them the news from Belfast. "The prosecution favoured a closed hearing in the interests of 'National Security'. My involvement enabled the American Consul, Tom Feely, to support the defence request for a hearing open to the public and the media. They're now battling over the inclusion of television. The more they try to impose restrictions the worse they look."

Jack acknowledged, "The Granart papers are the key, Paddy. The papers were presented and they've caused a considerable stir. Theresa's defence team and various human rights organizations are questioning the jurisdictional rights of the Northern Ireland diplock court system. The papers raised the question of the legality of the British occupation. Both these steps won support and interest worldwide. This could be Ireland's day of retribution. I just wish my father were here to see it all.

"The Northern Ireland Administration might be forced to release Theresa and Dan on bail due to a lack of prosecution witnesses – hearsay evidence. It's been moving that way in the past twenty-four hours."

Jack described a scene of uproar at the court hearings as Dan and Theresa gave their account of the shooting of the Seanache and the boy. Jack would be questioned later, as the prosecution tried to build its case.

A deal for the British was the inescapable option now, for them to lay the blame on the Australian, Tracker, rather than open the hearing to Dan, Bob or Jack's testimony. Following the shooting of the Seanache and the boy, Jack or Dan's right to defend themselves would be undeniable. Their testimony would expose more British FRU/MI5 collusion, damning evidence for the prosecution.

"Just this afternoon," Jack continued, "the testimony of those present at the Paris Embassy meeting has been requested, a sensational move by the defence. To our joy, the judge ordered your testimony, Paddy, by deposition or in person on your return.

"Among those summoned are DeVeere, regarding his possible illegal authorisation of Madam's plan Ajax. This will eventually lead to Bob's testimony, not only of the Seanache's death, but of the earlier shooting at Belfast Airport.

"Deicey of MI6 will also be summoned. The goal here is to lead up to the controversy over Michael Weatherby's accusations, and to Graham's possible links with the fate of the Weatherbys.

"The possible connection of DeVeere with PASS has been raised by the defence, with a view to exploring any role of PASS in the China Scheme. DeVeere protested any discussion of the meeting with Madam in Paris, on security grounds.

"Another story seems to have emerged from the hearings in Australia. The possibility of US National Security linked with MI6, with similar interests in relation to the China Scheme. Each day Belfast is packed with journalists and TV crews from all over the world chasing this sensational story."

Paddy nodded. What he'd suspected since his encounter with Victor Perry, and confirmed by Da Dias. Kerkorian and SEACO, with branches worldwide, the new and greater successor.

"Unless the international situation deteriorates dramatically," Paddy assured Jack, "the meeting with Kerkorian in Paris is on."

Jack agreed to meet them in two days, unless summoned to give evidence. "Gia Sao, you guys."

371

*

Minutes later word came of Ghubar's location. Ben, accompanied by Harry Shaiko and Arik Cohen, quickly departed for Mossad Headquarters. Ben arranged for Yossi and Sara to bring Paddy, An Luc and Terri to Mossad headquarters later in the afternoon.

They stood then, staring across the gardens of Herzliyya toward the Mediterranean, distant silver in the sunlight. Mesmerised by the solitude, no one spoke. Strategies of war on a day in peace - before the plains of Sharon, the mountains of Judah, in this, the Holy Land. The tide was out; the still pools, like tears across the landscape.

From far beyond the shoreline, whispers of longing, anguish and fear – the men, women and children, drowned in sight of the Homeland – fugitives from, or later, survivors of the Holocaust.

An urgent call for Paddy was quickly transferred from Apam, security, to Ben's home. The call was from Bob Thompson, in Northern Ireland.

"The situation here is changing rapidly." Thompson sighed audibly. "Graham was summoned to appear at the hearings. At first, he refused, for security reasons. His execution of plan Ajax could lead to his own prosecution. Now he's decided to turn King's evidence in exchange for immunity. Graham's using Tracker as a scapegoat, portraying himself as the innocent victim. Likely, he's been watching the progress of the hearings in Australia. The member of its Department of Defence who sponsored Tracker's assignment was indicted on several counts. A financial relationship's been established between this man and SEACO - SEACO intent in denying any wrongdoing."

Thompson hurried on. "Tracker and the foreign group are also now suspects in both Grey's murder and Lavery's. Graham's decision has caused uproar. No one trusts anyone. Appeals are now desperate for closed hearings. And there's more." Thompson hurried on.

"In light of the recent shootings in Northern Ireland, and the links, east to west, of the China Scheme, hearings at the

United Nations have commenced on the injustice and illegality of the British tenancy in the Irish State. The veto by the British representative was overridden. The demand for a hearing was assured by the United States abstention. This was a surprise. And with my own testimony coming up, will surely cause a further split in the US British relationship."

There was a pause. Thompson exchanged words with voices in the background. "Sorry Paddy, breaking news. Graham's lawyer claims Graham's actions were authorised by DeVeere, DDG MI6. A desperate or cunning stance for the prosecution. On grounds of National Security, DeVeere claims immunity from giving evidence in open court."

Another pause. "You're not going to believe this, Paddy. Not sure yet if it's even true; maybe to discredit Maloney since the uproar over his attendance at the Seanache's funeral. Allegedly, his secretary has been working for British intelligence. Maybe, a plea bargain – afraid Graham will tell the story. Apparently he knows something about Graham too. I'll have more on this later, when we get it all sorted."

This last comment was a dramatic revelation to Paddy. No wonder DeVeere and others at his interrogation had been so well informed. Maloney's secretary, on MI6's payroll? Had Geoffrey Gordon known that?

"And Paddy, the Australian economy is in trouble. In Hong Kong, desperate efforts are being made to shore up the currency. There are signs of a simultaneous implosion of the Russian economy. Strangely, the China Scheme is now shifting its base to the mainland. SEACO is still high on the exchange, despite the Australian government officials' acknowledged involvement in both the China Scheme and SEACO."

Paddy assured Bob he would be calling within the next twenty-four hours, giving as much notice as possible of his ETA in Paris. He hoped that developments would not prevent Thompson from joining them.

CHAPTER FORTY

"Long before nations' lines were drawn, when
no flags flew, when no armies stood, my land
was born."
Lines from "Anthem", a lyric from "Chess"

In Mossad Headquarters, Yossi Raviv brought them past
Security and into the main hallway. There Ben stood, talking
earnestly with Harry Shaiko. Paddy could see Ben's tense,
worried expression. They descended in silence to several floors
below ground level.

The elevator doors slid open to reveal a vast
amphitheatre, what appeared to Paddy to be a NASA
programme control room – with a complex array of control
panels and computers. Paddy, Terri and An Luc stared into a
surreal world, a bustling, dim lit city – an army of silent people
seated before flickering screens, or hurrying purposefully about
in the subdued half light. A sophisticated other world of eyes
and ears from cyber space, where the single eye determined the
fate of the multitude.

They followed Ben past the busy cubicles, joined by a
grim faced Arik Cohen. They entered a conference room where
they were greeted by agents standing before two luminous
screens that almost covered one wall. Someone handed them
dark eyeshades to protect from the harsh glare of the images.
A vivid glow suddenly appeared. Paddy was looking at a
clear satellite image, a brilliant, multi-dimensional map of the
northern borders of Syria and the luminous sweeping paths of
the Euphrates, the Tigris.

The view switched with extraordinary rapidity,
magnifying to instant close up. They were seeing through
the prying eye of satellites – coldly watching the arena where
Ghubar, they hoped, made his way homeward as the rescue

374

units closed in.

Two of the agents were pointing toward twin pinpoints of light located somewhere in the northern region of Iraq. Ben explained that computerised tracking devices activated the lights, monitoring the units tracking Ghubar. One blinked near Ghubar's last known sighting. The other, further west, was motionless. They all stared, mesmerised by the frail pinpoints of light, watching the silent, isolated drama of vulnerable human lives.

As Ghubar led his pursuers and the rescue team into futile confrontation, Paddy found himself distracted. Paddy could feel the desert heat, the same sands that had so quickly erased the passage of Alexander. According to Ghubar's urgent message, leading them to believe, now the home of Kerkorian.

He found himself remembering Ghubar's voice at the Seanache's wake, speaking for the more than one hundred million people of the Near East, all victims of the inherited evils and debris of colonialism. Ghubar had described the futility of sectarian strife, dividing the sons and daughters of Abraham against themselves – Jew and Arab and Turk, all the gifted peoples of the surge and flow of the Fertile Crescent, from the Euphrates to the Nile.

Like Ghubar, Safarov had ascribed the cause of both conflicts, in Afghanistan and in Ireland's northern counties, to the continuing colonial "great games".

Paddy again heard Ghubar's words at the funeral. "We are learning to focus more on what we share than what divides us. Truly the best of Judaism - the worst of Christianity; its mirage of deception deliberately obscuring the future for Jew and Arab – both too long, the unequal victims."

Paddy understood more clearly now. From Dan to Beersheba, it had been a desecration of all that the Semitic peoples could have shared in peace. All the children of Abraham now found their common heritage vandalised, denied.

There was a sudden shout of anguish from Ben. The twin lights had disappeared completely. They all stood, transfixed, not daring to look at one another – seeming to hear the primal scream, generation to generation. No sound came

375

from the awful vacuum of infinity. Ghubar, visionary from the stark cliffs of Massada, from the chosen people, alone in death. For Paddy, it seemed as though the world they lived in had little room for such a voice, such a man.

They later learned the rescue team from Sayaret Metcal had reached Ghubar too late. All had perished. Ghubar, it appeared, had been the bait for a cynical trap. In a small town on the Syrian border, in the sun dried, empty streets, they found him. Like Said before him, Ghubar had been crucified, mutilated. A message hung from his neck printed in Greek, "My way is not to fight my battles standing away from my enemies."

Curiously, the last enigmatic words were, "And so it will be!" Homer's defiant Achillean aniketos, invincible – a favourite quote of Alexander, and, Ben and Paddy instantly recognized, of Kerkorian!

Ben, Yossi Raviv and Harry Shaiko met with a clearly troubled Prime Minister. Later, Paddy was invited to tell the story of Kerkorian, the Algazi, to select members of the Israeli Cabinet, including the Department of Defence, a less sceptical group than Abdul Said and the Seanache had once tried to warn. At the conclusion of the intense exchange, the armed forces were put on full alert, a different enemy now in mind.

Ben transferred a call to Paddy from Bill Whitcombe in Hong Kong. Some hours before, Whitcombe had received an urgent message from Da Dias in Macao. Kuhn Sa, General Tung Giang, had been assassinated. They had found him in northern Laos, crucified and mutilated.

Shocked, Paddy quickly told Whitcombe the tragic circumstances for Ghubar. Whitcombe agreed the implications seemed obvious. Tung Giang, once Deevers' agent, ever in Kerkorian's shadow, knew too much. The manner of their deaths left its brutal message, to silence the informer, to warn the pursuer. The killings seemed a clear response, confirming Kerkorian's acceptance of the invitation to Paris, delivered by Da Dias through SEACO.

Short of time, they agreed to continue on to Paris. Harry Shaiko and Arik Cohen were assigned to accompany Paddy,

Terri and An Luc. French Intelligence Services were hurriedly briefed. Uncertainties did not permit contact with British MI6, nor with the US National Security Agency.

Unable to contact Jack Edwards in Belfast, Paddy reached Bob Thompson in London, updating him on developments, giving the ETA at Charles de Gaulle. Barring unexpected problems, Thompson felt sure both he and Jack could be in Paris in good time to meet Paddy. Paddy then called Jean Davost in Paris, giving him the numbers for Jack Edwards and Bob Thompson. Jean promised to call them as soon as he got off the phone.

"I am the lord of the dance, said he – and I'll lead you all, wherever you may be."
Sydney Carter, lyric from "Lord of the Dance." (1915)

Later that same evening, a private jet departed from a small airfield north of Tel Aviv. Arik Cohen pointed out the landmarks in the rapidly disappearing landscape beneath. Ben Harrari, Yossi Raviv and Harry Shaiko were less aware of the historic panorama below. Paddy, An Luc and Terri occasionally glanced to the distant plains of Sharon, each wondering what lay ahead.

In the immensity of the universe, among timeless fragments in the evolution of the galaxies they passed, the human presence a brief flicker in the stages of creation. Far below, beneath the dunes, the once Garden of Eden, scene of genesis, of redemption – hub of the successive flow and ebb of civilisations, each a regeneration of the human soul.

From the birthplace of the Carpenter's Son, they quickly passed the site of His crucifixion. His brief passage set an enduring memorial - for some, its unattainable aspirations. For others, its singular inspiration, to love or to war. To the north lay Tyre, witness to the brief succession of the more transient world conquerors, and of Alexander, to the site of Saladin's and his final defeat of the rapacious and misnamed Christian Crusaders.

Paddy felt again the unquiet spirit of Alexander, of the conquerors that succeeded him. Below and eastward, the historic lure of the oil rich littoral of the Persian Gulf – an unfortunate El Dorado of greed and death. To the endless reaches of the Arabian Desert – the immeasurable debris of nifak - the colonial divide. Gertrude Bell's, Lawrence's, seeds of future wars.

Terri listened as Paddy read how, for more than six thousand years the heavily silted Euphrates, mother of rivers, carried successive invasions. Those whose path Alexander had followed, and those who later followed - prophets and missionaries of morality, who left a legacy of wars and quarrelling religions. Those who built cities, and those who came to destroy them. Finally, the scene of Alexander's destruction of the Empire of Cyrus, of the Persians, and too soon, to be his grave.

Silent a moment, they shared the vision, heard the chorus of voices, the great peopling of Mesopotamia. Like Babel – each with their different dialects, language and culture, spoken in ancient tongues.

Terri smiled. "The story has a stunning impact, Paddy."

Paddy turned to glance at her. A remote coincidence had brought their lives together. Terri, from China to Laos, to An Luc, and so briefly, to Anna. He, following his own path to Ireland, to what had once been home in another time. The land of his family's heritage, the stolen entitlements he was ashamed of. The Seanache had known Paddy's story better than he did himself. He glanced again at Terri. Their worlds, once so far apart, now so close.

Paddy thought of Anna, then of Victor Perry and other victims, the passengers on the 747 over Scotland, the Weatherbys, Madam Prime Minister, the Seanache, Ghubar and now, Tung Giang. Each, 'crosses by the roadside' – yet each a death that had somehow led them closer to Kerkorian and his purpose.

Terri turned to see Paddy watching her. She smiled. "All will be well, Paddy." Her look became serious. "I had begun to believe that wars, sanctions, famine and disease were inevitable, our only natural course. Now, after speaking with Sara, I am convinced we are closer to what Aija described – caring for, trusting one another in a world truly without borders."

Paddy nodded. In that moment he saw Terri as he had seen her that night, as they left Da Dias' home in Macao. He reached for her hand. "It's been a long road, Terri, but somehow I feel we're nearly home."

CHAPTER FORTY-ONE

City of Love, City of Death

From the mansions of Neiully to the seedy pensions of St. Denis, from Le Bois to the Parc de Vincennes, on a clear day one can see the linden, the cypress, the sycamore and a profusion of flowers. And the resonance from the dissonant, boisterous chatter from Le Halle, the petulant shrieks from the Faubourg St. Honoré, to the symphonic splendour or the single, clear soprano from the Place de L'Opera. All, the song of Paris!

In her small garden Vera Beaudin Zebari knelt, busily tending her flowerbeds. The moss covered path felt cool to her knees, yet she also felt the invigorating warmth of the morning sun. She sang to herself as she pulled the predatory weeds or watered the still green buds.

With a painful grimace, she stood up, stretching her back. Shading her eyes, peering into the gnarled, ivy covered branches of the giant oak tree, she listened to a busy warbler. A breeze stirred the branches. Vera gazed around, cherishing the moment.

Vera's every movement was fondly observed by the older man, elbows perched on the window ledge above the cloistered garden. Rory O'Connor, ex-patriot Irishman, thought how far they'd journeyed together. She'd finally agreed to marry him, after all these years. As the first days of spring came they would walk in the parks, enjoying the flowers, the trees. The Bois de Boulogne or the Champs Elysées were often the site of his yearly proposal.

Always she'd responded with laughter. Marriage, she said, would reduce the magic, the romance they'd always shared, to the mundane.

Rory remembered their first meeting. A time of civil rights unrest, protests and violence. Near the Sorbonne, both were listening to speakers at a large and angry gathering. As they were jostled among the crowd, he and Vera had glanced at one another and smiled. The meeting quickly went out of control. In the melee Rory helped Vera escape through the nearby Luxembourg Gardens. They walked for hours, each telling their story. She to the blue-eyed Irish rebel with the quick, dry wit and the curious accent. He to his dark-eyed attentive companion, with the bright smile, the ready laughter.

They had dinner at a restaurant that was too expensive, on the Quai de la Tournelle. Later, Rory led her, laughing, across the icy pavements where they took refuge in the ageless warmth of Notre Dame, listening to the stark, clear, choral beauty of a boy soprano. Christmas Day they moved in together.

At first neither spoke of their work, only in brief reference, preferring to accept each other as they were, grateful and happy. Vera worked for SEACO, the same import-export company she had worked for in Vietnam. Since the recent hearings in Australia, increasingly controversial, the company faced an uncertain future.

Rory would tell her about Ireland, how he worked for the Irish national cause, requiring frequent absences. He referred to them as missions abroad, recruiting support. Vera never questioned him further. Always, she welcomed him home with joy and passion.

Both came to appreciate the uncertain future, the increasing risk. Moments of departure were confronted with an increasing air of bravado, false cheerfulness or an unhappy silence.

Some years before, the uneasy adjustment had come apart in a close brush for Rory. Rory's group had been ambushed in a sting by British SAS, with the collusion of RUC intelligence. Vera then learned the whole story of Rory's commitment. Rory Hennessey, alias O'Connor. Nothing stays the same. Rory, though wounded, had managed to evade his enemy. With him were two friends, Dan and Frank; their paths soon separated. Years later, Rory was shocked to hear news of Frank's death, fighting in someone else's useless wars.

Where possible now, Rory and Vera began to accompany each other on their various assignments. Their commitments intensified. They seemed to travel more.

They had learned of the meetings at the British Embassy in Paris, culminating in the assassinations of Madam and the Weatherbys, and other developments regarding SEACO. Vera wondered now, who authorised her assignments from SEACO? Were the accusations from Australia true - possible criminal proceedings for SEACO – the links to Hong Kong, to this new 'China Scheme'? Vera feared that she'd stayed with the company too long.

Rory and Vera felt they were losing control. Their careers had completely taken over their private lives. Rory wondered, where did the IRA's role begin and end? Events escalated with stunning impact – the shootings in the Mournes soon followed by the shocking news of the death of Rory's lifelong friend, his particular hero, the Seanache, Sean McCarton.

The weeks that followed brought more chaos. There were clear indications of internal conflicts within the British government itself, accusations and counter accusations. Recently, word that a member of MI6, Graham, had admitted he was "following orders" in the execution of Weatherby, and, accidentally, he confessed, the man's wife. Graham admitted being assigned to Ajax and its execution, but denied guilt in the assassination of the Seanache or the wounding of his grandson.

Rory and Vera seemed to see less of each other then. Vera, pursuing other assignments, was distracted. Rory was also troubled, being followed now himself by unfamiliar figures, he guessed possibly from British Intelligence. In Vera's absence there were phone calls to their apartment, voices of unmistakable non-European origins, leaving no message. Vera admitted she was uneasy about their role, at one point assisting perhaps, in some way, in Madam's assassination. Telling Rory she didn't understand some of the requests she was getting, the frequent phone calls to their apartment, she confessed that she felt tired, confused, older now.

For Rory, it had been the right moment. Again, he

proposed. This time, Vera accepted. She'd cried, then began to laugh. Rory had danced about, his game leg forgotten. Vera seemed like the young girl he'd first met. His girl now, forever!

Startled from his daydreams, Rory heard Vera's voice, saw her smile. Looking up at him, weeds and rake in her hands, she called, "Rory, my wild Irishman - this is the happiest day of my life!" Rory could only gaze down at her, biting his lip, smiling, tears in his eyes.

He felt like a boy again – hurried down the stairs in his limpy shuffle. Picking up the phone he called the maitre d' of another too expensive restaurant on the West Bank. Vera deserved the best.

"Monsieur O'Connor, we will be delighted! Flowers at your table? Yes, Monsieur, the table by the window, with the view of Notre Dame. The site of your first date - how charming, Monsieur. Everything will be arranged." Rory could hardly wait!

West of the city, in a more pastoral setting on the banks of the Seine, in the home of Jean and Nguyen Davost, Paddy awoke just before noon. They had arrived in Paris from Tel Aviv the previous evening. Jean had prepared for their reception at the airport, organising Security precautions. Word had just been received of the assassination of the new Russian Premier. Everywhere, everyone was on alert.

Bob Thompson had arrived from London some hours earlier. Jack Edwards flew in from Belfast. Both joined Jean Davost in meeting Paddy's flight. Jean had not seen either Jack Edwards or Ben Harrari since that fateful night in Phnom Penh more than thirty years before. Under heavy security they were quickly taken to Jean's home in St. Germain en Laye.

After a late dinner, Paddy and Ben brought Jean up to date on events since the DEA meetings. Jack and Bob Thompson described the developments in London and Belfast over the past twenty-four hours.

"Surely has to be an imminent resolution," said Jack. Wolsey won't let the chance or the challenge go."

Bob Thompson agreed. He had spoken with Wolsey

in the past twenty-four hours. Both Bob and Jack pointed out the challenges now evident with the Amnesty International and Human Rights hearings in Brussels, the UN hearings in New York, the Security Council with US support. They were convinced the British position in Northern Ireland was now untenable. The British team was seeking a marginally respectable path so as not to lose face. The Irish team, under Maloney's direction, was unrelenting in its request for closure on the trial of Theresa and Dan; unyielding in its further request for the newfound evidence in the Granart papers.

Bob Thompson described worldwide concerns over the transfer of nuclear material from Uzbekistan and the Ukraine, purportedly, to Iran. Ben Harrari reiterated Ghubar's fears of as yet unsubstantiated rumours in relation to Professor Senjaye's expertise, the threat of the use of biological weapons. "With the assassination of the Russian Premier, the substitution of rule by an alleged consortium of mob organisations," said Ben, "it is difficult to separate fact from fiction."

Bob Thompson had recently accepted a request from Wolsey to run for Parliament. He described his goals with obvious enthusiasm, "A new national image in the global village. No longer aspiring to the dominant role, but equal partners in the European community."

Commenting on his chances in the coming elections, his ultimate goals included a public referendum for a devolved Scotland and Wales. A new Britain, embracing the "new Europe" in its joint economic strategy. The decision for Irish affairs left to its own, all island decision - two or more systems, with one economic agenda. The new breed of Celtic tiger, he called it.

After carefully checking the preliminary plans for the encounter the following evening, Ben, Arik, Yossi and Harry Shaiko were driven to the Israeli Embassy, where they would spend the night. Bob Thompson, Paddy, An Luc and Terri stayed with Jean and Nguyen, turning in early for a well-deserved rest.

Paddy now gazed across the green lawns sweeping down to the tree-lined banks, to the placid, sun reflected surface of the river. What a peaceful, rustic setting, so at odds with the purpose of their visit. He heard the sound of dogs barking, of the front door opening, sounds of greetings and laughter. He turned away to shower and dress, listening to the sound of bells from the nearby village church.

Feeling refreshed, strangely exhilarated, Paddy stood in the sunshine before the open casement window. From the gardens below he could hear the voices of Nguyen and An Luc, Terri's quiet laughter. Paddy worried for her safety in the events that might follow. He wanted to reassure her, tell her all would be well.

Terri and An Luc were two of the few people who might be able to positively identify Kerkorian from the confused and multiple images he had deliberately projected. Their immediate recognition of him might be their only warning. If Kerkorian recognised them first, Paddy knew he would act quickly. As Paddy turned to leave the room, he glanced in the mirror. The breeze from the window stirred the curtains, reflected in the glass. He could have sworn for a brief moment he had seen the once familiar, grinning face, the taunting expression of Kerkorian as he had known him, beckoning, challenging. Paddy shrugged and turned away.

Descending the stairs, Paddy heard Terri's greeting. He paused to see her smiling up at him from the hallway, the French doors open behind her, sunlight streaming in. Paddy came toward her silently, reaching for her hand. Together they turned toward the garden. Ben and the others had already arrived.

Paddy moved among the friends he never thought he'd see again. Anna would never again be there - only in spirit perhaps. Briefly troubled, he glanced at Terri. Quickly her eyes were on his, a gentle smile of understanding perhaps.

Nguyen hurried into the house. In a moment she reappeared at the door, calling for Jack, an urgent phone call from Belfast. It was his cousin, Brigid, from the dark streets below the Cave Hill, telling him that young Sean had finally lost his battle. Jack turned toward the others, sadly shaking his head. "It's young Sean. He's just left us." The group on the terrace was shocked, Bob angrily muttering, "That's all we need! They'd better listen now."

Jack listened to Brigid, her tears and sorrow.

"We've had too many Irish heroes, Jack. But it's not over yet. Maybe wee Sean lost his battle, but he may have won the war for us."

There was more positive news. Amnesty International and the Human Rights bodies in New York and Brussels had achieved one of their goals, with Maloney's persistence. The prosecution was floundering. Dan and Theresa were to be released tomorrow. Apparently, Brigid told him, following Graham's shocking disclosure, the British administration's testimony at the hearings had finally admitted their responsibility in "inadvertently" activating the unauthorised undercover operation, use of SAS and RUC collusion, into the Mournes. They had denied the operation was an activation of Ajax - pleaded, a necessary step, following Madam's assassination.

As expected, they then tried to unload the responsibility on Graham as a "renegade agent exceeding his authority". This only brought Graham's testimony into focus. His denial of responsibility in the shooting of Sean McCarton turned media and public attention to the IRA's denial of any role in Madam's death, and to the others involved, including the Australian, Tracker, his origins and his mission, to the China Scheme, to SEACO. The British, dissembling, were in full retreat.

Telling Brigid he'd be there for Dan and Theresa's release and for young Sean's funeral, Jack ended the call.

An Luc, remembering his own family, for centuries victims of colonial strife, said quietly, "Sad for all of us, that the world must lose this brave boy. Yet, he has set the path. By his death, he has shown the way. At great cost to those of us left behind, he is the final hero."

Moments later the phone again rang. This time it was for Ben. Mossad had gathered information on Kerkorian from several sources. One response came from Military Intelligence in Hong Kong; another from Ben's contact in the NSA.

As the faxes were being transmitted, Jack received a call from Roger Moorefield. He had secured a copy of Kerkorian's transfer form in '72 requesting a move from Air America in

Cambodia, to Special Forces, Vietnam, specifically to "Spec 7". In submitting his request Kerkorian had scarcely hidden his eagerness for the assignment – compelled, it seemed, to explain his enthusiasm, the application revealing more of his background than requested.

It was incredible how Kerkorian, for reasons best known to himself, had written this near affidavit. Kerkorian had described his life, his search for personal redemption, he called it, on the battlefield. Moorefield promised to fax the document within the hour.

Paddy commented that there were obviously other reasons behind Kerkorian's eagerness to deploy. Moorefield agreed to meet with Paddy, in London, in the following days, to discuss Da Dias' account of the Vietnamese gold shipment, missing since '75.

It was past noon as Paddy, Ben, Harry Shaiko, Arik Cohen and Yossi Raviv once again reviewed Security measures for the confrontation with Kerkorian. Paddy relayed the communication from Da Dias, confirming Kerkorian's invitation had been received and accepted.

Over the past twenty-four hours, discreetly but in haste, French Security, DST and other special units had been alerted. Almost unnoticed, heavily armed groups of Agents de la Ville, gendarmes, city and other police, were doubled around many government offices, the Chamber of Deputies, the Hotel de Ville, an invisible cordon emerging. Paddy was concerned that the increased activity might arouse Kerkorian's suspicions and deny them their chance.

At Paddy's direction a special watch had been placed on the SEACO offices, personnel hastily investigated, lines tapped. Both Jean and Ben cautioned against excessive security activity in the areas of the fourth and fifth arrondissement. Kerkorian might choose to emerge, to his own advantage, elsewhere in the general area.

The sun now fell across the inner city and its two million inhabitants. As the day drew to a close, the metropolitan population surged busily to each of the twenty arrondissements, to suburbia, through the eight hundred miles of polluted city streets in an increasingly vocal, impassioned and impatient procession.

Twenty million tourists flowed by metro, bus and other transport, a human tide surging in and out of the city, above and beneath its streets, each on a different mission.

*

The golden half-light is distorted, deflected from a curious mosaic of empty palace museums and church steeples. The gargoyles, their sad stone eyes, stare blindly across the ancient, Celtic island fortress of Paris. Its two thousand years unfold in the sensuous coils of the Seine, now ochre and black in the pale even light. Singer of songs, weaver of dreams, birthplace of enlightenment, rebirth of reason and revolution.

CHAPTER FORTY-TWO

I loved you, so I drew these tides of men into my
hands and
wrote my will across the sky in stars.
To earn you Freedom, the seven pillared worthy
house, that
your eyes might be shining for me when we came.
T. E. Lawrence, Seven Pillars of Wisdom

On the terrace in the gardens of the old chateau, above
the incessant rustling of leaves, the gentle stirrings from the
river, Jack read from the copy of Kerkorian's application for
transfer. It was a strange tale, supplemented by Jean Davost,
from conversations he recalled with Kerkorian.

Alex Kerkorian was born in a small village near the
Serbian border. He had been secretly baptised Greek Orthodox
by his mother and father, both Christians, at a time of violent
religious oppression by the new Yugoslav government. Proudly,
with fervent hope, the young resistance fighters had named their
son Alexander Phillip. Kerkorian's father had died young, in a
skirmish with Albanian Communists, after World War II. Alex
was raised by his mother, a Greek ex-patriot, who had met his
father while both were fighting the Germans. A teacher, she was
passionate and strong willed. She taught him the earlier history
of the region, a tragic crucible of perpetual strife, and scene of
successive bloody sectarian and ethnic conflict.

Kerkorian described his father with obvious reverence.
Though Kerkorian was too young to have known him, his
mother had fiercely perpetuated his heroic memory. His father
was originally of Kurdish origin, descendant of the Macedonian
warriors of Alexander the Great. He too, had fought in many
wars against the Turks, the Russians, the Iraqis, to establish a

389

Kurdish homeland.

Kerkorian wrote of his mother reading to him as a child the tales of ancient Greece, of Homer, the Iliad, of Achilles, of his invincibility, arête. She described the young Alexander of Macedon's determination to eclipse the feats of his hero, Achilles.

Paddy's listeners were reminded of Kerkorian's misguided attempts to surpass Alexander's feats – that he too, might avenge his father. Jean Davost and Paddy both recalled Kerkorian's tales of Alexander's "companions", of flamboyant, reckless daring - the noblest of warriors. In Vietnam, Kerkorian spoke of his own "companions", his "special unit" - and something else apparent now.

Kerkorian wrote of the "softer life", the forces that weaken younger men, so that they forget their purpose. Perhaps written to encourage those who were reassigning Kerkorian, or perhaps, unconsciously, thought Paddy, trying to explain to himself the curious absence of women in the life of the celebrated Homeric warrior.

Paddy recalled from the book Whitcombe had given him, the history of the tormented Alexander, his incestuously distorted passions, obsessed mission. His future "companion and lover", Bagoas, gelded son of his murdered father, tortured sycophant and slave. Paddy recalled Kerkorian's isolation, his reckless daring, the absence of close friends, his disinterest in the notorious womanising of his fellow Special Forces warriors: at once at odds with his own striking physical attributes, the superficially gregarious, macho image he projected. Jean reminded them that in all the activities they had shared together on and off duty - macho hero as he was, women never seemed to figure in Kerkorian's life. The story was compelling – its telling deliberate, introspective.

Kerkorian wrote of his mother taking him to America while still a boy. There, they had lived with his grandmother, another fierce Greek matriarchal figure. Sorrowfully, he told how his mother died shortly after their arrival. She had made him promise not to forget his father's name, his birthright among the Kurdish people, to return to his people when he had accomplished great victories and could help them achieve independence. To attain real glory, she'd told him, must be his only purpose.

Kerkorian described his determined pursuit of the physical and academic excellence he ultimately achieved - graduating in the top third of his class at West Point. Vengeance and victory! The frightening achievements of the warrior hero - the conqueror, now indeed reborn - Alexander Kerkorian, his mother's goals never forgotten.

The sunlight fell further westward among the trees, the parks and steeples - its brilliant rays fractionate to shards of red and amber across the roiling surface of the Seine - a harsh reminder of the Paris of blood and retribution. From Montmartre, site of the early Christian massacres, to the Capetian, Isle de la Cite, once besieged by Attila the Hun, by the invading Celtic tribes. Further west, in battles with the Saxon, the mystical passage of the young Joan of Arc. In these very streets, three thousand men, women and children of the Huguenots, pitilessly murdered by the half crazed Duc de Guise and his followers to the mad carolling of the bells of the churches of St. Germain L'Auxerrois and Notre Dame. To the "Terror" then, another three thousand victims, the indiscriminate and bloody appetite of a busy Madame Guillotine, the remorseless chorus, "Au mort!" The city's endless theme of vengeance and violence, cries of the oppressor, cries of the oppressed. Paris, the city of death.

*

Rory was grinning like a schoolboy as Vera came into the room, radiant and smiling. Her lovely, dark hair, her deep, brown eyes, and the favorite red dress worn only for special occasions. In her hand she held a small bunch of red roses. Rory was speechless; Vera never seemed to age.

They headed for the nearby Metro. Despite her questions, Rory teasingly refused to reveal their destination. They found themselves among a noisy group of young people.

391

One told Vera they were on their way to listen to a rock band. They planned to escort the "Lives of Sin" as they were called, from their hotel to a gig at the University. Another crowd surged into the Metro. In the short ride to the hotel the singing, cheering fans stomped their feet to the loud, raucous beat of a music box.

Vera turned to Rory, laughing, saying something he couldn't hear. Rory put his fingers to his ears, grinning, shaking his head. As the train drew into the station, he took Vera's hand. They edged their way through the crowd.

Vera leaned close to his ear, shouting to be heard. "Rory, you devil you, I think I know where we're going!" He smiled, saying nothing.

Across the embankment, above the transient clamour and celebration, the massive and timeless spires of Notre Dame reached stoically for the early evening stars. Rory and Vera were swept forward, the crowd having increased, the noise louder now. Rory glanced at his watch. Holding Vera's hand tightly, he noticed the insidious increase in the number of Agents de la Ville, uniformed city police.

They struggled through a slower moving crowd growing more dense and unruly. Rory wondered anxiously about their reservations. He didn't look back as he pushed his way through. They were approaching the centre stage of a gala reception for the rock group.

The boom and percussion, the harsh twang of the amplified guitars, the unfamiliar rhythm, the wild harmony frightened Vera as she struggled to keep up with Rory. She too had noticed the increase, not unexpected, in uniformed police. Yet now, other plain clothed security and obvious military types were visible. She saw the flickering arc lights of television and other news coverage.

The crowd was now obstructing traffic, barely inching forward. Glancing toward the rooftops, Vera was startled to see figures, some discreetly crouched, intently scanning the crowd below. More alarmed, she saw that several carried automatic weapons. Security for rock stars, with automatic weapons? Something was wrong!

Vera tugged on Rory's hand as he pushed ahead. He

turned toward her, raising his eyes to follow her pointing finger. He looked back to Vera, nodding, his expression more troubled.

The mob surged around them. Rory and Vera pushed their way through with some desperation. The restaurant was near. Young couples, untroubled, moved aside, tolerantly allowing the older pair to move ahead.

Suddenly Rory stopped, pulling Vera toward him. He was pointing across the street. He leaned toward her, wide eyed, shouting something Vera couldn't hear. Suddenly, the crowd parted. On the steps leading up to the restaurant, Vera recognised the same British agent they'd shadowed in Paris and later, in London. Beside him stood a pretty, dark-haired Asian lady. The crowd surged, again blocking her view.

The night began to assume an unreal quality. Again, Vera glanced upward, Rory following her gaze. Both saw the single figures, their binoculars seemingly staring toward Rory and Vera. Confused, Vera turned to Rory. They both sensed an association with the British agent. Unable to hear what Vera shouted to him, Rory nodded as he stared up into the stark glare of the searchlights.

Rory suspected that they'd blundered into a "sting operation", some sort of British MI6, French DST collusion. Incredulous, he could only conclude they were after him now, to silence him for what he knew. Knowing there was pandemonium in Britain's "establishment" circles – that their stand in Northern Ireland was about to unravel, he should have known they'd be waiting for him sometime! Vera in sudden terror, looking wildly around, again glimpsed the MI6 agent standing on the steps, the girl and a short Asian man beside him. He seemed to be pointing in their direction now.

From the entranceway of the nearby hotel, the members of the rock group appeared. The screaming crowd surged toward them. As if on cue, a climax of carolling began across the city, the tolling of the great bells of Notre Dame.

No longer holding Rory's hand, suddenly Vera found herself free of the crowd, among the slowly crawling traffic. A long, Mercedes limousine stopped in front of her. The doors opened. A man wearing a flowing kaftan, his head and face almost covered in a chequered turban, moved quickly from the back seat. From the far side of the limousine, two others in similar dress followed. Horrified, Vera saw they all carried some sort of weapon. She stood motionless. The crowd, distracted by the appearance of the rock stars, the booming of the bells, seemed oblivious.

Behind Vera, Rory saw the limousine, the men emerging. In an instant, Rory recognised the stubby shape of a shoulder held rocket launcher. Suddenly, to all sides, the crowd began to scatter. My God - what is this? Rory was confused. Amid the pandemonium, his world stood still. Then, moving in slow time, the multitude vanished. A high-pitched scream, drowned by music and the carolling bells. In dread Rory reached for Vera. He saw her by the pavement, pushed further toward the car by the scattering mob.

From the restaurant steps Paddy felt Terri tugging on his hand, saying something he couldn't hear, pointing toward the street. Following Terri's gesture, Paddy saw the commotion among the crowd. Quickly he spoke into his hand held transmitter.

At that moment, An Luc grasped his arm, shouting, "Look Tuan, the older ones who watched us from Paris and London!" Paddy saw the older couple, who'd seemed to follow them from their hotel in Paris when they'd first arrived, and to Horse Guards in London the morning of their arrival from Northern Ireland.

Terri suddenly cried out. Paddy, startled, saw the figures emerging from the limousine. Even at that distance Paddy recognised him, unmistakable - even as An Luc shouted, "It's him, Tuan, both of them!"

Kerkorian, preceded by his "shadow", confronted the crowd. He raised a stubby automatic weapon, signalling the others, pointing toward the rooftops.

Vera also instantly recognised him. Almost thirty years ago, in Saigon in the weeks before the American evacuation. Her first job, secretary to SEACO, based in Saigon. The operation was run then by a member of the South Vietnamese army, in partnership with two Americans. Vera came upon both Americans late one night, in a loud argument. As the argument grew more violent, they had become aware of her presence. She remembered both men staring after her as she hurried from the office. In the short time left in Saigon, neither man had spoken to her again.

Little changed as he stood before her now, draped in the white kaftan, the handsome, blond, Greek American. Stunned, uncertain, she called his name.

He stared for a second, perplexed. For the blond, muscular man in the flowing white kaftan, the sudden appearance of Vera was a moment of startling déjà vu. He instantly saw this lady from Saigon as a dangerous witness to his identity.

Vera's startled shout, "Kerkorian!" was joined, like an echo, from the restaurant across the street. In the same instant, Kerkorian fired into the lovely face before him.

Disbelieving, Rory saw it, too late. Screaming in agony, rage and bewilderment, he stumbled toward Vera, calling her name. Within seconds, Rory joined Vera in the street, scattered wedding flowers lying between their lifeless, outstretched hands.

Paddy saw An Luc suddenly vault the railing, pushing through the crowd, toward Kerkorian. Stunned, Paddy saw Kerkorian's "shadow" carefully sighting a shoulder held missile launcher in his and Terri's direction.

Paddy instinctively pushed Terri aside, aware of An Luc's desperate challenging shout, the simultaneous explosion, just as he leaped toward the limousine, flinging himself onto the puff of smoke. The missile struck, almost as it left the tube; both An Luc and Kerkorian's "shadow", killed instantaneously.

For An Luc, the Khan Kong, samsara, his goals achieved – a promise realised. This simple Meo tribesman, a proud Montagnard, giving his life for his friends.

Ben and Harry Shaiko had watched the confrontation from inside the restaurant. No sooner had he seen An Luc disappearing in the explosion than Ben found himself rushing outside to face Kerkorian, now striding toward him. Suddenly he heard the big man shout.

"My way is not to fight my battles standing away from

395

my enemies!"

Reaching for the 9mm Beretta in his shoulder holster, Ben began to fire, watching the bullets hit Kerkorian, who kept advancing, the defiant expression, the contemptuous grin, the arrogant stride!

The big man advanced, blond hair blowing in the wind, blood now changing his white flowing robe into a dark red shroud. Amazed, Ben saw that Kerkorian carried no weapon.

Grinning, Kerkorian reached inside the neck of his garment. Thinking Kerkorian was reaching for a weapon, Ben fired again. In Kerkorian's now extended hand, something dully glinted; a chain he had drawn from around his neck. Suspended from the chain, shining in the arc lights, a small bright object. Paddy's seventh key! Still grinning, Kerkorian turned and flung the tiny symbol of death and untold riches high into the air, in a glittering arc, beyond the embankment toward the river. Kerkorian, young Alexander, his father's promises, his mother's dreams unfulfilled, crumpled sideways into the street.

For Kerkorian, his fantasy denied. Another mad conquest, stillborn. Only perhaps, Apocalypse postponed - the ultimate Armageddon - a heritage and tradition of wars. And, the price, as ever - decent, brave men, and the innocents.

The siren wail of emergency vehicles was challenged only by the reverberating toll of the bells from Notre Dame.

Above the quays, where seconds before the amplifiers' discordant percussion had prevailed, the air resounded with the cries of death above a quickly emptied stage. In the arc lights' cold stare the surviving players moved in a more dreamlike motion - the dead flung in helpless disarray. Above them, the ageless edifice of the Cathedral grew incandescent, glowing, like a giant offering of candles in the darkness, again the carolling witness to so much death throughout the years.

Somewhere from the streets of the once French quarter of a colonial city in Vietnam, from the quiet streets of La Villette where the batons mouches drift along the quiet waters of the canals, from the green granite glens and mountains of

the Mourne country in Ireland, a lilting clear soprano sings a
Romanian ballad - a song of love and remembrance, of violent,
unexpected death.

> If I'm going to die in a field of sweet smelling grass
> tell them to bury me, near here...
> so I may be with you still.
> Tell them that I got married to a beautiful queen –
> the world's bride – that at my wedding, a star fell.
> The sun and moon held my crown.
> Fir trees, maple trees were my wedding guests.
> Priests, the big mountains, players, birds – thousands of birds
> And star torches – at my wedding.

The flowers were delivered to the Tour d'Argent, almost
on time. The florist focused on his tardiness, otherwise oblivious
as he made his way through the debris and chaos in the streets,
through the security barriers, to the steps of the restaurant. He
was met by Monsieur Jacques, the Maitre D', waiting for his
special guests. They were also late, understandably, in view of
the tragic happenings. Monsieur Jacques paced worriedly from
the entrance, bringing the florist's offering to the table he had
reserved - the one with the view of Notre Dame, set with the
special champagne he had chosen. Only in the following days,
and a visit from a curious journalist, did M. Jacques learn of the
fate of the old couple - that they would never see the lights of
Notre Dame again. Forever, together now, Rory and Vera, in
peace, away from the shadows and the fears, and their sometime
world of flowers.

*

The following morning the survivors, the mourners,
and the storytellers gathered. Jean, Paddy, Ben and Terri joined
Jack in their immediate return to Belfast in time for Theresa and
Dan's release, and, after An Luc's burial, to attend yet another
funeral – that of young Sean.

CHAPTER FORTY-THREE

Number 10 Downing Street

In London at daybreak, shadows cast by the darkened Civil Service offices of Richmond Terrace and Whitehall crossed the wide expanse of Parliament Street and gradually receded with the rising sun. The side streets were empty and quiet. The city was awakening to another day of greater uncertainty, to a world at war. Nearby, the Cenotaph, a crumbling obelisk, its tattered floral wreaths celebrating the callous human debris, victims of a nation's imperial greed. In the words of young Kipling, "If any question why we died; tell them, because our fathers lied."

It was now just five a.m. Awakened earlier by the news from Paris, Sir Arthur Wolsey stood watchful from the upper floor of 10 Downing Street. An emergency meeting was planned prior to the gathering in the House of Commons later that morning. The most recent shootings in Paris would be the main focus.

For Wolsey the news was far reaching. The uncertainty of the information on those involved was disconcerting. The implications allegedly involved those in the China Scheme, its corporate corruption, and links to the threat of total war from the once Russian Republics.

Slowly wending their way past the security barriers, a succession of official limousines approached the Georgian facade of Number 10. Plain clothes and uniformed, weapons at the ready, the men from London Metropolitan and MI5 A, or Watchers, and regular police crossed the pavement to accompany each car as it slowly traversed the short distance from the entrance barriers. Since the assassination of the Russian Premier and of Madam and now the shootings in Paris, a mood of mistrust and growing tension had finally escalated to where Status "RED ALERT" prevailed.

On the roofs of the surrounding buildings Special Service troops scanned the area. Big Ben's sonorous chimes, suddenly echoing about the empty streets, added to the aura of gloom, of perceived threat, pervasive fear. Pending disaster was reflected at all levels, from the Prime Minister, Wolsey, peering from the upper floor of Number 10, to the uneasy figure of the recently promoted Sergeant of the London Metropolitan Police, Edgar Hennessey, now restlessly pacing before the steps below.

Hennessey hadn't slept too well. The call from his dad, the first in months, must have been around midnight.

"Edgar," his dad's voice was solemn, shaky. He usually addressed him as Ed. "It's my brother, your uncle Rory. You wouldn't remember him too well. He lived in Paris. Used to come and visit us when you were small." A sniffling sound, then, "He's dead. My only brother, shot and killed a few hours ago, an innocent bystander in Paris."

Hennessey had received a further call at 4 a.m. from Police Headquarters requiring his immediate attendance for extra Security at Downing Street. On his way to Downing Street he'd thought about his father's phone call. He remembered little about his uncle. He did recall that Rory's visits had become less frequent. His father and his uncle, he remembered, had once had a falling out. He became worried then, remembering something else about Uncle Rory.

It had come back to Edgar, cold and clear, as he rode the London tube to the City Centre. His Uncle Rory had been a member of an Irish paramilitary organization, forced to leave Northern Ireland. On the run then, he had changed his name from Hennessey, calling himself Rory O'Connor.

Edgar shuddered, thinking of the impact on his own career. He could see his recent promotion and future goals threatened if they learned of his family connections with Irish Nationalists, terrorists no less. Surely they would see him as a security risk.

The early morning worldwide news commentary focussed on last night's Paris shooting incident. The newscaster hinted of further disasters. The American press characteristically called it, *"Showdown – High Noon for the Terrorist Threat"*, or, *"Muslim Leader, Algazi Confronts the World."* As the story grew, the headlines changed.

Edgar Hennessey wondered about the shootings, vaguely ascribed to foreign terrorists. No end of such troubled groups of terrorists to blame. The Americans explained it as an extension of the Middle East conflict. The British media, true to form, blamed the IRA. For Wolsey, standing by the window of Number 10, checking his notes, the source of the threat had a wider impact.

At Downing Street now, Hennessey tipped his cap in salute to a succession of ministers and others, most of whom he knew by sight. He saw his old acquaintance, the Irish Chargé d'Affaires, emerge from a limousine accompanied by his secretary, a red-faced little man, arms loaded with files and other official baggage. They barely nodded a greeting.

Among the first to arrive was Geoffrey Gordon's successor, the former DDG of MI5, Maurice Stanfield. The Irish Chargé d'Affaires, Dermot Higgins, was followed by the Secretary of State for Northern Ireland, David Noonan, likely soon to go - already pursued by allegations of misconduct and misspending before and after his appointment. Next, an old party loyalist, then McClean, the Nationalist. Finally DeVeere, already facing charges, unwilling to confront his inevitable resignation or dismissal. His replacement, the interim appointee DG of MI6, was not far behind.

In his office above, Sir Arthur Wolsey, interim leader of this increasingly embattled Coalition Government turned from the window. Seating himself at his desk he scanned his notes for the coming Cabinet meeting, then distractedly glanced at the pages of his later speech, an emergency session of the House. This would be the appropriate time for his declaration of intent to run for election, to abandon the interim role as Prime Minister.

Wolsey had spent the night at Number 10 working till late, restlessly pacing the floor, making calls - wrestling with his tormented thoughts, hanging tightly to his growing convictions. He was still troubled by the call he'd received from the White

House the previous evening. The President had seemed anxious. In the coming weeks could they count on Britain's support at the UN, regarding their plans to protect the oil fields of the Caspian and the Gulf region?

The Brit/US partnership seemed less of an advantage now in the face of the failing American economy, clearly stumbling onto the path to an inevitable nuclear confrontation. His answer to the American President was evasive.

Wolsey recalled the shared concerns of Eisenhower, Truman and others of the unaccountable military lobby. Lincoln's warning to stay apart from Europe's wars, from the tyranny of the extreme right… corporations enthroned… corruption in high places that will surely follow. All were reality now.

A bad omen, the assassination of Ghubar, peacemaker of the Middle East, and of the Russian President. Awaiting further details from Paris on the recent shootings, Wolsey was less inclined to place Britain outside the European Alliance. His response was less militant now to the climax of disasters and the extending war in Russia. Was this all connected, Wolsey wondered, in some ominous way?

Wolsey glanced at the newspapers on his desk. Not since the death of Madam, of the Seanache, had anything shaken a watching world as much as the death of the boy, Sean McCarton. Like his grandfather some weeks before, his name was now known worldwide. The boy, once again centre stage. For many, especially those from third world countries, the funeral was the final straw. The boy's funeral refocused world attention less on terrorists, more on misrule by the Imperial powers.

This was one message Wolsey could convey. Perhaps this, he thought, is indeed the long sought excuse to break the divisive Machiavellian association with the "colons", whose warring feuds they had condemned or otherwise actively supported. The Irish territorial redoubt, isolated, untenable, a constant source of shame, blame and increasing debt – the focus once again of international attention was also a moment of opportunity. As Thompson, at both funerals had commented, "To persist in this incredible travesty is foolish and self-destructive. A source of shame to decent English people."

Wolsey pursued the tortured path, forced to come to terms with the escalating state of international tension, as now in Paris and once again in Ireland the news only seemed to add to an already explosive world situation. He remembered the words of Gladstone, Prime Minister from over a century before, "Ireland, source of all our troubled conscience - that cloud in the west - the coming storm, minister of God's retribution upon cruel injustice."

Wolsey had long foreseen the reunification of the island of Ireland. He realised it was the boy and his grandfather that had provided the timely opportunity to set the wheels in motion. For Wolsey, the European Family was the focus now - its economic and social aspirations, the future path for all. England must learn to live with it and within it. A new face – a new Britain, in a new European Community.

There was a knock at the door. The usually cheery face of his secretary, Margaret Haversham, showed concern. "There is a call for you. You're due downstairs in fifteen minutes," she reminded him.

Wolsey picked up the receiver. The voice sounded grim, without the usual greetings. "Word from Belfast. Graham's confessed to killing the Weatherbys. And there's more. Our Counsel has decided we'll have to drop the charges against the two IRA defendants. The United Nations Security Council has decided to open hearings based on the evidence from the Granart papers – the ones submitted by the Earl of Clanrickard."

Wolsey mumbled a quiet acknowledgement. He knew there was no alternative. As he rose, Margaret met him at the door, her arms loaded with papers. Standing by was Peter Marshall, his troubled looking assistant. They paused a moment looking at one another. Wolsey preceded them toward the stairs, wondering what the Americans would say as they watched the "special relationship" founder?

The phone rang. Wolsey impatiently shook his head. Margaret glanced toward Marshall – should they ignore it? Marshall hurried back, picked up the phone, listened for a moment. He croaked, "Oh my God!" Covering the mouthpiece, he handed Wolsey the phone. "Sir - it's the American Vice President."

Wolsey seized the phone and began a greeting, but his words were cut short. "I can't hear you," he snapped impatiently. "A terrorist attack? The World Trade Centre, the Pentagon? *The White House?* Good God! Impossible! What's that you say?" He listened for a few moments, turned to Marshall.

"They can't locate the President."

Lightning Source UK Ltd.
Milton Keynes UK
12 September 2009

143610UK00001BA/13/P